RITUAL MAGIC

EILEEN WILKS

BERKLEY SENSATION, NEW YORK

THE BERKLEY PUBLISHING GROUP
Published by the Penguin Group
Penguin Group (USA)
375 Hudson Street, New York, New York 10014, USA

USA | Canada | UK | Ireland | Australia | New Zealand | India | South Africa | China

Penguin Books Ltd., Registered Offices: 80 Strand, London WC2R 0RL, England
For more information about the Penguin Group, visit penguin.com.

RITUAL MAGIC

A Berkley Sensation Book / published by arrangement with the author

Berkley Sensation Books are published by The Berkley Publishing Group.
BERKLEY SENSATION® is a registered trademark of Penguin Group (USA)
The "B" design is a trademark of Penguin Group (USA)

For information, address: The Berkley Publishing Group,
a division of Penguin Group (USA),
375 Hudson Street, New York, New York 10014.

ISBN: 978-0-425-26336-5

PUBLISHING HISTORY
Berkley Sensation mass-market edition / September 2013

PRINTED IN THE UNITED STATES OF AMERICA

10 9 8 7 6 5 4 3 2 1

Cover art by Tony Mauro.
Cover design by George Long.

ALWAYS LEARNING   PEARSON

ACKNOWLEDGMENTS

While I might aspire to Lily's wonderfully anal-retentive and organized ways, at heart I'm more like the dog from *Up*: cheerful, sloppy, and easily distracted. No doubt this is why, when it's time to write the acknowledgments for a book, I'm so often surprised to find that *I have not kept a list.* As a result, I'm sure I have failed to acknowledge any number of helpful people along the way. This time, sadly, fits that general rule. I do have one thank-you to express, however. *Ritual Magic* has a large cast and my brain played hopscotch with the names of some of the minor characters. (And yes, if I'd kept a list right from the start this wouldn't have happened, but I'm pretty sure the dog from *Up* doesn't make lists, either.) My heartfelt thanks to the beleaguered copy editor who made sense of the jumble as well as keeping the timeline on track.

I also want to apologize to residents of San Diego for, once again, taking liberties with your city. In this story I mention several hospitals. Some you may recognize. Others have no analogue in our world, but I assure you they're just as I describe them in Lily and Rule's realm.

ONE

~

SHE blinked and swayed, so dizzy she had to reach for the wall to prop herself up. Could you pass out without falling down? That was what it felt like—like she'd blacked out. Which she'd never done, not in her whole life, but all of a sudden she was Sleeping Beauty and years and years had passed. Except she was still on her feet, so obviously years hadn't passed. The ladies' room was right behind her. She was still in the narrow little hallway of . . .

Of where?

Fear struck, quick and hot and dark, flapping its wings in her throat like a trapped bird. Where was she?

She didn't know. She didn't have any idea. She'd been . . . what? She couldn't remember. She remembered going to bed last night but not to sleep, not right away. She always had trouble falling asleep the night before her birthday. She'd sat up past bedtime—a sin overlooked on special nights—writing in her diary, with the light from her lamp warm and yellow on its lined pages and her lavender bedspread pulled up to her waist. She'd told her diary what she couldn't tell anyone, not even Kathy, and for sure not her sisters. Everyone was so "I can't wait" about being a teenager, but she was glad this birthday was twelve, not thirteen. She wasn't ready for thirteen, but that was okay because she had a whole year of being twelve ahead of her. That gave her lots of time.

But that was all she remembered. She didn't remember waking up or eating breakfast or lunch or supper. Was it suppertime? Had they come here instead of going to the roller rink like they were supposed to?

Had she somehow missed her whole birthday?

A burst of indignation burned through some of the fear. That wasn't fair. That wasn't fair at all, and she didn't understand, but here she was in some kind of restaurant. The air was thick with good smells—ginger and onions and fryer fat—and she could see a smidge of the room the hall led to. A man sat at a small, cloth-draped table, leaning forward and stabbing his finger at the air the way men did when they thought they were important and people should listen. The woman with him looked bored. They were both Caucasian, but this was a Chinese restaurant. She could tell from the smells and the crimson walls. Out of sight from her vantage point, someone was laughing a quick, barking sort of laugh: HA! HA! HA! Which made her think of Uncle Wu, who laughed in syllables like that, only quieter, huffing it out: Ha. Ha. Ha.

She was breathing really fast. Huffing like Uncle Wu. She clenched her fists and tried to make herself breathe normal. She needed something to be normal.

She felt tired. Tired and kind of heavy, the way she did when she had a cold. She sniffed experimentally. She wasn't stuffed up or anything. Had she been sick? Maybe she'd had a real high fever. A brain fever. Could brain fevers make you forget stuff? Maybe she'd had a terrible brain fever and got over it, but just now she'd had a relapse—that was why she'd been so dizzy—and—

"Excuse us, please," someone said behind her.

She whirled.

Two women had come out of the restroom. They were kind of old—maybe thirty—and they were dressed funny.

Both wore jeans, which was weird. Who wore jeans to a nice restaurant? One had on a big, sloppy sweater, but the other one wore a tight, stretchy shirt that showed *every-thing*, like she was a hooker or something. That woman had great big earrings and super-short hair like Mia Farrow and . . . good grief. She had a little gem in her nose, like it was pierced there.

Her mother wouldn't let her pierce her ears, and this woman had pierced her nose!

The two women were looking at her funny. She flushed. She was standing around like an idiot, blocking the hall. She stepped aside. As she did, her foot bumped something. She glanced down.

Someone had left her purse right there in the hall. It was a nice purse, too—black leather, the kind that's so soft you want to pet it. She should tell someone.

She'd taken one uncertain step when someone else came into the hall. A man. He was tall and probably as old as the two women and he was gorgeous. He looked like a movie star—kind of like Clint Eastwood, in fact, who was still her favorite, and she hated that *Rawhide* had gone off the air. Only this man's hair was all dark and shaggy and he had really dramatic eyebrows that weren't like Clint's at all.

The man looked right at her and tipped his head like he was puzzled. She felt a little flutter in her stomach. Then he spoke to her.

"Julia? Are you okay?"

LILY pushed the remains of her Kung Pao chicken around on her plate and tried to look like she was paying attention to her cousin Freddie, who was all excited about implied rates and parity and agio. What the hell was agio? Was that even a word?

She didn't ask. He'd tell her, and God knew how long that would take. It was some kind of broker-speak, though. Probably currency trading, which was his specialty. That was a large part of what he did for Rule these days. Rule's second clan wasn't affluent the way Nokolai was.

". . . not convinced the baht is on the rise, but . . ." Freddie broke off and chuckled. "Your eyes have glazed over."

"Sorry." She and Freddie got along better now that he'd stopped asking her to marry him. She'd even forgiven him for doing so repeatedly without mentioning that he was gay. Turned out he'd been in major denial about that and had only come out of the closet with himself recently. He wasn't ready for the family to know . . . by which he meant his mother.

Lily could understand that. Aunt Jei—who was technically Lily's second cousin, but Lily and her sisters called all their mother's first cousins "aunt" or "uncle"—put the passive in passive-aggressive. She was limp, needy, and full of sighs, a widow with only one child, whom she doted on, clung to, and controlled ruthlessly.

Poor Freddie.

Aunt Jei was probably the reason Rule had excused himself to go to the restroom. He'd been seated next to her, and even Rule could only take so much.

"That's all right," Freddie said kindly and patted her hand. "You're probably daydreaming about the big day. Only two weeks away now, isn't it?" He beamed at her.

"Two weeks and five days." After which, she thought with a smile, Rule would be officially related to Aunt Jei, Freddie, and everyone else at this table. Poor man.

They were in the larger of the two private dining rooms at the Golden Dragon, where the family held most such celebrations since it was owned by Uncle Chen—another "uncle" who was really a cousin. The party was smaller than usual this year. None of the children were here, and Grandmother's companion, Li Qin, had broken her foot two days before. It was still too swollen to cast. She was supposed to keep the foot elevated as much as possible, so Grandmother had insisted she stay home. Plus, Lily's younger sister wasn't here, though for a very different reason.

"I attended the wedding of a colleague's daughter recently," Freddie was saying. "Beautiful girl. It was a very modern sort of ceremony. They wrote their own vows, and when it was time for toasts . . ."

Lily nodded and let her mind drift. Her mother had told them firmly they were not to make a fuss: "With your wedding so close, it's too much to ask. Everyone is very busy." By "everyone," she meant herself. She and Rule were shouldering the bulk of the work involved in planning a major event, for which Lily was duly grateful. Perhaps a bit more grateful to Rule, true, because it was so obvious that her mother was having a blast.

Lily's father had wisely ignored his wife's instructions. Julia Yu loved being fussed over on her birthday.

That fuss had damn well better include presents, too. Lily's gaze slid to the table behind Freddie. The table held over a dozen gaily wrapped packages. She grinned. Freddie took her grin as tribute to his story about the groom's toast and chuckled and launched into a tale about someone else she'd never met.

Every year Julia Yu insisted she didn't need a thing, not a thing, but they knew better. She adored presents—the bright paper and bows, the whole unwrapping ritual. Lily would miss it herself if they ever did skip the gifts. Her mother might be picky and perfectionistic about all sorts of things, but presents were different. Her eyes lit with delight. She exclaimed with pleasure over everything, no matter how odd or humble, and held it up for everyone to admire.

"So what did you get Mother?" she asked when Freddie paused.

"Why, I got her a gift."

That meant he was dying to tell, but she was supposed to coax him. She glanced at her watch: 8:22. "Guess I'll find out soon. She'll be finished primping any—"

The first scream was loud and piercing and terrified. So were the ones that followed. Lily was on her feet and digging into her purse before the others got their dropped jaws working. She wasn't wearing either shoulder or ankle holster, but she didn't go anywhere unarmed. These days she carried a Glock 19—durable, reliable, accurate, and the clips held fifteen rounds. The pull was a bit long, but it was lightweight and she liked the grip.

By the time she slammed through the door, she had her weapon out and ready.

Barnaby and Joe were on their feet, faced out. "Hold your positions," she snapped. The other two guards, Scott and Mark, were already on the other side of the dining room and moving fast as only lupi can. They turned into the hall that led to the restrooms. Lily followed at a quick jog, veering around startled diners and a couple of servers. The screams cut off when she was halfway across the room.

Scott reappeared at the entrance to the hall and smiled at everyone. Scott cultivated the geek look. He wore glasses he didn't need and clothes a bit too large that turned his wiry frame skinny. If you didn't notice how well he moved, you'd think he never did anything more strenuous than tote a laptop. "I think she saw a mouse or something."

There were a couple of nervous laughs. Someone said, "Must have been a really big mouse." More laughter as the roomful of people began to relax.

Rule was in that hall. The mate-sense told Lily that as clearly as if she could see through the wall. Had some woman with a phobia about lupi seen him and freaked? Could be. His face was well-known. Whatever kind of trouble had triggered the screaming, though, she probably wouldn't need her Glock. Scott had put his back to the hall. He wouldn't do that if something needed shooting.

Still, she kept her weapon in her hand, down at her side. Scott gave her an odd look, but stepped aside without speaking. As soon as he did, she stopped dead.

Mark stood a couple feet into the hall. Either he hadn't drawn his weapon or he'd already put it up. A few feet beyond him, Rule stood with his arms around Lily's mother. She was sobbing. Her hands gripped his arms. He was stroking her back and murmuring something. He looked up from his soothing to meet Lily's eyes. He looked baffled.

"Mother?" Lily stepped forward cautiously. She'd never seen her mother come apart like this. Never. To do so in public . . . "What's wrong? Are you hurt?"

Julia Yu lifted her head from Rule's shoulder. Mascara

streaked her face in long black runnels. "I'm old! I'm so old!"

"You . . . you look great."

Julia shuddered and wailed.

"I was coming down the hall and saw Julia," Rule said carefully. "She looked upset, so I asked if she was all right. She reached up to touch her hair, then started patting her face. Then she screamed."

"Mother—"

"I'm not your mother! I'm not anyone's mother! I'm twelve years old and someone has stuck me in this old, old body!"

The last fifteen months had been difficult. Lily had killed. She'd died herself—or part of her had—and she'd seen someone die for her. She'd dealt with a wraith, too many demons, a Chimea, a crazy telepath, and a couple of really nasty elves. She had literally been to hell and back. But this . . .

For a long moment her mind was simply blank. Then she thought of psychotic breaks. Then she thought of magic. She swallowed hard and put her weapon back in her purse. "You're twelve, you said."

A vigorous nod. "It's my birthday."

Yes, it was. Only Julia Yu had turned fifty-seven today, not twelve. "Do you recognize me?"

"N-no. You look kind of familiar, though. Maybe we met sometime?"

"My name is Lily. You're Julia, right?"

Her mother sniffed. "Julia Lin."

Lin. Her mother's maiden name. "I'm an FBI agent. Would you like to see my badge?"

"A real FBI agent?"

"The real thing." Lily pulled her shield from her purse and held it out. "See?"

Julia Yu released her death grip on one of Rule's arms so she could lean forward to peer at Lily's ID. She didn't reach for it, though. "It looks real."

"It is. Have you heard about—" Noise behind Lily had

her turning. Her father and two of her cousins were at the hall's entrance. Edward Yu told Scott he'd better step aside right now.

"Edward," Rule said, "give us a couple more minutes. Please."

"I'm going to see my wife," Lily's father said. "Julia— are you all right?"

"Who's he?" Julia said, her voice wobbly. "He's not your husband, is he? He looks too old."

Lily almost lost it. She swallowed and blinked like crazy and prayed her voice wouldn't break. "Father. Give me a minute. Please. If magic's involved—"

"Magic!" Julia cried.

Edward Yu didn't answer, but he shoved at Scott. Who didn't budge, of course. Neither of them was a large man, but Scott was lupus.

"Edward." The cousins parted to allow a small, awesomely erect old woman to come forward. Her black hair was skinned back from her face and fastened in an intricate bun. She wore crimson satin, lavishly embroidered. Grandmother murmured something in Chinese that Lily didn't catch and laid a hand on her son's arm, adding in that language, "Something bad has happened. Julia does not know you. We will stay back so we do not overwhelm her."

Edward Yu frowned hard. His eyes were frantic. "Not long. I won't wait long."

Lily turned back to the woman who didn't know she was a mother. Who thought she was twelve years old. "I'm with Unit Twelve, Julia. Have you heard of that? We investigate crimes connected with magic."

"Someone put a spell on me, didn't they? That's what's wrong!"

"It's one possibility. I can find out if you'll shake my hand."

Julia's eyes narrowed suspiciously. "Why?"

"I'm a touch sensitive. If magic has been used on you—a spell of some kind—I'll feel it when we touch." Her mother was null, with not a whisper of a Gift. Any trace of magic Lily found would have been put there by someone else.

Julia cast a worried glance at Rule. He nodded reassuringly. "I guess that's okay," she said and held out her hand. It was shaking.

Lily took it in both of hers.

Julia Yu used to play the piano. She had the hands for it, long-fingered and graceful. Her manicure was immaculate, the polish a pale pink. The hand Lily held was covered in soft, well-tended skin and a hint of . . . something.

The sensation was so faint Lily wasn't sure she really felt it. She closed her eyes and tried to shut out every other sense, concentrating on her hands . . . yes. It was like the difference between air that's completely still and the merest puff of a breath, but it was there.

"You found magic." Julia's voice was high and quick. "You did. I can see it on your face."

"I found something," Lily agreed, opening her eyes. Something that bothered her, but she didn't know why, when she'd barely been able to discern that anything was present at all. Maybe her unease had nothing to do with her Gift and everything to do with whose hand she held. "I don't know what. It's very faint. Would you mind if I touched your face?"

"My face? I—I guess not."

Julia Yu was five inches taller than her second daughter. Lily reached up and laid her palm flat on her mother's cheek.

The skin was soft there, too. Pampered. Had she touched her mother's face at all since she was little? She couldn't remember. Julia was staring at her with such hope, as if Lily could fix things with her touch. Lily's eyes stung, so she closed them. Her hand. She had to focus on her hand.

Not as faint here. Still a barely there sensation, but a bit more present, just as she'd hoped. A spell that tampered with identity or memory should be more concentrated on the head. Only she still didn't know what she was touching. Magic always had a feel to it—slick or rough, intricate or smooth, oily or dry or whatever. This wasn't tactile. More like being in a dark room where you couldn't see a thing, but you knew someone was there. You didn't hear anyone or smell anything. Maybe you sensed the air move or the heat of their body, but you weren't aware of that. You just knew someone was there.

Lily opened her eyes and drew her hand back. Her right hand. Not the one with Rule's diamond. The one with the ring she'd had made to hold the *toltoi*, the charm the clan had given her when she'd become officially Nokolai. The Lady's token, they called it. "I think . . ." God, she could not cry. Not now. She had to be a cop, not a daughter, right now. She made her voice firm. That was what people needed from a cop—firmness, authority, even when said cop was clueless and wanted badly to curl up in a ball. "I did find something."

"Can you take the spell off? Make it go away?"

"No, I'm not a practitioner. We'll get someone who is, though. Someone who knows a lot more than me." Lily tried to smile reassuringly. She was sure it was a sad and sick failure. "Rule—"

"I'll call Cullen." He tried easing one arm away from Julia. She clutched at him. "I'm right here," he said soothingly. "I've got you. I need to call a friend of mine. He's very good with magic."

Cullen Seaborne was one of a kind, the only Gifted lupus in the world. His Gift was one of the rarest, too. He was a sorcerer, able to see magic much as Lily was able to touch it. He'd have some idea what to do.

Lily sure didn't. She drew a shaky breath. What now? If this had been anyone else, a stranger, what would she be doing right now?

"Lily," Grandmother said. "You will now tell us what you found."

All right. Yes, that was one thing she could do. But first . . . "In just a moment. Rule, I need to give your people some directions."

He had his phone to his ear. He nodded.

"Scott, I need the restaurant exits shut down. No one is

to leave. Julia, you'd probably like to sit down. You've had a shock. Grandmother, maybe you could take her to—"

"What did you find? What's wrong with Julia?" That was her father, who had waited all he could. Scott had moved away as soon as Lily gave him his instructions, leaving defense of the hall to Mark, who also didn't budge when Edward Yu shoved him. Her father's hands clenched into fists. "Move."

"Father, I don't know exactly what's wrong, but I know this is a Unit matter. I need to talk to Uncle Chen. Will you bring him here?"

His mouth tightened. He cast his wife one long look, then nodded and turned, pushing his way through the crowd gathering at the hall's entrance. It wasn't just relatives now—several customers had decided they needed to see what was going on.

"Everyone else—you will go back to your tables. Now." She whipped the last word out. Several people did back away. None of her family budged. "Mark, keep this hallway clear. Anyone who doesn't go sit down—" Quickly she amended what she'd been about to say. "Anyone other than Grandmother who doesn't go sit down will be taken politely but firmly to their table."

"Don't be absurd." That was Paul, her brother-in-law. "You can't intend for him to lay hands on any of us."

"This is a crime scene. I mean exactly what I said. I need you to go get Susan." Lily's older sister was a dermatologist, so this was way outside her field, but she could at least make sure their mother didn't go into shock or something.

Being given an assignment tempered Paul's indignation. He frowned to let her know he did not appreciate her attitude, but he left to get Susan.

"Cullen's on his way," Rule said.

Thank God. Though it would take him awhile to get here. He was at Nokolai Clanhome, well outside San Diego. "Grandmother, can you take Moth—Julia—into the ladies' room so she can sit down?" There were a couple of chairs in there.

"Who are all these people?" Julia said plaintively. "I thought I was here with my family, but I don't see them. Is my mother here? You need to call her. Mrs. Franklin Lin. She'll be worried. You'd better call her right away."

Lily met Grandmother's eyes. Her mother's mother had died forty-five years ago . . . two months after Julia's twelfth birthday.

Grandmother stepped forward. "You will allow me to worry about that. I am Madame Yu. I am not your grandmother, but you may call me that, if you wish. Come." She slid an arm around Julia's waist, gently but inexorably detaching her from Rule. She was a full head shorter than the younger woman. "You will sit down now. Someone will bring you a glass of water."

"Can I have a Coke?" Julia asked as she was steered into the ladies' room.

"A glass of Coca-Cola, then. We will not worry about caffeine tonight."

The ladies' room door closed behind them.

TWO

⁓

THE local cops arrived first—two patrol units that Lily put to work right away, herding the abundance of potential witnesses into separate groups. Her own people got there soon after. Ackleford came himself and brought three agents with him. The crime scene team, he said, was on the way.

Derwin Ackleford, aka the Big A, was the special agent in charge of the local office. His nickname did not refer to his size; he was five foot seven with an average build. Nor did it refer to his last name. Lily was convinced Ackleford had some sort of personality disorder. He was rude, crude, and hard to work with, and he always stank of cigarette smoke. He would never have risen to the position he held if he hadn't also been damn good at his job. The Big Asshole was a workaholic—painstaking, methodical, yet capable of brilliant intuitive leaps at times.

Those leaps were probably due to the tiny trace of a patterning Gift he refused to acknowledge. Ackleford was regular FBI, not Unit, which meant Lily outranked him in the ways that counted, if not on the organizational chart. But the man had a second saving grace: all that mattered to him was the investigation. He didn't give a damn who was in charge or who got credit. Or, as he'd put it the first time she'd had to work with him, "Every investigation's got problems. It rains before you get the casts of the tire prints or some asshole in headquarters loses the goddamn form you sent or some idiot chick promoted way past her competence shows up and gets put in charge." He'd shrugged. "Whatever."

In spite of his drawbacks, she was glad to see Ackleford. She briefed him and the other agents quickly, finishing with, "We don't know what we're dealing with. What I need first is names and addresses from everyone present and a brief statement. You know the drill. We also need to know if anyone left before I got the place shut down. Two of you take the family; two take the employees. Employees are in the kitchen." She nodded at the door to that region. "I'll start on the other customers when I can."

Ackleford looked skeptical. "You're saying this was some kind of spell."

"Maybe a spell, maybe something else, but magic is involved. For now, we will proceed on the assumption that what happened was intentional. A deliberate attack."

"The victim's your mother."

"Yes." Temper flared—but not, she realized, at Ackleford. Deep inside, rage had begun to burn.

"And your uncle owns the place."

" 'Uncle' is an honorific in this case. Chen Lin is my second cousin." Ackleford would be thinking that the husband was the usual suspect, or the kids—people who might inherit or who'd been nursing a grievance. "Whoever did this was Gifted. Of those present at the party, only two have the potential to use magic: my grandmother, Li Lei Yu, and my cousin Lin's husband, Mack Li. Oh, and one of the servers who waited on us has a slight empathic Gift, but it's completely blocked. I doubt she could use it if her life depended on it."

"What about your grandmother? What's her Gift?"

"Unique to her, I believe, so it's not named."

"Huh. And your cousin's husband?"

"A minor telekinetic Gift. Mack can't bend a spoon, but

he can nudge it a bit. To the best of my knowledge, however, he lacks any training in spellcraft."

"You left yourself off the list." That came from the newest agent at the office, a man Lily had met but hadn't worked with. What was his name? Fields? No, Fielding. Carl Fielding. "You can work magic."

"Idiots," Ackleford muttered. "Why do they always send me idiots? She's a touch sensitive," he told the man. "Feels magic if it's around, can't be affected by it, can't do shit with it herself. Go away. You and Brewer can make like you know how to interview witnesses."

"Uh—do we take the family?"

"No." Ackleford looked at Lily again, eyes narrowed. "Robert Friar's got a major hard-on for you."

And that was Ackleford. He'd earned his nickname of the Big Asshole, but he didn't settle for the obvious if it didn't fit. "I'd say he wants me dead, but dead probably isn't good enough. So yes, it's possible he's involved, but we've nothing to connect him at this time. I'd like you to double up on interviewing the family so we can release them as soon as possible."

Ackleford grunted. "Who's handling the woo-woo end of things?"

"I've got an expert headed here who can advise us on that."

"That Seaborne guy or the chick with the tattoos or the one with all that red hair?"

"The Seaborne guy. The family is in the small private dining room. I moved them from the larger room, where we—they—were eating. It's—"

"Lily!"

She turned. A tall, elegant woman strode toward her. She wore a simple blue sheath, low heels, and a determined expression.

"That one of your family?" Ackleford asked.

"My sister Susan. Susan Wong. She's a doctor. She and Grandmother have been staying with . . . with the victim in the ladies' room."

"I need to transport my patient to the hospital," Susan said crisply as soon as she reached Lily. "I've called an ambulance."

A jolt of fear made Lily stiffen. "Is she—"

"No, no—there's been no change. She's not in physical distress, but we don't know what was done to her. It was some kind of spell, wasn't it?"

"Magic was involved."

"It might have physical effects that haven't shown up yet. She needs to be checked out."

"Yeah, well, I need to talk to her first," Ackleford said.

Susan turned a polite frown on him. "Who are you?"

"Special Agent Ackleford, ma'am."

"Well, no one is interrogating my mother right now. She's suffered serious trauma, and questions increase her distress, potentially deepening the trauma."

"It's a funny thing, but the FBI doesn't let the victim's family determine who we talk to and when."

"In this case," Lily said, "the family member is also the doctor in charge. She's stated that the victim is not fit for questioning and is about to be taken to the hospital. Pretty clear rules about that. You might try to remember that I gave you an assignment."

Ackleford rolled his eyes. "C'mon, Parker. Let's get started."

"Second door on the right," Lily told him.

"Yeah, yeah. The one that's not being secured by the uniforms. I might've figured that out all by myself."

Ackleford stomped off. Rickie Parker—who was thoroughly female in spite of the nickname, which was short for Fredericka—gave Lily a single, sympathetic glance before following him.

"Who *is* he?" Susan asked, staring after them.

"He's in charge of the Bureau's office here. He is not, however, in charge of this investigation. He'll forget that several more times before we're through. Susan, how is she really doing?"

Susan sighed and looked tired and worried and not doctorish. "She needs a psychiatric evaluation."

"She isn't crazy!"

"We don't know what she is at the moment. I wasn't exaggerating about the trauma. Mentally, she's twelve years old. She remembers nothing later than February twenty-fourth, 1968. At a minimum, we need to monitor her for shock and determine if medication will be helpful."

Lily didn't like it, but . . . "I won't tell you how to do your job."

"Good. Rule will have to go with her."

"Rule? I mean, that's okay, but I would have thought Grandmother or maybe Aunt Deborah—well, no, not her." Deborah would be collapsed somewhere, sniffing damply. Aunt Deborah was as soft and huggable as a teddy bear, but she did not deal well with crises. "But Aunt Mequi—"

"Not Aunt Mequi," Susan said grimly. "She insisted on coming in to talk to Mother, but when Mother saw her, she freaked. I think she recognized Mequi, but the sister she remembers is fifteen years old, not next door to sixty. Even Grandmother couldn't get her calmed down. Rule did, though. He came right into the ladies' room and let her grab hold of him while he patted her back, and she settled down. Only now she's latched on to him like a toddler with a security blanket."

"Then he'll go with her. Have you called Beth?" Their youngest sister was in San Francisco. The day before the party, she'd claimed that a work emergency was keeping her from coming to San Diego. Lily suspected that Beth had decided the guilt involved with missing their mother's birthday celebration would be easier to deal with than the furor if she showed up with her new boyfriend . . . Sean Friar. Robert Friar's half brother.

"Dad did. She'll be here sometime tomorrow."

With or without Sean? Lily decided not to ask. She thought of someone else who had to be called. "What about Grandfather Lin?" Her mother's father was not exactly an involved parent, but he had to be told.

"Grandmother called him."

Lily's eyebrows shot up. "She used the phone?"

"Weird, isn't it? She demanded my phone and called him. He's going to make an appearance, but not right away. He's got some kind of important meeting."

Lily grimaced. Typical. "How's Dad holding up?"

"He's quiet. Really quiet."

Lily bit her lip and nodded. Edward Yu dealt with rough emotional waters by going silent. The quieter he got, the worse things were.

Susan sighed. "Thank God for Grandmother . . . and that's not something I say every day. But no one else could've gotten Aunt Mequi out of there so quick. She sure wasn't listening to me."

When the restaurant doors swung open, both sisters turned to look. It was the CSI squad. "My people, not yours," Lily said. "I have to go."

"I need to get back to her anyway."

"Over here," Lily called. She wasn't sure what good CSI would do. Magical evidence was hard for nulls to collect even if they could spot it, and it couldn't be tested in a lab. Which reminded her that she needed to call Ruben. Cullen was good, the best, but the courts only accepted magical evidence from accredited covens, plus there were some spells that needed to be a group effort. She had to get the coven the Unit used out here, and she needed to report.

Lily pulled out her phone and moved toward the squad so she could tell them to hold off until her magical consultant checked the scene.

Ruben answered right away. While she briefed him, two more patrol cars arrived; she broke off to direct the officers to start getting names and addresses of the sixty-odd customers in the main dining room. The ambulance arrived just as she finished reporting.

"That does explain the disruption I felt in the probabilities," Ruben said. "Which in turn suggests that Robert Friar may be involved."

Ruben was an off-the-charts precog. Friar was an off-the-charts patterner. The two Gifts worked differently, but Ruben usually sensed it when Friar was manipulating the probabilities in a major way. "Does that translate into a hunch you can share?"

"I'm afraid not, but the level of perturbation suggests this event may have wider repercussions than is immediately apparent. Lily, I'm going to allow you to remain in charge for now because you're on-scene, but you can't keep the lead. Not when the victim is your mother."

No. No, he was right. She was too damn angry. "I understand."

"Ida will send the coven to you ASAP. I'm going to send Abel Karonski. He's in Kansas City tying up the last dangling ends of a case, but that can be left to the junior agent he's been training. He should be there tomorrow. I'll have him contact you."

"Okay."

"I'm very sorry about your mother."

The EMTs were wheeling an empty gurney across the dining room. "Yeah," she said, her voice thick. "Me, too."

She'd barely disconnected when her phone gave a drumroll. That was Cullen's ring tone. She answered. "Yes."

"I'm pulling into the parking lot now."

"Good." She glanced at her watch, frowned. Maybe thirty, thirty-five minutes had passed since Rule had called him. "How did you get here so fast?"

"Rule said to hurry. I need you to have a chat with the guy who pulled in behind me. Surly-looking fellow. He's got a flashing red light on top of his car."

The patrol officer did not want to leave Cullen free to wreak havoc on the streets of San Diego. At the very least, he wanted to explain to Lily in detail how many traffic violations Cullen had racked up. "Officer, you can hang around and write tickets for Mr. Seaborne all night if you like, but you will have to wait to deliver them. I need my consultant *now*. Cullen, come with me."

As she turned and started for the front door of the Golden Dragon, she heard the officer mutter, "Goddamn feds."

"Rule said your mother suffered some kind of magical attack," Cullen said, keeping pace beside her. "What do you know?"

"Too damn little. She thinks she's twelve years old and that today is February twenty-fourth, 1968. I confirmed that magic was involved, but it . . . no, I want to find out what you see before I tell you what I felt."

He grunted.

The double doors opened just as they reached them. Mark held one of them wide. Rule held the other. Rule looked at her and nodded in a way meant to be reassuring. The gurney the EMTs pushed out those double doors was no longer empty. Susan walked beside it. Grandmother and Lily's father followed. His face was tight and pale and she didn't think he saw anything but the gurney carrying his wife.

Lily stopped moving. Someone had scrubbed some of the mascara streaks off her mother's face, but she still had the raccoon look going. Beneath the smeared makeup, her eyes looked lost. Bewildered.

"Hey," Cullen said as he stepped up to the gurney. "Hi, Julia. You've had a really rough night, I hear."

"Sir, you need to step away," one of the EMTs began.

"Susan," Lily said, "Cullen isn't going to question her. He just needs a minute."

Susan frowned hard, but she told the EMTs to wait.

Julia's jaw tightened pugnaciously. "I don't know you. I'd remember you if we'd ever met, and I don't."

Cullen was memorable. On the one-to-ten scale of male beauty, he was an eleven. Lily had seen passing strangers stop in their tracks to stare. Especially women, but men did it, too, sometimes. "Well, now," Cullen said with a smile, "if you don't want us to be on a first-name basis, you'll have to call me Mr. Seaborne. I'd rather be Cullen to you, but if you insist . . ."

Julia blushed. Lily had never seen her mother blush. "I—I guess that's okay."

"I'm going to make some funny gestures," he told her, "so I can get a better look at the magic used on you. You won't feel a thing, except maybe like giggling if I look silly."

Julia's eyes got big. "Can you fix me?"

"First I have to figure out what's wrong. What I'm going to do now . . . think of it like going to the doctor and getting a thermometer stuck in your mouth. He usually has to do other things, too, to find out why you're sick, like look in your ears and your throat. And sometimes that isn't enough and they have to do more tests. Right now, though, I'm just taking your temperature."

"Mr. Turner," Julia said, and tried to sit up, but they'd strapped her in. "Mr. Turner—?"

"I'm right here," Rule said and moved to her and took her hand.

She blinked up at him. "Is this your friend that you said was coming?"

"It is. Cullen is very good at magic."

"I'm the great pooh-bah of magic," Cullen assured her. He drew a sign in the air, whispered something, and put his two hands together, then separated them slightly, thumbs and forefingers extended and touching to shape a crude circle. He moved that empty circle around, staring through it, ending with it framing Julia's forehead. He frowned, muttered something that wasn't English, and shifted his hands a couple millimeters. Then he dropped his hands and smiled. "Thanks for staying so still, Julia. I'll see you a little later, okay?" He winked and stepped back.

"Is he going to be able to fix me?" Julia asked Rule as the EMTs got her moving again. She was still clasping his hand.

"Everyone is going to work together to fix you," Rule said firmly. "It may take awhile, though, so you'll have to be patient."

"I guess that's why they call a patient a patient," she said as they stopped at the back of the ambulance. "Because everything takes so long, and you have to be patient."

"You may be right."

Getting her loaded created a problem. Julia wanted Rule with her in the ambulance, and there wasn't room for both him and Susan, and Susan was the doctor. In the end Julia did let go of Rule, but he had to promise he'd do his best to be there as quickly as possible.

As soon as the ambulance doors shut, Rule came to Lily. He put his hands on her shoulders. They felt warm and large and familiar, and she wanted to burrow into him and hold on. She didn't reach for him. She didn't trust herself to let go.

"I'll stay with her," he told her. Just that. He didn't ask if she was okay or how she was doing, for which she was grateful. She wasn't okay.

But she was functioning. She'd keep doing that. "Go," she told Rule.

"I'll leave the car for you."

"No, take it. I'll have a uniform or one of the agents bring me when I'm through."

"All right." His hands fell away. "Mark, you'll drive. Barnaby, with me." He went from motionless to a lope in the blink of an eye, his guards trailing after.

This whole time, Lily's father hadn't said a word. He'd kept his eyes fixed on Julia, then on the ambulance as it backed up. As it pulled away, he turned and started for his car.

"Edward," Grandmother said, "you are not driving."

"I'm perfectly fit to drive," he said without looking at her. But he stopped at the Nissan he'd bought the previous year and didn't open the door.

She didn't answer, but walked up to stand in front of him. She put her hands on his arms and looked up at him—not very far up, for Edward Yu was not a tall man. For a long moment they simply stood there looking at each other. Suddenly his face crumpled, and he whispered something in Chinese that Lily didn't catch.

Grandmother reached up and patted his face, leaving her hand on his cheek as she answered in that language. "You will do what you have to, my son, until you can't. And then you will rest while others do what needs doing."

Edward Yu reached up and placed his hand over his

mother's. A stiff little smile curved his lips as both their hands fell away at the same time. He responded in English. "I will. And as I *am* fit to drive, I will begin by driving you to the hospital."

Grandmother's smile sparked briefly. "Ha! Everyone contradicts me." With that blithe disregard for truth, she went on to dispose of her troops—which in this case meant everyone within earshot and many who weren't. Lily was to pursue her work here. The rest of the family would remain here and obey the officers of the law. "We will leave now," she informed her son. "Sam will meet us there. It will take him two hours."

"Sam?" Lily said, startled. "I thought he was leaving for one of his sing-alongs."

Grandmother snorted. "Hardly that. In any event, he has postponed his departure."

Edward had opened the passenger door for his mother and stopped with his hand on it, staring at his mother in consternation. "Surely you aren't talking about—"

"Of course I am. Doctors are all very well." Grandmother slid into the car. "I do not object to doctors. But in matters of magic and mind, I think the black dragon will be more useful."

The car door shut.

"I hope she's right," Lily said too softly for human ears.

Cullen, of course, wasn't human, and he stood only a few feet away. He heard and moved closer to say softly, "You felt what I saw, didn't you?"

She wanted to tell him she had no idea. She didn't know what he'd seen, did she? Only she was pretty sure she did. "It's not exactly magic that was used, is it?"

"No. I'd hoped to see an intact spell in place, suppressing Julia's memories. That was the best-case scenario. Remove the spell and she's back to normal. Next-best case would be a potion that—"

"A potion could do that?"

"It's not likely, but there are some that cause forgetfulness. They don't make you lose most of a lifetime, though—more like a couple hours. I've heard of one that could make you lose up to a month, but . . . well, I'll skip the technical stuff, but theory doesn't support any potion causing the loss of more than a month because of the tie to the moon's cycles. But potions aren't my thing, so I wasn't going to discount the possibility. A potion wouldn't have been too bad. Sometimes their effects wear off spontaneously, but if not, there's the potential for an antidote."

"You're dragging this out."

"Yeah." He scrubbed a hand through his hair, making it stand up in spikes. "Worst case, I thought, would be a spell that had actually destroyed her memories rather than suppressing them. Just because I've never heard of such a spell doesn't mean it doesn't exist. And at first that's what I thought had happened, because the lingering trace of magic was so small I could barely see it. When I looked with my magnifying spell, though . . . whatever it is, it doesn't look like mind magic."

"Arguai," she said flatly. "That's what it felt like." She ran her thumb over the *toltoi* in her ring . . . which held *arguai.* Or so she'd been told. Her mouth twisted. "Not that I know what that means, but that's what the elves call it. Some kind of power that isn't magic. Magic can tell me it's present, but can't identify it."

"Arguai," he breathed. "Shit."

"You know what it is?"

"Oh, yeah. I can tell you that much, at least. We have another word for it. Spirit."

"That's just a word to me. What does it mean?"

"It means," he said grimly, "that you might need to find a holy man or woman, because I'm not going to be much help. Not any old monk or shaman or priest will do, either. If *arguai* was used on your mother, you need a truly holy person. A saint."

Lily wanted to grab her hair with both hands and yank. Or throw something. Or punch something. Her eyes welled up, and that infuriated her even more. "Any idea where I find a saint? They aren't exactly listed in the Yellow Pages!

Unless Miriam . . . she'll be here soon, with the coven. Does it have to be, like, a Catholic saint?"

"Holiness isn't dependent on creed, but if you're talking about Miriam Faircastle—"

"You know another Miriam? She's a Wiccan high priestess, so I thought maybe she'd do."

Cullen snorted. "Miriam's no saint."

"You don't like her?"

"Woman completely lacks a sense of humor."

It figured that Cullen would see that as a prerequisite for sainthood. "She's a bit intense, but . . ." Her voice trailed off as her eyes widened in shock.

Cullen spun to face the spot she was staring at. "What is it?"

"Mist." White mist that rapidly pushed out blobs so it was shaped like a starfish with a stump where the top limb should be. Four of the blobs coalesced into arms and legs as the one on top became a head and everything sprang into focus. A lean man with slicked-back hair stood there, smirking at her. He was as translucent as the mist he'd formed himself out of.

Al Drummond. Former FBI agent. Former bad guy, though he'd redeemed himself. Currently quite dead, but that didn't keep him from smirking at her. "Surprise."

"Son of a bitch."

"Don't get all soppy, now."

"Drummond—"

"I can't stay, but I wanted you to know, first, that Friar's in this up to his grimy neck. Second, I'll be working this one with you, but mostly from my side of things. I won't be able to chat much." Far faster than he'd come into focus, he winked out.

Lily stared in disbelief at the empty space. "I need a saint, and *that's* what I get?"

THREE

LILY had had plenty of experience dealing with a victim's family members when they were in the grip of grief or anger. She'd thought she understood their feelings. She'd been wrong.

Fury pulsed inside her like a second heart, driving her forward, but she could keep it in check. Use it. Over the next couple hours it flicked at her now and then, hot and raw like a flame licking up the side of a fire pit. But the job wrapped its constraints around her, telling her when to pause and take a breath, telling her not to respond to that sullen lash. As long as she could keep moving forward, she'd do okay.

But it was a good thing Karonski would be here tomorrow. A damn good thing.

At this point Lily knew pretty much exactly what she'd known two hours earlier. Her family had been questioned and turned loose; most of them had headed to the hospital. "Nothing," Rickie had told her. "The Big A and I got nothing from them worth repeating. No one saw or heard anything unusual until Mrs. Yu started screaming."

The coven wasn't here yet. Their head priestess had been in Mission Viejo, over an hour away, when Ida called her. CSI was still working the scene. Cullen was helping them by making sure everything they removed was magically inert. Ackleford and his people were interviewing the last of the restaurant's patrons. Lily had told him that Friar was probably involved. There were special procedures to be followed in a case involving Robert Friar. For one thing, he was a powerful clairaudient—a listener. Lily's Gift blocked him, as did Rule's mantle, but the regular agents would have to be careful about what they said.

And Lily . . . Lily was feeling increasingly useless. She was also running out of reasons to avoid going to the hospital.

She ought to want to be there, but, oh, God, she didn't. For once in her life, she wanted to play ostrich. She would put off going as long as she could, put off that moment when she looked at her father and her family, knowing she was probably the reason her mother had been attacked.

Coincidences happen, but this was not one. Not if Friar was involved. He hadn't done this just to get at Lily, though. He and his damn mistress were too goal oriented for that, and their goal was the biggest makeover ever, using *her* specs for Humanity 2.0.

Lily didn't see how robbing Julia Yu of most of her life gave them a leg up on the world-domination thing. Maybe this had been the test-drive of some new magical trick or device. A way to be sure it worked before turning it on his real target—Rule? Ruben? the president?—and to hurt Lily along the way. That made more sense.

No, it didn't. Why would Friar show his hand this way? Why alert them that such a thing was possible? Robert Friar wasn't stupid. He wouldn't risk having his real attack misfire just so he could shovel some pain into Lily's life. Did that mean that somehow Julia Yu's memory loss did help him? Had there been something in Julia's life—something she used to know, but no longer did—that could derail Friar's plans?

Whatever the hell those plans might be. She needed to stop speculating until she had more facts to build on. If she couldn't get a handle on *why*, she'd look at how. Which meant pestering Cullen, because Miriam and her damn coven weren't here yet.

She only hoped he wouldn't be too bloody careful with her. Some of the others were doing that, and it drove her crazy.

Cullen was perched on a table in the center of the main dining room, legs folded in half lotus, watching the busy CSI techs like a grouchy Buddha. Every so often he sketched something in the air, though his air-writing didn't glow like it usually did. Maybe he didn't like to do that around so many cops. Technically, sorcery was illegal, though the law hadn't been enforced for decades, and not just because most people didn't think sorcerers existed anymore. The law was based on such poor understanding of what sorcery was—and how magic in general worked—that enforcing it was about as reasonable as arresting people for leaving their Christmas decorations up too long. Which, she'd read, was illegal in Maine, but no one got arrested for it.

He saw her coming and stood, then launched himself from the table, leaping over a startled tech using a hand vac. The table rocked slightly. He landed easily and scowled at her. "I hope to God you've got something for me to do."

She should have known she could count on Cullen not to tread warily around her delicate feelings. "You can leave if you're done."

"No, I can't. I'm waiting on Miriam. There's a couple more elaborate spells I can try, but they require a full circle."

"While we wait, I've got a few questions."

"Of course you do." He ran a hand through his hair. "I've got precious few answers for you. Whatever was done to Julia, the spell or ritual took place elsewhere. No matter how carefully a spell or ritual is worked, it leaves traces. There aren't any here."

"You've abandoned the idea of a potion?"

"It's just so damn unlikely. If Friar somehow hooked up with another of Dya's people, someone who might be able to concoct a potion that would do this . . . but that's not at all likely, is it? Plus any potion would have to have turned magically inert afterward, since I checked every glass at the table. That's also hard for anyone but a Binai to pull off."

Dya's people made the most sophisticated potions known to the sidhe, which meant they were very sophisticated indeed. But the Binai were few and lived in the sidhe realms, and the two Queens came down really, really hard on anyone in their realms who so much as spoke the Great Bitch's name. None of the Binai would knowingly give aid to *her*.

All of which made it, as Cullen said, damn unlikely. "So what—ah. At last." Lily started for the restaurant's front door.

It had opened to admit five people. The one in the lead was a tall woman, what some might call statuesque, others lush. An insurance chart would likely peg her as thirty pounds above optimum, but she wore those pounds the way another woman might wrap up in a sarong.

Miriam Faircastle reminded Lily a bit of Nettie Two Horses. They were about the same age, two self-assured, forty-plus women who'd never married or seemed to feel the need. Mostly, though, it was the hair. Miriam's was every bit as long and frizzy as Nettie's and a similar shade of coppery brown. Their styles were vastly different, though. Miriam liked color. Lots of color. Tonight she'd pulled her hair back with a blue scarf. She put that with a floaty turquoise skirt, an orange tee, and a second scarf wrapped around her hips, that one mostly yellow with some green and blue. To make sure she didn't leave any part of the spectrum feeling neglected, she'd added several strands of bright red beads around her neck.

Lily had met three of the people with Miriam. The fourth was new to her—a short, square little woman with thick glasses and a blond braid. Lily gave the group a nod. "I know Jack and Gail and Warren," she said, "and this is—?"

"Abby," Miriam said and clasped Lily's shoulders in her hands, looking down at her with dark brown eyes. "Abby Farmer. You haven't worked with her before. She's new to the coven and is an extremely strong and capable Earth witch. Lily, I am so very sorry about your mother."

Sympathy affected Lily the way peanuts did some people. Her throat closed right up. She nodded stiffly. "Thanks. She'll be okay. Now, I'm sure Ida or Ruben briefed you, but—"

"It has to be terrible for you, working this as if it was just another case. Anything I can do to help, I will. We all will." Miriam glanced at the others, who murmured agreement or nodded.

She could start by not looming over Lily. Miriam's personal space dial was set to Italian or something. She always stood too close. "Thank you," Lily said again. *And if you hug me, I'm going to belt you.* "We need to know several things that I hope you can help with. First, though, I need you to certify that . . . damn." The electronic gong muffled by Lily's pocket was a ring tone she didn't hear often. Grandmother did not like talking on the phone. "I need to answer this," she said, pulling out her phone. "Cullen, could you brief Miriam and the others?"

"Sure. Here's the deal, Miriam. Once you've run the basic tests for the record, I'd like to try a variation on a seek spell with . . ."

Lily stopped listening, moving away as she thumbed the answer button. Her heart pounded. If it was bad news, surely it would be Rule calling, not Grandmother? "This is Lily."

"Do not be alarmed," Grandmother said crisply. "Julia is resting. However, there is disagreement about her treatment. I may revoke my approval of doctors. You are needed here."

RULE had always known his people were at war.

Long before his First Change, he and Steve and the others in their age cohort had killed thousands of dworg. Dworg made satisfying monsters because they were not wholly imaginary. Extinct, yes—or so everyone believed— but the clans had fought the real thing in the Great War.

Sometimes Rule had died heroically in those battles, like Arnos of Etorri, but mostly he'd preferred to emulate Kierran or Tel—heroes who survived to fight another day. Those ancient tales were the stories he'd listened to, played out, and grown up on. All lupi did.

Human history had no record of the Great War. Not surprising, given that it ended over three thousand years ago . . . or so its other participants thought. Not the lupi. War didn't end until your opponent was dead or had submitted irrevocably. The enemy they had been created to defeat was an Old One, as incapable of real submission as she was of dying. She might have been temporarily defeated and locked out of their realm, but the war hadn't ended.

For over three thousand years, each generation of lupi had been raised knowing they could be the ones called upon to resume the war. So Rule had always known that his people were at war, yes, and that his could be the generation called into battle . . . much as he'd grown up knowing the Russians might decide to drop nuclear bombs on his country. It could happen. It probably wouldn't, but it could.

Unlike the lupi's war, the Cold War had ended. And as year rolled into year it had been easy to believe that his generation, too, would live out their lives in relative peace.

One year and four months ago, the Azá tried to open a hellgate.

He and Lily and a great many others had stopped them, but they'd known *she* was behind the attempt. Persuading the other clans of this had been difficult until last September, when the Lady spoke through the Rhejes to announce the resumption of the war. In October, the battle had gone hot. Even humans knew a little about it now—at least, they knew about the battles at the Humans First rallies. Most had some idea of Friar's connection to that carnage, though they didn't know about the Great Bitch and her plans for their world.

A few did, however. At the FBI and in the White House, they knew.

It was one thing to know you might be called to war. It was another to fight it.

Rule leaned his head back in the uncomfortable chair beside Julia's bed and closed his eyes, relieved that she slept at last. Relieved for both of them. Dealing with a sad, frantic twelve-year-old was not easy. But with his eyes closed, the sickness came back, a sickness that pounded in him like a drumbeat.

Wrong, wrong, wrong.

What had been done to Julia was hideous, obscene, wrong on the deepest level. And his fault.

That wasn't true. He knew that, dammit. How could he have anticipated such a thing, much less kept it from happening? He pushed to his feet and then stood there, trying not to pace. Deep inside where that drumbeat pounded, words held no sway. Deep inside, he knew only that he'd failed. Failed Julia and failed Lily. Julia was part of the war because of him. It had been up to him to protect her, and he'd failed.

He took a slow breath to calm himself. God, he hated hospitals.

His eyes fell on the black leather purse sitting primly on the beside table. Edward Yu was a highly logical man, yet he'd insisted that Julia should have her purse. That made no sense. All the familiar detritus of Julia's life had no meaning to her now, but logic broke down under such an onslaught of emotion.

There was a slim leather folder tucked into one outside pocket of that purse. His heart heavy, Rule pulled out that folder. He knew what it held—a notebook containing all the plans for the wedding, written in Julia's slanting, impeccable script.

Lily often found her mother difficult, he knew. He understood why, but he'd enjoyed collaborating with Julia on the wedding. She was pushy, yes, and inclined to hold a very high opinion of her opinions. But once they'd established that Rule could not be pushed somewhere he didn't wish to go, they'd dealt with each other quite well. Julia was a natural organizer, and she'd taken such pleasure in arranging her daughter's wedding. Every detail interested her. Every detail mattered.

Every detail was written down in the notebook he held now. That was fortunate, for Julia remembered none of them now. Sorrow tightened Rule's throat. He tucked the folder into the inside pocket of his suit jacket.

On the other side of the door to Julia's room, Chris spoke. "Madame Yu is coming with a lady who looks like the one you're expecting."

"Very good. Admit them when they arrive." Grandmother had arranged for a family member with a nursing degree to relieve Rule. The woman had been chosen for her training, of course, but also because the twelve-year-old Julia hadn't known her. Julia was most distressed by those she'd known who were now so much older. Rule had asked Grandmother to escort the woman here herself. He had guards at the door to Julia's room and guards with the rest of her family . . . guards who would be useless against the kind of attack that had struck Julia, but it was all he knew how to do. All he could do.

Rule heard Chris's respectful greeting. He carefully smoothed out his face. The door opened, and Madame Yu entered with a woman in her forties with the kind of cushiony body that made children think of laps, hugs, and cookies.

Madame Yu looked at Julia, then at Rule. She frowned. "You must stop that."

He blinked. "Ah—stop what?"

"Never mind. We have no time now, but you and I will talk later. Jin, do you require anything?"

"Not a thing, Grandmother."

Madame Yu was not this woman's grandmother. Jin Zimmerman was the sister of a woman who'd married one of Lily's cousins. But "cousin" was an elastic term in Lily's family, encompassing first, second, and third cousins as well as their spouses, offspring, and sometimes other relatives. It could be confusing, especially since not all cousins were called cousin. Those of Lily's parents' generation or older were "aunt" or "uncle" to her generation—a more respectful title to indicate their status in the clan.

Not clan, he reminded himself. Family. The similarities between her family and his clan were obvious, but the differences mattered. Madame Yu might hold a position similar to Rho, but she had no mantle to enforce her will, nor would challenges to her authority be settled physically.

"Rule," Madame Yu said, "this is Lily's cousin Jin Zimmerman. Jin, this is Rule Turner. I go to the meeting room now. Rule, you will bring Lily there when she arrives." Having delivered her instructions, she left.

"It's good to meet you, Mrs. Zimmerman," Rule said.

"Make it Jin," she said placidly. "How's my patient?"

"Physically well enough. Sam says she'll sleep for at least eight hours, so your duties should be light."

"Who's Sam?"

"The black dragon. He put her to sleep."

"Oh. Yes, I was told about that. He will take some getting used to. I've never had a dragon treating one of my patients."

She didn't seem alarmed at the prospect. "I'm not sure one can get used to Sam. He probably won't bother you, however. I can't say the same for some of the doctors." Julia now had four physicians consulting on her case. He pulled out his card case. "You may want my number."

Jin took his card and glanced at the bed where her patient slept. "Anything else I should know?"

Rule, too, looked at Julia. She was curled up on her side, one hand tucked beneath the skimpy pillow the hospital provided. There were still traces of makeup around her eyes. Her eyelids twitched in some dream, but she didn't stir. He looked at her and all he could think was *Wrong, wrong, wrong.*

"I don't think so," he told her nurse. "Professionally, of course, you must obey the doctors. For anything that does not fall under their authority, heed what Madame Yu told you."

"Oh, yes," she said and settled into the chair Rule had spent too much time in. "I always do." She pulled yarn and knitting needles out of the tote she'd brought with her. "She said Julia imprinted on you."

Rule blinked. "She what?"

"Like a baby duck." She wound yarn around one needle. "Madame said you were the first friendly face Julia saw after being robbed of her memory, and that was that. She fixed on you, just like a baby duck. Should I call you if Julia wakes and asks for you?"

"She shouldn't wake before I return, but yes." Rule gave her a nod and left, closing the door behind him. Two of his men waited there. Two more waited near the nursing station. He nodded at the two who would remain on guard and went to speak with José, who was in charge of the squad. Rule checked quickly with the mate-sense to see how close Lily was. There was time to update his father, so he made that call first, then said, "Everyone is in place?" to José.

José nodded, so Rule gestured at Barnaby and the three of them headed for the stairs. Barnaby had point; José followed three yards behind Rule.

It felt good to stretch his legs. They were only on the eighth floor, so he wouldn't get to stretch them for long, but he savored the sensation. That was not the main reason he was avoiding the elevator, however. Their enemy could have tracked them to St. Margaret's, and a gunman waiting outside the elevator could spray the interior with bullets the moment the doors opened. Rule didn't consider a physical assault here likely, but why take a risk so easily avoided?

Especially when it felt so good to *move*. Defensive wars sucked.

Taking the fight to the enemy was sound strategy. Pity it had proved impossible so far. They had no way of reaching the Great Bitch, and her agent in this realm was a patterner, capable of twisting probabilities to his advantage. In other words, Robert Friar always had extraordinarily good luck. Neither the Bureau nor the clandestine group known as the Shadow Unit had been able to turn up a single lead to his whereabouts, so they were always reacting to their enemy's latest attack, never able to attack first.

Barnaby reached the door to the ground floor and signaled. Rule stopped. Barnaby stood in front of the door, listening and smelling—he had an excellent nose even when two-legged, which was why Rule put him on point—then eased it open and stepped out and quickly to one side.

Rule waited until Barnaby reappeared and gave the okay sign, then followed him into the lobby. The admissions desk was unoccupied at this hour, but several people were passing through the lobby on their way in or out. A couple of men lingered, however—Santos and Jacob. They very properly paid no attention to Rule until he said, "With me."

He hadn't signaled for haste, so they walked over. He checked with the mate-sense again. "Lily will be here in about three minutes. Santos, obtain and hold an elevator for us, please. Jacob, beside me." Eight flights of stairs were a pleasant way to stretch his legs, but a bit much for Lily when she was tired. The elevator should be safe. Their end point was secure; José had people stationed at the eighth-floor elevator. That wouldn't help if someone stopped the elevator on another floor, but Rule knew a trick to prevent that. He signaled Barnaby to proceed, and he and his men headed for the revolving door.

St. Margaret's main entry was in the newest part of the hospital and used the kind of oversize, automated revolving doors sometimes employed at airports and in large office buildings. When they reached it Rule waited while Barnaby checked with the pair of guards patrolling outside. Once Barnaby gave the all clear, Rule and Jacob went through together, with José following.

Rule stepped out into a cool San Diego night just as a black-and-white pulled up three cars away from the doors. It pleased him that he'd timed it so well. Lily was better than he at reading the mate-sense, but he was improving.

The patrol unit's back door opened. Scott stepped out, slid a slow glance around, then nodded that it was safe. Good. Lily had come to understand the need for guards, but with more resignation than real acceptance. She didn't always wait for them to check out an area.

Then the front door opened and the heart of Rule's world stepped out.

Lily wore a blue linen dress banded at the yoke and hem in bright green that stopped well short of her knees. Lily had amazing legs. The rest of the world didn't get to see them often, since her work wardrobe consisted of slacks—almost always black so she didn't have to think about it—with a tee or tank and a jacket to cover her shoulder holster. She liked dresses, though. With this one she wore bright green ballerina flats and her cop face.

"Thanks," she told the driver of the black-and-white and shut the door. Rule moved up beside her and they headed for the revolving doors together. Barnaby continued to hold point; Scott took Rule's left; Jacob walked on Lily's right side, blocking her from possible snipers.

"Have you learned anything?" Rule asked.

"Not much. I've sent people to talk to Friar's daughter and to Jones."

Armand Jones had been Robert Friar's West Coast lieutenant in Humans First. Jones claimed to have ended the association; he was a Christian man, he said, and Friar now worshiped a false god. Accurate enough, as far as Friar's allegiances went; Rule didn't assume that point of accuracy made it true. As for Friar's daughter, she was as much his victim as anyone, but it was possible he'd contacted her. Unlikely, but possible. "You assume Friar had something to do with this?"

"I'll tell you when we can't be overheard. Right now, Cullen's working up a spell he wants to cast with Miriam's coven. He's going to be at the restaurant for several more hours."

Her coolness didn't surprise him. Her expression had already cued him to what she wanted—keep things crisp, brisk, professional. Stay in control. She could have that . . . for now. "Yes, he told me."

"I wanted Scott to stay and guard Cullen. He refused."

The heart of his world was angry. But not, he thought, about Scott, who would have obeyed almost any order Lily gave, save that one. As she knew very well. "There are a lot of police at the restaurant, I believe. Perhaps they'd object if someone tried to shoot Cullen."

"You've suddenly decided that cops are adequate protection?"

"Better than nothing until the squad I sent there arrives."

"And you didn't tell me you'd sent a squad? You could have—no. Cancel that." She drew a sharp breath as they moved into the revolving cage that gave access to the hospital and didn't speak again until they emerged into the lobby. Then she said, "Could you please do something appalling so I'll have someone to yell at?"

"Okay." He stopped, took her arms in his hands, yanked her to him, and kissed her.

FOUR

～

SHARP pain stabbed down on his instep. A second blow took him in the ribs. Rule dodged the next blow and stepped back, pleased.

Unlike Lily. "Don't look so damn smug! I don't want to brawl in the middle of . . . no, I guess I do want to, but it isn't a good idea." She shoved her hair back from her face, looked around—a couple of people were staring—and sighed. "Is it catching? That desire all of you have to pummel someone to help you smooth out?"

As far as Rule could tell, the desire to pummel someone when you were upset wasn't a lupus thing. Humans did it all the time. Unlike lupi, though, they could cause lasting damage if they struck out in anger, so they couldn't afford to offer each other that simple means of relieving stress. "We could go out in the parking lot."

She looked at him for a long moment. Finally the corner of her mouth turned up. Not a full smile, but a wry acknowledgment. "I've relieved enough stress for now, I think."

He held out his hand. She put hers in it. Together they started walking again.

The ease was immediate. This, too, the mate bond gave

them, heightening the inherent comfort of touch. But it was love that made her touch rich, layered, full. Love was like smell, Rule thought. Smell was the most complex and dimensional of the senses, weaving together past and present, near and distant, motion and stillness. Love, too, was a weaver.

"Did Grandmother tell you what's up?" Lily asked. "All she told me was that she may revoke her approval of doctors."

"Madame Yu wants the family—the immediate family, that is—to hear what the psychiatrist advises. Sam disagrees with something the man said or with what he's thinking. I'm not sure which."

Lily glanced up at the ceiling as if she could see through all ten stories to where the black dragon circled overhead. Or perhaps Sam had landed on the hospital's roof again. The hospital authorities didn't like that, but Sam seldom concerned himself with human likes and dislikes. "She told you that? Or Sam did?"

"He hasn't spoken to me."

"Typical."

Lily had not wholly forgiven Sam for what happened three months earlier. She'd been in desperate circumstances and had managed, with great effort, to contact her mind-speech teacher—the black dragon. She'd needed help. She'd gotten three words of advice followed by a slammed mental door. The advice turned out to be good, as did Sam's priorities, once they learned why he'd cut Lily off. At the time, however, Lily hadn't known that Sam could not spare her a second's attention lest his shield around a psi bomb falter. Her sense of betrayal had been great. In her head, she knew now that Sam had done the right thing. Head and heart don't always agree.

The elevators were just ahead. Santos had obtained one and was holding it, as instructed, over the objections of an older couple. At least, she was objecting.

The man weighed at least three hundred pounds, with much of it hanging over his belt. He hovered protectively behind the woman, who weighed a couple hundred pounds less than he did. Her face was sharp, brown, wrinkled as a raisin, and determined. "We are not getting off, so you may as well let that door close," she told Santos.

"Ma'am, for security reasons I have to ask you to take the other elevator."

"The other elevator isn't here. This one is."

Rule let go of Lily's hand and stepped forward. "Ma'am, you are entirely within your rights to insist on taking this elevator. Are you here to visit a friend or a family member?"

She gave him a long, suspicious look before answering. "My granddaughter just had a baby. A beautiful little boy. I am now a great-grandmother."

A smile bloomed all through him. "That's wonderful. Congratulations. Naturally you're eager to see your granddaughter and your new great-grandson. Are they both well?"

"She's as well as any woman is after the travail of labor. He is perfect. Just perfect."

"I'm glad to hear it. Now, as I said, you have the right to use this elevator. But my man was right, too. You will be safer if you take the other one. In the past year the lady behind me and I have been shot, kidnapped, and attacked by demons, doppelgangers, a Chimea, and a wraith. We are going to take this elevator. Do you truly wish to ride with us?"

"No," the behemoth behind her said. "We don't. Come on, Marge."

"I do not think people should be allowed to get away with—"

"Come on, Marge." He put a hand on the small of her back. "Other one just got here, anyway." He gave Rule a cool nod as they exited.

"We'll see you on the eighth floor," Rule told José. It would be only a few moments alone, but he would give Lily those moments.

"You were aimed at the husband all along, weren't you?" Lily said as they changed places with Santos. "I thought you meant to charm her into getting out—and damned if you didn't nearly do it—but he was your target."

"He's protective of her." Rule smiled. It had pleased him to see a couple so clearly woven by time and love into a unit. "No, let me get it," he said when she started to push the button. "I've a trick to use. They're a lovely couple, aren't they?"

"You mean that. Just like you were genuinely delighted to hear about her great-grandson." Lily shook her head. "Which is why it works, I guess."

"Why what works?" He held down the eighth-floor button and the close-door button at the same time.

"Your other superpower. The one that gets people to do what you want. What are you doing?"

The doors closed. "Making this an express elevator. I hold the buttons down until . . . there." The elevator car started moving.

"That's an urban legend."

"No, but it only works on some systems."

"You're sure?"

"We checked it earlier." He moved behind her and wrapped his arms around her waist, holding her close. She didn't resist, but she didn't relax, either. Her muscles were tight.

"I'm not going to fall apart," she told him.

"No?"

"Not yet. I'd like to scream, though. Yell and scream and pound something. Not you, but something. How is she, really?"

"Asleep at the moment, thanks to Sam." He hesitated. What should he say? He had the sense that Julia was deteriorating, but what did he know? He wasn't even sure what he meant by that, except that by the time Sam had put her to sleep, she'd seemed more brittle. Less together, somehow.

And that was too subjective to pass on. Too uncertain. "Julia is very bright. She could see that everything around her was different—the clothes, the technology. She asked if this was 'the future.' Then she demanded to know what year it was. Madame Yu told her. At that point she concluded that she'd traveled through time and ended up in someone else's body."

"Grandmother didn't tell her the problem is with her memory?"

"Julia didn't believe her."

After a moment Lily said, "Once Mother gets an idea in her head, it takes an act of God to get it out. She is a stubborn woman."

"Stubbornness can be a survival characteristic. It makes good glue."

"I suppose. I need to tell you something while we're alone. Don't pass this on, but Cullen and I think that whatever was done to Mother involves the kind of not-quite-magic stuff that's in the *toltoi*. *Arguai*, the elves call it."

His eyebrows shot up. "I'm not sure what that means."

"Neither am I. Cullen says it's the same thing as spirit, but I don't know what that is, either."

The elevator slowed. Rule moved swiftly to stand in front of her. The doors opened. He saw Andy and Jeff and relaxed. "I'm feeling jumpy," he told Lily, more in explanation than apology, but he couldn't apologize for what he didn't regret.

She sighed, but as she joined him in the hall she put her hand on his arm to say she understood his need, even if she didn't like him shielding her that way. "One more thing. Drummond's back."

"What?" He stopped and stared at her.

"He popped in and told me he'd be working this one with me, but on his side of things." She'd thought her personal haunt was gone for good, not just for a couple months.

"What the hell is that supposed to mean?"

"I have no idea."

Rule glanced around. "Is he . . ."

"He's not here now. He told me that Friar was definitely involved and that he wouldn't be able to chat much. Then he winked out."

Lily didn't see ghosts . . . except for this one. And no

one else saw Drummond. Just Lily. Although there had been a couple of times before Drummond crossed over—or whatever you called it when a ghost went wherever the dead go—when the mate bond had made it possible for Rule to see him. Al Drummond had put himself through hell to get word to Rule when Lily was in Friar's hands. Without him, Rule wouldn't have found her in time. He'd done that, then vanished. For good, they thought.

Rule was aware how much he owed Drummond. That didn't mean he had to like him. His mouth tightened. Why couldn't the man stay decently dead?

"So," Lily said, "where are we supposed to hold our family council? And who all will be there?"

And he needed to get over the petty annoyance of Drummond's reappearance and pay attention to what mattered. Rule started walking again. "It's this way—a small conference room that Paul arranged for us to use." St. Margaret's wasn't the largest hospital in the city, nor was it the closest to the Golden Dragon, but it was where Susan's husband, Paul, worked in administration. That was why Julia was here rather than at another hospital. "Dr. Babbitt will be present, of course. He's the psychiatrist. Your father and grandmother. Susan and Paul. You and me. I believe your mother's sisters will be there, too."

"The cousins?"

"None of them."

"Thank God. Or maybe Grandmother."

"She does have a way. It was your father who set that particular restriction, though. Is holding a family council a custom of yours? Will everyone vote on what to do?"

That made her grin, albeit briefly. "You sound so appalled. No, this will not be an exercise in democracy. Dad always said, 'You get to be heard. You do not get a vote.' I guess I haven't talked about our family council meetings. It's been years since we did that. They were usually about where we'd go for vacation or if we should put in a pool—that one was a clear example of nondemocracy in action. We had a family council meeting once when Dad had been offered a really good job, but we'd have had to move to L.A. . . ." Her pleasure in the memory faded. "We never had one for something like this."

He took her hand again.

After a moment she said, "Doctors don't usually hold a conference with better than a half dozen family members."

"For that you may thank or blame your grandmother. Madame Yu informed him that he would do so. He's probably still wondering how he ended up agreeing."

They'd reached the conference room, where Todd and Jacob stood watch. Lily's aunt Mequi was just going in. The older woman stopped to frown at Lily. "I don't like having these guards everywhere. They're obtrusive. They don't help."

Rule answered before Lily could. "The guards are my contribution. Do you wish to discuss their presence now, or can it wait until after the family council?"

Mequi sniffed. "I suppose it can wait, but you need to send them away. It makes everyone very edgy to have them standing around watching like that." She turned and went into the room.

Rule was baffled. "The guards are supposed to make them feel safer."

Lily squeezed his hand and let go. "They didn't know they weren't safe until now. Come on. Let's go in and get it over with."

FIVE

As soon as they entered, Rule saw that his roster of who would attend had been incomplete. Julia's two brothers-in-law had been added to the mix: Jim Chung, Mequi's husband, and Feng Li Zhang, who was married to the pillowy Deborah. That filled every spot at the conference table save for two chairs waiting for him and Lily.

Most of those present were talking with each other. Edward Yu was not. He sat at one end of the table, as silent and stiffly erect as his mother, who sat at his right. At the other end of the table was the one person who was not a family member, a tall, stoop-shouldered man in rimless glasses: Dr. Babbitt. The psychiatrist's hair was thick and straight and gray, though his face was unlined. He smelled of baby lotion and hand sanitizer. Rule sat beside him.

Lily seated herself and immediately leaned across Rule to hold out her hand. "Dr. Babbitt? I'm Lily Yu."

He looked surprised but shook her hand. "I'm glad to meet you, Ms. Yu, but very sorry for the circumstances."

Lily nodded gravely and released his hand. "This is my fiancé, Rule Turner."

"Yes, we met briefly."

Lily leaned back and met Rule's eyes. She gave a tiny shake of her head to tell him she hadn't found any magic on the man.

Edward Yu spoke quietly. "We will begin now." The other conversations drifted to a halt. "Thank you. I have two decisions to make. Please understand that they will be my decisions, but I value your opinions. First I wish to make sure we all have the same information. Lily, is there anything you can tell us?"

Lily looked down at the notebook she'd set on the table, but she wasn't consulting her notes; the notebook was closed. She spoke slowly. "Not yet. I mostly have negatives, and they aren't confirmed."

Mequi's husband frowned. Jim Chung was a solidly built man with a sweet tooth and a fondness for crossword puzzles. He earned a good income as a tax attorney. Lily said that her uncle Jim made up his mind about as fast as glaciers traveled, but once it was made up, he never changed it. "What does that mean, you have negatives?"

"We're fairly sure it wasn't a potion, for one. And no," she said when her uncle started to speak, "I am not going to go through the list of things we think it wasn't."

Mequi spoke crisply. "You owe us more than that. It is clear that Julia was hurt because she is your mother. What other reason could there be? If we are in danger because of you—"

Edward's palm slapped the table hard. "Enough! We are not going to—"

"She has a point, Edward," Lily's other uncle said. Feng was normally a cheerful man, easygoing and sociable. He looked ruffled now. "If Lily's job is putting us and our children in danger . . ." He glanced nervously at Rule. "Or maybe it's her association with lupi. Whichever, we deserve to—"

"Deserve?" That was Madame Yu, her voice cold and sharp enough to cut flesh along with the others' speech. "You will tell *me* what you think you deserve, *bái mù*, for blaming the one who fights evil instead of blaming the evil she fights."

Rule didn't know the Chinese phrase she'd used. Clearly

Feng did. Just as clearly, it was an insult. He went white around the mouth.

Edward spoke into the sudden silence. "If terrorists in Afghanistan blow up a girls' school and kill the students, are their teachers to blame for teaching them? Are their parents at fault for wanting their daughters to be taught, or are the Afghan people to blame for not giving in to the terrorists?"

Feng spoke stiffly. "I was not blaming Lily."

To Rule's surprise, his wife, Deborah, said firmly, "Yes, dear, you were. Not in so many words, but that's what Mequi and you meant. And very upsetting that must be for poor Lily." She reached across the table and patted Lily's hand. "Pay no attention to them, sweetheart."

"Thank you, Deborah," Edward said. "I would like to stop wasting time now. We are going to hear from two experts who disagree about Julia's diagnosis, but first I must make you aware of a difficult decision I face. Some of you have met Dr. Babbitt already. He is a well-credentialed psychiatrist recommended by both Susan and Paul. He believes I need to have Julia declared incompetent."

"Oh, no," Deborah said. "Oh, no."

"That can't be right," Lily muttered. "I don't see how that can be right."

"It's not as bad as it sounds," Susan said. "Mother— well, she thinks she's twelve. She won't react the way she would if she were . . . if she thought of herself as an adult."

"Edward," Feng said. "You're considering this?"

Mequi looked severe. "Of course he is. What else is to be done?"

"I'm considering it," Edward said evenly. "I haven't decided. From what Dr. Babbitt tells me, the medical power of attorney I hold for Julia doesn't apply in the current situation."

"The problem is," Dr. Babbitt said gently, "that the law regards Julia as an adult. She's not comatose, nor does she fall under other established guidelines, so at this time we have to obtain her agreement to any course of action taken to help her. Given that she is mentally twelve years old and has no knowledge of what medicine is like in the twenty-first century, I don't believe she's capable of making such decisions. But even if you agree, this can't be implemented quickly. It would have to go before a court."

"I wanted you all to be aware that this may need to be done," Edward said, "though it can't happen right away. My immediate decision rests on the points on which our two experts disagree—diagnosis and treatment. Dr. Babbitt, will you present your diagnosis?"

The psychiatrist cleared his throat. "I can't call it that. As far as I can tell, Julia's case is unique, so we have no diagnosis that fits. I can give you my professional opinion, though, which is based on both my interview with her and on diagnostic tests." He looked around the table, making brief eye contact with everyone. "First, I'm told that her condition was magically induced. If so—"

"If?" Lily said.

He smiled apologetically. "I'm not questioning your expertise. In my field, we often express opinions conditionally. Psychiatry is a science, but not a precise one. We still know very little about how observational data correlates to physical data about the brain. In other words, I can readily diagnose schizophrenia, but not by using an MRI. Yet MRIs can still be useful. In your mother's case, the MRI shows no evidence of brain damage or other abnormalities, which is encouraging. It suggests that whatever was done to her, the effect was to suppress her memories, which—"

That is false.

The mental voice was as sharp and cold as a shard of ice. All around the table, eyes popped wide. Dr. Babbitt turned pale. Mequi said something in Chinese; Susan and Deborah gasped. Paul stiffened and Jim looked around suspiciously and Feng blurted out, "What the hell was that?"

"That," Grandmother said, "is the other expert we will hear from—Sun Mzao, known to some as Sam."

"The, uh . . ." Dr. Babbitt cleared his throat. "The dragon."

"Yes."

"Then that was mindspeech."

"Of course."

"I have never . . ." The psychiatrist shook his head. "How should I address him?"

Out loud. It is tedious to sort through the mental chatter that passes for thought in humans to abstract what you wish to say. Do not address me now. I will first correct your conclusion that a lack of physical damage to the brain means that Julia Yu's memories are being magically suppressed. They are not. The memories are either destroyed or unreachable.

Dr. Babbitt straightened his shoulders. "I, uh, suppose, sir, that you have examined her thoughts, but that would prove only that her memories aren't available to her."

The human tendency to settle on the convenient or comfortable answer is biologically based, as is the way you leap at conclusions like frogs jumping at flies. Resist this tendency. I recommend you review the work done by your Dr. Daniel Kahneman. It is flawed, but his metaphor of the two systems is a reasonable way for you to grasp the existence of your innate biases so that you may attempt to guard against them.

"Dr. Kahneman? I don't . . . oh, yes, heuristics. I've read his work on heuristics, but I don't see what that has to do with—"

You know I can read thoughts. You assume this is the extent of my ability to work with minds. You are wrong. You are also wrong about Julia's condition. Of course, you lack a basic grasp of the interrelation between memory, identity, and sovereignty, so your failure to comprehend her condition is not surprising.

"And you do comprehend it?" The doctor sounded both polite and skeptical.

Not fully. Unlike you, I perceive it, but my comprehension is limited. I have never encountered a mind damaged in this way. I will now address Julia's family. Do not interrupt. Edward Yu.

Lily's father didn't bat an eye. "Yes?"

Julia's memory is not being magically suppressed. Either the vast majority of such memories no longer exist or they are severed from her mind. She does possess some badly fragmented memories from beyond the day when she observed her twelfth birthday, but she is unaware of them. This suppression is her mind's own instinctive response. No effort should be made to direct her thinking toward those fragments. It is unlikely her mind would survive.

Lily reached for Rule's hand and held it tightly. She didn't speak.

"You are saying . . ." Edward's voice broke. "You say there is no hope."

There is no chance that conventional human treatments will restore her memory. There remains a slim chance of magical restoration. This depends on whether we can determine what induced her condition and on whether the memories have been eradicated or are somehow severed from her mind. Understand that by "mind" I do not mean brain or the ability to reason. Mind is the product of consciousness combined with memory. It is not a wholly physical construct, but its nonphysical components are largely inaccessible by humans. Ghosts are a projection of mind. Most are uninhabited by consciousness, but not all. Lily Yu.

"Yes." Lily's voice was husky, as if with unshed tears. She kept a tight grip on Rule's hand.

The ghost of Al Drummond contacted you. What did he say?

"If you know that much, why don't you know what he said?"

I sense the constructs you call ghosts, but I cannot hear them. I heard your speech to him. I did not hear his speech to you, which uses channels you would describe as spirit.

Lily grimaced. "Spirit again. He said Friar was involved and that he'd be working this case with me, but mostly on his side of things."

Good. You will need his assistance, limited as it is likely

*to be. You and Cullen Seaborne are correct in assuming
that the attack on your mother involves spiritual energy
rather than purely magical.*

"But what does that mean?" she cried, frustrated. "I
don't have any idea what it means when you say 'spirit.' "

*I congratulate you on awareness of your ignorance.
Spirit is capricious, personal, universal, and indefinable.
It can neither be shaped through will nor grasped by reason.
It is often spoken of in terms of good or evil, and observa-
tion suggests that humans in particular access it through
this polarity. It is both the product of and the ground for soul.
I understand very little about it.*

"You . . ." Rule closed his mouth before he finished that
statement—though Sam was probably well aware of what he
was thinking. Sam habitually claimed vastly superior understanding of pretty much everything, and not without reason.
If the first couple of millennia don't kill you, you probably
do know what you're talking about most of the time. If the
black dragon didn't understand spirit, who did? Rule kept his
voice level. "Do you have a recommendation?"

*Several. First, you need spiritual consultants. Dr. Nettie
Two Horses is an obvious choice. I suggest you seek others
as well. Second, you need to bring Julia Yu to me on the
roof of this building. I will ensorcell her and—*

The outcry was immediate.

"What?"

"Absolutely not!"

"No one is going to ensorcell my sister."

"If this is your idea of an expert, Edward, you need to—"

Madame Yu slapped one hand on the table. "Bah! Stop
bleating. You dislike the word 'ensorcell.' You understand
it not at all. It is a tool, like a surgeon's knife. It works for
good or ill depending on the wielder's intent and skill."

Sam's chill mental voice took over. *The surgical analogy is appropriate, although in this instance I would liken
ensorcellment more to the anesthetic than to the knife. I
propose to perform what you may think of as delicate and
complex mental surgery on Julia. Without ensorcellment,*

this would be as brutal as if a cardiac surgeon were to cut open a patient without benefit of anesthesia and saw through his ribs to gain access to his heart. Even if the patient did not die from shock, his screams and writhings would render a successful outcome unlikely.

That brought a few moments of profound silence. Edward broke it. "If Julia's memory is gone or—or whatever, what good will this surgery do?"

Julia's condition is fragile. Dr. Babbitt is aware of this. He makes several errors, but his observational skill is sufficient for him to recognize what I perceive more directly. He intends to propose that she be incarcerated in a facility where her environment can be regulated in an attempt to shield her from some of the shocks of adapting to a time, place, body, and people she does not recognize or understand.

Deborah looked horrified. Her voice wobbled as she addressed Dr. Babbitt. "You want to lock her away?"

The doctor's eyes were soft with distress. "This wasn't how I meant to bring it up, nor is that how I'd phrase it, but . . . yes. Essentially I agree with, uh, Sam about her condition. She needs to be in a controlled environment."

Such incarceration might delay the fragmentation of her mind. It will not prevent it. An accurate projection of when such fragmentation will become irremediable is not possible, but without my intervention, it may take place quite quickly. I am particularly concerned about the strength of her mother bond. Her mother died forty-five years ago. She is not aware of this.

"No," Grandmother said. "She asks for her mother. We make excuses. We have not told her that her mother died many years ago."

That is wise. I do not judge her mind capable of sustaining such a shock. Withholding this information is a temporary solution, however. She will either guess the truth or construct elaborate stories to protect herself from that. Already she has begun to do the latter. Eventually these stories will acquire permanence, and there will be no way to supplant them with observable reality.

Eventually Julia really would be crazy, in other words. Rule's throat went tight with sudden grief.

Edward spoke slowly. "You say you can prevent this. How?"

I propose to buttress certain mental constructs and alter others. I do not go into detail as you lack both the language and the conceptual background to understand, but several of them relate to her temporal sense. I will distort that to mimic the buffering provided by the passage of time. This will give her a better chance of surviving the blow to her mother bond and aid her in accepting her current body and other aspects of reality.

"A better chance," Lily repeated. Her voice was level. Her hand gripped Rule's so tightly his fingertips tingled. "How much better?"

Substantially better. I do not affix numbers to what is essentially unquantifiable. You should all be aware that, regardless of your individual or joint conclusions regarding competency, I will seek Julia's permission before proceeding.

Mequi's eyebrows lifted. "Mentally, Julia is twelve years old. You consider a child competent to make such a decision?"

Your species employs a far greater degree of custodial care for its young than mine finds either necessary or desirable. Respect for this species difference does not require me to violate my ethical standards. Julia Yu has done nothing that would entitle me to subvert her autonomy. I will not proceed without her consent. You should also know that delay is inadvisable. The sooner I am able to proceed, the better the outcome will be.

Edward Yu spoke. "In the interest of speed, then, we will now discuss which course to follow—that of Dr. Babbitt or that of Sun Mzao. We will go around the table. Mother, will you begin?"

"I prefer to go last, Edward."

"Very well. Jim?"

Mequi's husband didn't want to talk about the dragon's

proposed treatment versus the doctor's. He declared himself incompetent to make that decision—if that was meant as a joke, it fell very flat—and offered a short lecture on the legal means of declaring someone incompetent in California.

Mequi, next to him, said that of course Julia was not competent to make such decisions at this time, and that with all due respect to the black dragon, humans were obviously better able to determine what humans needed than he was. They should either follow Dr. Babbitt's advice or bring in additional doctors.

Lily's phone vibrated while Mequi was speaking. Her lips thinned, but she took out her phone to see who it was. Rule couldn't see the screen, but it must have been important because she interrupted. "I'm sorry. I have to take this."

"Good God, girl, can't you turn that thing off?" Jim exclaimed. "We're talking about your mother's—"

"Jim," Grandmother said, "enough."

"I was just going to—"

"You will do me the favor of shutting your mouth."

Wearily Edward said, "Lily is not chatting with her friends, Jim. The call must have something to do with the investigation. It may be urgent."

Rule was able to hear most of what the caller was saying to Lily in spite of the chatter at the table. Edward was right. It was about the investigation, and it was urgent.

Lily put her phone up and pushed away from the table. "I have to go. Rule, will you speak for me?"

He met her eyes. "What will I say?"

"That we're wasting time talking. There's no real choice to be made. If Sam says Mother has to have this procedure or her mind will come unglued, then she does." Then she added more intimately, *You heard what Officer Perez told me?*

Unlike everyone else at the table, Lily could use mindspeech. Not reliably, but sometimes. Rule nodded somberly. "You'll be in touch with Ruben."

"Oh, yeah." She looked around at her family, but her

gaze ended on Dr. Babbitt. "Doctor, the Bureau may wish to use your services as a consultant. I need your number so I can contact you if needed."

"Of course, but why? I'm already on your mother's case." He lifted up so he could pull his wallet from his back pocket. He took out a business card and handed it to her.

"Because it looks like Mother wasn't the only victim." She looked at Rule. "I'm headed for Scripps on Fifth."

"Take Scott and Mark."

She grimaced but left without arguing—or answering any of the questions her family hurled at her retreating back.

SIX

~

"**WELL**, I like that!"

"That kind of cavalier attitude—"

"I can't imagine you're going to let her behave that way, Edward."

"Of course he will not, Edward, I will go get Lily and tell her to come back here right now." Mequi scraped her chair back.

Rule had had enough. "Stop!"

Faces turned toward him—incredulous, startled, and displeased faces.

He looked at them one at a time . . . and he let his wolf rise just enough that they would see it in his eyes. They might not consciously recognize what they saw, but their hindbrains would. "I am tired of this. You are Lily's family. You love her—and you chide her as if she were a child. You have no grasp of her responsibilities or her abilities, and no respect for her authority. If she could have told you more, she would have. You are making a terrible time more difficult for her and for Edward. Stop."

No one said a word. Mequi was rigid with affront; Feng was frightened and trying to hide it. Paul was uneasy, which made him look especially wooden, and Dr. Babbitt flinched away from Rule physically. Susan's face flashed from alarm to disapproval. Jim frowned, but there was a thoughtful look in his eyes. Deborah was simply astonished. Madame Yu's eyebrows lifted. She gave him a small nod.

Edward's expression didn't change. Rule realized he'd been wrong. Edward's family wasn't making things worse for him. He was barely aware of them, save when they spoke directly about Julia. He had no energy, attention, or emotion to spend on anything not directly related to his wife's health. "Since Lily was called away," Edward said as if nothing had happened, "it is your turn to speak, Rule."

Speak about Julia, that is . . . who was why they were here. Who wasn't here with them, helping them make this decision. They'd already deemed her unable to participate in her own care regardless of what the law said, which Rule intended to point out to—

Do not.

Sam could direct mindspeech to one or many. This time, Rule was sure Sam had spoken only to him. Sam was well able to pluck the thoughts from Rule's head . . . or respond to his general confusion. Which was what he did next.

Do not point out that they have no legal authority to make this decision for Julia Yu. Li Lei would be displeased.

As far as Rule knew, only two beings called Lily's grandmother by her first name: Sam and her companion, Li Qin. Rule followed Madame's wishes when he spoke, not pointing out that they could not legally make this decision for Julia, so this meeting was pointless.

Why didn't Madame Yu want them to realize that?

The question all but answered itself. If Edward decided against having Sam treat Julia, his mother intended an end run. She or Sam would tell Julia what Sam proposed—and Julia was legally able to direct her own treatment.

You are slow, Sam said, *but you arrive at the obvious. Edward Yu believes he is keeping an open mind. He is not. He possesses a strong and visceral distrust of direct mental manipulation; he considers it an unholy violation of*

*sovereignty. Were he in a better mental state himself, he
would be able to reason that the violation has already
taken place, and what I propose is similar to the violation
of a surgeon's knife, made to repair what has been
damaged. He is not at this time capable of this level of
reasoning.*

*However, it is not Li Lei or myself who will persuade
Julia Yu to accept my proposed treatment. That falls to
you. She trusts you.*

Apparently persuasion did not violate Sam's ethical
standards.

*Direct mental manipulation without consent abrogates
choice. Persuasion does not.*

To a dragon, choice was the fundamental value. All vir-
tues and all sins flowed from it. The funny thing was that
dragons were also great meddlers. Rule had sometimes
wondered how Sam resolved the apparent contradiction.
Apparently the key lay in how one defined manipulation.

If Sam disagreed with Rule's conclusion, he didn't say
so. Rule finished the out-loud conversation by repeating
what Lily had said about them having no choice. Sam
was the only one who could help Julia. Edward listened
carefully, but without giving any sign Rule had convinced
him.

Dr. Babbitt was up next. He began to talk about his
proposed treatment—antianxiety drugs, talk therapy, and
sequestration in a mental institution. He padded that bleak
picture with a great many words.

Use whatever means seem best to convince Julia, Sam
told Rule while the doctor spoke. *This should not trouble
your own ethical standards. You are accustomed to making
decisions for others.*

Yes, but Julia wasn't one of his clan members.

*You are also accustomed to manipulating others into
making the desired decision themselves. Your father is better at this, but you have some skill. Lily Yu agrees that this
is necessary.*

That surprised Rule—both that Sam had already told

Lily and that she'd agreed, considering how unhappy she was with Sam at the moment.

Lily Yu has grown fond of me. When fondness grows in humans, an innate mechanism transfers expectations along with the emotion. Because this transfer occurs without conscious recognition, she is unaware of the foolishness of those expectations and experiences only their violation. She is, however, capable of setting this reaction aside to do what is necessary. Once you have persuaded Julia, I will put Julia to sleep again. Bring her to my lair.

Sam wasn't going to do this at the hospital?

I will need the protections at my lair. This will be a lengthy process and will leave me incapacitated in important ways. You do not see the ramifications. The Great Enemy is aware of me and at least some of my actions against her.

Dr. Babbitt finally finished. It was Paul's turn. He surprised Rule by saying only that he was out of his depth and would support whatever decision Edward made.

Susan was up next. She wanted to allow Dr. Babbitt to treat Julia with antianxiety drugs here at the hospital and to bring in other experts, get more opinions. While she talked, so did Sam. *It is reasonable to assume our enemy will be aware that I am partially incapacitated. Whether she can pass this knowledge to Robert Friar is unknown, but even if she cannot, his Gift will suggest to him that this is a good time to strike.*

Shit.

Susan finished by emphasizing the need to have more information before making a decision. Deborah stood and began meandering through a teary account of an event from Julia's childhood.

I speak to you now in your dual capacities as Lu Nuncio of Nokolai and as second-in-command of the Shadow Unit. You are aware that I monitor my territory in ways unavailable to those who are not dragon. You are not aware of various defenses I have in place, or of the matrixes I have established to alert me to sudden shifts in the probabilities. While I am treating Julia I will be unable to monitor my territory, any magical defenses outside my lair, or those matrixes. I will pass to Li Lei the monitoring of my territory. I do not explain the mechanism, which would be meaningless to you, but the senses involved in such monitoring are ill suited to her current form. She will change to her other form and she will be at my lair. I expect the procedure to take between fifteen and twenty-two hours. She will need to eat far more than usual during this period. She tells me she would prefer deer—whole but skinned, as she dislikes the hair, and freshly killed. You may leave the antlers on. She enjoys gnawing on them. Two small deer should do. The carcasses should be left immediately in front of my lair. Arrange this.

Ah . . . all right.

Deborah finished by surprising Rule. After wandering through various tales, ending with the story of how Edward and Julia first met, she sniffed and said that of course they would allow the dragon to do what he could for Julia, and she for one was very grateful to him.

If you consider any debt to be incurred for arranging for the deer, Sam informed Rule, *that is between you and Li Lei.*

There could be no debt where Madame Yu was concerned . . . although finding, killing, and skinning two deer might take awhile.

I recommend haste.

Deborah's husband, Feng, profoundly disagreed with her. No one should be allowed to go messing around in his sister-in-law's head, however good their intentions might be, and how could a dragon know enough about human minds to tinker with them, anyway? He continued to say much the same thing for some time.

I also wish the use of Cullen Seaborne. Note that I make no request of you and will incur no debt. I offer you the chance to act in defense against our common enemy, Robert Friar, by providing me the use of your man. You can agree to this, in your capacity as Lu Nuncio of his clan?

He could, but why Cullen?

I wish to pass to Cullen Seaborne the monitoring and control of some of the magical defenses in my territory. He will not be able to carry all of them, but I judge him able to accept those sites I deem most vulnerable to attack. He will not be damaged by this task, but he will be incapacitated both during and afterward. I estimate that he will be unconscious for at least twenty-four hours and is likely to experience depletion for two or three subsequent days. If you agree to this, understand that I will not allow him to retain full knowledge of my defenses. I may permit him to retain some of what he learns if he does not annoy me too badly.

In spite of everything, Rule's mouth crooked up. Cullen wouldn't just be okay with this—he'd be furious if Rule didn't give him the chance to drain himself into oblivion in exchange for learning something, anything, about Sam's mysterious "magical defenses."

Precisely. Sam's mental voice was, for once, not wholly unflavored. A whiff of wryness came through.

At last Feng stopped repeating himself and sat. Madame Yu did not stand to make her case. She looked at Edward. "You know my counsel. I have offered it to you already. I add only that there is no benefit in delay and much danger."

The room was silent as everyone looked at Edward.

He will not agree, Sam said coolly. *He is very torn, very muddy. He is aware of his muddiness and will delay, hoping for clarity in the future. Julia's condition deteriorates too quickly for such delay.*

Rule looked at Madame Yu. She met his eyes and again gave a small nod. Maybe Sam had directed that last bit at her as well as Rule. Or maybe Sam had been talking separately to her all along. He was capable of carrying on multiple mental conversations.

Edward looked down at his hands, clasped on the table. He looked at his mother, then away. "I thank you all for sharing your thoughts," he said slowly. "I appreciate Deborah's reminder that we must be grateful for what Sun Mzao has offered and I understand why some of you urge me to

accept that offer. I may do so later, but at this time I agree
with Susan. I do not have enough information to make a
decision. I will ask Dr. Babbitt to continue treating Julia
here for now, and also to give me the names of other experts who may be helpful. Sun Mzao, you said . . . earlier
you told me that sleep offers her mind some protection. If
you can keep her asleep for now . . ."

I can.

"Thank you. I . . . she is confused by my presence, but I
can at least be with her when she sleeps without upsetting
her." Abruptly he stood. "Dr. Babbitt, if you would get
those names for me . . . but you can give them to me later.
Text me or . . . I'm going to stay with Julia awhile."

"Father?" Susan said. "Do you want me to—"

"Not now," he said. "Not now." He left quickly.

Chairs were scraped back. Voices were kept low, as if
they were at a funeral. Paul began talking to Dr. Babbitt.
Feng and Deborah formed their own little knot of disagreement as Rule made his way to Madame Yu. He quirked an
eyebrow and spoke very softly. "Are we kidnapping her, or
do we do this openly?"

"Openly." She glanced at the door that had shut behind
her son. "This will be difficult enough on Edward. I will be
sure he lies down somewhere here to rest in an hour or so.
Sam will need that long to prepare. Then it is up to you to
convince Julia."

"In the meantime, I will arrange for deer."

"Good." Her eyes were troubled, but her voice was as
crisp as ever. "Skinned."

"But with the antlers."

She nodded, but he didn't see the flash of mischief in her
eyes he'd expected. "He is shutting me out," she said
abruptly. "Sons must do this with mothers sometimes."

"Mothers don't have to like it."

"No." The faintest of sighs. "I will speak with Mequi
now. She is more vulnerable than the others."

Mequi was more pigheadedly certain than anyone else
in the room.

As if she'd read his mind—which he was almost positive she couldn't do—Madame Yu patted his arm. "Certainty hides many things. You should know this. Mequi raised Julia after their mother died. She needs something to do."

Mequi wasn't the only one who needed that, he thought as he watched Madame Yu head for her daughter-in-law's sister.

He took out his phone. He'd speak with his father about the deer. There were three herds that included Nokolai Clanhome in their range, so the clan should be able to accommodate Madame's requested menu. Then he'd call Cullen. But where was Cullen supposed to—

At my lair, Sam said. *I will be there. I will now complete my warning.*

There was more?

My territory and some of the defenses will be monitored. There is no one who can monitor the probability matrixes. As second-in-command of the Shadow Unit, you need to be aware of this. There will be an increased vulnerability to attack by Friar and his organization while I am incapacitated.

Rule wondered if Sam had told Ruben . . . Lily's boss at the FBI, the head of Unit Twelve, who was also the creator and first-in-command of the Shadow Unit.

Mika has informed him.

Mika was the D.C. dragon. Rule frowned. Sam was going to an immense amount of trouble for Julia. Rule knew he'd already delayed his departure for some important gathering of dragons. He meant to render himself vulnerable, leave a possible opening for their enemy. If Sam considered that a debt was owed him for all this, it would be one whopping huge debt.

I do this for Li Lei, that cold, crystalline voice said. *There is no debt. There can never be debt between myself and Li Lei.*

SEVEN

~

THE coffee in Lily's cup was black, burned, and bitter. Suited her just fine. Maybe that was because it fit her mood, or maybe it was the comfort of the familiar. How many cups of bad coffee had she drunk when she was a local cop like the man who'd just handed her this one?

"If that doesn't work, you're gonna need toothpicks," Officer Perez said.

"It'll do. Thanks." They were in the tiny alcove of a room where visitors to the patients on this floor could get coffee or a soft drink. Scott and Mark—her designated bodyguards, though she preferred to think of them as mobile backup—were just down the hall. Lily had snarled her way into this abbreviated privacy after interviewing the newest vic, needing a moment alone to gather her thoughts.

A moment was all she'd gotten, too.

The second victim, Ronnie Winsome, was being moved up here from the emergency room, but hadn't arrived yet. Lily sipped nasty coffee. "Your sergeant clear you to help me out?"

"She did," Perez said. "She cursed, but she cleared it. She wants to be kept informed."

"She can know what you know. She won't be brought into the case further at this point."

Officer Ramon Perez wasn't quite a rookie, but his big brown eyes hadn't turned cop yet. He was a patrol officer, but he wanted to be more, and probably would be. Called to the scene of an ordinary rear-end collision with no injuries, he'd realized that the at-fault driver was confused. Lots of cops would have noticed that much, but Perez hadn't thought he seemed intoxicated, and the man had passed the breath test. Winsome hadn't wanted to go to the hospital, but Perez had persuaded him he needed to be evaluated.

Meanwhile, unknown to Lily, Ruben had been hit with one of his hunches. He'd instructed the SDPD to put out an alert for all units to watch for "impairment or memory loss of an unusual nature." They were to report same to FBI Unit Twelve. Perez had heard the alert about an hour after the ambulance carried Winsome away and he'd gone the extra mile, heading for the hospital to reinterview the man.

That was when he discovered that Ronald Ralph Winsome, known to friends and family as Ronnie, didn't know what year it was.

Winsome had only lost three years, not most of a lifetime. Lily didn't know of any connection between him and her mother, and the accident had taken place more than ten miles from Uncle Chen's restaurant, so there was no obvious geographical link. But the time fit. Winsome had rear-ended the car in front of him at roughly 8:15. Julia Yu had started screaming at 8:20.

Lily had just finished interviewing Winsome. He was upset by the memory loss, but otherwise seemed okay. She'd talked to his doctor, too. Amnesia was rare and the MRI didn't show any head trauma. The ER doctor was mystified, but he would have released Winsome with a recommendation to seek counseling if Perez hadn't persuaded him to hold off until Lily arrived.

Lily planned to take advantage of Perez's competence, his big brown eyes, and his bilingual abilities. "Winsome's wife is with him—Cara Winsome, fifty-one, brown and black, five-five and one fifty. She's the second wife. First wife is Anna Caraway. Winsome and Number One have one son, thirty-two, named Brian. Brian lives in Santa Ana and is on his way here. Cara has two daughters, both grown, both living here in San Diego. She says he's been under a lot of stress because of overwork—he's in management at a national clothing chain—and he worked late tonight. He was presumably on his way home when he had the accident, though of course he doesn't remember."

Perez nodded.

"I know that much, and that's all I know. I need more. Lots more. I want you to talk to the wife. She defaults to Spanish under stress. You said you're fluent."

He straightened unconsciously, looking very young and very serious. "You want me to conduct the interview in Spanish?"

"I want her comfortable so she'll open up. I think using Spanish will help with that."

"Anything in particular I'm looking for?"

"Connections. You know I'm a touch sensitive, right? When I interviewed Winsome I got his permission to check for magic. Found something, the same sort of something that was on my other vic. At this point, we've got nothing to connect the two of them but that vague trace of magic and memory loss. I want you to find out who Winsome knows socially. I need names, addresses, professions, and when and where Cara thinks her husband might have last seen each person. I want to know about his ex, her ex, and casual acquaintances. The guy who mows their lawn. Where they shop for groceries and go to church and fill up the gas tank. Find out where and how Winsome spends his time when he isn't at the office. Does he read a lot? Work out? Go fishing? Haunt the home improvement center? You get her talking, you'll get some of this without asking. Take your time. Get her comfortable with you. I'll send someone else to talk to his boss and coworkers, see if there's a work connection. You're going to focus on the personal."

"Okay. Who's the first vic? You have someone cross-checking there?"

"Her name is Julia Yu. She's my mother, so I'll be cross-checking on that end."

"Your . . . shit. I mean—I'm sorry, Special Agent. Is she okay?"

"She will be." Somehow. Getting her to Sam was the first step, and Rule would handle that. Lily didn't have a clue what the next steps were, but they'd find out. Somehow. "I'm going to—" Her phone buzzed. She glanced at it. "I have to take that. Get busy. You've got my number."

Officer Perez nodded crisply and left. The call was from Ackleford, who'd already conducted the interview with Winsome's boss. "She never heard of Julia Yu or any other Yu. I got the names of twelve of Winsome's coworkers from her. My men are calling them." One of Ackleford's charming habits was referring to the agents in his command as his men, regardless of their sex.

"Good. I've got a local cop digging for more names from Mrs. Winsome. He speaks Spanish, and she's more comfortable in that language. I'm going to contact more of my family to see if they know of any link to Winsome. I'm also going to alert area ERs to watch for cases of unusual impairment or memory loss."

"Fuck. You think there's more?"

"We'll find out, won't we?"

"Maybe this isn't about you, after all." He hung up.

Lily stood there a moment, holding her phone tightly. She needed to call Ruben, but she wanted to call Rule instead. There was no point in it. If Rule had persuaded her mother to let Sam treat her, he'd have let her know. He hadn't, so there was no reason to call him . . . but he'd have texted instead of calling, wouldn't he? Knowing she might be with the victim or a witness, he'd text so he didn't interrupt, and sometimes texts were delayed. She could call him and check and . . . maybe interrupt him when he was talking to Julia.

Lily stood there and breathed and couldn't make her

phone ring no matter how hard she tried, so she did what she was supposed to do and called Ruben. She had the authority to put out the alert herself, but Ruben needed to know about it.

"I should have done that when I alerted the local police," Ruben said as soon as she told him. "Any additional cases will probably be seen by the hospitals, not the PD. I'm relying too much on hunches, not enough on logic. I'll take care of it from here."

"You have any other logic or hunches to share?"

"I do. This is both. Karonski will be there at noon tomorrow to assume the lead, as I said. I've decided to place you in charge of the Shadow Unit's operations regarding this situation."

For a moment she had no idea what to say. Finally she managed, "You must be very confident that this line isn't being monitored." Normally Ruben didn't refer even indirectly to the Shadow Unit over the phone. Normally the dragons handled most of the Shadow Unit's communications. They weren't part of the Shadow Unit—dragons weren't exactly joiners—but they were allies, and mindspeech was perfect for a clandestine organization, being as untraceable and undetectable as it was uncanny.

Things were not normal, were they?

"Mika contacted me about what Sam plans to do to help your mother. While that is in process, Sam won't be able to handle communications for us, so I took certain measures. These measures are temporary and cannot be used often. This is our only chance to talk freely until Sam is able to handle Shadow communications again."

What measures? She didn't ask, much as she wanted to. Ruben would have told her if it was okay for her to know. "All right, but why me? If Karonski's in charge of the Bureau's investigation, shouldn't he be in charge of both? Or Rule could handle the Shadow end." He was second-in-command and knew a lot more about Shadow stuff than she did.

"You and he will function as a team, no doubt, but I

want you in charge. That's both hunch and logic. I think the Shadow Unit will be needed, but in parallel to the official investigation rather than in support of it. Both investigations will share the goal of finding the person or persons responsible, but the official investigation will of necessity focus on acquiring evidence to prosecute and convict. Your goal will be to stop the perpetrator, period. If that can be done through official means, good. My hunch—a strong hunch—is that it cannot."

"I'm not an executioner or assassin." Unlike Rule. He considered assassination a valid and moral tactic in war. Lily understood his reasoning intellectually, but the idea made her insides roil. "I know this is a war, but I . . ." Could kill whoever had done this to her mother. *Wanted* to kill them. The realization jolted her, then, oddly, steadied her. "There's a conflict of interest for me. Even more so than with the official investigation."

"There are others who can kill should it prove necessary, and I can make that call if you can't. But killing isn't the only solution the Shadow Unit can provide that our legal system cannot, just the most obvious. That's why I want you in charge of that end, Lily. Not in spite of what you call a conflict of interest, but because of it. Your awareness of that conflict, and your visceral distrust for such unilateral action, will make you work hard to find the less obvious solutions, if they exist."

Again she didn't know what to say. "Thank you" didn't fit. "Damn you" did, but was a little too revealing.

When Lily had first learned of the existence of the Shadow Unit the previous September, she'd been appalled. For law enforcement officers to be part of an organization whose very purpose was to operate outside the law violated everything she stood for. Grudgingly, she'd come to accept the need. The law simply didn't cover the sort of attacks the Great Enemy could wield and the wider world didn't even know there was a war going on, so the law was not going to be changed to apply to wartime conditions. She'd still wanted no part of it, personally. The Shadow Unit had to operate in secret. Secrecy eliminated accountability, and without that, abuse was all but guaranteed.

But Ruben had been right. She should have known he would be. Lily's boss was a precog, with the most uncannily accurate precognitive Gift on record. That Gift usually manifested as hunches, but for a time he'd had actual visions of the various ways the country was going to be destroyed if the Shadow Unit didn't exist . . . and if Lily didn't take her place within that Unit. In the end, she had.

If Ruben had a strong hunch the law would be unable to deal with this threat, he was right. She hated it, but he was right. "All right. I'm still lead on the Bureau's end of things for now, though, so I need to go deal with that."

"Of course. Abel is aware of your role in the Shadow investigation. He won't mention it unless you do, but he's aware. I haven't spoken to Rule about it yet. I leave that to you."

"Okay." Her stomach hurt.

"I'll see that hospitals in your area are alerted." He disconnected.

Lily lifted the cup still in her hand and sipped. And grimaced. She could drink coffee burned and bitter, but cold . . . no. She went to the small sink and poured it out, still holding her phone in the other hand. She had calls to make.

Then she just stood there, her head down and her eyes burning.

"You all right, honey?"

Lily jumped and turned. A woman in blue scrubs stood just behind her, watching her with a gentle smile. Her name tag read ELOISHA MORROWS, RN. "I'm good," she said automatically. The nurse must think she was an anxious and overwhelmed family member . . . which she was. Not of any of the patients here, however.

"Well, you just let me know if I can do anything." The nurse put a hand on Lily's shoulder and squeezed. "We're not too busy right now. If you want to talk, you come get me, okay?"

Lily wasn't up to explaining, so she thanked the woman,

who nodded and left. Thank God. Lily poured more hot sludge into her cup and hunted up Aunt Mequi's mobile number in her contacts list. Mequi and her mother were close, so she was an obvious choice to ask about Ronnie Winsome. If she'd never heard of him, Lily would have her ask the rest of the family, except for Lily's father. Lily would talk to him herself.

First she checked her texts. No word from Rule.

She wanted to be at the other hospital, where her mother was. She wanted Rule's touch. She wanted to be with her mother, who wasn't really her mother right now, but a girl named Julia. She wanted . . .

She called her aunt.

Mequi didn't know anyone named Winsome. While Lily was talking to her, she got a text. She got Mequi to agree to ask the others, disconnected, and read what Rule had sent: *Edward delays to consult other doctors. Sam says no time. Implementing Grandmother's plan, but I can't talk to Julia yet. Your father is with her.*

Lily heard a rushing in her ears. It was happening. They were circumventing her father. Rule would persuade Julia—he had to—and Julia would go to Sam's lair.

Would her father forgive them? He'd feel so betrayed . . . but they had to do this. And now she had to call her father and ask him about Ronnie Winsome. Knowing she was acting behind his back, knowing . . . *Do it,* she told herself.

Edward Yu didn't answer. Maybe he'd turned his phone off. He was with her mother, so that was possible. He wouldn't want to be interrupted. He might worry that the sound of the phone would wake Julia.

Did she keep trying? Send someone from the family to get him? She could have another agent conduct that interview . . . and that was pure cowardice. If this had been a normal case, she'd send someone to him to ask him to either call her or turn on his phone so she could call him.

Lily was about to call Aunt Mequi to do just that when her phone buzzed. It was the ring tone for calls forwarded from her official number. She answered.

The voice on the other end was crisp, female, and unfamiliar. She identified herself as Dr. Harris at UCSD Medical Center. Within moments, Lily had disconnected and was calling Ruben, not her father.

Dr. Harris had admitted a patient earlier that night, Barbara Lennox. Barbara Lennox was seventy-eight and lived with her son and his wife. At eight fifteen in the evening she'd appeared to suffer a stroke—or so her son and daughter-in-law thought when they called the ambulance. On arrival at UCSD Medical Center, she'd not reported any pain, but had been disoriented and extremely anxious. Brain scans had shown no sign of damage.

Barbara Lennox was now catatonic.

EIGHT

~⟋

THE room was cold and dirty. Julia couldn't see the walls. This was supposed to be her room, but she couldn't see the walls or her bed, and if she couldn't find the walls she couldn't turn the light on. It must be getting dark outside because it was sure dim in here.

She was supposed to get her room ready. They'd moved to this big, dirty house for some stupid reason, and she had to get her stuff unpacked. There were so many packing boxes . . . boxes piled up and tumbled around everywhere. Boxes taped up tight. Julia pulled and tugged and tried really hard, but she couldn't open any of them. "Mama," she called. "Mama, I need some scissors. Where are the scissors?"

Her mother didn't answer. That made her feel cold all the way down, so cold that she started shaking. Why had they moved here? Why couldn't they live in their old house? She couldn't remember. It didn't make sense and she couldn't remember and that scared her. "Mama?"

No one answered. Julia scrambled over some of the boxes and saw the door. She gasped in relief and yanked it open.

The hall was dark, too, even darker than her room, but

Mama was out there somewhere. Julia looked both ways as if she were crossing a street before she stepped out in that dark hallway. She couldn't see the end of it, but she could see doors on either side, so she opened one. More boxes. Big and little boxes, some in tidy stacks, some looking like they'd been tossed in every which way. All of them taped shut and she didn't have any scissors, so she closed that door and went to the next one.

Another room full of boxes. After that, another one, and she stopped calling for her mother, who never answered. She wanted out of this terrible house, but none of the doors led out, they just opened up on more taped-up boxes, and she was sobbing as she yanked open yet another door.

This room was different. These boxes weren't taped shut. The flaps gaped open in a spooky way that made her think of when her hamster died and its eyelids were stuck halfway open. She shivered and she wanted to close the door, but maybe some of her things were in those boxes. If she could just find some of her things, she'd feel better. Slowly she moved into the room.

The first box she peered into was empty. She started shaking because that was wrong. Horribly wrong. She grabbed another box and its weight told her the truth even before she looked inside. Empty. Another box, and another . . . empty, empty, empty.

All the boxes in this room were empty.

Julia staggered back, away from the plundered boxes. Horror stopped her breath and she didn't even want to suck it in again because everything was wrong, everything—the boxes she couldn't open and the boxes that were so very empty and her Mama wouldn't answer, wasn't here—either Mama was lost or Julia was lost and she wanted *out*, out of this terrible place, and—

"Julia!" a man said sharply.

She gasped and spun around.

Standing in the doorway was an ordinary-looking man. Everyone-else ordinary, that is, not Chinese ordinary. He wore an ugly suit and a big frown. He was kind of old, at least as old as her parents, with dark hair that started way back on his forehead. "Breathe," he said sternly.

"Go away!" she said, her voice high and shaking. "You're not supposed to be here!"

"Yeah, normally that would be true, but things aren't normal. I got special permission to come talk to you."

Her eyes narrowed in suspicion. "Who are you?"

He reached inside his suit jacket and pulled out a little leather folder and held it out. "Al Drummond. I'm an FBI agent."

She reached for the ID he was holding out—or tried to. Her arm moved, but somehow she couldn't quite reach him.

"We can't touch." It sounded as if he didn't like that. Like he was sad about it even if his face didn't look sad. "I have permission to talk to you, but that doesn't let us touch."

"I met an FBI agent once, but I don't remember when. I don't remember how come I'm here and my mama isn't. I hate it! I hate it so much! Why can't I remember?"

"Because a bad guy hurt you. That's why I'm here. I'll be working with that other FBI agent and some more people to catch the bad guy, and we're going to try to fix things for you, but it's going to take time. You're going to have to stay here while we're working."

Julia's lower lip quivered. She didn't know if she could do that.

"Look." He crouched down, which he didn't really have to do. She'd grown so much the past year that she wasn't much shorter than him. She was five feet, five inches tall now. Mama sometimes shook her head and said if she didn't stop growing she'd have trouble finding a man who was tall enough for her. Mama . . .

"It sucks, doesn't it?" the FBI man said. She nodded, not able to talk because she was too close to crying. "We've got someone who can make this place better. He can't fix everything, but he can make it so you won't be too uncomfortable staying here awhile. But you have to give permission. He can't help if you don't. Will you let him help?"

"Yes! Yes, where is he?" She looked around. "Can he make it not so dark and dirty and scary? Where is he?"

"His name is Sam. Remember that." He straightened. "He's not here right now. You won't meet him until you wake up."

"Wake up? You mean—you mean I'm dreaming? You're not real?" That was awful, because this place was real. She knew it was. Even if she was dreaming, this house was horribly real.

"I'm real, but yeah, you're dreaming. You need to remember . . ." He stopped and looked over his shoulder as if someone was behind him, talking to him. But no one was there. "I've got to go. Remember the name. Sam. You need to let Sam help you, okay?"

"Okay, but—wait!"

He was fading. She forgot what he'd said about touching and reached for him, but it didn't do any good. He faded out like he'd been nothing but smoke and a breeze had blown him away.

"Wait," she whispered. But it was too late. She was alone.

Julia.

That was a man's voice, too, but not the same man. She knew this voice. He was really nice and . . .

"Julia, I need you to wake up now."

She blinked her eyes and everything was bright again. Too bright for eyes barely awake, and she was staring up at a white, white ceiling and someone was holding her hand, so she wasn't alone, and that felt good, but . . .

"Back with me now?"

She could hear the smile in his voice so she turned her head on the pillow and there he was—the gorgeous man she'd first seen in the hall in the restaurant. The man who was the one good thing in her crumbling life. Mr. Turner. She managed to smile at him, but it felt wobbly.

She remembered some things now, and she didn't want to.

"You seemed to be having trouble waking up," he said, and he smoothed her hair back from her face in the way her mother sometimes did. Not her father. Father was as hard to reach as the FBI agent in her dream. Harder, because he never tried to reach back. "Maybe you didn't want to."

"No," she whispered. "It's okay you woke me up. I had . . . bad dreams."

He nodded as if he understood, and even though she knew he didn't, not really, it helped that he wanted to. "That's not surprising. Julia, we've found someone who can help. He can't make things right, but he can help, if you want him to."

"What—what's his name?"

"Sam."

"Yes," she said quickly. "Yes, please."

IT was after midnight when Lily stepped out of the brightly lit emergency room at Scripps Mercy to go to UCSD Medical Center, where Barbara Lennox lay in a coma. Surprise stopped her steps. It had rained while she was inside—not a lot, judging by the dearth of puddles, but enough that the pavement was wet and the world smelled wonderful.

She drew in a lungful of air scrubbed clean, perfumed with ozone and humus. Night air slid like cool silk over the skin on her face. Earlier she'd gotten her shoulder harness and a slightly wrinkled jacket from the trunk of Rule's car because she was damned if she'd work a case without having her weapon at hand. Now she wanted to take that jacket off and let the clean air wash over more of her. She didn't; people got jittery if they saw her weapon. But she did suck in more of that crisp air.

Scott made a motion and Mark loped around her. Mark would use his nose to make sure no one had messed with the car while they were inside. "You drive," she told Scott.

He nodded. "Where are we going?"

"UCSD Medical Center." Her feet didn't want to move. She didn't want to see the woman in a coma. Was that what awaited Lily's mother if she didn't allow Sam to help? Why was one victim comatose, another shaken but functional, and a third somewhere in between?

Stupid feet. Those questions wouldn't get answered by standing here in the parking lot. Lily made herself start for the car.

A wisp of fog drifted in front of her and quickly shaped itself into a man—a hard-faced man with dark hair wearing a dull gray suit with a wrinkled shirt. "It's Drummond," she said quickly to Scott, then: "You'd better not wink out right away. I didn't get to ask you anything, and—"

"Things are different this time."

"Different how?" She cocked her head. "You look younger."

"Never mind that shit," he said, but he ran a hand over his hair—which he had more of than he used to. He looked maybe forty, she thought. Not a lot younger than when he died, but some. The age he'd been before his wife died? "I'll mostly be working things on my side. I may not even hear you call me like I used to. I'm not tied to you the same way. Because we used to be tied I can find you, but I couldn't talk to you if not for the way you died once. You didn't tell me about that." He scowled as if she'd withheld facts pertinent to a case.

"So who did?"

He waved that away as unimportant. "Someone on this side. The thing is, having died once, you've got this little open place in you. It lets me get close enough for you to hear me."

She scowled. "I am not turning into a medium."

"Okay, fine. I doubt any ghosts are going to find that spot, anyway. Only reason I can is because of that tie we used to have."

"But if the tie is gone—"

"It left . . . call it a path. Or a habit. Same difference. Would you quit worrying about the shit I can't explain and pay attention? It's a lot harder for me to manifest this time and I can't do it for long, and there's stuff you need to know. First, you're dealing with something Friar got from that elf before he escaped from the warehouse. An artifact."

"Did you see it? What does it do?"

"I didn't see it. I felt it. It feels, uh . . . evil, I guess you'd say."

Lily turned that word over in her mind. "Evil is a pretty broad category."

"On this side, evil means something specific. Evil affects . . ." His mouth kept moving, but she didn't hear anything.

"Back up. I lost some of that."

He scowled. "There's stuff I can't say. Not won't. Can't. Just take my word for it—what Friar got hold of is evil in a way that upsets the heavy hitters on my side of things."

"Heavy hitters?"

He looked down and muttered. "Angels. Sort of. Not really, because they aren't . . . oh, hell, call them whatever you want, or don't call them anything at all. That might be best. The thing is, everyone on this side is real restricted in what we can do on your side. Even the heavy hitters. It's all about choice. Choice and time. On your side, time's like a funnel that lets only one drop of now through at a time, and choice is what you do with that drop. No one gets to take away the choices other people make—only, that object Friar got hold of does just that. I don't know how it works, so don't ask, but by wiping out memories, it robs people of all the choices they made."

Lily thought about her mother. All the choices Julia Yu had made over a lifetime, wiped out. Disintegrated. Her throat tightened. She managed to push a couple of words out through her tight throat. "Yeah. That's evil."

He nodded. "It affects this side of things, too. That's why I can be here. There's a . . . it's like a fissure or a crack. A break created by that artifact."

"But why you?" She waved vaguely. "I mean—there must be lots and lots of dead people who could—"

"Watch who you're calling dead. I died, sure, but I'm not dead."

"We'll talk about terminology another time. Why you?"

He shrugged. "Mostly because I can. Most folks on this side can't interact with your world at all, but because of the way I died, that tie we used to have, I've got a toe in the door. All that death magic stirred things up, plus there's the way I . . ." His mouth kept moving, but silently.

"You went mute again."

"Shit. The stuff I can't say . . . anyway, I'm not as rooted on this side as I'm supposed to be. I could've gotten that fixed, but I'm needed for this. I'm small enough that I can slip through that crack to work with you on your side. The heavy hitters can't. They . . . there's so much of them, see. They're part of your world, but it's just their shine you get, not all of them. They can't be squeezed into the funnel of time without breaking it."

"So instead of an angel, I get you."

He grinned crookedly. "That's pretty much it."

"You grinned."

That brought back the familiar scowl. "What the hell are you talking about?"

"I don't think I ever saw you grin. Smirk, yes. Grin, no." She tipped her head. "Did you . . . there at the last, I mean, at the warehouse, you said her name. Just before you poofed out. Sarah. You found her?"

"Yeah." Softness seeped into his face the way light seeps into the sky at dawn. "Yeah, I did. I don't remember much, but I know I found her."

"You don't remember? But that—that's like my mother—"

"No," he said firmly. "It's not the same at all. My memories of that other place don't fit into this place, that's all. They aren't gone. They're sort of packed up, waiting for me."

A cold hand gripped Lily and squeezed. "Then my mother's memories are gone. Not damaged or lost. Gone."

"Not exactly. I mean, they're gone, but . . ." He ran a hand over his hair. "I can't explain, mainly because I don't understand. The idea is to get her back to being herself. To get all of them back to themselves. I don't know how we do that. I don't know if that's something that can even happen on your side of things. Might be the missing pieces can't be returned to her until she's on my side."

"Until she dies, you mean. Even if we do everything right, she may not get her memory back while she's alive."

"Yeah. Yeah, that's what I mean. I know that's hard to hear, but it's one possibility. Lily, there's a lot more affected than your mom. A lot more than you've found so far."

God, could it get any worse? "How many? Who are they?"

"Can't tell you that. And remember, when I say *can't*, that's exactly what I mean."

"What can you do?" she cried, frustrated.

"Not much. I can watch your back. I think I'll know if I get near the object. It has . . . I don't know what to call it. A spiritual signature or color or . . . see, on this side we use spirit instead of light to see things. Sort of. It isn't really seeing, but you can think of it that way, and that's how I'll know if the artifact is nearby. Otherwise . . . they didn't exactly give me a training manual, so I don't know what all I can do. No, wait, there's one more thing. I should be able to let you know when your saint shows up."

"My saint? What the hell are you—"

He smirked at her. "You wanted one. Pissed you off that you got me instead."

"Yes, but—hold on a minute." Lily's phone dinged to let her know she had a text. Her heart started pounding. She snatched her phone from her purse.

It was from Rule. She read his message quickly, then read it again. Her shoulders slumped in relief.

"Good news?"

"My mother . . . Julia agreed to let Sam help her. They're checking her out of the hospital now."

NINE

~~~

THERE were thirty-one hospitals in the Greater San Diego area. By 2:45 A.M. Lily had been to eleven of them and was pulling into the ER parking of hospital twelve. Drummond had accompanied her at first, but after the fourth stop he'd said he had stuff to do "on his side." He hadn't explained and she hadn't seen him since.

Eleven hospitals meant two false alarms and fourteen victims that she'd confirmed by touch. None of them had an obvious connection to the others. Fourteen victims, and they had no idea what they were dealing with or how many more might be out there.

Lily had talked to Ruben again on the way here. He'd decided it was time to wake the president up.

Hospital twelve was City Heights. She'd put it next on her list because it was more or less on her way back to St. Margaret's, where they had two more possible cases.

Her mother wasn't at St. Margaret's anymore. She was at Sam's lair. Lily had heard from Rule about that. She'd also heard from her father about it. She'd heard him out, then she'd shut what he said out of her mind so she could do the job.

Things get to be clichés by being true over and over. The ER at City Heights Hospital fit every cliché of an inner city emergency room. Even at this hour, it was crowded and noisy. It reeked of disinfectant with a whiff of eau de homeless guy, and the overworked staff got through their shifts on a mix of adrenaline, bad coffee, and black humor. Some were burned out. Some were still fiercely idealistic, though they hid it behind a heavy veil of cynicism.

In other words, it was a lot like a cop shop. Lily felt right at home as she walked up to the nurses' station. "I'm here to see Festus Liddel," she told one of the women behind the counter, holding out the folder with her ID.

"Liddel?" The woman's braids flared as she turned her head sharply. "God, Denise, don't tell me you called the FBI about Liddel! Plackett is gonna have a cow."

The other nurse was twenty years younger than the first and at least twenty pounds heavier. She propped her hands on her ample hips. "And why shouldn't I call them? That's what that bulletin said to do, isn't it?"

"Liddel's memory got washed away by alcohol years ago."

"This isn't the same. You know it's not the same. He doesn't even sound like himself. And Hardy says—"

"Hardy!" The first woman rolled her eyes. "Now, listen, sweetie, I know you like Hardy—though God knows why. He creeps me out. But—"

"That was a coincidence! He couldn't have known."

"I'm not talking about that, though it was pretty damn weird. I'm talking about the way he looks at you. As if . . . well, it creeps me out, that's all. What are you going to tell Dr. Plackett when he finds out you called this nice agent? You going to explain that *Hardy* thought we should call in the FBI?"

The second woman giggled. "It would almost be worth it to see his face."

The first woman sighed and shook her head and looked at Lily. "I'm afraid you got dragged out here for nothing, Special Agent. Festus Liddel is one of our regulars. He can't remember what day of the week it is most times. Denise thinks his poor, pickled brain is malfunctioning worse than usual tonight, and maybe it is, but that's not saying much."

"I'm here, so I might as well see him." And touch him. That was the quickest way to know for sure if Festus Liddel was victim fifteen.

"I'll take you to him," Denise said. "You can see what you think, but he is not his usual self."

"What kind of unusual is he?"

"You'll see." Denise came out from behind the counter and started down a well-scrubbed aisle between examination cubicles separated by curtains. A Spanish-speaking family were clustered in the first one, spilling partly out into the aisle, all of them talking at once. "He's this way, down at the end. Hardy's with him."

"The message I got said your patient didn't know what year it is."

"He thinks it's 1998. To be fair, his memory's always iffy, so I understand why Hillary thinks I shouldn't have called you."

"That's exactly the sort of memory problem I need to know about. I'll need to talk to that doctor—the attending?" Lily searched her tired brain and couldn't come up with the name. "He won't be happy that you called me, I take it."

Denise snorted. "Plackett doesn't want us to take a piss without his say-so."

In the next cubicle a baby cried, thin and sad, in his mother's arms. The mother looked about fifteen and exhausted. They passed an emaciated young man with gang tats being hooked up to an IV, an old man on a heart monitor, and a middle-aged couple exchanging worried words in what sounded like Vietnamese.

"I ought to tell you about Hardy," the nurse went on. "*I* don't think there's anything wrong with his cognition." Her defensiveness suggested that others did. "But he can't communicate normally. He was beaten real badly several years ago, see. Brain damage."

They had to stop and move aside to let an enormously

obese woman make her way slowly down the hall with the aid of a walker, breathing heavily. She wore two hospital gowns—one to cover her backside and one her front—and a look of grim determination. As the woman struggled by, music arrived. Harmonica music.

It was a hymn of some sort. Lily knew that much, even if she couldn't put words to it. Lily had been exposed to religion as a child, but the battle between her parents over which faith system their daughters would be raised in— Christian or Buddhist—had made her decide to opt out of the whole subject. She'd been studious in her inattention whether dragged to church or to temple, and eventually her parents dropped the subject, too.

The woman beside her obviously recognized the song. She was humming along, smiling. "That Hardy," Denise said as the obese woman finally passed them. "He can sing most anything—well, old songs, anyway. I never heard him sing any of the newer ones. But he only ever plays the same three hymns on that harmonica of his—'Blessed Assurance,' 'Amazing Grace,' and 'In the Garden.' We hear those over and over. He does a real pretty job with them, though."

Blessed Assurance. That was what the hymn was called. Mildly satisfied with having put a name to it, Lily followed the nurse to the last cubicle on the right.

The small space held two men. The one in the bed was white, unshaven, and scrawny, with a potbelly and mouse-colored hair. His eyes had the yellow tinge of a failing liver. The one standing beside the bed was over six feet tall and gaunt, though muscle lingered on his wide shoulders. His skin was unusually dark, the kind that takes on a bluish tinge under fluorescent lights, and his hair was grizzled. He wore a faded flannel shirt and baggy gray pants. He, too, could have used a shave.

"This is Agent Yu," Denise announced. "She's with the FBI."

"The FBI," the man in the bed said in a marveling way. "Imagine that, Hardy. That pretty girl is with the FBI."

The other man lowered his harmonica to look at her in delighted surprise, as if they were old friends but he hadn't expected to run into her here. "'I'll be calling you . . . ooo,' " he sang. " 'You will answer true . . . ooo.' " His voice was deep and true, but rough. Maybe the beating that damaged his brain had included a blow to his voice box.

"It's mostly songs with Hardy, see," Denise said. "Sometimes rhymes, but songs are easiest for him. Music is stored differently in our brains than language, see? He makes himself understood pretty well. Right, Hardy?"

The broken man smiled at Denise with the sweetness usually reserved for very young children, then held out both hands to Lily, still smiling.

Lily didn't pass up a chance to get a reading on people. She moved closer and learned that he probably lacked the chance to bathe often. She put her hand in his. Not a trace of magic. His dark eyes were filmed at the edges with cataracts. "You're Mr. Hardy?"

He shook his head.

"He likes to be called Hardy," the man on the bed put in helpfully. "No 'mister.' "

Hardy nodded, but his smile faded. There was something odd about his eyes, the intent way he looked at her . . . suddenly uncomfortable, Lily thought about her third grade teacher and felt a pang of sympathy for the other nurse. Mrs. Hawkins had been kind of creepy, too.

Hardy frowned. "H-h-hard road, heavy load. You true, you blue." He still held her hand in one of his, but reached up to pat her cheek with the other. He started humming—a pop song this time, one she knew, though the words eluded her. It wasn't recent.

"Hey, Hardy, you aren't the only one who wants to hold hands with the pretty girl," the man in the bed said. The crooked smile he gave her might have been charming many years before, when he still had all his teeth. "I'm Festus Liddel, miss, and I guess you've come to see me."

"I guess I have," Lily said, disentangling her hand from

Hardy's. "And I'd be happy to shake your hand, too, Mr. Liddel."

"Well, I got to go check on my patients," Denise said, smiling at all of them, "but you come talk to me later, Agent Yu."

Festus Liddel had dry, cracked skin, a deep scratch on the back of his hand, and he smelled worse than Hardy. A lot worse. He also had a trace of an empathic Gift. It was weak, but it was wide open. "How can you stand it here?" Lily exclaimed before she thought.

Liddel flinched. "What do you mean?"

Lily cursed herself for introducing the subject of her Gift—and his—so poorly. She must be more tired than she'd realized. "I apologize for giving away information you might not want revealed. I'm a touch sensitive, and—"

"Get away! Get away! I don't have anything to do with magic!"

Liddel, it turned out, had been raised in a fundamentalist sect that hated magic even more than they did gay sex. It took time to find that out—time, and Hardy crooning country music lyrics about how he believed in love, music, magic, and you. By which he meant *Yu*, Lily supposed, since he put his hand on Lily's shoulder when he sang that part. He seemed to want Liddel to relax and trust her.

Amazingly, it worked. Liddel did calm down and let Lily explain and apologize for speaking about his Gift. "I understand that many people don't want others to know, and I deeply regret mentioning it out loud. I was concerned. A hospital is a miserable place for someone with . . ." She paused, hunting for a way of referring to empathy without using the word in front of Hardy so she wouldn't give away even more than she already had. And realized Hardy wasn't there. "Where did he go?"

Liddel shrugged. "Guess he was called elsewhere."

Lily was used to noticing things. Her job depended on it; sometimes her life did, too. It bothered her that the big man had slipped out without her noticing. "You've known him a long time?"

"So they say. To me, I just met him tonight. Guess I must have met him after 1998. That's what year it is for me."

Startled, she said, "But you trust him. You seemed to be relying on him."

"He's a man of God, isn't he? Doesn't matter if he doesn't have a church of his own. I've never been around anyone who felt like . . . like he's true, all the way down, the way Hardy is."

Lily had a sinking sensation. "Almost like a saint."

"Well, the Brethren don't hold with all that papist stuff, so that's not a word I'd use. But I guess if you were Catholic, you'd call him a saint. You Catholic?"

"Ah—no. But the subject of saints has been on my mind recently. You seem very calm about losing a large part of your life, Mr. Liddel."

"I was upset at first, but after Hardy reminded me how God has a plan for each of us. Besides, it looks like what I lost was the worst part." He chuckled. "I probably wouldn't remember much of those years anyway."

EMPATHS are not all alcoholics, nor are all alcoholics empaths, but Liddel wasn't the only person who started drinking to drown out an empathic Gift. Alcohol, Lily had been told, didn't so much shut down empathy as numb the brain to it. Unfortunately, it required larger and larger doses to work. Lily wondered how many of the homeless were empaths who'd never developed the sort of unconscious block their more functional brethren did. Shields were the best solution, but most people didn't have access to the kind of training that would let them learn how to shield. Besides, many low-level empaths didn't realize they were Gifted. If you don't know what the problem is, you don't look for solutions in the right places.

Festus Liddel had passed out a fifty-some-year-old drunk. He'd come to with years missing from his life and a body ravaged by alcohol. And he was happy about it. The way he saw it, God was giving him a chance to do things differently. He'd have to detox—blood tests showed he still had a lot of alcohol in his system, which Lily supposed was why he wasn't swamped by the pain and anxiety of the patients around him. Detox would be bad, he figured, but if he could get through that, he had a second chance.

Lily needed to talk to Liddel's doctor. She needed to leave so she could check out the next report on her list. But after she asked the usual questions, looking for some connection to any of the others who'd been stricken, and getting the usual answer—he didn't remember any of them—she talked to Liddel about his Gift. Detox was going to be extremely difficult for him. His Gift would awaken as the alcohol left his system, and he'd be around others experiencing the pain and confusion of detox. He had to tell his doctor about being an empath. She could put him in touch with people who could teach him how to shield, but he had to get sober first.

"No way. I don't have any truck with magic."

"Learning how to shield keeps magic from messing with you."

He considered that and agreed that he would pray on the matter, maybe ask Hardy what he thought when he came back—"since," he told her, "I don't have a shiny track record for figuring out the rights and wrongs of things on my own."

Could a brain-damaged man without any touch of magic understand how imperative it was for an empath to be able to shield? Even if Hardy did understand, what song could he sing to persuade Liddel to give it a try? "You do that. I'm leaving you my card. Call me if you want that contact I told you about. Call me if you remember anything, or if anything happens you think I should know. I need to be able to reach you, too."

His grin was lopsided, given that he lacked two teeth. "Should be easy enough for the next couple three days. I'll be in detox."

Lily tracked down Denise in the break room, which gave

her the chance to meet the infamous Dr. Plackett. Plackett—
Dr. John L. Plackett, according to his name tag—was about
five-five and puffier than the Pillsbury Doughboy. He didn't
even glance at Lily when she entered, too busy giving the
nurse a dressing-down for having phoned in "a false alarm."

Lily took some pleasure in identifying herself, correcting him, and commending Denise for having called her.
Denise flashed her a grateful smile and escaped.

Lily and the Doughboy doctor then exchanged information. Plackett informed her there was nothing wrong with
Mr. Liddel "aside from the ruination of his body and brain
through excessive drinking," and she informed him he was
wrong. She had by then perfected a spiel to give physicians.
She opened by speaking of "magically induced trauma
with potentially serious medical repercussions," made a
suitably ominous reference to a potential state of emergency due to the number of victims, and concluded with the
need to keep his patient hospitalized and avoid drawing
media attention. Since most hospitals hated media attention, the last bit was usually easy for doctors to agree to.

A few were reluctant to agree to the first part, about
admitting the patient. Everyone had a budget. That was
when Lily told them about Barbara Lennox. Most doctors
were too conscientious to risk releasing a patient who could
lapse into a coma, and the rest were too worried about
lawsuits.

Plackett proved to be the exception. "I assure you this
patient is not on the verge of a coma."

"If you know something about the spell that damaged
these people that leads you to that assumption, you need to
share that information. If you don't, how can you assure me
of any such thing?"

He smiled with such vast superiority that she was reminded of an elf she'd once known and hadn't killed. "I am
a board-certified emergency room physician with over eighteen years of experience. You may rely on my assurance."

"I understand Mr. Liddel plans to go through detox."

"Ah—yes." Plackett pursed his lips. They were puffy, too. "I will, of course, make the proper referral, but we are not set up for that here."

"It's very important that I keep track of him. Please see that my office is informed of where you transfer him." She handed him one of her cards. "While you're looking for a spot for him, you'll keep him here, of course. Given the possibility of coma, he must have ongoing medical supervision."

Plackett took her card and huffed out a breath. "Do you have any idea how hard it is to get a bed at a detox facility for an indigent? There are waiting lists. Long waiting lists."

"I understand that you are reluctant to admit him while you search for a bed, but—"

"Reluctant? I can't keep him here. Medicaid won't pay for it. Unless there's a new diagnostic category I don't know about—one for admission based on magically induced trauma with medical repercussions?"

"You're pretty good at sarcasm. Not top of the line, but pretty good. Who has the authority to admit him, if you don't?"

That chapped his ass. "I have the authority. That doesn't mean I'm going to jump when you say jump. If the FBI wants Festus Liddel hospitalized, the FBI can pay for it. Or you could put him up at the Hilton with a private nurse. Or take him home with you. I don't care. Keeping track of him is your problem, and I will not be bullied into making it mine."

"He's your patient. I've told you he's at risk for coma, and that's not your problem?" She shook her head. "If you have the authority but lack the willingness, I need to talk to your superior. Or maybe I should cut to the head of the line. I get to do that. Who's the CEO here?"

"You arc not going to wake up the CEO."

"Be a shame if I had to do that, wouldn't it? He might think one of his staff should've shown a little initiative so he could get in his eight hours without being pestered by rude federal agents."

Plackett caved. He knew he was caving and hated it and

hated her, but he agreed to admit Liddel until the man could be transferred to a detox facility. Then he stomped out of the break room.

Someone else entered. "You made an enemy there."

With a sigh of relief Lily turned to face Rule. She'd wanted him with her for hours. "Yeah, I'm all torn up about that. What are you doing here?" Her throat tried to close up. "If you have news—"

"No, nothing like that." He came to her and put his hands on her shoulders. "Julia is with Sam. We won't hear from him for at least another twelve hours, probably longer. I came to get you."

"I don't need to be fetched, but if you want to go with me, I'm headed back to St. Margaret's next."

"It's three thirty in the morning. You're headed to bed."

"Oh, that's going to work—pop in and tell me what to do. I've got . . ." Her brain felt sluggish. Too sluggish for math. "Last time I checked, thirty-two possible cases had been reported to the Unit. I've confirmed fourteen of them—no, fifteen with Liddel—and eliminated two, which means—"

"That someone else will have to check out the other fifteen reports, plus however many more have come in."

"Who?" she snapped. "Cullen is tending to Sam's mysterious security measures. No one else can tell if magic was involved. The traces left by whatever happened are too weak."

"But others can interview the victims and their families and make educated guesses, which you can confirm after you've slept. You can't do it all yourself, Lily. If you try, you'll make mistakes."

Because she was too tired to think straight, he meant. Rule could go all night and into the next day with no real problem. Sometimes that was handy. Sometimes it irked the hell out of her. "You're right, and while that is deeply annoying, I'm not as mad as I should be. Why is that?"

"Perhaps because you vented some of your spleen on the unfortunate doctor."

"That *was* fun." Reluctantly she started moving—toward the coffeepot, not the door. "I need to keep my brain working long enough to delegate intelligently."

"I can't believe you're going to drink that."

"It's not quite thick enough to chew, so yes, I'll drink it." She poured a half cup. "Ruben's still up. He's like you." Lupus, in other words, and not in need of sleep the way mere humans were . . . though he'd not arrived at that state in a way anyone could have expected. "With me having to run around to verify reports, he's been coordinating things from D.C. I'll check in with him and—shit, that reminds me." She took a sip of sludge and grimaced. Nasty. "Are we private?" His ears would tell him more than hers could.

"Reasonably. Scott will hear."

Scott knew about the Shadow Unit, so that wasn't a problem. "You know Ruben's putting Karonski in charge of the Bureau's investigation. He decided to put me in charge of the other one."

Rule didn't say a thing. Not a thing. He was way too still.

She frowned. "Is that a problem?"

"I'm not sure why he didn't tell me himself."

"Extreme busyness, I imagine. He knows you and I work together anyway, so . . . this bugs you. It's not just that he didn't tell you personally. You have a problem with me being in charge instead of you."

"Nonsense. I don't object to your doing what you do best, certainly far better than I could. But Ruben should have told me."

"Is this a lupi thing? He committed a sin against the hierarchy?"

"He treated me like a subordinate. Not like a Rho."

"You are his subordinate in the Shadow Unit."

"I am his second, but I am not of his clan, and I'm a Rho. He misstepped. I'll explain this to him when there's time."

"He's very new at being a lupus."

"I know. Drop it, Lily."

There was something off about Rule's reaction. She couldn't put her finger on it, and admittedly, she didn't know everything there was to know about lupi and their fixation on hierarchy, but she knew Rule, and he was . . . watching her patiently. Not looking at all like he'd had his oh-so-dominant toes stepped on.

So maybe she was wrong. She rubbed her face. She was tired enough to be wrong about half the things she thought right now. "Okay. Calling Ruben."

Ruben was very interested in hearing about Hardy, who might be the saint that Drummond thought would show up, but he agreed that details could wait until morning and seconded Rule's suggestion that she get some sleep. He would coordinate the ongoing work with Ackleford himself for now.

"You had another chat with Drummond?" Rule asked when she disconnected. He had, of course, heard both sides of the phone conversation.

"Yes, and I need to fill you in about that. Drummond says this is connected to an artifact that damn elf gave Friar. He called it evil. But first . . ." She frowned. Something was nagging at her. Something about Hardy that had floated back into her head while she talked to Ruben, then floated out again. What . . .

Oh, yeah. "What's this song?" She hummed the tune Hardy had hummed to her.

" 'Mother and Child Reunion.' Paul Simon."

"Son of a bitch." Adrenaline worked even better than caffeine. She headed for the door double-quick.

Rule kept pace. "What is it?"

"I need to find a nurse. Denise. Brown hair, one-sixty, five-five or so."

"I haven't seen her. Why do you need her?"

"To help me find someone." As they headed for the nurses' station she told him briefly about Hardy, ending with, "Drummond told me I was getting a saint. I thought . . . well, you'd have to meet Hardy to understand, but there's something otherworldly about him. Plus, it seemed like it would be just my luck to get a brain-damaged, singing saint who can't answer questions straight out. But he was humming that song to me. He patted my cheek and hummed that song. How does it go? Something about not giving false hope on a 'strange and mournful day,' then the refrain about the mother and child reunion. How could Hardy know how well that fit?"

"I don't know. Because he's a saint?"

"Or because he's anything but."

TEN

DENISE was gone. While Lily had been talking to Rule, the shift had changed. Plackett, too, had left. Lily checked to make sure the doctor had admitted Liddel, then tried to find out more about Hardy.

Everyone in the ER knew the man. He came to the ER at least once a week, but not as a patient. They didn't think they'd ever treated him for anything. He sang, he played his harmonica, and he listened to the patients, especially the homeless or otherwise abandoned. Sometimes he brought in patients. Some of the homeless showed up at the ER regularly, like Liddel, while others resisted medical care until they were in bad shape. Those were the ones Hardy could sometimes persuade to come in for treatment.

Everyone knew Hardy. Most of them liked him. No one knew anything about him. Was Hardy his first or last name? No one knew. Did he have a regular spot to eat? To sleep? No one had a clue.

"They don't like to tell you where their flops are," one nurse told Lily. "I asked Hardy once—the weather was really stinky and I was worried about him—but he just smiled and sang an old hymn about everyone gathering by the river."

San Diego was lacking in rivers, so that wasn't much help. Lily thanked him and turned to Rule. "I'll bet the shelters know him. He'd have been too late to get a bed tonight, but—"

"Lily."

"I know, I know. I can check with them in the morning. But first—"

"Call whoever you need to from the car."

"But . . ." She closed her eyes. The brief shot of adrenaline had worn off. She felt downright dizzy with fatigue. "Okay. All right."

Lily's mobile backup fell into step behind them as they left the ER. "Where's your team?" she asked Rule.

"José is at the car. Barnaby is going to see if he can find out anything about Hardy. He knows some people. Jacob is watching our room."

She hadn't even seen Rule talk to Barnaby. Clearly her brain had gone to sleep ahead of the rest of her. "What room?"

"I've rented a room at the Hilton for tonight to cut down on driving time." He opened the door of his Mercedes and waited for her to climb in.

"The Hilton? I mean . . . there's always Motel 6."

"Ah, well, there are other ways to cut back on expenses, aren't there? Take the downstairs bathrooms. Do we really need to buy everything new? I'm sure, with a good scrubbing, the old toilet would be—" He broke off at the look on her face and touched her arm. "Joking, Lily. Joking. If you're too tired to know that, maybe we'd better leave before you keel over."

Lily sighed and got in the car, scooting over so Rule could slide in next to her. The Hilton would certainly be closer than driving all the way home, though Lily's commute wasn't as long as it had been when they were at Nokolai Clanhome.

They'd bought a house.

It lay about halfway between the city and Nokolai Clanhome and came with forty acres and a small, derelict motel, which was being turned into housing for the guards and others from Leidolf. That clan was, in a roundabout way, the reason they had to buy the place, so they'd put a rush on getting the extra housing ready. It was nearly finished.

The house wasn't. It was in bad shape, too.

The setting was pretty—rolling hills that screened them from their neighbors on two sides, with the back shielded by an abandoned orchard. There were a couple of ley lines running beneath the land—not that any of them could use ley lines, but like Rule said, you never knew when such a thing might come in handy. The house had been built in the thirties in the Spanish Revival style, with lovely high ceilings. It had also had hideous shag carpet, holes in some walls, scabrous kitchen cabinets, an ancient roof, and faulty electrical. But it was structurally sound, and Rule had negotiated a really low price.

It was also big. Really big. Two stories plus a partly finished attic and a full basement. Lily didn't trust the basement—what Californian wants to be underground when the earth starts to rock and roll?—but it was being reinforced. Originally, the ground floor had held a large living room, small dining room, and huge kitchen; a study with hideous wallpaper, a fireplace, and beautiful built-in bookshelves; and a bedroom intended as the master. The second floor was all bedrooms—six of them—plus the house's only bathroom.

What kind of nutcase built a house with seven bedrooms and *one* bathroom?

That was being changed, as was so much else. Not on the second floor, not yet, because they were living there while the first floor was gutted and rebuilt.

The new roof, windows, and steel beams were in place. One of the walls that had come down was load bearing, which had made Lily nervous, but the architect assured her that steel beams would do the trick. The kitchen was maybe half-done, and they'd just finished framing in the new walls. Lots of electrical and plumbing still to do before they could put up drywall, but the study would end up as the dining room. The original dining room, which adjoined the master bedroom, was slated to become a luxurious master bath plus a walk-in closet.

The floor was finished, at least—and hadn't that been a hassle, deciding what to use! Lily had leaned toward bamboo. Rule had been torn between the beauty of a dark-stained hardwood and the practicality of carpet, which offered better traction to a wolf's paws. In the end, they'd gone with stained and polished concrete. It looked great, was highly customizable, and wouldn't get scratched up by anyone's claws.

Lily's brain got constipated when she thought about what all this was costing, so she tried not to. She might have signed the mortgage papers along with Rule, but he was covering the renovations, so she didn't have to contemplate it. If he said he could afford it, he ought to know. She ought to trust him. She did, but it was a godawful amount of money, especially when added to the cost of their wedding . . . which was supposed to happen in two weeks and five days.

"What is it?" Rule asked.

"I . . . the wedding. Should we postpone it?"

Rule went still. "Do you want to?"

"I don't know. It seems like we should, but . . . Mother won't be able to . . . and I don't know who's doing what. I don't even have the final guest list."

"I have all that information. I can do what needs doing, but if it hurts too much to hold the ceremony with your mother's situation so uncertain, we will postpone it. Is that what you want?"

"I think I should want it, but I don't. Only there's the trip, too. Our honeymoon trip. How late can we wait to cancel our reservations? And the plane tickets. Did we get the refundable—"

"It doesn't matter. We can decide about that later."

"Okay." She drew a shaky breath. "Do you think Mother will want to be flower girl instead of mother of the bride?"

"Ah, *nadia*," he said and gathered her to him.

She rested her hands on his chest, keeping an inch of

space between them. "Don't do this. If you do this, I'm going to—"

"Relax?" He stroked her hair. "Behave in an un-cop-like manner? Fall asleep?"

Fall apart, more like. Exhaustion was melting outward from her bones to her muscles to her brain, taking down what few defenses she still had. "I don't want to stop doing the job. Without the job I'm just a daughter. Nothing good is happening with me-the-daughter. My father's very angry."

"Yes, he called me."

"Did he yell?"

"Not precisely. Did he yell at you?"

"He said he would forgive me eventually, but for now he didn't want to see or speak to me. Then he hung up."

Rule kept petting her. He didn't say anything.

"I've never . . . in all my life he's never . . . I don't know what to do with that. I don't know what to do."

"He's a good man. He's hurting and scared and angry. He thinks you made the wrong decision, but he's a good man. He loves you."

She couldn't have hurt him so much if he didn't. "There's no one to hold him the way you're holding me. He's got Susan, I guess, and Beth when she gets here, but he'll want to be strong for them instead of letting them be strong for him. And he's too angry at Grandmother to let her help. He said she'd gone too far this time. What did he tell you?"

"It was a difficult conversation. I had to tell him that Julia wishes to stay with you and me when she leaves Sam's lair."

"When she . . . God. I hadn't thought about that. I hadn't thought of it at all. I just assumed she'd go home, but she doesn't know it's her home, does she? But that's what she should do. As hard as it will be on my father to have her there when she doesn't remember him, it would be worse if she wasn't there."

"Hmm."

"What does that mean?"

"Julia says she won't live with Edward and we can't make her. She understands that we consider him her husband. That frightens and angers her."

"But he's not going to do anything that . . . mentally she's a kid! He knows that. He would never take advantage of a twelve-year-old girl."

He rubbed his cheek along her hair. "What did you want when you were twelve, Lily?"

"To be a cop."

She felt his smile in the way his cheek moved. "Let me put it this way. Suppose when you were twelve, strangers forced you to marry a man more than forty years older than you. Would you have felt okay about being married to him, living with him, as long as he didn't touch you?"

"Yech. No. I would have . . . if for some bizarre reason no one could help me, not even Grandmother, I'd . . ." Probably have found a way to make herself a very young widow. But at twelve, she'd had issues her mother didn't. Julia was unlikely to turn homicidal if forced to live with Lily's father, but running away was a real possibility. Lily sighed. "We've got extra bedrooms. No kitchen and only one bathroom, but plenty of bedrooms."

"Which is fortunate, because Madame Yu and Li Qin will also be staying with us."

ELEVEN

~

SHE was chopping carrots when the mouse ran across the counter.

She was dreaming. She knew that, but it didn't make what she did less important. There were so many carrots, a huge mound of them, and she had to get them all chopped. She'd come here to complete a task, but this wasn't a safe place. She wanted to get the carrots chopped quickly so she could leave.

But then a dirty little field mouse, all quick dun-colored nastiness, ran right over that mound of carrots. She exclaimed and swatted at it. Then another one ran right in front of her, and another was on the floor at her feet, and another . . . where were they all coming from? So many mice . . . She started counting.

She'd gotten to twenty-one when she heard him calling.

It was the call of the wind, alone on the heights. The cry of a mother grieving her lost child. His voice was the sound of tears turned to ice and unable to fall, sorrow frozen in crystal drops. It was beautiful beyond words and terrible beyond hope.

Her hands shook. Her vision blurred. A mouse ran over her foot.

She cried out in anger and swiped at the mouse with her knife. The mouse raced away untouched. She stabbed her own foot. Blood welled up along with pain.

She dropped the knife and yanked her foot off the floor, frightened. It would be bad to get blood on the floor, very bad. This was a dangerous place to spill blood. If her blood touched this floor, something terrible would happen.

He called again.

She'd heard him before. She knew that suddenly—not a memory, but a bright, clear knowing. At other times, in other places, he'd called and she'd tried to find him, but she always failed. She hadn't been able to reach him from where she was.

Tonight, she could. She was in a different place tonight.

Her heart began pounding. That was why she'd come here. Not for the carrots. Why had she thought they mattered? She had to find him and free him from the crystalline trap of his loneliness.

She turned and there was the door, right where she knew it would be, though this wasn't her kitchen. But the door was where it should be, and he was outside, somewhere out there in the darkness. She walked to the door and opened it, leaving bloody footprints behind.

The black dome of the sky held neither moon nor stars, yet she had no trouble seeing the ground, pebbled and bare, and the trees she must go to. A tiny, shrill voice at the back of her mind gibbered warnings. There should be a moon . . . but the ground itself held a glow, as if it had soaked up enough moonlight over the eons that it was willing to share some of that radiance with her.

Eons . . . yes. This was an old place. A very old place. And he was calling. She walked into the dark forest.

The trees of this forest were black, truly black, not simply hidden by night, and very tall. She knew that, though she could only see them lower down, where the ground gave light. Over her head black trees merged with the sightless dark of the sky. At another time, she would have feared those trees and what they meant. She felt no fear now. Only urgency.

He was calling. He was calling *her*. It was her name she heard in this windless place, her name carried by echoes and darkness and the hoarded light of the moon. Her heart lifted in joy and terror.

And then, between one step and the next, he was there.

Her heart skittered. Her breath caught and held. The beauty of him wrapped around her and made breath unimportant. He stood ten feet away, pale god of the dark forest, garbed in his own glowing skin over muscles taut with life's heat. His hair was tousled and friendly, hair one might touch, or at least dream of touching. And he saw her and smiled.

His smile lit his face with whimsy and mischief, and his eyes were the dark of the sky overhead, his full lips curved up—oh, full, yes, ripe and full his mouth was. Full of wicked suggestions. She fell to her knees, smitten by awe and the rush of desire.

He walked up to her, and his penis was full and engorged, saluting her merrily as he crouched on one knee. "You came," he said softly, and his voice echoed inside her as he reached for her hand.

Why had she thought it her foot she'd hurt? It was her hand that bled, throbbing along with the heat in her loins. She tried to pull it back, embarrassed by the untidy blood welling up.

"No," he told her. "No shame, nothing held back." He kissed her hand gently and pulled her to him, whispering, "You can share anything . . . everything . . . with me."

TWELVE

~

THE San Diego International Airport handled fifty thousand passengers a day. It cozied up to the ocean without being quite on the shore; international flights came in over the water. And it looked, Lily thought, pretty much like every other airport. Lots of glass, lots of concrete, lots of cars jockeying for position on that portion of the concrete designated for passenger pickup.

She swerved in front of a bright yellow muscle truck to snag a spot by the curb. The pickup's driver didn't appreciate her vehicular dexterity. He leaned on his horn. She did not shoot him the finger. FBI agents don't do that sort of thing. Besides, she didn't need to. She'd won. He'd lost. Ha ha.

The white Toyota following her lacked a parking spot. Mike was driving it, with Todd riding shotgun . . . well, not literally shotgun. Todd had a Smith and Wesson M&P9. Nice weapon, if a bit large for her hand, but not a shotgun. Mike stopped smack in the traffic lane, forcing the line of cars to veer around him. Those drivers didn't appreciate him, either.

She could have let Mike drive her. Probably should have.

But she'd wanted to be alone. Just for a couple-three hours, she'd wanted to be alone. Being alone in San Diego traffic might not be optimal, but it was better than nothing.

After five hours' sleep, she'd woken up to another twenty-seven reports of possible victims. Ackleford—who'd apparently not even gone home last night, grabbing a nap on the couch in his office—had flagged those cases she needed to check out personally. The rest fit so well in terms of symptoms and time of onset that she could skip them for now. She'd checked out six victims this morning before heading to the airport to pick up Karonski. Four of the six got added to their victim tally.

Her mother was still at Sam's lair. Her sister Beth had arrived and was staying with their father, who still wasn't speaking to Lily. Her sister Susan was staying with him, too. Susan was speaking to Lily. She'd had plenty to say, mostly about how Lily had stabbed their father in the back and how it was all on Lily's head if Mother didn't do well following Sam's so-called treatment.

Lily had suggested Susan yell at Grandmother, too. Susan had hung up.

Rule had just left Clanhome, according to the mate bond. Headed for St. Margaret's Hospital, according to the text he'd sent. He was bringing Nettie with him. Nettie Two Horses was Rule's niece and age-mate. She was also a physician, healer, and shaman with ways of examining patients not available to her medical colleagues.

Rule had spent the morning at Nokolai Clanhome handling a disciplinary action. Discipline was one of his duties as Lu Nuncio, and there were a pair of young Nokolai in need of formal rebuking. His father would have let him reschedule, but Lily had told him not to bother, not on her behalf, at least. Then she'd had to persuade him she wasn't playing martyr by urging him to follow through with his duties. Rule didn't really understand her need for time alone. He accepted it, but he didn't share it. Lupi don't feel crowded by the presence of other clan.

Lily glanced at the dash clock. Five till noon. Karonski's

flight was on time, so he'd be out PDQ. Alone time was almost up. She sent Karonski a quick text so he'd know where to find her.

She could easily have delegated picking up Karonski, but she wanted to talk to him without other ears around. He'd want to talk to her, too. Ask questions. Ruben had briefed him, but the key word there was "brief." However competently you deliver a verbal report, you're summarizing. To spot a pattern, you need to dig down into the details, and when Lily talked to Karonski just before his flight was called, he hadn't yet read her report. There'd been a last-minute snafu with the case he was passing to his trainee that had kept him busy. By now, though, he would have read it and the various reports attached to it.

Maybe he'd spotted something that had eluded her. Maybe not. Either way, he'd have questions.

Lily pulled out her iPad. She, too, had reports to read. And questions. Maybe something in one of the new batch of reports would nudge her in the right direction. There was a pattern, some commonality that linked the victims. She just hadn't spotted it yet.

Halfway through the transcription of an interview with the daughter of victim twenty, she got a nudge . . . a teeny little poke that set up a vague itch between her eyes. She frowned and skimmed back through a couple other accounts . . . and called up the database someone at headquarters had set up. It held the basic stats about all the victims. A quick sort of that database turned the itch into a quiver, like a bird dog on point. She switched to her browser and asked Google for some statistical data. It obliged.

Knuckles rapped on the windshield. She jumped, wished she hadn't, and popped the trunk. She opened her door and started to get out.

"Sit, sit," the man who'd knocked on her windshield said. "The day I need help with my bag from someone I outweigh by a hundred pounds, I'm retiring." He wheeled his suitcase back toward the trunk.

He didn't outweigh her by a hundred pounds. Seventy,

maybe, and alas, not all of it was muscle. Abel Karonski looked like he'd been born middle-aged and rumpled. Rumpled hair, shirt, skin. The hair was brown and thinning on top, the skin was pale verging on pasty, and the shirt was white with a reddish stain not quite covered by his tie. Strawberry jam, probably. For breakfast Karonski liked to have a little toast with his strawberry jam.

She felt as much as heard his suitcase thump into the trunk. A moment later he slid into the passenger seat and slammed his door. "Any word on your mom?"

She shook her head and started the car.

"You want me not to talk about her?"

"I'm trying to keep all that stuffed away. Stay focused on the job. It helps if I can focus on the job."

"Okay." He patted her shoulder. Karonski wasn't a toucher, so from him, that was a hug. "So tell me why you were thinking so hard you didn't see me until I banged on the windshield."

Lily put the car in gear and pulled away from the curb. This was made easier by the way Mike's Toyota blocked oncoming traffic. "I finally noticed something. Maybe you already spotted it. All forty-six of our likely or confirmed victims are adults. Twenty have adult children. Twenty-two of them are fifty years and up. That's almost half. In the general population, only one in nine people is over fifty."

"Huh. That means something. I don't know what, but something." He chewed that over and nodded. "Schools. I didn't see any mention of them in your report. Have you asked what grade school or middle school the vics went to?"

Excitement fluttered in her gut. "That's good. That's a good possibility. I've got some info on colleges, but they didn't all go to college. We didn't ask about lower grades."

"You drive. I'll call Ackleford." He took out his phone. "We headed to the Bureau's office?"

"Yes."

"Good. I need to let you know that . . . Ackleford. This is Karonski. I'll be there in fifteen or so. I know you can't wait to see me again, but . . . heh-heh. Good to know you're still the same shining wit I remember, though what you suggest is anatomically impossible. Listen, I've got something for you to do to fill the empty minutes till I get there."

Lily listened to Karonski's instructions with half an ear as she began winding through the concrete maze that led away from the airport. After a pause Karonski shook his head and said, "My, but you do get cranky when you're short on sleep. Just how short are you?"

She'd tried to send Ackleford home earlier. He'd waved her off.

"That's what I thought," Karonski said. "After the press conference . . . hell, yeah, I'm holding a press conference. One thirty. Ida's arranging it, so you don't have to sully yourself by talking to any damn reporters. Once that's done, I'll try to struggle on without you while you catch some shut-eye." A pause. "Because I want you on nights, that's why." Karonski glanced at Lily, his eyes crinkling with amusement. "Because I've got other shit for her to do. Yeah, yeah, but I'm the son of a bitch in charge, so you'll have to live with it." Another pause. A chuckle. "You do that."

"He wouldn't go home when I told him to," Lily said.

Karonski put his phone back in his jacket's inside pocket. "You're genetically compromised in his eyes, being as how you lack that magic Y chromosome. In spite of that, he damn near complimented you. Wanted to know why I didn't leave 'that Yu chick' in charge nights, seeing that you're halfway competent."

"You actually like him, don't you?"

"Smartest asshole I know. He's pissed because he didn't think of the age slant or about checking where the victims went to school. Made it hard for him to argue that he was doing fine on almost no sleep."

"So why are you holding a press conference? The piranhas of the press haven't tumbled to the story yet."

"Two reasons. First, they're tumbling, even if they haven't put anything on the air yet. Ida's fielding calls about that bulletin to the hospitals. Won't be long before someone opens his big, fat mouth to a reporter. Second . . ." His voice turned grim. "We've got to. Your mom lost her memory back to when she was twelve. That's the most years any of the victims lost, with the possible exception of the one who's in a coma. Maybe that's what went wrong with her. Maybe she lost too many years. Even if that isn't what happened, what if there are others like her? We need people to check on their friends, their relatives, their neighbors."

"Hell." Lily's hands tightened on the steering wheel. "People who live alone. I didn't think of that. I didn't think."

"Yeah, so take a good thirty, forty seconds and beat yourself up about that. Or you can do like Ruben and save it for a later brood, when you've got more time for that sort of thing."

So Ruben hadn't thought of the possibility, either. That was some comfort. But Lily knew she'd missed that horrible possibility because she was distracted. Because it was her mother who was the first victim. Her mother who'd lost the most . . . so far. "I'm glad you're here. What did you have in mind for me, since you want the Big A in charge at night?"

"You tell me." Plastic crinkled as he opened a pack of peanuts. "You've got your own investigation to handle."

"Right now, I don't have anything. Nothing the Bureau can't do better and faster. The only angle I can see is to keep looking for what connects the victims, and that takes manpower. That's the Bureau's thing."

"Guess you need some thinking time, then." He crunched down on a handful of peanuts. Chewed, swallowed. "Heard from the coven yet?"

"They didn't learn anything at the restaurant, which isn't surprising. Whatever spell or rite caused this wasn't performed there, so there weren't any traces from it for them to find. They're going to work with one of the victims, though. She's Wiccan, so she isn't weirded out by having witches chant over her. They hope to find out something about what was done to her. What caused all this."

"You don't sound hopeful."

"If Sam doesn't have a clue, is the coven likely to figure it out?"

"If this had been a magical attack, I'd say no. If it's spiritual, like the dragon and Seaborne say . . . Lily, you've got to stop thinking of this the way you would a magical attack."

"I don't have a way of thinking about spirit."

"Spirit is . . ." He flopped his hand back and forth. "It can be good. Can be evil, too. I'm betting this shit lands on the evil side."

"Do you believe in evil?"

"Yep. Do you?"

"I don't know," she said slowly. "Evil like the devil? Not so much. Evil like some—some vile, insentient force? Maybe." She thought about it. "Death magic. The way that feels . . . I guess I do think evil is real."

"If evil exists, then good does, too."

"Do we have to talk about this?"

"Yes. Have you thought about the fact that your Gift doesn't protect you from spiritual energy?"

Her mouth opened. Closed. Her stomach went hollow. "No. No, I hadn't thought of that."

"You'll need to draw on what you know about good to protect yourself. Religion is no guarantee of protection, but it helps. You don't have a faith, a spiritual practice, so you need to think about what you do believe in. What you know in your gut about goodness." He crunched down on another handful of peanuts. "Do dragons have a spiritual practice?"

"I—I don't know. The subject hasn't come up." She thought that over, frowning. "Sam said spirit was capricious and personal and universal. That it was often spoken of in terms of good and evil. He said he couldn't define it and didn't understand it."

"I like him."

"What?"

"The dragon. He's arrogant as hell, but too smart not to realize that and allow for it. In my branch of Wicca, we call spirit the great mystery. Buddhist koans point toward spirit. That's all you can do, point in the general direction. You can't corral it in words. You can't use spirit the way you use magic or electricity. You can channel it, but you can't use it, and to channel it, you have to submit to it. Not surprising Sam doesn't understand spirit. Dragons are not good at submission." He glanced at her, his mouth twitching up. "You aren't, either. Plus, you want rules. Spirit doesn't follow them. Not exactly."

"Not exactly? What does that mean, not exactly?"

"Probably what your dragon meant when he called it capricious. There's what you might call guidelines— religions are full of 'em—but they don't come with guarantees. You can follow the hell out of the guidelines and get a different result from one time to the next."

Great. She drummed her fingers on the steering wheel. "Cullen said we need a saint. Drummond said I was supposed to get one. I may have found him, but I lost him again."

"That homeless guy in your report."

"Hardy. I don't know if that's his first name or last."

"He hummed 'Mother and Child Reunion' at you."

"And how did he know that song would fit? God told him?"

"Not impossible."

"I am so not happy with the God-talk."

"Then call it spirit instead."

"Which can be either good or evil . . . though I still think the simplest explanation is that Hardy's connected to the bad guys, and that's how he knew about my mother." She brooded on that a moment. "That's where I need to start, I guess. I need to find Hardy. Whether he's a saint with a mysterious source of knowledge or a bad guy, he knows things I need to know."

"Glad you got that figured out." More rustles from the plastic bag. "Damn. That's all my peanuts. We'd better have lunch delivered PDQ. Don't have much time. Mexican okay with you?"

"Fine, but I don't see—"

"I don't intend to talk to the press on an empty stomach. You shouldn't, either."

"Me? You don't need me to—"

"Sure I do." He tossed her a heartless grin. "Your face is better known than mine. Prettier, too. You're gonna be right beside me at that press conference."

THIRTEEN

~~

TRAFFIC was unusually annoying on I-5. Rule drummed his fingers on the steering wheel and did not curse or contemplate a judicious culling of the herd. Not much.

The slow creep was aggravated by the fact that he couldn't switch lanes aggressively. Impatience was not sufficient reason to risk losing the car tailing him. He glanced at the woman beside him. Nettie had asked him to let his guards follow in another car for the ride into the city. He was still waiting to find out why she'd wanted the privacy. He'd used the drive to tell her more about the situation, but that was nothing that his guards couldn't hear. She hadn't said anything they couldn't hear, either.

Nettie was reading Lily's report now, her head down, a pair of readers perched on her nose. It was a strong nose that went well with the copper skin and bladed cheekbones that were her heritage from both sides of her family. Benedict was half Navajo; her mother was full-blood.

Her hair was a throwback to Rule's great-grandmother on his father's side, or so Isen claimed. Not at all Navajo, that hair. Today she'd braided the unruly mass that, let loose, would have spilled in frizzy waves to her waist. As a teen, Nettie had hated her hair. She'd chopped it all off in medical school and kept it short until, when she turned thirty, it began turning gray. Somehow that change reconciled her to it. She'd worn it long ever since.

Rule had known his niece since she was in diapers. He'd studied women for years. He knew hair held meaning for women, that it affected how they saw themselves. He had no idea why its turning gray had made Nettie like hers. He was glad it had, but he didn't understand it.

He eased forward another few feet. His phone chimed that he had a new text. He reached for it.

"You are not going to read text messages while driving," his passenger informed him. "And yes, this speed still qualifies as driving."

"Of course not." Rule held the button down briefly without looking at his phone. "Read the text, please." The automated voice complied. The text was from Lily, who wanted him to know that Abel—whom she insisted on calling Karonski, that being the preferred cop mode of address—was holding a press conference in thirty minutes. Abel wanted her to perform with him.

"That's the damnedest thing." Nettie shook her head. "Your phone reads your texts to you? Not that you should be using it at all when you're driving."

"I don't do it at highway speeds."

"You shouldn't do it at all. And I don't want to hear about your super-duper lupi reflexes. Even if you can avert a crash at the last minute, you shouldn't put yourself in that position. Or me. Or the drivers around you."

He wasn't feeling charitable toward the drivers around him at the moment. There were too damn many of them. "I wouldn't risk you."

"Try not risking yourself, too. May I see your toy? How do you get it to talk to you?"

He handed her his phone and instructed her briefly in how to access Siri. Nettie had one of the oldest still-functioning cell phones in existence. It was another point of bafflement for Rule. She was no Luddite, yet she disliked cell phones and refused to upgrade.

While she played with Siri, they eased forward a bit faster. Maybe the bottleneck was breaking up at last.

Nettie handed him back his phone. "Maybe I should break down and get a smartphone."

"I'll get one for—"

"No, you won't. Note that I said maybe *I* should. Not you. Feeling especially Leidolf and territorial today, are you?"

"I *was* feeling generous. Now I'm feeling annoyed."

"Surely you know that lupi claim territory by giving presents? Leidolf's especially obvious about it, but you all do it."

That shut his mouth. Did he do that? Did his father? "The way you claim territory by constantly correcting me?"

Nettie chuckled. "It's not constant, but if you're going to be wrong so often—"

"Careful."

"Not to mention prickly. What's wrong?"

Rule gave her a look.

"You're worried about Lily's mother, of course. I know that. But I was raised by a champion brooder. I know a good brood when I see one. Something else is eating at you."

"If I'd wanted to talk about it, perhaps I would have found a way to introduce the subject myself."

"Did I ask if you wanted to talk about it?" Though her words were as tart as ever, her voice was gentle. She reached out and squeezed his arm. "Do you know what's bothering you?"

Rule sighed. "I've found a new level of pettiness in myself. I'm not happy about it."

She made a humming noise that was supposed to encourage him to keep talking. When he didn't, she did. "I'm not just being nosy, Rule. I'm wearing my shaman hat. If we're dealing with a negative spiritual incursion—"

"A what?"

"A negative spiritual incursion into our world. Or you could call it the dark side of the Force. Or an evil god."

"You mean the Great Bitch."

"Actually, I don't. Not necessarily. First, not all gods are Old Ones. Second, wouldn't your mantles have reacted if *her* power was used directly against Julia Yu?"

"I think so, but if Friar is using an artifact, the power isn't coming from *her* directly."

"I don't know much about artifacts." Nettie thought about that a moment, then said, "Directed, focused spiritual power—to me that speaks of those we've traditionally called gods. But whether we're dealing with a god or an artifact, spiritual power is involved, and spirit is different from magic."

"So everyone keeps saying, without defining that difference."

"Spirit can't be pinned in place with a definition, but the difference . . . I can take a stab at that. Magic is inanimate and morally neutral, like electricity. Spirit is morally active and volitional."

"It's alive?"

"Not precisely. Spirit is what life is built from. That's why Lily's Gift doesn't block it."

"You need to tell Lily that."

"Do I? All right."

"Sam said that humans speak of spirit in terms of good and evil. Is that what you mean by morally active?"

"Close enough. My point is that if there's a lot of really bad spiritual juju around, we have to be careful about our spiritual hygiene."

He snorted. "Spiritual hygiene."

She shrugged. "Evil infects. It's like a virus. We encounter all kinds of viruses and bacteria every day—and spread them, too, without meaning to. Most people, most of the time, don't get sick beyond a head cold or stomach upset. Similarly, most people, most of the time, fight off most of the infections caused by evil. But if we encounter the spiritual equivalent of the plague, we're in trouble."

"You're afraid we're dealing with the plague version."

"I don't know what we're dealing with. That's why I'm pestering you to talk about whatever is bothering you." She squeezed his arm again. "It's like lancing a boil. If you can't talk about it with me, then find someone else."

Lily. He wanted to talk to Lily. Unfortunately, she was the one person he couldn't discuss this with.

He hadn't known there was anything wrong until this morning, when jealousy reared its snaky head. Lily had told Rule to go tend to his clan business. She wanted to be alone, she'd said. He'd caught himself thinking that she'd arranged to be alone with Abel.

That was so absurd it got his attention. Why would he think that, even for a moment? The answer had come immediately: because she was shutting him out. It wasn't just that she hadn't wanted him with her this morning. It was how she felt when she was with him. Closed down. Shut down. Shutting him out. And he resented it.

And that was a nice bit of irony, wasn't it? Lily had pointed out how often he shut her out when he was troubled. She didn't like it. Now he knew how she felt. He didn't like it, either, but he wasn't going to whine to her about it now. Not when she was dealing with very real grief. In effect, Lily had lost her mother. Julia was still around, but the twelve-year-old version of her was not anyone's mother.

Unlike with most deaths, however, there was a chance Lily could get her mother back. A slim chance, maybe vanishingly small. But Lily being Lily, she would believe it was up to her to put things right. This had to push her anxiety into the stratosphere, and he worried about how hard she'd be hit if they weren't able to—

His phone rippled through the violin music he used for Lily's ring tone. He grabbed it. "Yes?"

"The press conference is postponed. Karonski and I are on our way to Balboa Park. Can you meet us there?"

"Of course. What's up?"

"The locals found Hardy for me. He was crooning over a dead body."

* * *

BALBOA Park was a big place—roughly twelve hundred acres—but it was an urban park, not a wilderness area. The zoo took up a big chunk of those acres, as did the Naval Medical Center and the Morley Field Sports Complex. There was a history center, a science center, fourteen museums, assorted other buildings, and the pavilion. The Old Globe theater complex. The amphitheater. Multiple gardens, running from Alcazar to Zoro.

In spite of all the cultivation, there were also hiking and biking trails. Lily squatted on a rocky outcrop about a hundred yards from one of those trails, looking down into a ravine. It was a blue-sky day, the air soft with early spring. Birds called each other, gossiping about the two-legged intruders in their midst.

Off to her left, mostly hidden by scrub, she could hear the city's CSI team. They were working on what was probably the path the perps had taken. Below her, in the ravine, were two men. One was alive. One wasn't.

The living man stood with his back to the dead one, chanting softly as he studied a small mirror he kept tilting this way and that. The dead man ignored him as thoroughly as only the dead can.

He'd been fifty-five or sixty. Caucasian, and a really pale one now, with so much of his blood gone. What she could see of his features looked regular; the lower half of his face was hidden by the black cloth they'd gagged him with. Blond hair going gray, a bit of a paunch . . . which she could see because his killers had stripped him before staking him to the ground with four big iron spikes. One through each hand, one through each foot.

He'd still been alive when they did that. Alive, too, when they drew some kind of rune on his chest with a knife. They hadn't cut his throat until after they pinned him to the earth like a human bug. He'd struggled. Damn near pulled one of his hands free in spite of the spike, which spoke of strength and desperation and guts. It took guts to do that to yourself. He'd ripped his hand apart, trying to get loose.

Lily's gut cramped. Whoever he was, he'd been a fighter.

"What's your buddy doing?" the cop behind her asked.

"Investigating," Lily said. That came out too terse. Angry. She tried again. "I don't know any more than what he told Detective Erskine. I don't know spellwork myself."

"Huh. I thought all you Unit types did the woo-woo stuff."

Lily sighed. You'd think she'd be better at waiting. She did enough of it. "We all have different areas of expertise. I'm a touch sensitive. I can't work magic, so I never learned spellwork. I'll be checking for death magic after he's finished." There were special protocols for dealing with a body and a scene involving death magic, so they needed to know for sure before the Bureau's CSI team got started.

When Lily and Karonski got here, the city's crime scene team had started working the scene, though they hadn't gotten beyond taking pictures and video. Karonski had set them to working on the path and relegated the rest of the SDPD to searching the nearby area, maintaining the perimeter, and watching Hardy and the boys. The guy with the lead, Detective Erskine, was not happy about that.

It would have to be Erskine, Lily thought glumly as she rose. Not T.J. or Brady or even Laurell, but Erskine. She turned to face the patrol officer. Officer Daryl Crown wasn't middle-aged yet, but if he stood on tiptoe he'd bump his head on it. He was Caucasian, brown and brown, with tired eyes and, from the smell, a nicotine habit. He'd been first on-scene, and Lily had wanted to question him while Karonski did his thing, so she'd asked him to escort her here.

She cocked her head. "The boys who found the body— Ryan and Patrick, right?"

"He likes to be called Pat."

She made a mental note of that. "They said they were on the bike trail and heard Hardy singing."

"If Hardy's the guy who doesn't talk, then yeah. They also said they never take their bikes off the marked paths, but they made an exception this time."

"I guess they don't usually cut school, either." She exchanged a look with him. "They're brothers. The parents here yet?"

"I'll check." He clicked his mike and asked someone about that. "The dad just arrived. Mr. Samuel Springer."

"If Karonski doesn't finish up pretty soon, I'll—"

"I'm done," called a voice from below. "Come on down. Carefully."

Lily didn't waste any time following that order.

The ravine wasn't deep, but it was steep and covered in bushy growth. Only one good way down, so they weren't using it. The perps probably had. The next-best access was about ten feet to Lily's right. She headed there, sliding the strap of her purse across her chest messenger-bag style so she'd have both hands free. That let her scramble down quickly, hitting the bottom of the ravine several yards from the body.

Karonski met her. His face didn't tell her much. The lines were grooved deeper than usual, but that might be fatigue from the spell.

"Well?" she said.

"We'll share notes after you've checked things out your way. Stay back as far as you can. Don't cross the circle."

"It's not active, is it?"

"No, but don't touch it. Just touch one of his hands for now."

She nodded, slipped booties on over her shoes, and advanced carefully. She'd already mapped out her route from above.

The circle around the victim had been drawn with a thick line of powder the color of unburned charcoal. It was scuffed in several places. Inside it—in addition to the body—were simple runes sand-painted on the earth. They were a pale, chalky yellow. It looked like there'd been nine of them, though several had been obscured by the arterial blood that had fountained up and out, covering a large swath of the ground . . . except in one spot, near the victim's head. The place where his killer had squatted to cut his throat.

Blood splatter doesn't show up as starkly on dirt and rocks as it does on a white wall, but from above Lily had been able to map out a fairly clear path to one staked hand. She sniffed as she drew near and frowned. She'd expected the sour, butcher-shop stink. There was a lot of blood. Some had soaked into the ground, but the ravine was rocky. Not enough soil to absorb however many quarts he'd lost before his heart quit pumping it out.

She had not expected the faint stink of decay. Visually, the body seemed fresh. Some lividity, sure, but while that didn't hit maximum for six to twelve hours, it set in pretty early. No signs of animal depredation, and while the day was warm, it wasn't hot enough to speed decomposition. Last night had been cool.

Well, figuring out time of death was the ME's job, not hers. She stopped and crouched. Someone had a very sharp knife, she observed. They'd sliced his neck open with a single stroke. No false starts. Took a good blade and some strength to do that. Might take some practice, too. Had they used the same blade to carve that rune on his chest? If so, it was fairly narrow.

She could reach one of the staked hands without crossing the scuffed circle. She did that, pressing her fingers to one mutilated hand.

And fell back on her butt.

FOURTEEN

~

"LILY?"

"I'm okay." Embarrassed, but okay. Lily put both palms flat on the ground, patted around, and felt nothing but dirt and rocks. So she pushed back into her crouch, steeled herself, and stretched out her right hand to touch dead flesh again.

When she'd learned everything she could, she stood and walked back to Karonski, digging in her purse with her left hand for a wipe.

"Obviously you felt something. Death magic?"

"I don't know. That first touch . . ." She repressed a shudder and started scrubbing her right hand with the wipe. She wished she had some holy water like Cynna used sometimes. Clorox didn't seem like enough. "Maybe it's a variation on death magic. Is there such a thing? This stuff is every bit as repellent, and the sensation is similar, but not quite the same. Mushier. Whatever it is, there's a lot of it, and it . . . it's in motion. It's crawling around on that body." This time she couldn't keep from shuddering. "It tried to crawl up my hand."

"Son of a—Lily, are you—"

"I'm okay. It couldn't stick to me. It tried, but it couldn't. Take my hand." She held it out.

"I didn't touch the body," he said, but he let her check anyway. His palm was firm and slightly moist, and the only magic she felt was the kind he'd been born with. Karonski's Gift was a variant of Earth magic called psychometry—the ability to read emotions from objects. A strong psychometor could pick up images and thoughts if they were connected to strong emotion. Karonski's Gift wasn't that strong, but he was exceptionally well trained. When Lily touched him, she felt moss-covered stones. Stones were Earth; the mossy sensation was how her Gift interpreted both his particular variant and his years of training.

When she dropped his hand he asked, "Is this stuff anything like what you touched on the amnesia victims?"

"I don't know. What I'm aware of touching is magic—nasty, icky magic, and lots of it. Trying to find some *arguai* mixed in with that would be like trying to spot the Big Dipper when the sun's up. I can't do it. Karonski, we need to make sure no one touched that body. The first-on-scene said he didn't, since the vic was obviously dead, and I shook hands with him. I didn't feel any trace of magic. But the boys and Hardy—the boys say they didn't touch him, but we need to know for sure."

"Shit. You don't feel any magic in the air, do you?"

"No, and I checked the ground. The dry ground, that is. Nothing there. I can't say about the blood-soaked area. I didn't think I should touch it."

"You'll probably need to, but later. Let's go."

She tucked the wipe in a pocket and started up out of the gully. Up was harder than down, and she needed both hands for the first part. The paramedics were going to have a fun time getting the body up if they used this route . . . if the body could be safely handled. "How do we keep the icky magic from crawling on people?"

"Silk, maybe. It's worth a try. I'll need you to check to see if it can get through silk."

That was going to be fun. "What did your spell tell you?"

"Two spells, actually. The first one should have let me see if there was any death magic in the area."

"Should have?"

"The results didn't make sense." He was huffing a bit from the climb. "You want the long version? It's technical."

"Later. What was the other spell for?"

"It's a way to contact the vic's ghost, if there's one around. Nonverbal, since ghosts mostly aren't good with words. That spell would have let me see what the ghost remembered about his death."

"It didn't work?"

"No ghost this time. Speaking of ghosts . . ." He paused to catch his breath. "Have you heard from yours?"

Lily scrambled up the last bit and saw Officer Crown waiting. He looked very curious. She grimaced. She hated it when people referred to Drummond as her ghost. "Not since last night. I could try calling him. He said that wouldn't work as well this time, but I could try."

That was too much for Officer Crown. "You've got a ghost?"

"I have occasional contact with one. Karonski? Should I call Drummond?"

He heaved himself up onto level ground. "Probably, but you need to check out the kids and Hardy first. Officer, I'd like you to stay here, where you can keep on eye on the scene. We've got a serious magical contamination problem. No one can approach that body but me or Agent Yu for now. No one. The mayor shows up, you keep him away."

Crown's eyebrows lifted. "Yes, sir."

Lily and Karonski set off at a quick jog. "I'm betting on at least two perps. You?"

"Probably. The vic looks to weigh around one eighty. He could have been unconscious or drugged, so one person isn't impossible, but it's unlikely."

"The gag suggests they wanted him alive and aware when they started hurting him."

"Yeah." His words started getting spaced between breaths.

"Theoretically one guy . . . might have done the staking . . . if the vic was unconscious. But they had to get him down there first. Hard for . . . one person . . . to do that."

"No drag marks."

"Exactly."

"Why here, do you think? Plenty of dogs, bikers, runners in this park. They performed their little ritual as far from the trails as they could, but still. Why not head outside the city altogether?"

"Ley line. Might be some other . . . significant factor but . . . the body's smack on a whopping big ley line that's . . . close to the surface. That isn't . . . as easy to find as you might . . . look, you go on. I can't talk and run, and I need to . . . call our people about . . . the contagion."

They weren't running. They were jogging. "You okay?"

"I'm pathetic, is what I am. Go." He flapped a hand at her as she stopped. "I'll call your Detective Erskine, too."

She gave Karonski one more dubious look, but he didn't seem to be having a heart attack. He was just really out of shape. She nodded and set off. The ground was too rough for real speed, but she could pick up the pace.

Lily had started running in college because it was a cheap, quick way to get in a workout. When crunched for time, she could get in a run, shower, and dress in thirty-five minutes. Forty-five, if she dried her hair.

She'd discovered she liked it. Needed it. Running cleared her brain better than anything, with the possible exception of the kind of cardio that took two people. She'd run in exactly one marathon, and while her time hadn't sucked, she'd decided she wouldn't do it again. It brought out her competitive instincts, and that messed up the experience. Made her think about the wrong things. This turned out to be a good decision, because these days she usually ran with Rule or one or more of the guards. No way a human could compete with lupi, so it was just as well she hadn't built her runs around the idea of winning.

She wasn't winded when she slowed as she neared the

bike trail. A uniform was stationed there, making sure no one wandered toward the scene. She told Lily that a van from a local TV station had shown up at the parking lot.

No doubt more reporters were on their way. Lily grimaced and picked up her pace again. The trail wasn't paved, but it was a lot smoother than the ground. She didn't have to pay such close attention to where her feet landed. She could think about other things . . . like how many perps were involved.

It would have taken at least two people to carry the victim down into the ravine, all right. Or one lupus. Lily hadn't mentioned that possibility. She gave it less than one chance in a hundred. Lupi were as capable of wrongdoing as humans, but no lupus would knowingly help the Great Bitch, and if Friar was involved, the Big B was, too. Of course, Lily didn't know for certain that this victim was connected to the amnesia victims. She had a strong suspicion, yeah. If you have two creepy-freaky things happen close together, you suspect they're connected. But suspicion is not fact.

Rule would be able to tell. As soon as he got here—and a quick check of the mate-sense told her he was close and getting closer. Good. He'd be able to sniff out how many perps were involved and if they were all human. Or not. No point in raising that particular issue unless she had to.

Black-and-whites with their strobing red lights were clustered at one end of the parking lot. They'd used the cars to section it off, keep the civilians away. A thin woman trailing a cameraman was arguing with one of the uniforms on the civilian side of the patrol-car fence. Lily had no trouble picking out Erskine in the crowd of cops on the near side of that barrier. He looked like a pudgy, faded leprechaun in black-framed glasses. He frowned when he spotted her.

Erskine was a good cop. Lily had worked with him sometimes back when she was in Homicide, so she knew this. More by-the-book than brilliant, maybe, but competent and thorough. She hadn't liked him back then, but that was mainly because he hadn't liked her. She'd never been sure what about her rubbed him the wrong way, but from day one it was clear something did. They'd put up with each other for the sake of the job.

These days he couldn't stand her. He blamed her for Mech's death.

Sergeant Homer Mechtle had been a good cop, too. And a friend. He'd committed suicide last year. When Lily killed a telepath named Helen, the psychic backlash had killed or damaged a number of the people she'd been controlling, aided by an ancient staff. Mech had been one of them.

Sometimes Lily blamed herself for Mech's death, too.

The uniforms parted to allow her to jog up to the detective. "I need to—"

"Your boss told me," Erskine said curtly. "I talked to Springer. He okayed you checking out his boys. The boys don't know about any possible contagion. Keep it that way."

Well, darn. And there she'd been looking forward to scaring the snot out of them. "My consultant will be here soon. Rule Turner. Karonski told you about him."

"Is that what you call him? Your consultant?" Erskine could sneer without moving a muscle on his face. It was a good trick, especially on a face like his. Erskine had one of those round faces that look boyish no matter how old its wearer gets. "Yeah, Karonski mentioned him. You want to keep chatting with me, or would you like to find out if those boys are okay?"

Her lips tightened. She turned without a word.

"Agent Yu!" a woman called. "What can you tell me about the murder?"

That was the reporter. Lily ignored her with the ease of long practice.

Samuel Springer and his sons stood near a large oak, well away from the patrol-car fence and the eager reporter. He was a tall, skinny man with dark hair, a luxuriant mustache, and glasses. One of the boys looked exactly like him, done smaller and without the mustache. The other was sandy haired and lacked glasses, but had the same sharp features. Springer had his arms around both boys. He watched warily as she approached.

"Special Agent Lily Yu," she said, holding out her hand. "You're Samuel Springer?"

The man eyed her hand a moment, then turned loose of one of his sons to accept the handshake she was silently insisting on. "I am."

No magic. Lily released his hand and looked at the taller of the boys. The dark-haired one. "Are you Ryan? I've got a friend named Ryan." She held out her hand to him, too.

He glanced up at his father uncertainly. Springer nodded. "Go on."

Ryan took her hand. She shook with him solemnly, but inside all kinds of knots relaxed. No magic. Not a trace. "Good to meet you, Ryan. You've had a really rough day." She turned to the younger boy, the one with sandy hair. "And you're Pat, right? Again she held out her hand.

This one didn't hesitate. He put his hand in hers and pumped it like a politician. "Yeah, and you're an FBI agent? For real? I guess you're investigating the dead guy, huh?"

"I am." No magic here, either. At least none to worry about. He had a tiny trace of a charisma Gift, but that was all.

"Cool."

"I didn't let him see . . . it." That was the dark-haired Ryan, assuring her that he'd done his duty by his younger brother. "I got him away from there."

"I did, too, see! You kept getting in the way, then you dragged me back to the bikes, but I saw the singing man and—and the other man."

And maybe now he wished he hadn't, but pride would not let him admit this. Lily looked from one young face to the other, then up at their dad. She gave him a small, reassuring smile and a nod to let him know his sons were okay. His face sagged a little in relief. "Mr. Springer, boys, I think we'll be able to let you go home pretty soon. I'll need to talk to you first, but before I can do that, I have to have a word with the man who was singing."

" 'The Old Rugged Cross,' " Ryan said.

"Pardon?"

"That's what he was singing, which was pretty gross. Considering."

He was right. It was pretty gross, considering. "I'll be back in a few minutes. You need anything?"

"They said they didn't have any Coke," Pat said hopefully. "The police officers, I mean. Just water. Do you . . ."

"I'm afraid I don't have any Coke, either."

"Stupid," Ryan informed his brother as Lily turned away. "As if FBI agents carry Cokes around with them everywhere."

His brother said hotly, "You know who's really stupid? People who don't even bother to ask!" Their father was shushing them as Lily reached Erskine.

"They're clean," she said. "Where's Hardy?"

"You're sure?"

"Ninety-five percent. To be one hundred percent, I'd have to touch them everywhere, which would be scary and intrusive. But magic tends to—to spread or leak or something like that when it's in a living organism. Even if only one part of the body is affected, there's almost always some trace of it on the skin."

"Almost always," he repeated. He glanced over at Springer and the boys.

"Best I can do." They needed Cullen. Seeing magic was better than feeling it for some things, but Cullen wouldn't be available for hours, maybe days, depending on how hard covering Sam's security arrangements hit him. And that made her think about what Cullen was doing right now, and what Sam was doing, and how much longer it might be before they knew if it had worked. Her stomach knotted up in a sick lump. She forced those thoughts back down. Buried them nice and tight. "Hardy?"

"In Delacroix's squad car." He nodded at the black-and-white at the end of the row. "We put him in there so we could take the cuffs off. He behaved himself once we got him away from the scene. Didn't want to leave it, though.

Got pretty agitated, according to Crown. That 'person of interest' notice you people issued said this guy can't talk."

"Brain damage, I'm told. Something that affected the speech center. Music is stored differently than speech, so he can sing, but he can't put together a sentence."

"Well, we tried getting him to write something out for us, but he couldn't or wouldn't do that, either. Seems to understand us when we talk to him, though."

"Hey!" shouted one of the uniforms.

The thin woman had slipped between two of the patrol cars while the uniform wasn't watching. She trotted up to Lily. "Special Agent, why is the FBI involved? Was this a ritual murder? Is there a connection with the amnesia victims you've been visiting?"

Well, damn. Looked like the story had broken after all. Lily recognized the reporter now. Milly Rodriguez was young, ambitious, and pushy as hell. That was her job, but she hadn't figured out how to push without crossing the wrong lines. "Ms. Rodriguez, if you'll wait where you were told to, I'll speak with you as soon as possible. If you won't, you go on my list. The list of reporters I do not take questions from. Ever."

The woman considered briefly, then nodded. "Fifteen minutes."

"No guarantees. As soon as I can."

"I won't wait forever," she warned, but she retreated.

Lily and Erskine reached the patrol unit where Hardy was locked up. Erskine nodded at the patrolman sitting in the driver's seat. "Open up."

The moment Lily opened the door Hardy turned to look at her. He didn't try to get out, but he turned in the seat and stretched out both hands urgently.

Automatically she bent and took his hands.

No icky magic. She exhaled in relief. No blood, either. At least none she could see.

He kept hold of one of her hands, patting it as if reassuring her. Lily gently tugged it free. "Hello, Hardy. Please step out of the car so we can talk without me bending over."

He climbed out. He wore the same blue flannel shirt and

worn gray pants she'd seen him in the night before. He stood there looking down at her sadly.

"You understand that it looks bad, don't you? You were found with that body. You didn't want to leave it."

He started humming.

"I'm sorry. I don't know that song."

"'Washed in the blood,'" he sang soft and slow, "'washed in the blood of Jesus.'"

Lily didn't react, but it wasn't easy. "You wanted to wash in the blood?"

He shook his head and frowned at her as if she'd disappointed him. Then he tried again. This time he sang an old commercial ditty.

"Mr. Clean? You, uh . . . you were trying to clean something?"

He nodded quickly, then sang, "'Move, Satan, move on out of my way.'"

"You were casting out the devil?"

He cocked his head as if considering her word choice, then nodded slowly.

Weird. The body really did need cleansing or the casting out of devils, or something along those lines. Hardy's singing hadn't done the trick, but he'd tried. Or claimed he had, she reminded herself. It was harder to think of him as a possible bad guy when she stood in front of him. "Was that man alive when you first saw him, Hardy?"

He shook his head, his eyes dark with sorrow.

"Did you see anyone near the body?" Another head shake. "Do you have any idea who did it?" Another. "Do you know who the murdered man was? No? Ever seen him before? Okay. I can't think how to make this next one a yes or no question. How did you find the body?"

He hummed a few snatches of tunes, as if he were hunting for the right lyrics, then started singing about coming into a garden alone where a voice that "'the Son of God discloses . . . bids me go.'" He stopped, switched tempo and key, and added, "'Angels we have heard on high, sweetly singing o'er the plains.'"

"Jesus told you about it? Or an angel?"

He nodded.

"Which one was it?"

He spread his hands. Shrugged.

"You don't know?" He nodded and she looked at Erskine, raising her brows to see if he wanted any more questions right now. He shrugged. When she looked back at Hardy she saw Karonski wending his way to them through the cars and officers. She told Hardy she'd talk to him some more later. "Do you need anything? Some water?"

He nodded and smiled.

"I'll see that you get some. Oh. One more thing. Is Hardy your first name? No? It's your last name?" He nodded. "All right, Mr. Hardy, I'll—" He was shaking his head again. "Okay. Just Hardy, no 'mister.' "

Karonski arrived and gave a little jerk of his head. Erskine told one of his men to get Hardy some water and get him back in the patrol car, then walked with her to where Karonski waited.

"I called the coven," Karonski said. "We need a strong circle set around that body while we figure out what we're dealing with. You learn anything?"

"No contagion on the boys or Hardy." As she summarized what she'd learned from Hardy, she felt the subtle easing that meant Rule was here. She glanced at the entrance to the parking lot and saw his Mercedes pulling in. "Does that conform with what Hardy told you, Detective?" she asked Erskine.

"You got more from him than I did." He snorted. "Jesus told him to do it."

"You're jumping to conclusions. There's no blood on him."

Erskine gave her a scathing glance. "So he stood back while his partner did the slicing. He's a brain-damaged man who hears voices, for God's sake."

Lily wasn't about to tell Erskine that Hardy might be a saint, but she didn't like the way Erskine was zeroing in on the homeless man. "We're not dealing with your typical crazy-guy killer. Whoever murdered that man knew exactly what he was doing, and he generated a whole lot of bad magic doing it. Hardy doesn't have any magic on him."

"So he didn't get any of the magic his partner cooked up. Doesn't prove anything. There's clearly a religious twist to the killing, the way that body was staked out like they were crucifying him. Your buddy over there has religion on the brain."

Karonski had taken out a piece of gum while they talked. He folded it into his mouth. "Religion may be involved, but not necessarily Christianity. There are well-established ritualistic reasons for using some form of a crucifixion pose. Did you think the Romans invented that? People were doing that to each other long before Jesus of Nazareth came along. Doesn't prove Hardy wasn't involved," he added, "but it doesn't link him, either."

Erskine looked dubious. "The magic part is your deal, I guess. But there was more than one person involved. I don't see any reason Hardy couldn't be one of them."

"Or any reason to think that he was," Lily said. "Being brain damaged is not a reason."

"Being found singing to the body just might be considered significant." He looked away dismissively to ask Karonski something about the body.

Rule had parked while they were talking, trailed by a familiar Toyota that disgorged four guards. Lily nodded in that direction to let Karonski know where she was going. He broke off what he was telling Erskine about containment procedures to say, "Good. Looks like Dr. Two Horses came prepared. Bring her over here, would you? I'd like her take on this."

"Who's that?" Erskine asked.

"Shaman," Karonski said as Lily started for the other end of the parking lot. "Damn fine one, too."

Rule and Nettie started toward Lily. Nettie held a tote bag, not her medical bag. She was saying something to Rule, who'd tucked a small woven rug under one arm. Lily's eyebrows lifted. Nettie had brought the big guns. That rug had been woven by Nettie's great-great-grandmother. Family magic, Nettie called it, though the rug held no magic Lily's fingers could detect. And the tote held bottles of the colored sands that Hatałii—medicine makers—had used for countless generations.

Lily knew only bits and pieces about Nettie's religious practices, but she did know that sandpainting was done on the ground, not the upper floor in some building. How had Nettie known she'd need the sands today? She'd expected to be headed for the hospital, not an outdoor murder scene. Nettie was no precog. Had she been tipped by her deities?

Lily did not like that idea one bit, and not just because of her little phobia about organized religion. If actual gods were involving themselves in the situation, it made things large. Downright vast. Vastly less predictable, too. She moved faster.

Milly Rodriguez had spotted Rule, too. She was making a beeline for him, cameraman in tow, and she was closer than Lily. She got there just as Lily passed the car holding Hardy. Lily could hear her badgering Rule.

Rule was used to this sort of thing. He said something to Nettie and stopped, smiling at Milly as if he'd been waiting all day for the chance to chat with her. "Ms. Rodriguez. It's been awhile. I hope you're well?"

Nettie kept going. One of the guards went with her; the other three stuck with Rule.

Behind Lily, Hardy screamed.

She spun. Hardy was banging on the window of the patrol car and yelling wordlessly.

A white shape materialized between Lily and the agitated Hardy. Drummond pointed off to the right. "Stop him! Stop him!"

Lily spun back—and saw Officer Crown. He stood about twenty feet away grinning like a kid in a candy shop as he snatched his weapon from the holster and lifted it in the approved two-handed grip—

"Stop!" Lily yelled, grabbing for her Glock, her gaze flicking in the direction Crown's weapon pointed, where

Nettie was headed toward Lily and Rule stood next to his car, talking to the reporter. Scott leaped in front of Rule, his jacket flipping up and one hand reaching inside it for his weapon—

Crown fired twice. Double-tapping.

Nettie went down. Not Rule. Nettie.

Officer Crown pivoted, gun still held out, aiming—

Lily exhaled. Squeezed her finger. And shot him.

FIFTEEN

~

RULE skidded and dropped to his knees beside that still, crumpled body. The iron-sweet scent of blood flooded him. He couldn't smell anything else. Just blood. Nettie's blood.

Shouts. Some wordless, some not. He ignored them. His men formed up around him and Nettie, weapons out. "Andy," Rule snapped, "get a blanket. Joe, lie down and warm her." Couldn't let her slip into shock. Humans went into shock easily. So much blood . . .

Blood on her head. Blood on her chest. The head wound was bleeding like crazy, but it looked like a graze. God, he hoped so. The chest wound—that was bad. At least it wasn't spurting. No artery involved. He tore off his jacket and shirt, ripped the shirt in half, and made two pads. One for her head, one for her chest. His hands were steady, as if they knew what they were doing. His wolf was howling and howling, in his head, in his gut—*Out! Out! Kill, guard, protect!* As Joe curled up on Nettie's other side, lending her his body's heat, Rule pressed one pad to the side of Nettie's head. The other was for her bloody, ruined chest.

Her heart beat. He felt it faintly beneath the pad. He

couldn't hear it, not with all those noisy humans around. Noisy, dangerous humans.

Out, out!

The bullet had gone in beneath her left breast. Below the heart. Looked like it had smashed into a rib. Her lung. Her lung was there. Was it even now filling up with blood? What if it collapsed? *Dammit, Nettie, you're the doctor. What do I do? I don't know what to do.*

"Shit, shit, shit." That was Lily. She'd run to check on the man she'd shot. The man who'd shot Nettie. He couldn't see her. Scott and Andy were in the way. Guarding him. Blocking his view. "Rule?" she called. "Is Nettie—"

"Unconscious. Your target?"

"The same. Stay back," Lily told someone sharply. "Don't touch him."

"You get back," another voice said. An angry voice. "You shot Daryl. You'll step away now."

Nettie was so still. Her eyes were rolled back, leaving little white smiles beneath the lids. She was alive, though. She didn't move, but she lived.

Out! Out!

"Mr. Turner! Mr. Turner, who is the victim? Is she alive? Do you know why—"

He snarled at the woman who'd startled him. She'd shoved in close. Too close. The Change rose in a hot rush, earth reaching through him to touch moonsong—beautiful beyond words, promising pain and joy. Welcoming him. Beckoning him . . . but muted. Dark moon was only two days away, so moonsong was distant. That distance slowed his headlong rush into Change, let him hold it back. Mostly. But though he didn't pass through that door, he slid close. Closer to wolf now than man, but not truly either one. That was dangerous. He couldn't remember why, but he knew it was.

The woman—*she's a reporter,* the man insisted, feeding him/them on words instead of action. That mattered, but he couldn't remember why. The reporter-woman fell back, her face bleached by fear. "Get her away," he growled, holding the pad to Nettie's chest. "Keep everyone away."

"Goddammit, I don't have time for this!" Lily again. "Put up your weapon, Officer."

"Scott," Rule said. "Go." That was all he said, but Scott knew what he meant and leaped up. Someone wasn't obeying Lily. They would now.

It was hard to think. Hard to pull up words, and that wasn't right. The wolf wasn't as verbal as the man, but they both knew words. He fought to press the wolf back, to pull up the man . . .

There was a yelp, the sound of a scuffle. Rule found two words. "Mark. Report."

"One cop had his gun pointed at Lily. Scott took it away from him."

Rule growled and slid toward wolf. But not all the way.

"Scott is handing the gun to another man," Mark went on. "A guy who just got there. Short, glasses, red hair. Looks like a cop, but he's not in uniform."

"Thank you," said a new voice, very dry.

The angry man who'd told Lily to step back announced, "You are under arrest for assaulting—"

"Shut up, Marlowe," said the new voice. "No, I'll keep your weapon for now. Idiot. Agent Yu. You want to tell me what the *hell* just happened?"

"Officer Crown is contaminated."

"He's fucking wounded."

"Yes, in the shoulder. It shouldn't kill him while we figure out—"

"It shouldn't fucking knock him out, either, but he's unconscious. What the hell happened?"

Andy came racing up. He had the blanket Rule kept in the trunk of the car, and that association pulled Rule a bit closer to the man. Enough that he remembered what the blanket was for. Enough that he remembered why it was dangerous to linger in the hinge between man and wolf . . . because you couldn't bloody *think*. When you were neither one nor the other, neither way of thinking worked right.

"What happened?" Lily repeated. "I saw this officer draw his weapon and aim where there was no visible threat."

Rule closed his eyes and breathed slowly. Deeply. He focused on the sound of his mate's voice, using it to pull himself back.

"I drew my weapon and shouted for him to stop. Officer Crown then shot Dr. Two Horses. He pivoted to aim at this end of the parking lot. Not at me. Maybe at you, maybe Karonski, maybe someone near you. I don't know. I shot him." Lily delivered all of that flatly, but Rule heard the shakes trying to squirm out from beneath the iron lid she'd clamped down over her feelings. "He is contaminated. It's the same magic I felt on the body, and it's probably why he shot Nettie, and it can transfer to anyone but me who touches him."

THE surgical waiting room was crowded. An old man sat across from Rule with what seemed to be his entire family—five adults and two teens. Two young women kept each other company. A middle-aged woman had brought her knitting. A jittery young man kept getting up to pace.

Rule wanted them all to go away.

Twice he'd had to work off tension by heading to the stairwell to run up and down the stairs. His guards had gone with him. They were in the hall outside the waiting room now. Some of them were, that is. He'd sent Andy back to the guard barracks.

Andy had been assigned to Nettie. He hadn't seen the threat. No one had except Lily, who'd been tipped off by a saint and a dead man, but when Lily called out, Andy had frozen for that first, critical second. He'd been as useless as the other three guards, but those three had been following instructions to stick with Rule.

Scott's instructions, but Rule could have overruled Scott. Why hadn't he overruled Scott?

Rule leaned forward and scrubbed his face with both hands. "They had to shave a lot of hair off. She'll wake up halfway bald. She's going to hate that."

"She was a bald baby," Benedict said. Like Rule, he kept his voice low so the humans around them wouldn't hear. "Bald and red-faced, with great lungs. The midwife didn't have to spank her. She started screaming all on her own." His mouth quirked up a fraction. "She still does, when necessary. Just doesn't dial up the volume as high."

Benedict sat on Rule's left. Arjenie sat on Benedict's left. Arjenie Fox was pale, skinny, and freckled, with extravagant hair—red, long, and curly. She was a devout Wiccan, a near genius, and Benedict's Chosen. Rule was damn glad his brother's mate was here. He tried not to think about how much he wished his mate was here, too. Lily's duty lay elsewhere for now.

"That sounds like Nettie," Arjenie said. "She'll grumble about her hair, I'm sure. But maybe she already knows. Didn't you say she woke up in the ER?"

"So they told me." He hadn't gotten here in time to see her. They'd taken her to surgery so quickly . . . "She was conscious long enough to insist on Dr. Sengupta for her surgeon, anyway."

Arjenie nodded. "I looked him up. He's a thoracic surgeon. Young, but with excellent credentials. Graduated at the top of his class from Harvard Medical School and served his residency at the Good Samaritan in L.A."

"What time did you say they took her into surgery?" Benedict asked.

This was the third time he'd asked that. Benedict looked normal. He sounded normal. He wasn't. "One forty."

"Over three hours, then. Nearly four. Should it take this long?"

"Yes, it should," Arjenie told him firmly. "The chest is crowded. Repairing damage there is painstaking work. You don't want them to rush."

"No." Benedict lapsed back into silence.

Benedict and Arjenie had reached St. Margaret's shortly after Rule did. Nettie had already been in surgery by then. After Rule passed on what little the doctors had told him,

Benedict had been silent for a long moment, then said, "We shouldn't both be here."

"I know," Rule had said. Rule was heir to Nokolai; Benedict was the only other possible heir. Friar would love to take them both out. Benedict had brought additional guards, but having them both exposed was an unacceptable risk. "I'm staying anyway."

"Good." Benedict had sat down. "Tell me what happened. Tell me exactly what happened."

Rule had spent the next hour doing that, then answering his brother's questions. Painstakingly thorough questions. Benedict could undoubtedly draw an exact map of where everyone had been, with notes on when they'd moved, what they'd done.

Since then, Rule had gotten up twice to run the stairs. Arjenie had stood and stretched a few times. Benedict hadn't moved. Rule knew why. Benedict lived closer to his wolf than most, and Benedict's wolf was infinitely patient . . . on a hunt. What was he hunting now? Answers? The moment when the surgeon emerged and told them his daughter had made it through surgery and would be fine?

"You need to decide what to do about Andy," Benedict said abruptly. "You didn't accept his submission before sending him away."

"I was too angry."

Benedict nodded. "Understandable, but too much time to brood on his failure will destroy him as a guard."

"It will be a physical punishment, obviously." Nothing else would let Andy move beyond his guilt and shame. "I was thinking of letting you rebuke him."

"No. I want to kill him. He doesn't deserve it, but I want to."

"Ah." Rule glanced quickly at Arjenie to see if she was upset by her mate's bloodthirstiness. Apparently not. She rubbed Benedict's shoulders and made a sympathetic sound. Rule sighed. "I'll do it, then. Scott can take care of the others, but Andy's failure cost too much. I have to deal with him myself. He froze. Only for a second, but a second is too long."

"Scott reacted immediately."

"Yes." Rule scrubbed his face again. "Maybe because you've worked with him, unlike the others. If I'd had some of your people with me—if the guards had been Nokolai instead of Leidolf—"

"Maybe it would have made a difference, maybe not. No point in dwelling on it. Scott's reaction proves you've got your best man in charge. That's good."

"Being in charge means he feels this failure, too, but he isn't to blame."

"No. He isn't. I taught him what I teach Nokolai guards. Their first priority is always the Rho. Second is the life of their Lu Nuncio. When Scott signaled for only one guard to stay with Nettie, he was doing what he'd been taught." Benedict paused. "What I taught him."

"Good," Arjenie said.

Rule stared at her in outrage. Benedict simply looked astonished.

"It's about time you two talked about why you blame yourselves. Neither of you has any *good* reason to do so, but I'm not going to argue with you. I know very well it won't help. No one is going to oblige either of you by ripping you up so you can bleed out your guilt like you're planning to do to poor Andy, but you can at least figure out that you don't blame each other."

"Benedict doesn't blame himself," Rule said. "He wasn't even there."

Arjenie snorted. "You cannot have been his brother all these years without noticing that there is no end to what Benedict can blame himself for. He thinks it's his fault because of how he trains the guards, plus he wasn't there, proving that he isn't psychic. And you think it's your fault because you didn't see the threat in time, plus you failed the psychic pop quiz, too."

Benedict and Rule looked at each other uneasily. "I should have kept two guards on Nettie," Rule said.

Benedict stole a quick glance at his mate. "I think that falls under Arjenie's psychic quiz. You couldn't have known. You did what duty requires. You're heir to one clan, Rho to another. Duty requires you to be guarded."

"And duty requires you to train the guards to keep me alive. Dammit to hell."

"Yeah." Benedict sucked in a slow breath that shuddered on the way out. "I should call our father again. Nothing to report, but he's got the hardest wait, back at . . . what is it?"

Rule had straightened, his head turning. "Lily's here. Not just at the hospital, but on this floor. It surprised me because I hadn't noticed. Her experience of the mate-sense is more acute than mine, but normally I'd notice before this."

Arjenie reached across Benedict to squeeze Rule's hand. "Things are not normal. I'm glad she's here."

So was he. "We haven't heard anything from Sam yet." Lily would be stretched so taut by her own long wait . . .

"No, and that has to be hard on her. But it's better to wait together."

Rule heard Lily speaking to Scott in the hall and stood. A moment later Lily walked in, walked straight to Rule, and put her arms around him.

Something held tight inside him unclenched. The sudden loss of tension left a dull smear of pain in its wake. His closed eyes stung. He'd needed this. Needed her, and now she was here. They leaned into each other. He inhaled deliberately, breathing her in.

She smelled of coffee and Lily, with citrus notes from her shampoo and almond from the lotion she'd applied after her shower. Also the tinny, astringent odor of anxiety.

Rule's wolf did not consider fear and anxiety the same emotion. Their scents were from the same family, but quite distinct, just as roses do not smell like violets. Fear was more sour, anxiety more bitter. Wolves consider fear a healthy emotion, but anxiety makes them . . . anxious. Rule immediately tried to soothe Lily, stroking a hand up her back.

It was like stroking a guitar string. Tight, tight, from the base of her spine to the nape of her neck, and when he started to knead those tense muscles, she pulled away. She stretched out both hands to his brother, who'd finally abandoned his chair to stand. "Benedict." He took her hands and she told him, "You're okay."

His eyebrows lifted slightly. "Am I?"

"Yes. You're okay and Nettie's going to be okay." She spoke with suppressed ferocity, as if her will alone would make it so . . . or make Benedict believe it.

Benedict's expression didn't change. "You've learned something."

"A few things. No trail to follow yet. And I can't talk about the parts we do know, not here. Too public. They're going to—"

"Agent Yu?" A man in a very nice charcoal-colored suit stood in the doorway. "I've spoken with your, ah—with your man out in the hall, as you requested. We have the room ready. If you'd follow me?"

"Of course." Lily looked tense and tired and a trifle smug as she explained. "The hospital has agreed to let us use a small lounge. We'll be the only ones there, so I can discuss confidential matters."

Benedict frowned. "Will the surgeon know where to find us?"

The man in the suit answered. "I will personally make sure of that."

"Mr. Reddings is the executive assistant who works directly under the hospital's president," Lily said. "He knows how to make sure."

"Kind of them to offer us the use of this lounge," Arjenie said as they left the crowded waiting room. Scott was clearly expecting the shift; he fanned his men out, half in front, half behind, as the four of them followed Mr. Reddings.

"They were supposed to offer it to you two hours ago. I called and explained about the security issue—someone could drop in and try to kill some or all of you, and wouldn't it be a shame if they gunned down a few innocent bystanders in the process? I should've done that right away. I didn't think of it." She shook her head at this omission. "The admin guy

I spoke to agreed it would be best to park you someplace private, but on the way here, I found out that hadn't happened. Seems the only private spot is the VIP lounge, and some multirich bastard was using it while his wife had various bits lifted and tucked. He didn't want to leave. The admin guy didn't feel up to making that happen."

"No doubt you were persuasive," Rule said.

"I wasn't in a persuasive mood. I sicced Ida on them."

"Poor souls," Arjenie said. "Have you ever been present while she removed some unsuspecting roadblock?"

"A time or two." Lily exchanged a knowing look with Arjenie. "Mr. Reddings here was waiting for me when I arrived. He's been very helpful."

Lily did not hold Rule's hand as they proceeded to the elevator. She seldom did when she was in cop mode. She had, he thought, been in cop mode ever since her mother looked at her and didn't know who she was.

And that was the problem. Not that she was shutting him out. Oh, he did not like that, but he'd already noted the pettiness of his reaction, hadn't he? The real problem was that she was shutting herself out, too. That was why she reeked so of anxiety. She'd been jamming her emotions down, down, ignoring them, shoving them aside. Sometimes you had to do that, but you couldn't keep it up for too long. If you did, something broke inside you.

That kind of break healed slowly, and not always well.

Rule knew what Lily needed. She needed to fall apart, and soon. If she'd been one of his men, he'd see to that. It would be both his right and his duty. But she wasn't, and he'd vowed not to try to make her choices for her anymore.

What would his father do? Could he use that wily old manipulator as a standard?

Rule thought about dragons and sovereignty and his father as everyone but the guards stepped into the elevator. Six of them. Six people in that small, cramped space. The elevator doors closed and his heartbeat skyrocketed and his mouth went dry . . .

Out, out, out.

He was so damn tired of this. Tired of hurt and fear and handling himself. Tired of war and people he loved being damaged, endangered, killed . . . and Lily wasn't taking his hand the way she always did in elevators. She wasn't thinking about his fear because she was tired, too, exhausted by worry and fear and people she loved being damaged and endangered and . . .

A warm hand slipped into his.

Lily didn't speak. She didn't look at him. Her expression remained inward and closed, but she held his hand as they rode up to the top floor. The elevator doors opened.

Spiritual hygiene, Nettie had said. Rule still didn't know what that meant, but he suspected his soul could use a good scrubbing. He didn't know how to do that, but holding on to Lily wasn't a bad substitute.

Dammit, Nettie, you'd better not die. I am going to be so pissed if you die.

SIXTEEN

~

THE VIP lounge was to the other waiting room as a memory foam mattress is to a sleeping bag. Both served the same function, but they did so with vastly different levels of comfort. Rule had Scott sweep for bugs before they entered; the delay could have been engineered to give their enemies time to plant a listening device. Mr. Reddings observed this precaution with some alarm.

No bugs. The helpful Mr. Reddings seemed relieved and rather rushed as he pointed out the room's amenities—a cushy sofa that let down into a bed, a fruit basket, a well-stocked bar, a refrigerator . . . and a brimming pot of coffee that smelled like it had been brewed from freshly ground beans. Costa Rican, Rule thought, inhaling appreciatively. Lily headed straight for that amenity as the executive assistant asked if there was anything else he could do.

"Thank you," she said, filling one heavy white mug, "but no."

This clear dismissal sent the man out the door. Rule could hear Scott asking him a question after it closed.

Lily held out the filled mug to Rule.

His eyebrows lifted. "That's real love, offering me the first cup."

"True. But not, you'll note, the last one. That you'd have to wrestle me for." She poured a cup for herself and sipped with her eyes closed. "God, that's good."

"Never mind the damn coffee," Benedict said. "What have you learned?"

Rule looked at his brother. Whether it was the effect of physical movement after hours of immobility or the promise of something, anything, to distract him, Benedict's patience had evaporated. Without it, he was . . . intense.

Arjenie moved up behind him and laid a hand on his shoulder. Lily looked at him over the rim of her mug and answered crisply. "I'll give you the key points first. One, the artifact last seen in Friar's possession was used to ritually kill our John Doe. Two, the icky magic I found on the body, which transferred to Officer Crown, is some sort of residue from that ritual. Three, that magic isn't just icky. It's evil. And no, I don't know what that means exactly, but it matters."

"Are those suppositions or facts?"

"Expert opinions based on observation. Drummond and Hardy—"

"Drummond?" Arjenie said. "You mean your ghost? He's back?"

Rule had forgotten to tell Benedict and Arjenie about that.

"He's not my ghost," Lily said, "but yeah, he's back. He, uh, was sent here to help. He says spirit is visible on his side." Her hand waved vaguely to indicate the nebulous direction involved. "The artifact leaves an obvious spiritual mark or color, which is how he knows it was used in the ritual killing of our unknown victim."

"No ID yet?" Rule asked.

"No, and we may have trouble getting one. I'll tell you about that in a minute. Drummond says that the bad magic—the contagion—is evil. Seems there's a clear definition for evil that he can't tell me, and he can't tell me why the contagion fits that definition. But it does. Hardy agrees, if I'm interpreting his hymn choices correctly. Which reminds me—"

Benedict broke in. "Hardy is the supposed saint."

Lily cocked her head. "You don't believe he is one? Or you don't believe in saints?"

"I don't know. I don't know what the word means."

"I don't, either, and no one . . ." Lily used both hands to push her hair back. "*No one* will define anything for me! Saint, spirit, evil—all that shit's tossed into the mix and I'm just supposed to guess what it all means! Though Cullen did say a saint was a holy man or woman . . . God, I wish he was here." The moment she said that she shook her head. "No, I don't. He's needed with . . . but his ability to see magic would sure help right now."

Rule glanced around. Uselessly, of course, but he couldn't resist the impulse. "Is Drummond here?"

She shook her head. "He hung around awhile, then said he had places to go, things to do."

"You're accepting his statement as fact? Even if Drummond's on the side of the angels now, he isn't one himself. I don't think ghosts are infallible."

"True, which is why I'm calling it expert opinion, not fact. But all three of my experts agree that the contagion is evil, so I'm considering that as established."

"Drummond's one of your experts. And Hardy?"

She nodded. "The third is Miriam."

Rule had met Miriam. She was the head priestess of the coven the Unit called on in this area. "Not Karonski?"

"He said no, not for this. Since spirit, not magic, is the—"

"Discuss their credentials later," Benedict snapped. "Rule has described the shooting to me in detail. Nettie was not a random victim. She was targeted specifically."

"So we concluded. *We* meaning me and Drummond and Karonski. Not Miriam. She thinks the overdose of evil caused Crown to commit evil acts, but without a specific target. In other words, he just started shooting, didn't matter who he killed. I don't agree. If all Crown had wanted was to kill people, he would have kept firing at the ones near Nettie. He didn't, which tells me he had specific targets in mind. He was turning to shoot the next one when I dropped him."

Had she shot to kill and missed? Probably. That was her training. As she put it, when your target was using deadly force, you did, too. Or, as Benedict put it: In battle, take the easiest shot. You'll do well to hit at all. Don't make it any harder to win than it has to be.

"Who was the other target?" Arjenie asked. "Do you know?"

"Drummond thinks it was Karonski. That's based on his observation of the shooter, not on some special ghostly knowledge, but he was a cop for a long time. He may be right, but another possibility is—"

Benedict broke in. "But Nettie was primary. He had time to select his first target, and he chose her. Why?"

"We think it's because she's a threat, and she's a threat because she's a shaman. This goes back to the contagion being evil. That's a spiritual quality, and spirit is what Nettie works with. Wiccan and Native practices both have spiritual aspects, but with Wicca the spiritual part is sort of fenced off."

Arjenie frowned. "I wouldn't put it that way."

"I probably said it wrong. Here's what Karonski told me. That Wiccan star of yours—Earth, Air, Fire, Water, Spirit? They're the points or arms of the star, and they're all tied to the Source, which is represented by the open space at the center. But spirit is only one aspect of the Source. That's why so many unbelievers can use Wiccan spells. And—again, this what Karonski said—a lot of Wiccans don't work with spirit that much, except during your major rites, because it's so unpredictable. With Native practices, it's different. Spirit is at the center. It's the way they access power, so Nettie's used to working with spirit directly."

Arjenie nodded. "Okay, that makes sense. Not that I know a lot about Native practices, but that fits what I do know."

"Sam said we needed Nettie." Lily sighed. "Maybe she

could have dispelled the contagion. Karonski can't. The coven can't."

"What?" Arjenie's eyes widened. "But—but if the usual cleansing techniques weren't effective, surely Miriam tried an elemental cleansing. Not everyone can handle those, but she's extremely competent, and she's got strong Gifts in her coven to channel each of the elements."

"She did try. It didn't work."

Arjenie's brow pleated. "I don't understand. I've never *heard* of an elemental cleansing failing. I don't understand that at all."

"Miriam doesn't, either, and she took that failure personally. But she thinks it has to do with the way spirit and magic are all tangled up in the contagion. Spirit doesn't follow the rules."

Arjenie nodded. The worried pleat remained in her forehead.

Lily looked at Rule. "I need to ask you something. I said that Drummond thinks the secondary target was Karonski. That fits what I saw, if we assume I fired the second Crown had his target lined up. But if we scrap that assumption . . . if Crown had turned a bit more, he would have had me and the patrol car behind me in his sights. Maybe he was going to shoot me, but Hardy was in that car. If Crown was after the, uh, the spiritual heavy hitters, then I'm betting on Hardy for his other target. I've taken him into protective custody. I'd like to park him at Clanhome."

Rule's eyebrows lifted. After a moment he nodded. "If we need a saint and Hardy is one, then the other side would be eager to deprive us of him. You'd like me to speak to Isen about this?"

"If you can't okay it yourself, then yes."

"I could admit him to Clanhome, but whether he stayed would be the Rho's decision. Best to just ask." And speaking of asking . . . "You've been unable to learn anything from the officer himself?"

Lily's gaze slid away. "Officer Crown hasn't regained consciousness."

And that told Rule what he needed to know. Half of it, anyway. Lily had shot a fellow officer of the law who'd turned out to be the victim of evil, not a bad guy himself. She'd done what she had to, but she was twisted up about it. If he pressed on that spot, she'd break down.

Would that be helping or taking over? God knew it would piss her off.

Arjenie asked, "What's been done for him? If the contagion can't be cleared . . . did you find a way to block it?"

"Crown is here at the hospital, in quarantine. Unconscious, but stable. Miriam advised them on how to—" Lily stopped, huffed out an impatient breath. "I'm doing this out of order. When you left, Rule, we were trying to find out what would block the contagion so the EMTs could work on the poor guy."

He remembered that. "Silk didn't work."

"Right. Turned out the icky shit crawls all over anything organic. We think that's what happened to Officer Crown. He'd been left to guard the body and the contagion followed organics in the soil to get to him. Some disagreement on that," she added. "We agree that it probably traveled through the soil. I think it went to him on purpose. Miriam thinks I'm nuts. Magic isn't sentient, doesn't have plans and intention."

"Well, no," Arjenie said mildly. "It isn't and it doesn't."

"This stuff is different." Lily spread her hands. "I don't know how else to put this, but it feels malignant. Like it *wanted* to crawl all over me. Miriam thinks I'm projecting. But whether it transferred through some natural process or went to Crown on purpose, it used organics to get to him. That's what trial and error suggested, and Miriam did some kind of test that confirmed it."

Arjenie looked unhappy. "That's a property of spirit. It can adhere to inorganics, but only when the object involved is spiritually significant, like a cross." Her hand went to the small silver star she wore around her throat. "Or a Wiccan star. So it pretty much confirms that the contagion is some unholy mix of magic and spirit."

Lily frowned and tapped her fingers on her thigh. "Miriam didn't tell me that. She's being prickly. Or maybe it's me. We've worked together fine in the past, but something about this case . . ." She huffed out another breath. "Maybe it's me. Anyway, the EMTs were able to prep Crown for transport using caution and latex gloves, and they didn't pick up any trace of the nasty stuff. I confirmed that. The doctor who dug the bullet out after he arrived . . ." She paused. "I haven't checked him myself. One of Miriam's people rode in with Crown, and he checked everyone involved, using a spell to detect magic. He's sure they're clean, but I wasn't here to check."

"Who did the detection spell?" Arjenie asked.

"Jack. Jack Weysmith."

"Oh, Jack's very good. He's Water-Gifted. It's hard to hide magic from a Water witch."

"I'd prefer impossible." Her frown deepened. "Maybe I should check out the ER doctor and nurses, whoever came in contact with Crown. Just to be sure."

Rule didn't want her to. He wanted her with him for both his comfort and hers. He rested a hand on her shoulder, prepared to argue—and changed his mind. Her muscles were so tight. "Will you come with me a moment?"

She slanted him a look half-puzzled, half-annoyed. "Why?"

"I would speak with you privately."

"There's no such thing as privacy around here. Unless you plan to take over the ladies' room or something—"

"We won't go quite that far." He used the hand on her shoulder to urge her toward the door. She allowed that, annoyance blending into concern.

Their guards were in the hall. He signaled that he wanted privacy. They split up and spread out down the hall in both directions. They couldn't go far, but they stopped with their backs to Rule and Lily.

Humans were so visual. Lily wouldn't even think about what the guards smelled. She'd know the guards could hear them, but it probably wouldn't occur to her that Benedict could, too. He thought that, as long as they weren't being watched, she'd feel a measure of privacy.

Sure enough, when he gathered her into his arms, she didn't resist. She circled his waist with her arms and hugged him.

Ah. He understood now. She thought they were out here for his sake. He explained her mistake by using one hand to knead the nape of her neck while he anchored her with his other arm.

Abruptly she leaned back and frowned up at him. "Rule—"

"Shh." He continued rubbing her neck. So far it wasn't having much effect.

"I don't need a damn massage. I need to finish telling you about the case. Both cases."

"You need to let go of the cop for a few minutes."

"I don't. You think you're helping, but you're wrong. I thought you needed a minute, but if you're just going to—"

"Well, that's the thing. I've been trying to understand where your needs end and my need for you to be okay begins. I couldn't figure it out, so I'm asking you to let me help you. For my sake, Lily. This is what you can do to help me."

She quivered. "I can't. I'll come apart, and I can't do that right now. Not now. Not here."

"You won't. I've got you, and I won't let you come apart. All you have to do is be in your body." His other hand joined the first one at her shoulders. "You aren't letting go or letting down your guard. You aren't letting in all those thoughts you don't want to think. You're just going to be in your body for a few minutes, and I'm going to help you do that." He smiled down at the objections he saw gathering in her eyes. "Sex would be better, but I felt sure you'd consider that inappropriate."

"Oh, just ever so slightly, yeah. Rule, I don't . . ." She made a small sound of surprise.

His thumbs had finally found the right spot. He dug in with his thumbs, then stroked up and out with both thumbs.

Her head fell back involuntarily as at last, at last, she began to relax.

He might not be sure where the line lay between helping and interfering, but he had figured out a few things. First, he wasn't his father, so no trickery. He had to be honest with her. Second, Lily wasn't one of his men. He'd known that, but hadn't followed that knowledge deep enough to reach real understanding.

It was all about control. With one of his men, he had both the right and the duty to assume control if theirs was endangered—and the ability to do so, through the mantle. This freedom to surrender control was a deep comfort for a lupus . . . unless that lupus was a Rho. A Rho was responsible, always, for his own control. Lily was neither lupus nor Rho, but she was responsible for her own control. No one could or should attempt to usurp that, no matter how much he loved her and how certain he was that she needed to *let go*. To let herself fall into tears or rage or whatever lay on the other side of the walls she'd put up.

Lily could not be touched by any mantle. She also couldn't Change. The Change was one reason it was safe for him to shove one of his men over the edge. It was a release all by itself, but part of that release was shifting into a thoroughly physical self.

The body exists in the here and now. It's the mind that spins anxiety from thoughts of otherwhere and otherwhen. Rule couldn't give Lily the ease of the mantle or a wolf's perspective, but he could make her body more compelling than her mind. He could offer her respite.

Wonder of wonders, she accepted it.

He rubbed and kneaded and she leaned into him, even making little sounds now and then—a low groan, a wordless *mmm*. Her muscles went lax and loose and warm beneath his hands. And if his body responded to that physical surrender, if the scent and feel of her filled him and stirred him, what of it? He was no randy adolescent. Desire could be enjoyed for itself. It didn't have to be acted on.

He knew the moment her body responded with something

more than ease. He knew it a second or two before she noticed—and stiffened. Not pushing him away, but not willing to feel what she did, either.

Still, she didn't move away, didn't so much as lift her head, leaving it tucked down. She muttered into his shirt, "I trust you're feeling better now."

That made him smile. "I am." He felt much better now, with her limp and relaxed against him. He pressed a kiss to the top of her head. "Thank you."

She sighed and straightened. "You are so strange sometimes. Why did we come out in the hall for this? You could rub my neck in front of Benedict and Arjenie."

"I could, but if we'd stayed in there, you wouldn't have stopped thinking." She would have been too aware of Benedict and his fear, which would have made her think about Nettie, which would set her to thinking furiously about her investigation . . . where she had some control. Or thought she did.

Lily's mouth twitched in a grimace that might have been agreement. "Well, my little hedonistic interlude is over. But, Rule . . ."

"Yes?"

She smiled faintly and stretched up and kissed him lightly on the mouth. "You're welcome."

SEVENTEEN

~

WHEN they went back into the plush little lounge, Benedict was pacing. Arjenie stood out of his path, watching him with worried eyes. Rule took one look at his brother and inhaled sharply. What he smelled told him more than simply watching the leashed ferocity of Benedict's movements.

Benedict's control was flawless, but it was not endless. "Benedict."

Benedict kept moving without a word or a glance.

Rule pulled on the Nokolai mantle. "Benedict."

This time Rule's brother stopped and looked at him. His face was blank, all expression smoothed out. His eyes were wild. Wolf eyes.

"I give you a choice." Only once had Rule felt the need to pull mantle on his older brother—when Benedict had been magically shoved into *fuerta,* a berserker state. He pulled just as hard this time. "Change now, and await news as a wolf, or go run."

For a brief moment Benedict looked at him with the eyes of a wolf—keen, sharp, and thinking. But not thinking as a man does. Then relief shivered through those dark eyes.

He lowered his head, acknowledging Rule's authority. And Changed.

Humans weren't able to see the Change fully. Perhaps you had to hear moonsong in order to see the way it threaded itself through a man, reaching out to grasp Earth so that together the two could fold him up through a place that was not here, yet was eternally present. For a second, the song of the moon reverberated through Rule, so clear, so pure . . .

Then a large black wolf stood atop Benedict's clothes.

"I guess you didn't want to risk missing the surgeon when he gets here," Arjenie said briskly, stepping up to thread her fingers through Benedict's ruff. "Is this better?" she asked her mate. Benedict nodded once.

"He probably also didn't want to split our guards," Rule said. He inhaled thoughtfully. Good. Benedict wasn't easy, far from it, but he was better.

Arjenie looked at Rule. "He was okay, then suddenly he wasn't."

"He pushed himself too far. The problem with having excellent control is that we grow accustomed to it always being sufficient. We can confuse what we think should be true with what is." Plus, Rule suspected that Benedict, whose mate bond with Arjenie was still new, had relied on it to shore up his control more than he should have. Rule pulled on the mantle again. Not hard, but enough to reassure his brother: *If you can't do what you know is necessary, I will make you.* "Benedict, your duty now is to wait. I prefer you do so in this form. Scott will let us know when the surgeon approaches so you can Change to a less threatening form."

Benedict nodded again, heaved a windy sigh, and lay down.

"I hope Scott can let us know in time for Benedict to pull on his pants after he Changes," Lily said. "Dr. Sengupta might be rattled by a naked Benedict."

"A lot of people would be," Arjenie agreed. She'd folded herself to sit on the floor beside Benedict and was rubbing behind his ear.

Rule used his phone to let Scott know that they wanted a few moments' warning of the surgeon's arrival. Scott knew what the man looked like; he'd looked him up on Facebook earlier and confirmed it with the helpful Mr. Reddings. Rule put up his phone and repressed a sigh.

Respite was, by definition, temporary. Lily was pouring herself another cup of coffee, though caffeine was the last thing she needed. She looked like she needed the run Benedict hadn't chosen. "Did you decide not to check on the ER doctor now?" he asked.

"Yes. I guess. I don't know." She ran a hand through her hair. Her other hand clutched the coffee cup as if it were a security blanket, but she didn't drink. "I should trust Jack, I guess. Spells aren't as precise as Gifts, so it's possible he'd miss some tiny little trace, but that's unlikely to be an issue. We have reason to think the contagion doesn't transfer partially."

"What reason?" Arjenie asked.

Lily's gaze flicked to her. "While I was doing the trial-and-error thing, Karonski pulled the CSI team farther away from the body. He thought the contagion must have spread, seeing that it had reached Crown, who wasn't that close to the body. Once we were pretty sure Crown could be treated, Karonski sent me to see how much it had spread. Turned out it hadn't. It took awhile to confirm that. I had to cover a lot of ground barefoot, but in the end, I didn't find any trace of it."

"None?" Rule's eyebrows shot up. "But the body—"

"That's the thing. The body was gone."

"If whoever stole the body caught the contagion—"

But Lily was shaking her head. "When I got back to the scene I found bones and hair and clothes, some scraps of sinew. No flesh or muscle. Creeped me out. By the time I left to come here, even the bones were dust. It's like he was never there at all."

"That's—"

Mike spoke through the door. "Surgeon's coming."

Benedict Changed so quickly that, even as he thrust to his feet, he ended by standing on two of them, not four.

"Rule?" Lily asked.

"The surgeon," he said tersely.

Lily moved to him and took his hand.

Arjenie handed Benedict his jeans. His thrust one foot in, then the other.

Mike opened the door.

Benedict pulled the jeans up.

Dr. Sengupta was short, wiry, and young. He smelled of blood, though his blue scrubs were clean. No doubt he'd changed. His eyes were bloodshot. If he was startled to find one of the family members zipping up his jeans, it didn't show. He spoke quickly. "Dr. Two Horses made it through the surgery and is in recovery now. In addition to the pneumothorax, there was herniation and perforation of the left colonic angle in the pleural cavity and both diaphragmatic and abdominal damage. I chose to bring in a specialist for the abdominal repair. We were fortunate that Dr. Ransome was able to postpone the elective procedure he'd scheduled. He is a superb surgeon. You may speak with him later, if you wish, but he had another surgery and couldn't meet with you now."

Benedict's voice was so low it was nearly a wolf's growl. "What kind of abdominal injury?"

"Her stomach. Dr. Ransome believes that was the only area to sustain significant damage, and that he repaired it fully. Do you want a full description of the path the bullet took?"

"Not now," Rule said. "What's her prognosis?"

"Fair. Her injuries are grave, but surgery went well and she's stable. It is possible she will make a full recovery, if we do not see any complications in the next few days. I understand she's a healer."

"Yes. A very good one."

He nodded. "That works in her favor, certainly. Even without her conscious direction, her Gift is probably operating at a low level to sustain her. However, she must not attempt more." The little surgeon frowned sternly. "Healing is physically draining. Her body cannot afford that drain. In a few days, I may allow her to attempt some limited healing under my supervision. That is very important. She is to wait until I am present."

"I should be with her," Benedict said. "In recovery. I can make sure she doesn't try to use her Gift."

Sengupta pursed his lips. "And you are . . . ?"

"Her father."

The surgeon's eyebrows shot up. Benedict looked slightly younger than Nettie. "That is . . . a remarkable claim."

Benedict's lip lifted in a snarl.

"He's lupus," Rule said smoothly. "Our age doesn't always show. He would certainly be the best one to ensure that Nettie doesn't try to use her Gift."

Dr. Sengupta cast Rule a look, frowning but with some curiosity mixed in. "Very well. I will arrange it. Understand that she'll be fuzzy-headed and in pain. Her instinct will be to heal herself. You must impress on her on how dangerous this would be. You must be firm."

Benedict nodded once. "Where do I go?"

As the little surgeon gave directions, Rule considered the man's surprising familiarity with the instincts and limitations of healers. He turned to ask Lily to find out if the man had a trace of that Gift.

She stood absolutely motionless, one hand still clutching the mug she'd filled and forgotten, her face a blank mask—save for the tears slipping from her eyes, shining damply on her cheeks.

Fear leaped up, lodging in his throat. His hand tightened on hers. "Lily?"

"I . . . it's Sam. He just told me. My mother . . ." Now she turned to look at him. "He's finished, and it worked. Her mind is stable."

EIGHTEEN

~

LILY rubbed the back of her head with one hand and tried to concentrate on the copy of Karonski's report she'd gotten from Ida. It appended reports from the Big A, Erskine, the crime scene squad, and the coven. She had it spread out in hard copy with the database about the amnesia victims called up on her laptop.

Her head hurt.

It was one of those sneaky headaches that starts small so you won't notice it and take action, but the little guy with the big crowbar had clocked in at some point and was hard at work prying open her skull. The little guy is industrious. As long as you're still, he can keep working. If you move, it jostles him. That makes him mad and he whacks you with the damn crowbar.

The doorbell chimed, Lily raised her head and the little guy whacked her. She winced. Maybe she'd better take something.

She was in a tiny corner bedroom of the house that would get around to feeling like home one of these days. The bedroom on one side of her held Grandmother and Li Qin. Apparently Grandmother was no longer pretending Li

Qin was just a companion; that room had a double bed. On the other side was the temporary master bedroom, with Toby's room just beyond. They were using this one as an office, though instead of a desk it held the dining table that used to sit at one end of their apartment. Lily still didn't understand how they'd gotten the table in here. It barely fit. Rule's stuff was spread out over one end of the table. Lily sat at the other.

Downstairs she heard voices. Rule's, for one. The other one was too faint for her to identify, but it was male. She listened intently a moment, but no one sounded upset. Not bad news about Nettie, then.

Benedict and Arjenie had stayed at the hospital along with a half dozen guards, whose presence was probably stressing the hospital personnel. Nettie had come around in recovery and done exactly what the surgeon had said she would—tried to use her Gift. But Benedict had been there and told her to stop it. Nettie wasn't one to take orders and she'd been too fogged by drugs and pain to listen to reason, but he was her father. That voice had reached her on a level no one else's could. She'd stopped.

It must be one of Rule's men downstairs, Lily thought, rubbing the back of her neck. Though they didn't usually ring the bell. She frowned, wondering if she ought to go find out, but the question didn't seem as pressing as her headache. She had a bottle of water already and there were ibuprofen pills in her purse. She dug them out, swallowed two, and forced her attention back to the report.

Several minutes later, the stairs creaked as Rule came up. He didn't come into their makeshift office, though; she heard a door open and felt him move into the bedroom at the other end of the hall. The one that held her mother.

Rule could move silently when he wanted, but it wasn't necessary. Normal noises wouldn't wake Julia up. Grandmother had said she would sleep at least eight hours and probably ten or twelve. Grandmother had looked so tired when she arrived. Drained. Julia had looked . . . the way she always did. No makeup and her hair was down, which was unusual, but she'd looked like Lily's mother. As if she ought to wake up and be fine.

She wouldn't. She'd wake up, sure, but she wouldn't know Lily or her husband or anyone. She—

Shut up, Lily told herself and rubbed her neck and wished the damn pills would kick in. She needed to focus. There had to be some clue, some trail to follow . . .

"It's midnight," Rule said from the doorway.

"Yeah?" Surprised, she glanced at the top right corner of the screen: 12:07. "Someone rang our doorbell at midnight?"

"Paul brought more of your mother's things."

She didn't want to think about that. She needed to get back to the report, but . . . "This late?" Susan had packed a bag for their mother earlier and brought it here; Li Qin had put the things away. "What did he bring that was so important?"

"Your father found a few of Julia's childhood keepsakes. He thought she'd feel better if she has some familiar objects nearby when she wakes up."

"Oh." That was the kind of thing her father would do, too, spend however long it took to unearth a few old treasures that might comfort his wife in her odd and altered state. Edward Yu wasn't a demonstrative man. Lily didn't think he'd said "I love you" to her since she went off to college, and not often before, but she knew he did. He lived his love instead of speaking it.

Of course, now he wasn't speaking to her at all. Would he still be silent at her wedding? That would be jolly. Her mother twelve years old, her father not speaking to her . . . she turned back to her computer screen.

"Lily." Exasperation rang clearly in Rule's voice. "It's midnight."

"We covered that already."

"You need to come to bed."

"Not yet. You go on."

He growled. It was an honest-to-God growl that ought not to come out of his throat unless he was furry. "I'm wiped out, and I need a good deal less sleep than you do. Sleep, Lily. You do remember what that is?"

"I need to figure out *why*. Look." She twisted in her chair to look at him. "Motive isn't always the answer, but it's sure as hell part of the question. Friar didn't do all this just to swipe at me. That may be a bennie, but it's not the reason. Not his goal. What's he after?"

"Beaucoup power, for starters."

"He already has power. We don't know how much, but we know the Great Bitch supercharged him. There are now seventy-nine amnesia victims. Seventy-eight of them aren't connected to me, but something connects them. That's where I'll find the *why*, in that connection." Angrily she shoved her hair back. "I just can't spot it."

"And you think staying up all night when you're already short on sleep will help you do that?"

Lily made a noise in her throat. It did not sound like a growl. "That is so frustrating. Why can't I growl the way you do?" She turned back to the computer screen. "Go away."

"I have been careful." He said that calmly. "I have done my best not to overstep or push or take over—and I am *by damn* tired of it! I'm sick of being careful with you when you refuse to be careful with your own bloody self!"

Lily had her mouth open to yell back at him when her chair jerked backward. Two hands landed on her shoulders and plucked her out of it, stood her on her feet, and spun her around. Rule glared down at her. "Would you bloody tolerate it if a subordinate refused to stand down and get some rest when he needed it?"

"Subordinate?" The word sputtered out as rage ignited. "You think I'm your subordinate now?"

"In the Shadow Unit, you are."

"I can't believe you said that. Is that what we've come to? You ordering me to go to sleep because you think you can?"

"Lily." His eyes closed. He took in a breath slowly before opening them again. "How many times have you read those reports?"

A couple. Well, three, if they were talking about Karon-ski's report. More with the database, but that hardly counted. You couldn't absorb all those details at once, so you had to keep going back over it and over it . . .

"You can barely focus on that bloody screen. You're in pain—I saw it in your eyes the moment I—"

"It's just a headache. Humans get them, you know. If—"

"—and you are exhausted and determined to make yourself more exhausted. You are setting yourself up to make mistakes. Mistakes can get you killed. I understand why you're doing this. You're determined to shut out every-one and everything but the investigation because that's the one thing you think you can control, but—"

"Thank you so much for your dime-store psychology, Dr. Turner." She planted both hands on his shoulders and shoved. He let go of her, but didn't allow the shove to move him back. He still loomed over her, and it infuriated her. "And thank you for making me so mad I feel downright bright-eyed and bushy-tailed now. I think my headache's on the way out, so if you'll just get out of my fucking way, I can get back to work."

"Your headache is better?"

"Yes, though you don't get the credit for that. Contrary to what you seem to think, I am not a child. I took some ibuprofen, so you can take your orders and—"

"Good." He seized her head in both hands and slammed his mouth down on hers.

Apparently he was done being careful with her.

The kiss startled her, but the real surprise, the thing that undid her, was the wash of heat that rolled up from her belly, liquid fire that lit up every nerve at once. Like plug-ging in a Christmas tree, she thought dimly as she grabbed him back and dived into that kiss. Every nerve at once, all of them singing and stinging, and oh yes, that's *good* . . .

He was sucking and licking at her neck. She arched into him and got the first button undone on his shirt. "This is not makeup sex."

His *mmm* sounded vaguely inquiring.

"I am still mad at you."

This *mmm* suggested agreement.

"And you have too many buttons on this shirt. You don't need all those buttons." She tugged, but her angle wasn't great and Rule bought quality clothing. No buttons popped off. "Dammit." But she had opened up a bit of chest with that first button, and she wanted it. Wanted the taste of him on her tongue, so she aimed her mouth there.

This dislodged Rule from her neck, but his gasp suggested he didn't mind. She couldn't reach his neck very well—he was too tall, dammit—but she could get to the little hollow at the base of his throat. A thought intruded. She paused with one hand at his waist, the other headed south. "Did you do that on purpose? Make me mad on purpose?" He'd done it before, hadn't he? Tripped her into temper because he thought she needed the outlet.

"No, that was unpremeditated assholery. I . . . mmm." That low hum came from what she did next, not what he was saying or thinking. Or not thinking, she hoped. "This is not an order, absolutely not an order, just . . . ah, that's good, that's lovely. But unless you want to do this on the table—?"

Wrong room. They needed to move this one room over. "They're all downstairs, right? The guards?"

"One downstairs. The rest outside, patrolling, or at the barracks."

"Let's go, then." And not worry about the bits of clothing undone or . . . wait, when had he done that to her shirt? How could she not have noticed? Hastily Lily tugged it back down and grabbed his hand.

The hall was dark. Rule flicked off the light in their makeshift office, and the whole house was dark. Dark and silent. Though his eyes would find light hers didn't, and his ears probably picked up all sorts of small sounds from the others in the house. Who were all asleep, but . . .

"You're thinking," he told her and lifted her into his arms.

"Bad habit," she agreed, and now she could reach his neck just fine. She did that as he carried them into their bedroom, closing the door behind them.

It wasn't as dark here. The blinds at the windows were old and ugly as sin, with bent and missing slats, so mostly they left them pulled up. Outside, the sky was full of stars. No moonlight, but enough starlight to lessen the dark. It was just as quiet, though, so quiet she could hear the slight rush of Rule's breathing as he set her on her feet and the rustle of fabric as he slid his hands up her sides beneath her shirt.

Rule would hear the catch of her breath. Did he hear her heartbeat pick up, too? Could he hear those sleeping nearby? Grandmother and Li Qin and Toby and the woman who wasn't a woman now, but a young girl . . .

"Shh," Rule said as if she'd spoken that thought out loud, and he stroked soothingly down her hips.

. . . her mother, who wouldn't wake to hear her daughter having sex because she didn't have a daughter, and besides, she'd been placed in sleep by the black dragon after he knit together her fraying mind. She wouldn't wake for hours. Julia Lin—no longer Julia Yu; there was no Julia Yu—would not be sleeping in this house now, her plundered mind wandering whatever dreams were left to her, if not for Lily. Her destruction might be no more than a pleasant perk for Friar on the way to whatever goal he'd set, but she had been included among the victims on purpose. Because of Lily.

A shudder took her.

Rule's hands paused. "Lily?"

"Don't let me think." She pulled his head down and kissed him hard, and if there was more desperation than desire in the kiss, she didn't care.

Rule did her bidding, but not as she expected. Instead of a hot, hasty race to the top, he was thorough and deliberate and ruthless. He stripped her quickly enough and laid her in their bed, but then he wanted to taste. With mouth and teeth and touch he took her up and shoved her off that high sensory peak—then dragged her back up the cliff so he could do it again. This time with him inside her.

Oh, he was ruthless, all right. And deliberate and thorough. Also effective. For a long time she didn't think of anything but sensation, need, and Rule.

In the cool, close darkness afterward, with her skin slick with sweat and her breathing beginning to steady once more, she lay with her head on his shoulder. "I'll probably go back to work in a minute."

He was stroking her back. "Will you?"

Her head moved in the tiniest of nods. Her eyes were heavy. She'd rest them for a bit. "She never wanted me to be a cop, you know."

"So you've said."

"She wanted all of us safe, but also . . . prestige. Wanted us to have prestigious careers."

"Many parents do want that for their children." He kept stroking in long, slow slides.

"For us or from us. Do right by the family, y'know." The outer darkness was seeping in, dragging her down, making a mumble of her words. "I never thought about the price. The price to me, yeah, but my choice, so I pay the price, that's okay. Didn't think about the price others would pay. Expected them to pay it, but didn't think about it."

"No one could have thought this would happen. That it even could happen."

"Not the point." What was the point? She couldn't remember, not with all that heavy darkness dragging her down . . . oh, yeah. "Can't face her. 'S my fault. Can't look at her like this."

"Okay."

That roused her. "What d'you mean, okay? I've got to. She's my mother, and she's *here*."

That soothing hand never stopped petting. "But you won't be, most of the time. You'll be busy working yourself into exhaustion again. That's why Madame Yu and Li Qin are here. Let the rest of us deal with her. You don't have to."

There was a flaw in that reasoning. She was sure there was a flaw, but the relief was so intense it unmoored her. With a sigh, she let go and fell off into sleep.

NINETEEN

~

SHE lay in an exhausted heap against his side, and even now, flattened by a succession of climaxes, the warmth of his breath on her skin made her tingle with longing. It took so little for her senses to be overwhelmed by him . . . all of them save one. His skin was smooth and warm and slightly damp with sweat, but she couldn't smell it. Couldn't smell at all in this place.

"You are troubled," he breathed into her ear. "Tell me."

"It's wicked to allow any sadness in when I'm with you."

"And yet, you do." He sat up abruptly and fear spiked sharply—she'd displeased him, angered him—but no, he was smiling down at her. His face was always his somehow, though it changed to suit his whim. Tonight his skin was dusky, his nose long, and his hair as brown as a mink's, only curly. His eyes remained fathomless black. "By your own logic, then, you are wicked. Confess to me."

She had to smile back. "I'm foolish. It's just that when I wake, you won't be there. You won't be anywhere in my world, and the ache grows hard to bear."

"Ah." He touched her nose playfully. "But that time is almost over. Soon you will bring me fully into your world."

"Soon?" Her heart lurched. "I don't experience time as you do . . ."

He laughed. "Very soon, even as you measure time, my sweet mortal. Tonight I will give you the rest of your instructions. Pay close heed, for after I act I will be too weak for a time to call you to me."

Alarm stiffened her. She sat up. "Too weak? You didn't tell me—oh, beloved, don't spend yourself too freely and leave yourself open to—"

"Do not?" he said very softly. All the light and laughter fled as winter rushed into his face, his voice—a chill as absolute as the empty sky above them. "You would tell me do or do not?"

She hung her head, shame mingling with terror. "I fear for you. It makes me foolish. That's no excuse, but I . . . I'm so flawed. You've blessed me beyond reason with your loving. I should make my life a song of gratitude, and instead I—I spoke as if you weren't so far beyond me that—"

"Child." Not winter in that voice now, but no merriment, either. He placed a hand beneath her chin and tilted her face up. "I will not punish you this time. It would distress me to do so, I admit. Already you are dear to me. But you will remember, won't you? You must not speak so to me."

She nodded, dizzy with fear and relief. She listened carefully as he told her exactly what she must do . . . and what he planned to do. Some of it he'd told her before. Some he hadn't, and parts of it frightened her deeply, and yet . . . she peered at him out of the curtain of her hair. "You said you must do this in order to wrest the path from the other one, the one *she* wants. You have to—to tip that path toward you before I can act. I know that's true, but I think it—it's not the entire truth." Breathless with daring, she let her own small portion of mischief tilt her lips up. "I think there are many ways you could do that, some of them easier, less costly. But this will be more *fun*."

And his laugh rang out merry and full, rewarding her for having risked so much. "It will, oh, it will. I give her all that she wants, or thinks she wants . . . in a way she will surely hate." He stroked her cheek. "You do delight me. We will make much pleasure between us, you and I, when you are my high priestess and we meet body to body."

Heat shivered through her, lust as pure and potent as whiskey, and sweeter by far. They would make love in the flesh . . . surely she would have that much, before he betrayed her. For he would, one day. From spite or anger or simply because that was what he did. What he was. He might laugh then or mourn, just a little, for he said she was dear to him . . .

"Ah, sweetheart," he whispered as he stroked her between her legs, "do you not yet know that much about me? I can do both."

TWENTY

JULIA woke up in yet another bed that was not hers. There was a window by this one. It didn't have any curtains, so sunshine poured in. Early morning sunshine, the kind that looks like it's been brewed up fresh for the day. On the other side of the glass, birds were making a fuss about dawn.

Stupid birds. They were used to not remembering much. For them, everything was *now*. They didn't have much *then*. But she bet even a bird would be really sad if you took him out of his place and put him someplace else, a place where everything was strange and he didn't know any of the other birds.

Somewhere a floorboard squeaked. She heard voices, but not clearly. Not enough to tell for sure if one of them was Mr. Turner, but probably so. This was his house.

Julia didn't remember coming here, but Sam had told her she'd wake up at Mr. Turner's house. She'd forgotten so much, but she remembered everything Sam told her, which was funny because it felt like she'd learned those things a long time ago. She knew it was just yesterday, but she felt as if months and months had passed. Sam had told her she would feel this way. She remembered that, too.

Most of what he'd told her was pretty awful.

Mama, I miss you so much. I wish you were here. I wish it a lot.

That thought was familiar, as if she'd had it thousands of times. The grief was familiar, too, like an old blanket worn thin by use and washing. So was the way her eyes leaked some of her sorrow. There was comfort in that familiarity, like knowing where the cracks were in the sidewalk she walked every day to go to school. Even when a path took you somewhere you didn't much want to go, knowing where the cracks were made you feel a little better. But there'd be no more counting the sidewalk cracks for her, would there? No more school. At least she didn't think so. She was fifty-seven years old, even if her memories were only twelve. They didn't make fifty-seven-year-old women go to school, did they?

Someone turned on a radio or a stereo. Music, anyway. It was the classic kind of music her dad liked, so she pretended to like it, too. Not that it seemed to matter to him.

Why couldn't it have been him who died, and not Mama?

Guilt bit hard. She sat up and started to throw back the covers, wanting to run, just run, until she didn't feel so much of everything. And she saw Fluffy.

He'd been pink once. Now he was a dingy sort of no-color that just looked old. But the scrap of ribbon around his neck had held on to some of the pink, and his face and the insides of his ears were black—faded, but still black. Someone had left him here for her. Someone had put him on the bed next to her pillow. Julia grabbed the little stuffed lamb and hugged him tight.

She was way too old for stuffed animals. She didn't care. Memories were stacked up in him, piled up in layers she could feel, weighty and dense, when she hugged him. She didn't think, *remember when*. She held that memory, all sorts of memories, in the rough, tactile form of a scruffy stuffed lamb.

There was a TV table next to the bed. It held a flashlight and a glass of water. The flashlight made her eyes sting. It made her a little bit mad, too. That had to be Mequi's idea. Mequi was the only one other than Mama who knew she'd slept with a flashlight until she was ten, but she wasn't ten anymore. Either way you counted up her age, she was too old to need a flashlight to feel safe in the dark. Mequi shouldn't have told anyone she needed a flashlight, and besides, she didn't anymore.

But maybe Mequi didn't remember exactly when Julia stopped needing a flashlight at bedtime. For her, that was a very long time ago.

Julia sniffed and scowled and reached for the glass of water because now that she thought about it, she was really thirsty. She drank most of the water and sighed. Now she'd have to find the bathroom.

She put Fluffy on her pillow and got all the way to the door before she realized she'd almost gone out of the room in her pajamas. In someone's pajamas, anyway. They were white with little blue flowers, and they weren't what she'd been wearing when she went to Sam's lair, which meant someone had put them on her while she was asleep. That creeped her out.

She bit her lip, then put her ear up against the door, wanting to know who was out there. At first she didn't hear much, but then someone spoke, and it was him. Mr. Turner. She couldn't hear very well . . . mumble, mumble, *few more minutes*, mumble. Then someone else spoke. A woman. Her voice was familiar, but even if it hadn't been, Julia knew who it had to be.

Miss Yu. Lily Yu. The FBI agent she'd met yesterday . . . no, not yesterday. Two days ago. Sam said he'd spent twenty-six hours fixing her, then she'd slept, and now it was morning. So it was two days since she found herself outside the restroom in the wrong body.

Miss Yu lived here, too. She was Mr. Turner's fiancée.

Julia's stomach felt sort of clenched and curious at the same time. Miss Yu was living in sin with Mr. Turner. He said people didn't think of it that way anymore because the sexual revolution had changed things. Well, he hadn't said those exact words, but she thought that's what he meant. Julia's mother had not approved of the sexual revolution. She said it was just a bunch of silly hippies who thought they'd invented sleeping around, when really people had been misbehaving that way for thousands of years only they didn't talk about it all the time.

Miss Yu was trying to find the bad guys who'd hurt Julia, which meant Julia ought to like her. But she was going to marry Mr. Turner, which made Julia not like her very much, even though that was silly. Julia was either too old for Mr. Turner or too young, depending on if you went by her body's age or her real age, so there was no point in being jealous. But that wasn't what made her straighten away from the door, rubbing her stomach.

Miss Yu was supposed to be Julia's daughter.

This body . . . this too-tall, too-old body . . . had had sex. Had borne children. Three of them, she'd been told. Three daughters. This body knew about those things and Julia didn't, and when she thought about that her stomach felt weird, like it couldn't make up its mind if it was sick or excited.

She wished she was still sleepy so she could go back to bed. But she wasn't, not even a little bit. And she really did need to go to the bathroom. She might as well get dressed. She sighed and looked around the room.

It was small and clean and didn't look finished. The bed she'd slept in was a double, and it had sheets and a blanket, but no bedspread. No rug on the scuffed wooden floor, either. No curtain on the window, and only that TV tray for a bed table, and no mirrors. She was glad of that. She didn't like looking at herself.

There was a chest of drawers, though. With a bunch of stuff on top. Familiar stuff. Julia's feet took her there without her even thinking about it.

There was her Magic 8 Ball and the little porcelain figure of a Chinese girl that her grandmother on her mother's side had given her for her ninth birthday and the silver-plated mirror her grandmother on her father's side had left to her when she died three years ago. Forty-eight years ago, now. Next to them were two books—the little-kid storybook her mother used to read to her, with stories about Peter Rabbit and the Little Red Hen, and *The Secret Garden*, which she'd read three times. On top of the books sat the white New Testament she'd been given when she was confirmed in the church, and below them were two photo albums.

When Julia was nine, her parents had given her a Polaroid camera for Christmas and a photo album. After Christmas, she and her mother had put the snapshots in the album together. That was the album on top, with a pink velvet cover. The other album was from their trip to Disneyland last year, or forty-six years ago, depending on how you counted. She'd bought that album with her own money and had embroidered "My Trip" on the green brocade cover ever so carefully, but she wasn't very good at embroidery. The letters leaned all over the place.

Everything looked old. Old and tired. Except for the sheet of folded white paper on top of the books. She picked it up and opened it. The writing was small and precise, almost like printing:

When I met you, you were twenty-one and long past needing help to ward off the darkness. We dated for several weeks before you trusted me enough to tell me that you used to sleep with a flashlight under the covers. Perhaps the darkness has become frightening again. If not, please forgive me for guessing wrong.

You're obviously past the age for needing Fluffy, yet I know you cherished him. I hope having him and a few other familiar things nearby will help a little as you adjust to what has to be a very strange new life.

It was signed *Edward*.

It hadn't been Mequi who thought of the flashlight. It had been him. Edward. The man she was married to. The man she'd made those three daughters with. Her stomach felt tight and anxious, but some other part of her felt easier. She didn't understand.

He sounded like a nice man, though. Maybe that was why she felt a tiny bit better. She didn't want a husband, nice or not, but Edward Yu seemed to know that.

Still, she didn't want to think about him. She folded the note up again and tucked it inside the Christmas photo album. She was not ready to look at the pictures in either album. She was glad she had them, but she wasn't ready to see how faded and old those pictures looked. She picked up the Magic 8 Ball and thought hard: *Will I get all of my memories back?* And shook it.

First it said, "Reply hazy, try again." When she did, it said, "Better not tell you now." That made her mad enough to throw it across the room, but she didn't. She didn't have many things from *before*. She wouldn't break one just because it made her mad.

Her bladder reminded her that she still needed to get dressed, so she opened the top drawer. Pajamas. Panties. Bras. She grimaced. She'd started wearing a bra this past summer, which was really a whole bunch of summers ago. She hadn't especially needed one, but all the girls wore them, so she had to, too. But these bras were bigger than what she'd been wearing.

Of course they were. She had boobs now. When she'd gone to the bathroom at the hospital she'd checked them out. They were not very good boobs, being kind of droopy. That made her mad. At some point she'd probably had great boobs, but now she didn't remember it.

Funny. She didn't exactly like her body, but she didn't hate it as much as she had at first. Maybe Sam had done something about that, too.

A bra would help with the droopiness. She sighed and took one out.

Even though she didn't remember this body, it seemed to know what it was doing. It was taller than she remembered, but that didn't make her trip over things. Muscle memory, one of the doctors had called it. Her muscles remembered how to walk, and it turned out they remembered how to put on a bra, too.

The panties were not the plain white cotton she was used to. These were grown-lady panties, several of them with lace, a couple of them nothing but lace. She pulled out a pair of black ones and put them on the bed, then looked for stuff to wear on top of the bra and panties.

The next drawer held shorts and tops. Good enough. She got out some khaki shorts and a green top.

Someone knocked on her door. She jumped. "Yes?"

"It's Lily Yu," a female voice said. "The FBI agent. Rule says you're awake, and I . . . may I come in?"

A little thrill of panic shot through her. "If he knows I'm awake, how come it's you instead of—" She flushed. "I'm sorry. That was rude."

"It's okay. I know you're more comfortable with Rule, but I wanted to talk to you before I leave."

"I'm not dressed."

"There's a robe in the closet."

Lily Yu wasn't going to go away. She lived here. Reluctantly Julia went to the closet. It was small and full of clothes, but not like anything she'd ever worn. Grown-up clothes. They made her sad, so she was glad when she found the robe. That was pretty—lots of fuzzy watercolor flowers all over, and silky. Maybe it was real silk. She slipped it on and stroked the slinky fabric. Real silk was expensive. Was she rich? Or maybe her . . . maybe Edward was.

Julia scowled. She was not going to think about him. "Okay," she said to the stranger on the other side of the door.

It opened. The woman who was supposed to be her daughter was wearing black slacks and a stretchy black shirt under a bright blue jacket. Her hair was long and shiny, but she'd pulled it back in a plain old ponytail. It didn't look like she'd used any makeup. She really ought to. With a little effort she'd be gorgeous. Right now she mostly looked tired.

She did not look anything like Julia. Julia had a heart-shaped face. Lily Yu's face was more oval, plus she had a better chin. Julia hated her chin. "Hello," Julia said cautiously.

"Hi. I, ah . . . this is pretty weird, isn't it?"

"It is super weird! I mean, I'm supposed to be your—your—" She couldn't even say it.

"But you aren't." Miss Yu's voice was matter-of-fact. "You look just like my mother, but you're someone else. Someone named Julia Lin, who I never really had a chance to know. We both have to get to know each other, don't we?"

"I guess so." Julia tucked her hair behind her ear and wished she'd had a chance to brush it. Lily Yu looked very pulled together, even if she wasn't wearing any makeup. "Miss Yu—"

The woman winced. "Could you call me Lily? I know that's not what you're used to, and I know we're basically strangers, but it sets off my freak-o-meter for you to call me Miss Yu."

Freak-o-meter. Julia liked that. She repeated the phrase mentally so she'd remember it. "I'll try, but you have to promise not to get mad if I forget."

"Deal."

"I asked Mr. Turner if I could stay here, but I didn't ask you if that was okay. I should have."

"Don't worry about it. You didn't have a chance to ask me, did you?"

"Because you've been working. Trying to find whoever did this to me."

She nodded. "And to some other people, and I have to leave pretty soon so I can keeping working on it. Rule will stay here today, unless something happens that changes things. I know you feel better when he's around."

Julia nodded, feeling awkward.

Miss Yu smiled a little bit. It was the kind of smile grown-ups use when something's sort of funny, but mostly *oh, geez.* "I feel better when he's around, too. Ah . . . I wanted to see you before I left, only now I'm not sure what to say. What to do."

That made two of them.

Miss Yu—Lily—looked around the small room. Her gaze lingered a minute on the bed. "I see you found something to wear. The woman you grew up to be is . . . was a bit of a clotheshorse. Very stylish. But her clothes probably aren't the sort of things you're used to wearing."

"They're pretty, but they aren't . . . they just . . . I don't know how to be an old woman!" All at once she felt horridly close to tears.

"Then don't try. You don't have to make yourself fit what you think your body says about you." This smile wasn't *oh, geez*, but it wasn't happy, either. "You may want to get some different clothes later. Are you hungry? The kitchen's out of commission right now, but we've got—"

A ridiculously loud noise interrupted her. "What's that?" Julia had to raise her voice to be heard.

"I think it's the wet saw. They use it to cut tiles. Rule did tell you that the house is a disaster area, didn't he? We're having a lot of work done. Most of the work's downstairs, but they'll be up here, too, trying to get at least one of the bathrooms finished. That's why you don't get eggs this morning. No kitchen. But we've got croissants and fruit and cereal and bacon."

"How do you fix bacon if the kitchen isn't working?"

"In the microwave. Um . . . I guess microwaves are new to you."

"I've heard of them," she said, indignant. "That's another word for electronic oven, isn't it?"

"I don't know. Want to see how it works?"

"I guess." Some bacon would be good, too. Her stomach didn't feel icky anymore, but it did feel empty. "I need to get dressed. There, uh, there seems to be a lot of people here."

"Grandmother is staying with us, too, and her companion, Li Qin. They're still asleep. You met Grandmother."

Julia nodded. "She said to call her that, even though she isn't my grandmother."

"Then you probably should."

"That's okay. I kind of like her." For one thing, Grandmother was really old—even older than Julia's body, which made her feel less of a freak. Plus, she made Julia feel steadier. Not the way Mr. Turner did, but it was like you knew you could count on her. She'd boss you around a lot, but you could count on her. "I thought I heard Mr. Turner talking to another man, too."

"That would probably be Scott. He's one of the guards. Did he explain why we have guards?"

Julia's eyes were big. "Guards? Does it have something to do with him being . . . uh, I think I'm not supposed to say werewolf."

"They prefer to be called lupi. He told you about that?"

"Sam did. He didn't tell me about any guards, though."

"Rule is the Rho of one lupus clan. That means he's their leader. He's also sort of the assistant Rho for another clan. Rhos always have guards. You don't seem upset about him being lupus."

Julia shook her head. When she thought about Mr. Turner being able to turn into a wolf it made her feel like when she stood in line for the roller coaster. As if something exciting was going to happen, even if she wasn't sure if she'd like it. But it didn't upset her.

"I guess I'd better let you get dressed." Miss Yu—Lily—moved to the door, but then stopped with her hand on the doorknob and looked at Julia. Her face said there was more she wanted to say, but instead she shook her head and smiled in that I'm-making-myself-smile way and left, closing the door behind her.

Julia didn't go to the bed and get her clothes. She grabbed the almost-empty glass, drank the last of the water, and went to the door. She put the glass on the door and her ear on the bottom of the glass. She used to do this at Mequi's door when her sister and her friends were giggling about boys. You could learn a lot that way.

On the other side of the door, Lily Yu dragged in a deep breath that broke in the middle, like when you're trying not to cry. Then Mr. Turner said something quietly, but he was close enough that Julia heard him. "Was it as hard as you feared?"

"Yes. How did you trick me into doing that, anyway?"

"I didn't."

"I was pretty fuzzy last night, but I remember enough. You tricked me."

"No, but I did expect you to change your mind. You're not very good at refusing to deal with things, *nadia*. It took everything I had to persuade you to stop dealing with every damn thing long enough to get some sleep."

"*That* was the trick."

"Mmm," he said, which was not an answer but seemed to satisfy Lily Yu, who didn't sound mad when she said she had to go if she was going to stop by the hospital first to check on Nettie. They moved away from the door then, and though they were still talking, Julia couldn't hear what they said.

Julia straightened, feeling guilty for eavesdropping and angry for no reason she could tell. And alone. So horribly alone. There were people on the other side of that door, and some of them knew her and seemed to care about her. But she didn't know them. She didn't want them.

The people she wanted didn't exist anymore. Even the ones who were still alive—like Mequi, who looked so old—weren't the people she remembered.

Someone knocked on the door. "I'm not dressed," she said crossly, but she grabbed the clothes again.

"If you don't let me in," a young voice said, "Dad will be back upstairs in a minute and he'll make me go away. He didn't tell me I *couldn't* talk to you, but that's what he meant when he said it wouldn't be a good idea. He thinks I'll say something to upset you."

Everything upset her. Some dumb boy probably wasn't going to make it any worse. Julia yanked up the khaki shorts. "Hold on a minute."

Shorts fastened, T-shirt tugged down, Julia opened the door. The boy who slipped inside was a lot shorter than her. How old had Mr. Turner said his son was? Nine, she thought.

A big tomcat slinked in behind him. The cat was orange

and missing part of one ear. He ignored her to stalk past and jump on her bed.

"Is that your cat? Does he have fleas?"

"Of course he doesn't have fleas. Dirty Harry is really Lily's cat, but he's adopted me. That's what Dad says, anyway."

She watched the cat making himself comfortable on her bed. Mama didn't like cats, especially not in the house. Houses are for people, not livestock, she said . . . used to say. Julia frowned at the boy. "I've forgotten your name. Mr. Turner told me, but I forgot it."

"I'm Toby. And you're . . . well, I used to call you Mrs. Yu, but now you're just Julia, I guess."

Toby looked a lot like his father done up smaller, with a softer face. "How come you aren't in school?"

"It's Saturday."

Saturday. Saturday was for cartoons. She still watched *Tom and Jerry*, anyway, with Deborah, who was little enough to watch a lot of cartoons. Saturday was also for getting together with Ellen and Ji after she'd done her chores, and . . . and Ellen and Ji were old ladies now.

"Are you going to cry?"

"Maybe." But she jutted her chin out instead. "So what did you want? Curious about the freak?"

"I thought you might like to hang out with another kid. Maybe you're not sick of being around grown-ups every minute. I would be, but maybe you aren't."

Her stomach loosened up a bit. "I guess I am. I haven't even seen another kid since . . . since everything changed."

"I guess you're all weirded out. Do you know about PS3? I really want a PS4, but Dad says not yet, which means wait for my birthday. I've got some cool games. You might like *Ratchet and Clank* or *Lego Pirates* or *Skylanders*. *Skylanders* is my favorite. Or we could play online stuff, though Dad won't let me sign up for a lot of those games. He says no graphic bloodletting on-screen until I'm old enough to understand about bloodletting in real life, and then I probably won't want the on-screen kind, which kind of sucks. But that's what I do when I'm upset if I can't go run or something."

Julia's forehead wrinkled in confusion. "What's what you do?"

"Play games on my PlayStation or computer."

Whatever that was. "Why did you say that about blood-letting?"

"Did I upset you? Grandad says humans think about that sort of thing different than we do 'cause they sublimate their violence. Wolves don't sublimate very well."

She blinked. "Are you a . . . I forget the word, but like your dad?"

"Yeah, but I won't turn wolf for another couple years. Do you want to play *Skylanders*?" He studied her a moment. "You don't know what I'm talking about. C'mon. I'll show you."

TWENTY-ONE

~≥

"**SHE'S** what?" Lily wedged her phone precariously between her shoulder and her ear while she hit send. Another day, another damn report. This one was short because she didn't have much to add to the one she'd sent last night, just a summary of the false lead she'd chased that morning.

It was noon. She was in the conference room at the Bureau's San Diego office, which shared a building with the ATF. The two organizations were a tad competitive. ATF was currently all-over smug because of a recent raid on a militia group that had netted them all kinds of illegal weapons, which made them harder than usual to get along with. But mostly the two agencies managed to cohabit reasonably well . . . except when it came to parking. They fought over the limited parking spaces like a pair of starving cats with a single mouse.

Lily had a tiny office of her own, but it was downstairs in what was mostly ATF territory, so she preferred to commandeer the conference room in spite of certain drawbacks, like having the men's restroom on the other side of one thin wall. She heard every flush. But the women's restroom was close, too, which was handy, and so was the break room. And there was enough room to set up a murder board here.

Through the closed door, Lily heard a phone ringing. She also heard Fielding's iPod, which was playing "Hotel California" for the sixteen-thousandth time. In a minute it would change to "Dani California," then Chuck Berry's "California," then "California Dreamin'." Fielding—a recent transplant from Massachusetts—had the office closest to the conference room, and he really liked songs about California. His playlist, however, was sadly limited. Lily didn't understand why no one had accidentally spilled coffee on the man's iPod.

Eleven more people had been admitted to hospitals with some level of amnesia. Two of those already admitted had slid into coma. Two more were on life support. The database of their victims' lives had finally provided a connection. Fourteen—including Lily's mother—had gone to the same high school. One of them had been close friends with Julia for two of her high school years, though according to Aunt Mequi the friendship had soured the summer before their senior year. Something to do with a boy. Two agents were at that high school now, poring over records.

The murder board for the ritual killing hung on the north wall of the conference room. They still didn't know whose face starred in the crime scene photos, it being tricky to get an ID without a body. They did have the man's fillings—two gold, two composite—and the scarf he'd been gagged with, but the scarf was a cheap import available by the thousands, and even the best forensic dentist couldn't learn much from four fillings.

That fit right in with the trend on this case. All they had were negatives. Their John Doe hadn't been reported missing. He didn't have a police record in California or those states participating in the NGI program, and Homeland Security was pretty sure he hadn't been a terrorist. Either he hadn't had much of an online presence, or what showed of his face above the gag wasn't enough for facial recognition software to ID him using Google and Facebook. Although they'd turned up enough near misses that way to keep a couple of agents busy crossing those people off the list.

"Playing *Skylanders* with Toby," Rule repeated. "I had to drag her away to eat breakfast."

"That's good, I guess. Surprising, but good." Lily's mother wasn't a complete tech illiterate, but she didn't much like it. Or didn't approve of it, anyway. God knew she considered texting some kind of major social sin. "At least she isn't, ah, quite so dependent on you." Following him around in a moony, preadolescent way, that is.

"Mmm. She seems to have caught on to the game pretty quickly. The two of them are currently arguing about tactics."

"That's . . . good?" Lily thought about it. "It is good. It means that Toby really does see her as another kid. He badgers adults. He doesn't argue with them."

"True. Which is why I let him stay after he snuck in to see her—which, as he pointed out, I hadn't explicitly forbidden. She informed me that he was no more upsetting than any other dumb boy, and she liked playing *Skylanders*."

In a weird, twelve-year-old way, that sounded just like her mother. "How's Grandmother?"

"Still asleep. She must have been awake at some point, though, because Li Qin had a message for me from her. Grandmother wishes us to know that Sam has decided we need information about the artifact. It's a sidhe artifact, so he sent an agent to speak with a sidhe historian."

Startled, Lily put down her coffee. "He did? What agent? Where exactly did he send this agent, and how?"

"That's the total message, I'm afraid. Li Qin tells me I must address my questions to Sam or to Madame Yu, neither of whom is likely to wake soon. She added that tigers, like wolves, often sleep heavily after a difficult hunt."

"How's Li Qin's foot? Is she getting around okay?"

"The swelling is down and she's supposed to get a boot for it tomorrow. She'll still need to stay off it as much as possible, which she says is fortunate, because then Julia can help her."

"That's fortunate?"

"What she actually said was, 'Who does not need to be needed? There is little that helps us forget our pain so much as giving aid to another.'"

Lily found herself smiling. Li Qin had that effect even when she wasn't around. "Speaking of giving aid to another—that florist called this morning. Bob or Bill or whoever it is Mother found. I let it go to voice mail, but maybe you could call him and see what the problem is."

"Of course. He shouldn't have called you. They've been told not to. I'm considering hiring a wedding planner to assist with some of the arrangements, if you don't object."

"No, it was my mother who didn't like that idea." Julia Yu had been appalled at paying someone to do something she was sure she could do better . . . something she'd been enjoying the hell out of doing until she'd been robbed of most of her life. Lily changed the subject. "Did you know your father put Hardy up in his own house instead of a guest cottage?"

"I didn't." And it clearly surprised him. "I doubt Benedict liked that."

"Probably not, but he wasn't there to object." She'd seen Benedict and Arjenie when she stopped by the hospital to check on Nettie, who remained stable and in fair condition but was heavily sedated. She'd woken repeatedly during the night, and every time she did, she instinctively started trying to heal herself. She'd stop when Benedict told her to, but even such brief drains weren't good for her. When her surgeon made his rounds that morning, he'd decided to increase her dosage to keep her knocked out.

Lily sipped at her fourth cup of coffee. "Isen says he's questioning Hardy in his own fashion, and he'd prefer that I leave him to it. He also said he's sending me something, although it goes against his own better judgment."

"Did he say what?"

"No, that would have been too easy."

"Have there been any results from the press conference?" Rule asked.

She snorted. "Thank God calls from the concerned public are being routed through D.C., or we'd never get anything done." Only callers with some slight potential of aiding the investigation were passed on to the team—which this morning meant Lily. Of the two dozen individuals Lily had talked to, only one had sounded promising . . . at first. "The best lead from the public so far was this woman who claimed she'd had a vision about the murder in Balboa Park. She had details the press doesn't, so I gave in to temptation and went to talk to her, seeing that she works only a few blocks away. Turns out she's a null."

"Nulls can, in rare instances, have visions."

"Yeah, but ninety-nine percent of the time they involve hallucinogenics. Pretty sure this particular vision was not part of the one percent. Unless you smelled kittens at the murder site and forgot to mention it?"

"Kittens."

"Hundreds of them, she said. They pinned that poor man down and smothered him in adorable."

"A gruesome end. I'm wondering what details she could have gotten right when her vision featured death by cuteness."

"The location. She knew that up, down, and sideways, but it turned out she's a Night Gazer."

"A what?"

"There's seven of them, seven being such a mystical number and all. They believe in gazing fearlessly into the night, only they don't like to do it at night"—she paused because Rule was laughing, then resumed—"because the park's too dangerous after dark. So twice a month in broad daylight they go to that very spot to conduct their rites, which I gather they make up as they go along, aided by the occasional illegal substance."

"You've had quite a morning."

"Yeah." She sighed. "My afternoon is likely to be more of the same. I'm holding down the fort while Karonski checks out the murder site. He's hoping to reconstruct the runes used in the ritual, with help from Abby Farmer from the coven. Seems the spell he wants to use is best cast by a strong Earth witch, and Abby is that, but she's inexperienced at this sort of thing. He has to teach her the spell first, plus there's a lot of prep involved. He said not to expect him until I saw him."

"Why didn't he have Miriam do it with Abby? Surely she knows the spell."

"She's at the hospital trying to figure out a way to remove the contagion from Officer Crown. He . . ." Her voice drifted off as the door to the conference room opened. Her eyebrows shot up. "You look like hell. Are you what Isen sent me against his better judgment?"

"I doubt it," Cullen said. "That's probably the person right behind . . . no, she's stopped to talk to someone."

"Is that Cullen?" Rule asked.

"Unless we've got more doppelgangers running around."

"Not funny." A short pause. "I hear Mark downstairs. That will be lunch, so I'd better go pry Toby and Julia away from the computer. You need to eat, too."

Lily had given up trying to persuade Rule that she ate regularly even without being reminded. For lupi, staying well-fed meant staying in control. One of the most basic things they did for each other was to offer food. Frequently. "Sure. You, too. See you whenever." She disconnected.

Cullen had wandered to the end of the room where she'd set up her murder board. He was studying the photos taken before the body dissolved. "How come you're awake?" she asked. "Sam thought you'd be unconscious at least twenty-four hours."

"That would be my doing," said a familiar voice from the doorway. An amazon stood there grinning at her through the spiderweb whorls tattooed on her face and pretty much every other bit of skin that showed.

"Cynna!" Lily's heart lifted. She and Cynna hadn't started out as friends, which just went to show how lousy first impressions can be as predictors of anything important. She shoved back her chair, suddenly sick of sitting. "I'm glad you're here, but why are you? I thought you'd be in lockdown, under the circumstances. Where's Ryder?"

"To answer your first question first, I gave Cullen a pick-me-up. He might come in handy, even if he is still too weak to light a candle."

"Hey," Cullen said without turning away from the murder board. "I could handle a candle. Maybe even a piece of paper."

Cynna's grin flickered. "Besides, he'd be royally pissed if I came here without him. Answering question two—or was it three?—I pumped out some milk for Ryder, who's staying at Clanhome with the tenders. I'd be there, too, if Isen had his way. But he ain't the boss of me." Her smile was impish. "He needs to be reminded of that sometimes."

"What she means," Cullen said dryly, "is that neither Isen nor I could argue her out of coming. She claimed she had a nudge from the Lady."

"I did not. I said I had a feeling I was needed. It might be the Lady giving me a nudge, it might not, but either way, she didn't nudge me to stay put. So it's okay for me to get out of Clanhome for a while."

Cynna Weaver was a Finder who wore her spells on her skin. She was also Cullen's wife, a new mother, former Dizzy, practicing Catholic, former FBI agent, and the Nokolai Rhej. A Rhej was the clan's connection to the Lady, more wisewoman than priestess, and keeper of the clan memories. She was able to draw on the magic of the entire clan, though Lily wasn't clear on whether that power came from the mantle or from each clan member. "You zapped Cullen with clan power?"

"I did. He's still as weak as a sweet little butterfly—"

Cullen snorted. "You could make that weak as a tired old tyrannosaurus or a gorilla with a bad cold. But no. You—"

"Grumpy as a gorilla with a bad cold, maybe. Anyway, it seemed like with him being able to see magic and me being able to use it, we might be useful. And I needed to tell you something." She came closer and held out her hands.

Puzzled, Lily took them and touched leaves and moss. That was how Cynna's Gift felt—like the intricate patterns found in a leaf, the organic growth of moss.

"I'm so sorry about your mother."

Lily's eyes stung. She blinked fiercely. "I know. I mean, of course you are. I mean . . . dammit."

"And it's pissing you off that you're about to cry, and I get that, so I won't say anything more. We're going to figure this out. So, ah . . . do have something in mind for me to do? Anything I could Find for you?"

"I don't know. We've got our vic's fillings. Could you use them to Find the dentist who made them?"

"Nope. Any of them gold?"

"Two."

Cynna brightened. "Excellent. Forget about Finding the dentist, but gold picks up and holds its wearer's pattern real well. Since your victim is dead and oh-so-thoroughly gone, I can't Find him, but I might be able to Find other objects that hold his pattern."

"Really? I didn't know you could do that. What sort of objects?"

"His home is the most likely."

"I was already glad to see you. Now I'm really, deeply glad."

"If he's just moved, I may not pick up his new place."

"If you get anything, it's more than we have now." Knowing who Friar had killed would either answer some of Lily's questions or point her at new ones. "Good chance, you think? Fair?"

Cynna shrugged. "It depends on how much of his pattern I can get from the fillings, on what the house is made of, and on how long he lived there. Brick and stucco absorb pattern well, but slowly. Wood absorbs pattern fast. Doesn't hold on to it well, but he hasn't been dead long enough for that to be an issue."

Lily headed for the door, opened it, and leaned out. "Fielding!"

His office was diagonally across the hall from the conference room. She could see him at his desk, eating from a foam take-out carton. Mexican, she thought, judging by the amount of cheese smothering it. He didn't look up. "What?"

"I need you to bring me the fillings. John Doe's fillings." They were at the morgue, since they were the only remains the victim's family would be able to bury. If they ever found the victim's family. "*Now* would be good."

"All right, all right." He shoveled a last forkful of cheesy whatever into his mouth, shoved back his chair, and grabbed his iPod from the speaker it had been plugged into.

Blessed silence. Lily closed the door, pleased. Two birds, one stone.

"Tell me what you know," Cullen demanded suddenly.

He'd been quiet so long Lily had almost forgotten he was there. "In a comprehensive mood, are you?"

"About that, of course." He waved at the murder board.

"Precious damn little. I need lunch first," she decided. "Unless you learned something I need to know right away?"

"Not urgent, but I—"

"Then it can wait a few minutes. Anyone want something to drink?"

"No, thanks," Cynna said. "We just ate."

"Okay." Lily headed for the door. Her lunch was in the refrigerator in the break room.

Right after they moved into their new house, Lily had started packing her lunch. She'd gotten a look at one of Rule's spreadsheets. The one that tracked his expenses for their Leidolf guards. Their salaries weren't large, but there were twenty-four of them plus Scott, who was Rule's second and had his own line item in the budget. Add that to a fortune per week in groceries, the insurance and upkeep on the five vehicles Rule provided for the guards, and ammo and withholding and utilities and something called WCP—

"Are you hyperventilating?" Rule had asked.

"No, but—but you can't possibly afford that!"

"I don't pay it. Leidolf does."

"But you said Leidolf's finances were a disaster."

"I never said the clan was broke." Rule had leaned back in his chair. "Stop and think, Lily. Leidolf is the largest clan. Not all of them pay *drei*, but most do. At the moment, seven hundred and forty-five clan members are providing Leidolf with an income of nearly two hundred thousand."

"Yes, and if I ever pulled in two hundred grand a year I'd think I was swimming in money, but that's, uh . . . fifteen thousand a month? Sixteen? That's barely a third of—"

"Lily," he'd said patiently, "I'm talking about monthly income, not annual."

Oh.

"Obviously that's gross. After-tax is more like a hundred forty—at least it is now that we've paid off that damn tax bill. We do get some income from other investments, but not much. Leidolf owns only two small businesses outright, and only one of those is profitable, and then there's the tax bill on the North Carolina land and . . . and you don't want to hear all that, do you? Basically, Leidolf has about one-third of Nokolai's net income and half again as many clan members to provide for. I've started a college fund, but it's badly underfunded. There are other obligations that can't be stinted on . . . still, one of those obligations is maintaining an adequate number of full-time guards. I've increased that number, true, but we're at war. I'd already increased it before bringing the guards here."

Two hundred thousand. A month. Per year that would be . . . two million, four hundred thousand. Lily was used to thinking of Leidolf as *poor*. Two point four million a year was not poor.

And all of it went to Rule. A clan's wealth was held by its Rho. Rule didn't think of it as his money, but the IRS would. Add that to what he managed for Nokolai and . . .

Rule's mouth crooked up. "You have such a funny look on your face."

"My mind does not deal well with numbers that big when they're preceded by a dollar sign. How could Leidolf's finances be such a mess with that much income?"

"Victor, like many of those who don't understand money, alternated between pure liquidity—by which I mean keeping everything in a bloody checking account—badly chosen loans, and throwing money at whatever took his fancy. He didn't keep proper track of his assets, such as they were, and at one point he decided to save money by not reporting most of the *drei* he received for a few years. That worked about as well as you'd expect. He ended up owing nearly three million in back taxes, which the idiot was making monthly payments on instead of—are you all right?"

She'd assured him she was fine, and the color must have come back into her face, because he'd accepted that. In an effort to sound rational she'd asked, "I saw the entry for ammo, but nothing about the AK-47s you bought recently." Those would come in handy if they ever found themselves up against a demon again. Not as much stopping power as the Uzis Isen had, but machine guns were illegal in hell. She'd settle for the AK-47s.

"Those are capital expenses, which are budgeted separately."

"Oh." She glanced at the spreadsheet again. "What's WCP?"

"Workers' Compensation Pool."

TWENTY-TWO

~

LILY grinned as she pulled her lunch sack out of the fridge. Workers' comp for werewolves. Rule hadn't understood why she found that so funny. It was state law, he'd pointed out. He'd explained—in rather more detail than she required—how he'd been able to pool that obligation with Nokolai, who already self-insured their workers' comp. "Self-insuring is a better deal than buying it elsewhere," he'd assured her.

Lily believed him about that. She believed him when he said Leidolf could afford the guards, too. She still started taking her lunch. She had a mortgage now. Saving a little money couldn't hurt. Besides, as she'd told Rule, it also saved time.

The break room was just across from the conference room. Lily pushed open the door to the conference room. Cynna was telling Cullen how she intended to use the fillings. He nodded and said something about the rashies—at least, that was what it sound like. It was probably Sanskrit or something. Then he looked over at her with sudden interest. "Roast?"

"I don't know." She set the insulated bag on the table and popped the tab on her Diet Coke.

"Roast," he said with certainty. No doubt his nose had informed him of this. "Have any extra?"

"Undoubtedly. Either Rule told the Kitchen Carls to double my portions or—"

Cynna hooted. "Kitchen Carls? As in Isen's houseman, Carl?"

Lily nodded and opened the bag. Sure enough, there were two fat sandwiches, two apples, and a baggie with a half dozen cookies. Lupi just couldn't get their minds around the idea that a single sandwich could be a meal. "That's what I call whoever has kitchen duty. They always put in way more than I can eat." She took out one of the sandwiches and tossed it to Cullen.

He caught it, sniffed. "This has a mother lode of pickles."

"I like pickles. Want some cookies, Cynna?"

"No, thanks. I thought you didn't have a kitchen yet."

"Rule and I don't, but the guards do." Their new property consisted of the house, several acres of land, and a barracks that had been a cheap motel in a former life, then sat derelict for several years. It had been renovated before the house. Friar wanted them dead and he was tenacious about it, so Rule wouldn't move into their new home until he could house his men. As a result, the barracks had a working kitchen. The guards rotated cooking chores among themselves.

"They were already sending over supper most nights," Lily said, sitting down and unwrapping her sandwich. "And they buy in bulk to save money, so when I decided to start packing a lunch, I asked Scott to add a few things to the grocery list for my lunches and let me know how much I owed. He agreed. Early the next morning that week's Kitchen Carl sent me a packed lunch. They've been doing that ever since." She snorted. "And they're all remarkably bad at numbers. Not a one of them can figure out how much I owe for my share of the groceries. I finally quit asking."

Pot roast, she discovered when she took a bite. With

butter pickles. Yum. She swallowed and chugged down some Diet Coke. "What did you learn from the crime scene pics?"

"The sigil on his chest looks like a sidhe rune."

Lily didn't quite spit out her Coke. "God, no. Not another evil elf."

"Probably not. Not many in our realm know sidhe runes, but they aren't completely unknown, either. I'll need to check my source materials to be sure, but I thought I recognized a couple of the runes drawn inside the circle, too. They look more like ancient Sumerian."

Lily's eyebrows went up. "Someone's blending disciplines, you think? I could send copies of the relevant photos to Fagin, see if he can ID them." Dr. Xavier Fagin was the preeminent authority on pre-Purge magical history.

"Good idea. He's got an impressive library still in spite of those assholes and their firebomb. Now tell me what you know about the ritual."

Lily filled him in between bites, ending with their failure to identify the body they no longer had.

"Huh." Cullen frowned. "Let me know when you get the labs back on those samples."

He meant the samples taken from the substances used to draw the circle and the runes. "Okay. Keep in mind that the lab may not get consistent results. There wasn't much magic left on—"

"I thought you said all the magic was gone."

"The contagion was completely gone. There was still a tiny tingle of magic in the circle itself—about what I feel if I walk in Isen's house barefoot." Which was not, as she used to think, entirely from the traces of magic left on the floor by so many lupus feet. There was some kind of stealth node under the deck behind his house—one that didn't give off the usual drifts of stray power that Cullen called sorceri. Whenever she asked Isen about it, he smiled and changed the subject. Isen could be really annoying sometimes. "And no, it didn't feel like *arguai*. And no, I can't describe the difference, but I can feel it."

Cullen's frown tightened a notch. "Describe the contagion again. Your experience of it."

"Icky. Gooey. Like something that had been dead a long time and was soft with corruption. A lot like death magic, really, only mushier, and without the ground glass. And it moved. Maybe that's why it seemed alive to me, as if it had intention. As if it really wanted to crawl all over me."

"Huh." He thought about that a moment. "Maggots?"

"What?"

"What was the movement like? Like maggots crawling around inside the corruption, or like the magic itself was in motion?"

She had to stop and think. "More like it was made up of maggots—soft, putrid, dead maggots that were still moving and wanted to get on me."

"Now there's an image I didn't need to have in my head," Cynna said.

"Tell me about it." Cullen had fallen silent, as if she'd given him something to think about. She couldn't imagine what. "Why did you want to know, Cullen?"

"Trying to figure out if something was moving the contagion or if it moved on its own."

"Miriam thought I was projecting. She said the contagion couldn't have intention."

"Miriam lacks imagination sometimes," he said absently, bending to pull a small spiral notebook out of Cynna's purse. "If something's never happened before, she thinks that means it can't happen."

Lily tended to think that, too, but she'd had enough evidence to the contrary in the past year to understand how wrong that was. "I figured you'd ask me about the body dissolving." That being the spookiest thing she'd ever seen.

He didn't answer, busy thumbing through his little notebook.

"How can you figure out if the contagion was moving on its own without looking at it?"

"I'm thinking. Stop talking to me."

"See? Grumpy as a gorilla with a cold," Cynna announced.

"It won't bother him if we talk because he won't notice, and *I* want to know about the body dissolving."

"It seemed to go through all the stages of decomposition, only on fast-forward. They ran some tests on the soil and found the kind of organic traces you'd expect to find in a burial site . . . about fifty years after the burial."

Cynna's forehead wrinkled. "Do you think it was a way of getting rid of the evidence? They couldn't have expected the body to be found as soon as it was, so they could have done something to make it self-destruct. Not that I know of any way to do that, but it happened, so it's possible. If Hardy hadn't gone looking for the body—oh, that reminds me. I've got a message for you from him."

Lily's eyebrows shot up. "You do?"

"Isen wanted me and Cullen to meet Hardy, or for Hardy to meet us, or maybe he thought Hardy would talk me into staying at Clanhome. Or maybe, being Isen, he had something else in mind altogether. I went along with it because I was curious. I've never met a saint."

"Do you think you have now?"

"I don't know. I liked him, even though he's got this way of looking at you as if he's been reading your diary. Not that I've ever kept a diary, but . . . how do you know if someone's a saint or not?"

Lily had no idea. "He seems to know things he shouldn't. Not without getting tipped by, uh . . . someone or something. The question is what side is tipping him off."

"Even people without magic can have visions. If drugs or magic aren't involved, then spirit is. Would that mean he really is a saint?"

"It means that he had a valid warning for me once, so if he gave you a message for me, I'd probably better hear it."

"Oh, yeah, right. Hardy kept singing 'I'll be calling you,' emphasis on the 'you,' until I asked if he had a message for you. He nodded a lot, then he went like this." She hummed the refrain from "Riders on the Storm," then switched to singing, " 'There's a killer on the road . . . da-da-da . . . squirming like a toad.' Just like that, with some of the words left out."

Lily huffed out a breath. "Unless he's trying to warn me about a killer toad, I don't get it."

"Me, neither. Isen told him that probably wasn't enough information to help, so . . ." Cynna launched into another song.

Lily stared. "The candy man? He's warning me about killer toads and the candy man?"

"He added a few bars from something called 'I Want Candy' by the Strangeloves."

"That can't be a real band."

"I never heard of them, but Isen has. I guess they're an older band."

Lily shook her head. "I suppose Hardy means well—saints have to mean well, right? But I don't see how that helps. Unless he's not a saint and is getting his information from the dark side of the Force, in which case he doesn't mean well. And it still doesn't help."

"Don't be an idiot," Cullen said.

Surprised—and too inured to Cullen's habits to be any more than a little annoyed—Lily looked at him. He'd put away his little notebook. "Was that a general suggestion, or were you actually listening?"

"I meant," Cullen said with exaggerated patience, "that of course the man's a saint. Isn't it obvious?"

"No. And you wouldn't be my first choice for spotting holiness."

"He made me want to squirm. Made both of you feel like that, too, didn't he? When he looks at you, it's like he's shining a light right through to the back of your skull. Shine a light in a dark place and you get roaches scurrying for cover. We'd all rather think we weren't full of roaches." He raised his eyebrows. "What, did you think saints were supposed to make you feel good about yourselves? That's *Sesame Street*'s job. Saints make people uncomfortable, which is why people usually kill them."

After a moment Cynna said, "He has a point."

It was more insight than Lily was used to from Cullen, and it made her uncomfortable. Kind of the way Hardy had.

Which was practically proof Cullen was wrong, because she was abso-damn-lutely sure that Cullen Seaborne was no saint.

"What spell is Abel planning to use to reconstruct the runes?" Cullen asked.

"Something that requires an Earth witch. Beyond that, I have no idea."

"Probably one of the variants on Cyffnid's Dire," Cynna said—which set her and Cullen to arguing in technobabble about the Law of This and the Quadrant of That and synchronicity. Lily tuned them out and thought about a saint who couldn't talk. Was Hardy's message supposed to be a warning? The "Riders on the Storm" made her think so, that being such an ominous song, but maybe it was intended as a clue about the killer. Or the victim's identity? Maybe their victim had written the damn song back in his younger days. Hell, maybe he'd been the lead singer in The Strangeloves.

No, not that. Hardy communicated through song lyrics, not by playing some kind of music trivia game. So . . . assume it was a warning. What did he mean by singing about the candy man? Should she be on the alert for a Willy Wonka lookalike? If she spotted one, was he supposed to help, or was he the killer toad? Toad-on-the-road . . . roadkill. Candy roadkill. A smashed chocolate bar. Smashed into the shape of a toad. Don't take candy from strangers, little girl . . .

The door swung open and Fielding entered, carrying a small plastic bag. "Here they are. What in the world are you going to do with them?"

"Cast spells," Lily said, standing up and grabbing her Coke.

"Huh. You Unit people are weird. Can I watch?"

Lily exchanged a look with Cynna, who shrugged. "All right, on one condition."

"What's that?"

"You leave the iPod unplugged the rest of the day."

*   *   *

CYNNA needed to go outside to set her circle, since she couldn't draw on carpet. First Lily notified her guards. They—Santos, Joe, and Andy today—were waiting for her in the public reception area. They'd prefer to be a lot closer, but she'd tried bringing them into the offices once. Lily could have put up with the comments and funny looks she got for having bodyguards, but the men were just too much of a distraction. Because they were lupi, yes, but also because they weren't FBI. Civilians aren't supposed to hang around in law enforcement offices unless they're witnesses or under arrest.

She notified Santos of where they were going and why. That was part of the deal, that she let them know if she was going to stick her nose out the door. Cullen had already headed for the conference room door; Lily, Fielding, and Cynna followed.

The Big A ran into them in the hall. "Fielding. Why don't I have that wit report yet?"

"Uh—I thought, after making that mistake about Agent Yu's Gift, I'd better learn more about how the Unit operates. I wanted to—"

Ackleford rolled his eyes. "Get me that wit report."

"Yes, sir."

Ackleford shoved open the men's room door and went in.

Fielding said quickly, "I'll be right out, okay? I've almost got the report done. I'll be just a minute."

"He's eager," Cynna commented.

"He's new," Lily said dryly. "He's still trying to get on the Big A's good side. He hasn't figured out that the Big A doesn't have a good side. Why do you need a circle?" She'd seen Cynna cast for a pattern plenty of times without setting a circle first.

"There's a wee chance that if Miriam is able to banish the contagion from your officer, it will sort of rebound into the fillings."

"Mind you," Cullen put in, "it's a very slim chance. The resonance would be very slight, considering how little the fillings had to do with generating the contagion and, I suspect, with containing it until it was called or decided to move out. If the—"

"Don't explain." Lily looked at Cynna as they turned into the hall that led to the stairs. They'd go out the back way, which was really on the side of the building, but everyone called it going out the back. "Is this going to be safe for you?"

"Ought to be. I'm not impervious to magic the way you are, but I've got pretty heavy-duty protections these days. And I set one hell of a circle. I won't open the baggie until the circle's set."

Just how much power did Cynna have available as Rhej? She probably shouldn't ask. Rhejes kept a lot of things secret. "How much power do you have now, anyway? On, say, a scale of one to dragon."

Cynna grinned. "Less than Sam, certainly."

She hadn't said less than a dragon, but less than Sam, who was the oldest of the dragons, and presumably the most powerful. "Does that mean—"

"It means," Cullen said, "that your question can't be answered. In the first place, magic isn't electricity. You can't break it down into neat little quanta like ohms or volts or whatever. In the second place, the real question is how much power someone can safely handle. There are casters with minor Gifts who can cast quite powerful spells because they've mastered the use of external power. Abel Karonski, for one. Then there are people with powerful Gifts who can't channel external power worth a damn. Like you."

"But—"

"And then," Cullen said as they reached the door to the stairs, "there are a few rare souls like me." His grin flashed. He swung the door open with a flourish. "Strong as hell and masterful, too."

"Not to mention pretty," Cynna said, patting him on the cheek as she passed. "But not modest. Somehow he missed the modesty gene altogether."

"I thought about adding modesty to all my other wonderful qualities, but decided it would be too much."

"Couldn't squeeze it in past your ego, you mean."

Lily smiled, but she couldn't help noting that, between the minilecture and the banter, Cullen and Cynna had done a fine job of changing the subject. Rhejes did get to have secrets, she reminded herself as she started down the stairs. But Cullen didn't. "Why did you say I can't channel? I can't, of course, but doesn't that go without saying with a Gift like mine? I can't use magic, period."

"You can't use spells. You use magic all the freaking time. You soak it up, mostly unconsciously, but you've done it on purpose, too, though that nearly killed you precisely because you couldn't dump it fast enough. I don't understand why Sam hasn't taught you how to avoid that."

"Oh, gee, maybe it's because I can't do it."

"You probably can't learn to channel, but you can learn to get rid of excess magic. You already do, just not consciously."

"No, I don't." Her Gift soaked up magic and made it hers, which was how she was able to read magic with a touch and why she couldn't be affected by it. Throw a spell at her, and her Gift ate the power. And yes, like he said, she could use it to suck up magic on purpose, although doing so bothered her. But . . . "That's why I can't cast spells. You told me that yourself. To cast a spell you have to be able to use whatever magic you've got, you said, and mine isn't available for that. My Gift hangs on to all the magic it absorbs."

Cullen snorted. "Why is it that your brain works fine on other subjects, but not about your Gift? I said one of those things. The other is your unconsidered assumption. Think about it. Your capacity to absorb magic is not unlimited. Your experience with the Chimea proved that. So why didn't you exceed your capacity years ago?"

Lily's mouth opened . . . and closed again.

"You must be shedding excess magic somehow. I don't

know what the mechanism is, so I can't teach you how to use it consciously. But Sam ought to be able to."

Thoroughly uncomfortable and not sure why, Lily didn't respond.

They'd reached the bottom of the stairs, which opened onto a short hall with locked doors on either side—one to the parking lot, the other to the rest of the building. Both doors required key cards; Lily moved to the front to use hers.

"Weird weather," Lily said as she stepped outside. The air was heavy with moisture and smog. Humidity was always a surprise, and usually the wind off the ocean was a tidy and tireless housekeeper, sweeping the city's air clean of man-made murk. The air was utterly still today.

A few steps out, Lily stopped and shook her head. "Cullen."

The parking lot was deep but narrow, with a single central lane and parking slots arrayed along the federal building on one side and an insurance company on the other. The spaces were reserved for Bureau and ATF employees, and there weren't enough of them. And smack-dab in ATF territory, occupying not one but two spaces, sat a black behemoth of a car. A glossy Lincoln Town Car, to be precise, with armored sides and bulletproof glass. Three less-than-glossy men lounged nearby.

"What?" Cullen said. "You don't think Cynna should have bulletproof glass between her and possible snipers?"

"Using the tankmobile is a great idea. Parking it illegally, not so much. Isen would be pissed if it got towed."

"You wouldn't let them do that."

"ATF is hugely unimpressed by me. If one of them sees it, they'll have it towed before I can blink. Hi, José," she said to one of the men near Isen's tankmobile.

José had a quick, appealing smile. "It's good to see you, Lily. Ah . . . Isen said I was to mention the chain-of-command issue."

Lily looked at the *other* three men standing about ten feet away . . . Santos, Joe, and Andy. Her Leidolf guards.

José and the guards with him were Nokolai. The two clans had been enemies for at least two hundred years. Rule was now Rho of one and Lu Nuncio of the other and was trying to mend that, but some habits were hard to break. At the moment no one looked hostile, perhaps because they were avoiding looking at each other at all. "Right. Santos."

"Yes?"

"This is José"—she pointed—"and Casey and Steve. While we're all together like this, José's in charge."

Santos's dark eyes flickered with outrage. He glanced at José, who was a head shorter and about fifty pounds lighter. A decade older, too, but that didn't show. His response was carefully courteous. "May I ask for your reasoning?"

"First, I'm not going to put you over someone who's been subordinate to your boss, and Scott was under José in D.C. Second, I'm told you're good. I believe it, but I know José better than I know you. I know what to expect, how he thinks, how he reacts when the shit hits the fan. That's an edge I don't intend to give up just to smooth your ruffled fur."

Santos didn't like it. That was obvious in the very blankness of his face, but he nodded.

She glanced at Joe and Andy. She didn't expect any problems there. Santos was pricklier and more dominant than the other two. They each nodded.

Good enough. Lily turned to follow Cynna and Cullen, who'd headed about a third of the way down the parking lot, arguing cheerfully—something about a ley line. José gave low-voiced instructions for how the men should station themselves. Lily carefully did not check to make sure Santos and the others obeyed. That was José's job.

"I still say you're too close," Cullen said to Cynna, "but have at it. Just because I was playing with ley lines before you were born doesn't mean you should listen to me."

"Glad you realize that." Cynna set her tote down.

He looked at Lily. "José could kick Mr. Macho's ass."

"When they're two-footed, yeah." Two-footed wasn't Santos's best form for fighting, and Lily had seen José take down fighters who outweighed and outmuscled him every bit as much as Santos did. As a wolf, though, Santos was supposed to be one of the best. Lily had heard Benedict's assessment: superb in wolf form and potentially excellent on two feet, though mishandled and mistrained. Currently a pain in the ass.

Santos had issues. A lot of issues. Rule hoped to reclaim him. He said that Victor, the previous Rho, had wanted to make a weapon of Santos, alternately petting and punishing, trying to obliterate the man's sense of right and wrong so that the only "right" was Victor's word. Victor had been a grade-A son of a bitch. "But Santos has to be able to take orders from people who can't kick his ass. Me, for one."

"True."

The door into the building opened and Fielding hurried out. "Have you started?"

"Not yet. There won't be much for you to see," Lily warned him.

"More than I've seen until now," he said as he moved to join them. He glanced around, obviously noting the guards. "What are they—"

"They're my men," Lily told him.

He grimaced, but didn't comment out loud. Maybe he didn't consider lupi men, or maybe he didn't approve of her having bodyguards. Either way, he didn't want to make her mad. He really wanted to watch the magic happen.

Cynna was drawing her circle with her special chalk, using a piece of string.

Fielding whispered, "Is it okay if we talk?"

"Sure," Cullen said. Not whispering.

"Why the string?"

"Same reason you used a compass to draw a circle back in geometry class. Circles don't have to be mathematically precise, but the cruder the circle, the more power is needed to close and maintain it."

Cynna finished drawing, crouched, and touched the chalked line to set the circle. She moved to its center and opened the plastic baggie, shaking the fillings out into the palm of her hand. She spoke a Swahili word and made a quick gesture with her other hand. After that, nothing at all happened, to Lily's eyes.

Or to Fielding's. "What's she doing?" he asked.

"Copying all the patterns imprinted on the gold," Lily said.

"What exactly are these patterns?"

Lily gestured at Cullen. "You try. I don't understand it myself."

"You might think of patterns as words. Both are representations of something, not the thing itself. The analogy isn't precise, of course. A word is like a basket that lets you carry the idea of the thing around. Patterns actually partake of the nature of the thing, which is why they're so effective for all types of sympathetic magic."

Fielding looked at Lily. "Do you understand what he just said?"

"Not really."

Cullen sighed. "It's magic."

Fielding nodded, satisfied.

Cynna made another gesture and then just sat there with her eyes closed.

"Whatever patterns are," Lily said quietly, "she's doing the heavy lifting now. First she copied the patterns that relate to those two fillings. Now she has to get rid of everything that isn't part of the pattern for the victim."

"Huh." Fielding thought about that a moment. "How does she know what to take out?"

Cullen took over again. "Part of it is plain old hard work and experience. Part is art. She'll recognize some of the elements she wants to keep, like 'human' and 'male,' because she knows them pretty well. She'll spot some that she wants to remove that way, too. But the art . . . that's what makes her such a helluva Finder. She's got a sense for how a pattern flows, what belongs, what doesn't. She'll know when she's got something she can work with."

Fielding smiled. "She's your wife, right? I can tell you're proud of her."

"Pride would suggest I played some part in what she can do. I didn't. In other areas, maybe—I've beaten a little theory into her thick skull—but not this. She's just damn good with patterns."

Lily smiled. Yeah, he was proud of her.

Now and then Cynna gestured or spoke in Swahili. Fielding began to fidget. He dug into one pocket and pulled out a crinkly cellophane bag. It rustled as he dug into it and popped something in his mouth. "Want some?" He held it out.

It was some kind of virulently green candy shaped like . . .

Cynna's eyes opened. She dropped the fillings back in the bag, sealed it, stood, and stretched. "Well, I've got something, anyway."

Lily grabbed the bag out of Fielding's hand and held it up. It was full of frog-shaped gummies. Or maybe they were toads. Candy toads. *The candy man can. There's a killer on the road—*

"Lily!" José called sharply. "Ten o'clock and twenty feet up! What the hell is that?"

TWENTY-THREE

❧

"**So** that's going to be your secret tunnel." Julia crouched next to the earthen trench, impressed. Big metal bars were rammed into the dirt along the walls every few feet and the floor was outlined by boards called forms because they'd form the way the concrete would go when they poured it. That was what Rocky had told her. He was the foreman or crew boss or something like that, and she ought to call him Mister Something, but Toby hadn't told her the man's last name. Toby called everyone by their first names no matter how old they were.

The trench ran about twenty feet from the house's base-ment to what was going to be a big garage, but right now was a big mess. They'd knocked down the original garage, because it had been in sorry shape, plus it hadn't been big enough. Two men and a woman were working to clear away the mess. The woman was operating a backhoe—a ma-chine with a big scoop on one end that Julia really, really wanted to drive, but they wouldn't let her. The woman used it to scrape up chunks of cement and broken-up boards from the old garage. Then the men used their shovels to toss smaller pieces of broken stuff into the scoop, and then the machine would pivot and bump along several feet to empty its load into a dump truck.

They wouldn't let Julia drive the dump truck, either.

"Want to see the other one?" Toby asked.

"Other one what?"

"Other secret tunnel."

Julia sat back on her heels, indignant. "You get *two* secret tunnels?" One secret tunnel was cool. Two was like having two swimming pools or two maids picking up after you or—or doubles on anything that was just too much.

"Yes, because maybe our enemies will explode the garage, or maybe that won't be a good way to go 'cause there's too many of them in that direction, or maybe they'll find this one. So there's one the other side of the house, too. It's not finished, but it's closer to being done than this one." He popped to his feet. "Come on. If the cement truck shows up, we'll hear it."

Maybe it wasn't too much after all, Julia thought as she followed the boy. Or else it was too much of the wrong thing. If you had to worry about your enemies blowing up your garage . . . "Will we be able to see the cement truck if it does come?"

"We'll hear it, anyway. But Rocky didn't think the truck was gonna make it today."

Rocky was the foreman, who'd gone into the house with a couple of his men to eat lunch when they found out there was a problem with the cement truck. Watching them pour the cement was supposedly the reason Mr. Turner had chased them outside. She bet, though, that if they tried to go in, he'd make them leave again. He was working on his computer, which looked a lot like Toby's computer, but he was reading stuff on it instead of playing stuff on it.

She sighed. "I guess grown-ups are all the same about some things. Like wanting kids to go away when they're busy."

"Dad didn't want us to go away. He wanted us to stop playing computer games. He thinks too much gaming isn't good for me. That's usually okay because I usually have plenty of other stuff to do, but since we moved here . . ." He shrugged and kicked a small rock. It skittered several feet.

"You don't like it here?"

Toby shrugged. "It's okay. It's just that there's more to do at Nokolai Clanhome and lots of kids to do it with. Maybe they'd let you go to Clanhome with me tomorrow. Do you like to fish or rock climb?"

"I don't know. I've never done either one."

"Not ever?"

"My father doesn't like fishing." He probably wouldn't have taken her and her sisters even if he went fishing every week, but she didn't want to say that. Not when Toby had the coolest father ever . . . even if he had chased them outside after lunch. "I don't know if I could do rock climbing. I used to be pretty strong for a girl, but I don't know how strong this body is." They rounded the corner of the house. "I don't see a tunnel," she said, frowning.

Toby grinned. "They did a good job, huh? It's camouflaged. That's why I'm not supposed to play on this side of the house, in case I forget what to look for and accidentally fall in."

"Are we going to get in trouble for being here?"

"We're not playing, are we? And you ought to know about it so you don't accidentally fall in."

"And that is what you plan to tell your father if he finds out."

"I'll tell him anyway. I don't lie to him . . . well, I can't, because he'd smell it if I tried. But I don't hide stuff from him, either." He paused. "Usually."

Was he pulling her leg about Mr. Turner smelling a lie? She looked at him suspiciously, but decided it might gratify him too much if she asked. He was okay, for a boy. But he did think he was pretty special. "So where's the tunnel?"

He showed her. It was well hidden, all right. They'd put plywood on top and put sod over the plywood, so all you really saw was a kind of bump that ran out to a small grove of trees. They ambled along in that direction.

"This tunnel is a bigger secret than the other one," Toby

said. "See, if someone's tracking what we do here they'll spot the other one and think they know what we're up to. So you can't tell anyone about it. No one at all."

"Okay." It was a really tricky way to do things, which she had to admire, but it made her stomach feel tight to think they might need this much trickery. "It looks like it's been here all along. The grass and weeds look like they grew up all by themselves."

"They used magic to help with that."

"Did Mr. Seaborne do the magic?"

"No, he's not that good with plants, because of him being so good with Fire. Grandmother did most of it, but she taught Cynna how so Cynna could do it, too."

She looked at him, astonished. "Grandmother? You mean the old lady who . . ." Julia had to think for a minute to recall the relationship. "Mr. Yu's mother?"

"I guess you don't know about her anymore." His brow wrinkled. "I'm not sure if I should tell you, but . . . well, she's got what you might call a really special Gift, but it's a big secret. She knows some spells, too, and one of them makes things grow."

Julia frowned, studying the slight hump that indicated the tunnel-to-be. "So why do they worry about you falling in? You don't weigh enough to break plywood."

"Oh, it isn't plywood everywhere. There's places where it's just a bit of tarp and not much dirt. See that scuffed spot by that dead-looking bush? And I think there's one close to us, too." He studied the ground, then squatted and brushed at the dirt. "See?"

The edge of a yellow tarp showed through beneath a thin coating of dirt. "But that's not enough dirt to grow things!"

"That's why they needed magic."

That was some pretty cool magic. Julia sighed. She'd never thought about magic much before, but now she found herself sad because she didn't have any. "So why did they use a tarp in some places?"

"So they can get in and out to work on it, which they mostly do at night."

"They really are working hard to . . . hey, what's that?"

"What?"

"Up there." Julia pointed at a patch of sky between them and the house. "See where the air is all wavy and funny?"

"YOU'VE seen the greenhouse, the store, and the rec center," Isen said. "Shall we visit the babies now?"

Hardy's face lit up. " 'You are my sunshine,' " he sang. " 'You make me happy when skies are gray.' "

Isen chuckled and turned down the path to the clan's day-care center. "Babies do that for me, too."

He had learned quite a bit about his unusual guest today. Some of it was obvious. Hardy couldn't use words normally, but he understood them just fine. He had a vast repertoire of songs and commercial ditties from before 1975. Most likely, then, he'd been hurt in 1975, or close to it.

Isen had also learned that Hardy loved dogs, chocolate ice cream, and hot water. That last item was probably not a pleasure he could indulge in often, but he certainly had this morning. He'd been in the shower a full hour. He also knew that Hardy had a bad knee, a child's curiosity, and a clear and flexible mind. Humans might not notice that. Without language, Hardy wouldn't think the way they did, so sometimes he would baffle them, or vice versa. But Isen was accustomed to new wolves who'd temporarily lost language . . . and old wolves who didn't always bother to put words to their thoughts.

He might be the most nearly fearless man Isen had ever met.

Not completely without fear. He'd been anxious about the message he wanted passed on to Lily, but otherwise he lived in the moment, sunny and untroubled. Certainly lupi didn't worry him. Once he understood the nature of his hosts, he'd been fascinated. At Hardy's request—rather elliptically posed, but Isen had figured it out—Isen had Changed in front of his guest. Hardy had watched intently, then he'd grinned and sung out that God had "you and me, baby, in His hands"—a clear proclamation that Hardy considered Isen one of God's children, even when he was four-footed. Interestingly, he'd assumed that Isen would still understand him.

Hardy also walked with angels.

That was how Hardy thought of it, at least, and who was Isen to say he was wrong? They'd had a good conversation about it. Hardy didn't actually see the beings he called angels, but he felt their presence. Sometimes they spoke to him, and the way they . . .

What was that? Isen stopped, all his senses alert.

Hardy grabbed his arm and sang so quickly that the words all smeared together. "Running-just-as-fast-as-we-can!"

The mantle in Isen's gut twisted as some part of Clanhome *ripped*. Isen looked toward that breach and felt the wrongness and knew precisely where it had occurred—the node halfway up the rocky slope of Little Sister. He pulled hard on the mantle, tipped back his head, and bellowed, *"Fighters—to me!"*

SEVEN floors up at St. Margaret's Hospital, Benedict pushed to his feet. He didn't suffer from claustrophobia the way his brother did. He had a touch of discomfort in very tight, enclosed spaces, sure, but almost all lupi did. Nettie's room was small, and at his insistence, it lacked a window. But it wasn't small enough to trigger that response in him.

So why was he on his feet, pacing?

Arjenie looked at him over the top of her laptop. "Oh, for heaven's sake. Go run the stairs again."

"I'm fine."

"You're restless and anxious and sick of this room. You're also accustomed to a lot of physical activity, and you haven't been getting it."

Benedict stopped to smile at his mate. "Know me pretty—"

Thud.

He froze.

"What is it?" Arjenie whispered.

He made the sign for silence and listened keenly. Then he spun. Quicker to take the bed with Nettie in it than to disentangle her first from the various tubes. He pulled his hunting knife from the sheath on his calf. "We're evacuating. I'll get Nettie. You get her IV."

She didn't hesitate. She put her laptop on the floor and hurried to the IV stand.

Thud.

She must have heard it this time, too. Her eyes widened.

"Bill, Tommy!" he snapped. "Get in here. Rearguard!" He laid the knife beside Nettie and shoved her bed, aiming for the door, which opened to admit the two guards. Arjenie kept pace with the IV stand. "Something's on the wall outside. Something big. It—"

Thud, thud, crack!

"—wants in."

LI Lei Yu woke suddenly, sat bolt upright in her borrowed bed, and did something she never did. She yelled. "Rule! The children! *Run!*"

TWENTY-FOUR

～

"IT'S a gate!" Cullen cried. "It's a goddamn gate!"

"Weapons!" Lily snapped at the guards, drawing hers. "Fielding, go get backup. Lots of it, with the most heavy-duty weapons you've got."

"But we don't know if—"

She shoved him. "Go!"

He ran.

"Hold your fire," Lily called, "until we—"

Something leaped through the gate twenty feet in the air, nearer the street than the building. It was big and squat and looked like the ugliest centaur ever—only someone had substituted "bug" for "horse" in the thing's ancestry. Segmented like a caterpillar and armored like a dinosaur, it was a mottled dun and gray with a barbed tail at one end and a gorilla's chest and arms at the other, and way too many legs in between. As it twisted in midair Lily got a glimpse of a face like a demented gargoyle.

"Dworg!" Cynna screamed.

The guards opened fire.

The creature landed on the roof of a Suburban. It was damn near as big as the Suburban, and metal crunched and crumpled beneath the impact. Instantly it leaped off, as quick and easy as if the bullets had all missed—leaped and landed on pavement with that muscular tail held curled up over its back like a scorpion's. And raced straight at Lily and Cynna.

Fast. Ungodly fast for such a large creature. Lily had her weapon out and aimed. She squeezed the trigger twice.

It kept coming.

Cynna hurled something at it. Something invisible.

It stumbled and grunted what sounded like words— God, did it *speak*?—but recovered immediately.

A wolf with fur the color of cinnamon landed on the armored back. Another one, gray and black, darted in to clamp his jaws on one rear leg, and that at last got the creature's attention. It stopped abruptly, sending the wolf on its back tumbling to the ground. Those gorilla arms ended in claws like a bear's, and the thing twisted to rake at the fallen wolf with those claws while its tail whipped out at the other wolf.

It was so damn fast! But so was Cullen, who'd already danced aside. She couldn't see what had happened to the black-and-gray wolf—and couldn't stand around watching.

"Cynna—come on!" She scrambled onto the nearest vehicle, a Ford just like hers, and Cynna vaulted up there with her. Lily jumped to the next one—a shiny black Mustang. Cynna landed beside her and together they scrambled onto the small car's roof so they could vault over to the minivan beside it, while behind them wolves snarled and José shouted a quick stream of orders: *"Joe, Steve, Santos— keep it busy—"*

Lily jumped to the next car, an old Dodge Colt. "You sure that's a dworg?" They were like a cross between a troll and a demon, Cullen had once told her, only meaner and harder to kill. Of course, he'd also said they all died over three thousand years ago. But Cynna remembered things from three thousand years ago—

José: *"Go for the legs—"*

Cynna landed beside her. "Hell, yes! I stopped one of its hearts but—"

"—*Cullen, help Andy. Casey, with me!*"

Another jump, onto another government Ford.

"They've got four hearts," Cynna said. "And it took a hell of a lot of power—"

White Nissan.

"—to knock out just one. They're—"

Government Ford.

"—resistant to magic and they heal ungodly fast and I can't draw too much power or I'll faint."

They'd gone far enough, Lily decided, to pause and see what was happening, so she did—just as Santos leaped onto the Ford with them. "What the—you're supposed to be helping Joe and Steve!"

"I'm supposed to protect you!" He grabbed her arm. "Come on—keep moving!"

She tried and failed to pull her arm away. Several cars back, two wolves harried the dworg. José stood at the trunk of the tankmobile with Casey, but he looked up and saw Santos and his lips moved in what might have been a curse. He gestured at Casey, who Changed. Cullen had switched back to man form and was dragging a bloody and unconscious wolf—God, she hoped he was unconscious—away from the action. One of the harrying wolves darted in suddenly and clamped his jaws on one of the dworg's too-many legs, but that muscular tail smashed into him, sending him flying. He landed crumpled and still.

"You son of a bitch," Lily said to Santos, her voice low with fury. "You will follow orders. Get back there. *Now.*"

He grabbed her and dumped her over his shoulder in a fireman's carry and jumped down off the car, which drove his shoulder into her gut. Her air whoofed out and she gulped in a breath. She needed to get her Glock turned around so she could clobber him with the butt and—

Metal crunched loudly.

This time it was accompanied by the crash of glass breaking, and she couldn't fucking see what was happening from her upside-down perch over the shoulder of the idiot who thought he was fucking *rescuing* her.

Suddenly magic blazed all over her skin, a blast of fur-and-pine prickles. And there was no shoulder in her stomach. There was no anything beneath her but air.

She didn't land well, but somehow did manage to keep her head from connecting with the pavement. Instead her left hand did. Pain shot up her arm from that impact, but training had her rolling away, rolling and pulling herself into a low crouch, her weapon still clutched in her right hand.

A huge dun-colored wolf stood on Santos's clothing, hackles raised and growling at the dworg that had fallen out of the sky onto an ancient Pinto—the one just across the center lane from where Cynna still stood on the government Ford. Right fucking next to Lily. This close, she got a good look at the face—rubbery skin, too-loose lips stretched in a grin that showed a row of shark teeth. This close, she could smell it—eau de rotten meat and vomit. And gasoline—?

Two more dworg fell out of the sky. A goddamn pair of dworg, who landed one behind the other on the pavement between her and the other lupi—and immediately turned to face her.

She was so screwed.

SEVEN floors above the ground at St. Margaret's Hospital—one floor above pediatrics—two monstrosities clung to the brick like enormous caterpillars. One pounded the wall with its rearmost legs while the other clawed at the hole the first had started, widening it.

The hole was about a foot wide. Not monster-size. Yet.

THIRTEEN miles outside the city, a monster fell from the sky. Toby froze in a thrill of terror so absolute he didn't recognize it as fear. He scarcely noticed the woman-sized girl beside him screaming. All he could think was, *That can't be, it can't be* . . . He'd heard the stories about monsters like this one, but they were about the past. Way, way back in the past.

When glass shattered on the second floor and an orange-and-black streak leaped through the window to the ground—when his dad came racing around the side of the house four-footed, going flat-out fast—when a second monster landed beside the first, and a third—he knew that whether it could be or not, it *was*.

Dworg.

Run. Hide. Evade. Find a weapon. Fight.

Those were the priorities for what to do if he was attacked and there was no adult with him: *Run* if you can get to a safer place. *Hide* if you can't run. If you can't run or hide, *evade*. Only then look for a weapon, because for kids, *fight* was the last resort.

Toby bent and grabbed the tarp covering the trench and yanked it back. "Come on!" But Julia didn't unfreeze, so he grabbed her leg and yanked, making her stumble, which got her attention. "Down here! Hurry!"

He jumped down into the darkness, scampering aside immediately so Julia wouldn't land on top of him, and then thought he should have pushed her in first because for a second it didn't look like she was going to follow—but she did. She landed on her hands and knees, panting in fear. "They—another one came and the wolves—and a tiger—" She gulped.

Toby felt a rush of relief. *Wolves,* plural, meant the others had Changed and followed his dad, and Grandmother was there, too. Dad wasn't fighting alone. "Come on," he hissed, because even though plywood wouldn't stop a dworg, it was better not to stay in the same spot they'd entered. They scuttled farther down the tunnel and stopped. Listening.

Toby's heart pounded so hard. Anyone could hear it, he thought. Any*thing*. Maybe those creatures weren't really dworg, but something else that looked the way those long-dead monsters were supposed to have looked. Either way, he'd done the right thing. He thought he had. He hoped. He couldn't just run away. If the monsters were dworg, they'd be too fast, and besides, they'd been between him and the house, so where would he go? That left *hide* and *evade*. This was more evading than hiding, because they'd probably seen him and Julia jump down here.

But the monsters were big and the tunnel was narrow. Maybe narrow enough they wouldn't fit. Maybe.

Then he thought of something else. He should have had Julia go the other way, away from him. Because even though she was really a kid, the dworg wouldn't know that, with her having such a grown-up body. He'd thought he was helping her, but if those were really dworg . . .

Dworg had this instinct, this drive. That's what all the stories said. It's what had made them so horrible, but it was also their weakness. They didn't always do the smart thing, didn't always follow orders, because this instinct sometimes took over. A feeding instinct.

Dworg ate kids.

TWO minutes and twelve seconds after Isen summoned his fighters, the klaxon was blaring, calling for the immediate evacuation of Clanhome. A few cars were speeding away already, with more car doors slamming at this house and that one as dworg poured over the crest of the hill on the north side of the meeting field. They'd come from the big node, the one not tied to the mantle.

Twenty-two dworg, Pete had just informed Isen. Twenty-two nightmares from a past so distant humans knew nothing about it. Nightmares that his people had fought in the Great War—fought with tooth and claw, yes, but also with swords. There weren't many ways to kill a dworg, but cutting off its head worked every time.

Isen had used every one of his hundred and thirty-two seconds. In the old days, it had taken between ten and twelve lupi to bring down a single dworg. Isen didn't have enough fighters to pit ten or twelve against each dworg. He didn't have half of that, and those he had weren't all here. Some were on patrol. Some he'd sent to the barracks to retrieve weapons stored there. Most of the rest were deployed around the day care, which was where he'd sent Hardy. That's where Pete now watched from the roof, coordinating their defense. Isen had kept one squad with him.

Not that six lupi could do much against twenty-two dworg. "It's in your hands now," Isen said crisply into the phone he'd borrowed. He'd left his at the house—bad habit, that, and one he should have abandoned the moment they knew themselves at war.

"Rho, please—" Pete began.

"No." Isen had neither time nor patience for argument. He disconnected and tossed the phone down. He wouldn't be able to use it in a moment, anyway.

Isen had used every one of his hundred and thirty-two seconds, but that wasn't much time. Not enough to devise an entirely new strategy against creatures who weren't supposed to exist. He had to hope these were traditional dworg against whom a traditional plan might work.

According to the tales, no one could hide from a dworg, for they directly sensed the lives around them because it was life itself they fed on, along with the flesh of their prey. But they had one weakness: their hunger. It held them always in a pack, that being the only way they could maintain focus on their task. Sometimes a few would become distracted anyway and begin to feed before they'd achieved their objective, and then the rest would turn on those few. That could be exploited, though Isen preferred that they not be given the chance to feed at all.

They hungered most of all for children.

Not all of Clanhome's children were at the day care, but many of the youngest ones were. Four babies, three toddlers, and ten between the ages of three and nine. Seventeen babes and children currently being loaded into a pair of minivans behind the day care. At the last drill, it had taken the tenders just under six minutes to evacuate the day care. The dworg would be here much sooner than that.

According to the tales, the Great Bitch had often sent dworg to kill the Rho or Lu Nuncio of a clan, for dworg could sense the mantle just as they sensed the bright flame of life in children, and so could always find their target. So if these were nice, traditional dworg, they were here to attack Isen. But they'd be distracted. Rushed, wanting more than anything to get to the children.

As the monsters reached the green grass of the meeting field, Isen's fierce grin broke out. "Now!" he shouted. And Changed.

A second later, Isen led six wolves as they streaked across the green—not running directly away from the charging monsters, but at a teasing slant: *Come get me, come get me—you can do it!* And yes, praise the Lady, the dworg immediately shifted direction to flow toward them. Their gait was oddly smooth, like a centipede's. And fast. Ungodly fast.

Lupi in wolf form were faster than any born-wolf, reaching speeds around fifty miles an hour.

According to the tales, dworg were faster.

TWENTY-FIVE

～

LILY didn't think about raising her weapon. Didn't have to. Her hand did that all by itself and sited on the dworg standing on the smashed Pinto, though she couldn't use a proper two-handed grip because her left wrist was either broken or badly sprained. This close, it shouldn't matter—might not matter if she missed, either, considering how little notice the other dworg had paid to bullets so far.

Cynna shouted a string of nonsense syllables.

The dworg standing on the remains of the Pinto flew backward to crash into the wall of the building in a spray of gore.

On the other side of the dworg twins, an Uzi opened up in a quick, deafening burst.

José had gotten the trunk open. Thank God.

Lily went flat. A big, hairy wolf landed on top of her.

She heard shouts and a howl and a second quick burst from the Uzi, but from a different spot. José had probably fired the first burst high because the idiot who was now trying to shield her with his stupid hairy body had put her in the line of fire, which meant one or both of the goddamn pair of dworg were still alive enough to pursue him. She squirmed over onto her back—not easy with a hundred seventy or so pounds of wolf on top of her—and jammed the barrel of her gun in Santos's throat. "You will go to Cynna," she growled. "She probably fainted from saving my ass after you dragged me into the line of fire."

Wolves' faces do show emotion, if you know what to look for. This one looked really startled.

"You will Change and get Cynna safely to the Toyota. Then you will get the AK-47s from the trunk"—and why the hell had she thought it was okay for the guards to park so far away? Stupid, stupid—"and come back here as fast as you can." When he just stared at her she pushed the gun deeper into the fur and flesh of his throat. "You. Will. Obey. Me."

He must have believed her. He launched himself across the open center aisle in a burst of speed, staying low, not pausing to Change until he reached the limited sanctuary of the space between cars.

Lily took a second to check out the dworg Cynna had sent flying. It lay motionless atop what was left of the Pinto. It looked like its chest had exploded from the inside out. White rib bones stuck out through ripped and bloody flesh.

Turned out their blood was purple.

Lily flipped back onto her stomach and crawled under the nearest vehicle—a panel van with a nice high clearance. High enough for her, anyway, but too low for one of those oversize centaur-bugs. Once she had herself under cover—freeing José to fire as needed, which he may have noticed because there was another burst of fire—she scooted toward the back of the van so she could see what was going on.

There was a dworg blocking her view. A dead one. At least she was going to assume it was dead, because the head, neck, and shoulders had been thoroughly pulped by some portion of the Uzi's six hundred rounds per minute. The shiny purple blood made the scattered bits of brains and flesh look weird.

Two down, then, and two to go. One was chasing José—

another burst of fire from the Uzi, this one closer to the street, and how many rounds did he have left, anyway? And one she guessed was still being harassed by wolves. How many wolves? She'd seen two of them knocked out or killed. Were the rest still . . .

Metal creaked. Something grunted loudly a couple of times, like the huffing grunt of a bear. Something on the Pinto next to her cozy retreat under the van.

Shit. Not two down, after all.

Lily sucked in a breath, trying to calm her racing heart. Trying to think, dammit. And noticed that gasoline smell again.

Now her mind raced along with her heartbeat.

Years ago, Pintos had been notorious for the way their gas tanks ruptured on impact. Lily had read that subsequent studies showed that they weren't any worse in that respect than a lot of cars in their class, but most patrol cops still approached a rear-ended Pinto with caution.

She needed a match. She didn't have one. Or a lighter. Cynna's tote might hold one or both, as she routinely packed it as if she expected to need to camp out for a week. But her tote was on the other side of the central lane and several spaces back. If Lily tried to get it she'd get in the way of the lupi fighting that dworg and could easily get in José's line of fire again. Besides, she hadn't missed the way every dworg immediately aimed itself at her when it arrived. Sneaking was likely not possible.

All she had was her Glock and the thirteen—no, twelve—rounds still in the clip. In the movies people routinely shot a bullet into a car's gas tank to make it go boom. Pity that didn't work in real life. Supposedly it was possible to skip a bullet across a rough surface like concrete and create enough of a spark to ignite gasoline, but talk about iffy! And while Cullen might have enough juice to light the gasoline, he was back at the fight, and needed. She didn't—

A gray snake as thick around as a small elm whipped under the van.

Lily scrambled forward as fast as she could. If the bony

barb at the end of the tail hadn't gotten stuck on one of the tires, she wouldn't have made it. But it did and she did—only now she was out in the open again, and the damn dworg grinned its shark's grin at her from its perch atop the smashed Pinto. Its chest was covered in gore. Some of the blood was still wet, but the wound had closed.

There was a wet gleam at the Pinto's rear end that wasn't blood. It was clear and vaguely iridescent. Without thinking, Lily sighted on that and squeezed the trigger once, twice, again—

Fire whooshed up, instantly engulfing the car and the beast crouched on it.

Son of a bitch. It worked.

A hand grabbed her arm. "Move it!" Cullen shouted as he jerked her up—and threw her. Again she landed badly, this time even losing her grip on her weapon as she tried to keep her weight off her damaged left wrist. And saw Cullen standing perfectly still holding a sword—a sword, for God's sake, not a big knife, and where in the hell had he gotten that?—as the fiery dworg launched itself at him or her or both of them. And the Uzi roared again.

The monster's head exploded as its burning body fell on top of Cullen.

The fire winked out. So did the Uzi's roar.

Another blast of gunfire erupted—not the sustained howl of the Uzi. Semiautomatic fire this time. And someone screamed, high and agonized.

Lily spun.

The backup she'd sent for had arrived. The dworg was eating one of them.

From somewhere behind Lily, the Uzi fired again—and stuttered to silence all too quickly. José was out of ammo.

But another dworg was down. Dead or temporarily down, she didn't know which, but there was just one active dworg left. Where? Lily spun to see, and oh, God, there was José leaping from the top of a panel van to another car, but the dworg was too close! The dworg pulled ahead and jumped onto a car in front of José and—and glass broke again.

But not on the car. From up above someplace. Lily looked up—and shoved to her feet and yelled at the dworg, which just that second caught José with a blow from one of those clawed arms. "Hey! You ugly asshole idiot monster! I'm right here! You want me? I'm right here!"

The dworg charged her.

Lily threw herself to the ground and covered her head with her arms.

From the broken second-floor window—the window to the Big A's office—the RPG she'd glimpsed fired almost straight down.

She didn't see the grenade hit. She sure as hell heard it. And felt it.

THE explosion nearly deafened Toby. It shook loose clods of dirt and made Julia shriek and grab him. The way she hung on to him, sort of bent over, Toby wasn't sure if she was trying to shield him or trying to make herself little enough to be shielded. Either way was annoying. It was his particular job to keep any kids near him from being too scared, and how could he do that if Julia could feel how he was shaking?

So he shoved at her. "You're squishing me!" he whispered loudly.

"Sorry, I'm sorry." She loosened her hold but didn't let go. "Should we stay here? If they're blowing things up and the tunnel collapses—"

"It didn't collapse, and that'll be the only explosion."

"How do you know?"

"Because we only had one trap laid. I *wish* I could see how many it killed!" Some, anyway, because they wouldn't have set it off if they hadn't been able to maneuver some of the dworg near what looked like a utility box near the driveway. But how many?

"But—"

"Shh!" Toby listened intently. He'd been able to follow what was happening a little bit by listening, even if his ears were still only human. There'd been shouts and, once, horribly, a scream. Lots of gunshots. The coughing roar of a tiger.

Now he heard his dad. He couldn't hear what Dad said, but it didn't matter. His eyes filled up with tears. Dad was alive and he was giving orders and . . . and then he didn't hear much of anything. Silence for several long moments, but his dad was *alive* . . .

"Toby!" his dad shouted. "Toby, answer me!"

"Here!" he yelled, shoving to his feet. "I'm down here, Dad, and so's Julia, and we're okay!"

SEVEN floors up at St. Margaret's Hospital, Benedict cut off another foot.

On the floor beneath the hole in the wall, a collection of toes, claws, and now three grisly feet lay in a spreading pool of purple gore. Some of his own blood mixed in, too. Nothing major.

A machete would have been better, but his hunting knife did well enough. He was damn glad he'd worn his leg sheath. At the moment, he had the advantage. In order to widen their hole, the dworg had to expose their weakest spots—their legs and feet—and they couldn't get at him well enough to do much damage.

The advantage was temporary. He'd slowed them. He couldn't stop them.

A clawed hand gripped the edge of the hole and pulled. Benedict sliced at it. This time he didn't do much more than hurt the monster's feelings. A little blood, that was all.

In the hall outside the room, he heard all sorts of commotion. They were trying to evacuate the hospital. They weren't going to have even just this floor emptied in time, rate they were going. "Time for you to—" Benedict interrupted himself to dodge one of those clawed hands, swiping at him through the hole, and immediately lunged. This time he got a chunk of flesh. "—pull back," he finished.

"No," Bill said.

He'd kept Bill with him as communicator. Bill had Ruben Brooks on the line now, keeping him posted. He'd sent Tommy with Nettie and Arjenie. They ought to be out of the building by now. "Not room for both of us in here, once they're through." Another grabby claw. This one connected, laying his skin open along one forearm—and keeping him back long enough for the other dworg to pull a chunk of masonry away. "They'll be through soon."

"You need me to—"

"Fall back."

As Bill reluctantly obeyed, one of the dworg hammered the wall with its hind feet. That was something Benedict couldn't counter. He didn't dare lean out the hole himself—

That would be a bad idea, a cold voice said in his head. *Stay back.*

The entire building shook as if there'd been a quake. Through the hole Benedict glimpsed black scales and one enormous, taloned foot as it closed around a dworg. Even Sam's feet weren't large enough to fully encircle the monster, but the talon pinned it long enough for his other foot to come up—and rip off the dworg's head.

That took about one second. Then Sam was falling away, there being no perch for a dragon on the side of the building. The great wings beat hard. Benedict felt the wind from those buffets.

The other one flees. I will stop it.

The mental voice was as crisp and cold as ever, yet something else reached Benedict along with those words— a single flick of delight as keen as the blade of Benedict's knife. Delight he recognized as the heady bloodlust of a predator watching his prey run.

Benedict moved up to the wall and looked out the hole. The remaining dworg was scuttling down the wall, trying desperately to find cover before death stooped upon it.

Benedict smiled. *Not going to make it, are you?* He spoke to Bill, who had stopped in the doorway when Sam hit the building. "Tell Ruben we won't be needing the army, after all."

*   *   *

BATTLE still raged at Clanhome. Not for much longer, Isen thought, grinning through a beard sticky with sprayed blood—some purple, some red. Twenty-two nightmares from another time had rained down on them. Two remained.

There was much to be said for the traditional, he thought as he watched one of the last two dworg pitch to the ground. Especially when it was your enemy who fought traditionally. The natural weaponry of the dworg, combined with their unholy healing, inborn armor, and resistance to magic, had been devastating three thousand years ago.

But the world had changed since then, hadn't it?

It had been a near thing. Four of the six from his squad were injured, and Rob was dead. He'd lost some blood himself—head wounds do bleed like crazy—but nothing important. But he and his squad had drawn the dworg within range of those he'd sent to the barracks. The grenades had killed about a third of the dworg outright. When they were followed by devastating fire from six Uzis, those dworg still alive and mobile had tried to flee.

Uzis have an effective range of about two hundred yards. They hadn't made it.

The machine guns had run out of ammo, however, so his men were finishing the last two monsters the old-fashioned way—tooth, claw, and swords. "Don't rush," Isen had told them. "No point in taking chances. There are sixty of you and two of them. Take your time."

TWENTY-SIX

~~

SANTOS returned with the pair of AK-47s while Casey was chopping off the head of the last dworg José had shot with the Uzi. The one that had started eating. It certainly didn't look alive, but no one was willing to take chances. He used the sword Cullen had found in the depths of the tankmobile's trunk.

Cullen was too busy to wield that sword himself. He was trying to keep José alive.

Lily looked at Santos for one long moment. "How are you in hospitals? Is your control up to spending time there?"

"My control is good."

"First, go get Cynna. Take the AK-47s back with you. Then you'll ride in with Cullen. He has to go to the ER with José and Andy. I don't want him unguarded."

Santos's expression didn't change, but she saw his throat work when he swallowed. "What about Steve?"

"Steve's dead. So is Agent Fredericka Parker."

RULE wasn't answering his phone. Lily tapped in a quick text—*I'm okay. Cynna's okay. Attacked by dworg.*

Casualties. Call me. She'd just hit send when her phone chimed. It was Ruben. "You're being psychic, I guess."

"I've had no hunches today, unfortunately. I'm calling to tell you that Benedict, Arjenie, and Nettie were attacked at the hospital by a pair of what I'm told are called dworg. Benedict held them off until Sam arrived. Sam dispatched them."

Lily was silent for a long moment. "He held off a pair of them? All by himself?"

"They had to break through the exterior wall. That provided him with a tactical advantage, and he had a hunting knife."

A second ambulance pulled up next to the first. "I have to go. We didn't do as well as Benedict. We've got two dead—one Bureau, one Nokolai—and several wounded, three of them critical." Andy, who'd been the black-and-gray wolf who'd leaped to attack the first dworg with Cullen. José, whose guts Cullen had packed back inside the hole a barbed tail had ripped in him. And Fielding, whose heart had stopped once while they were loading him into the first ambulance, due to shock from blood loss. Fielding hadn't been injured by a dworg, but by shrapnel from the RPG.

Lily knelt beside Andy. He'd just come around, which was both good and bad. Bad because the pain had to be terrible. Good because it let him change back into a form the hovering EMTs were willing to transport.

Andy didn't look as bad as Fielding and José. No blood. But his chest was caved in. One lung was collapsed, and Cullen thought there was damage to his heart, too. If he hadn't been lupus, he'd be dead. He still might be. At any moment, he could lose this fight.

They'd brought in a helicopter for José and were loading him now. He was still alive, too. That counts for a lot with a lupus, Lily reminded herself. If they both held on another thirty minutes. Even twenty. Shit, fifteen. Every minute helped.

"Didn't . . . freeze . . . this time," Andy whispered. He smiled.

That smile hurt all the way down. She touched his cheek.

"You were fantastic. Cynna and I wouldn't be alive if you hadn't acted." She looked at Cullen and nodded. With a touch, Cullen had Andy asleep again.

"How in the hell did you get your hands on an RPG?"

"Interagency cooperation," the Big A said.

"It's from ATF's raid?"

"Yeah. I'm sure the assholes would have cooperated like crazy if I'd asked." He looked around. "This is one goddamn fucking mess, you know that? Rickie . . ." His jaw worked. Then his gaze sharpened. "Goddamn vultures."

Lily followed his gaze. The press had arrived.

"**. . . BROUGHT** Cynna back here," Lily told Ruben. As soon as the wounded were on their way, she'd called Ruben back. "Cullen checked her real quick before he left. He says she'll probably wake up with a bad headache soon, but she's okay. I'm going to head to the ER now. Ackleford's willing to take the scene until Karonski gets here. Then he needs to go to the hospital where they're working on his man."

"I'm afraid you'll have to talk to the press first. People are likely to panic if they don't hear something."

She grimaced. "Yes, sir."

"Keep it brief."

Brief was good. Maybe she'd get through it without falling apart. Can't alarm the public by falling apart on camera. "Yes, sir." She disconnected and started to rub her face, but noticed her hand was shaking. That didn't make sense. She was sure she'd burned through every drop of adrenaline her body had pumped out.

Why hadn't Rule called her yet? It had been . . . she glanced at her watch. Seventeen minutes. Not that long. Obviously he was away from his phone for some reason. Hell, maybe he was in the shower. "Casey," she said to the only one of the guards—other than Santos—who hadn't been badly hurt, "do you have keys to the tankmobile?"

"I've got a set, yeah."

"Okay. I'm going to talk to the press, and then we're

heading to the ER." She took a couple of steps, stopped, and turned. Casey was right behind her, guarding her still. He was built chunky. Solid. His hair was mouse brown, his eyes a faded blue. She didn't know him well, just enough to put a name to his face, plus a vague impression that he was on the quiet side. He could have died today. "Casey. You did well. All of you did extremely well today."

She wondered if it was anger that tightened his mouth—who was she, to tell him he'd done well? But it might have been grief. He'd cried earlier, about Steve. "José will be okay," he told her, as if she'd been the one asking for reassurance. "You'll see. He's a fast healer."

Her phone chimed. It wasn't Rule, but she answered automatically anyway. Maybe because she had no idea what to say to Casey. "Yes."

"Miss Yu?"

"Who is this?"

"Philippe. Have I called at a difficult time? My regrets, but this is urgent. I've left several messages for your mother, but I'm afraid she hasn't returned my calls. It's about the *feuilles de brick avec fruits de la passion.*"

"The what?"

He sniffed. "The pastry I make for you with the passion fruit. I am sorry to give you difficult news, but we are going to have to adjust the menu." He launched into an account of perverse suppliers, the weather, and the impossibility of using any but a certain farm's passion fruit.

She interrupted. "You're supposed to call Mr. Turner, not me."

"No, no, I have found it is much better to speak with the bride. What does the groom know, eh? Always I speak with the bride. It is her day. I must have *your* decision, Miss Yu, in order to proceed. Now, we will make a substitution. Let me explain what your options—"

Rage bubbled up in Lily. Why could no one follow directions? Orders, even. They thought they knew best and ignored what you told them to do, and people *died*. "You want my decision."

"I have said so." He was becoming testy. "Please listen. The options I offer you—"

"Okay, I've decided. You're fired."

She had to stab the phone twice to disconnect. That was when she noticed that her face was wet. She was crying? Oh, God, she was bawling, and she was supposed to talk to the goddamn press and not fall apart. Too late. She rubbed hard at her face.

"Here." Casey had pulled off his T-shirt and was holding it out. He stood close—protectively close, she realized, blocking her from view as much as possible. "It doesn't have much blood on it. You can clean up with it." His faded blue eyes looked worried.

Casey and the others—living and dead—had fought with her and for her today. Now he was literally giving her the shirt off his back. Never mind the goddamn press and the worried public. Lupi needed to know their leaders were in control. She'd pull herself together for Casey's sake. "Thanks," she said, and her voice didn't wobble or break. She dried her face dry with the unbloody portion of his shirt and handed it back.

He nodded once and pulled his shirt back on.

Lily took another slow breath. She was okay. She could do this.

When her phone rang this time, it was Rule. At last.

TWENTY-SEVEN

~~

RULE was talking on his phone when he returned from visiting his clansman in recovery. He handed Lily one of the coffees he'd brought from the hospital's gift shop, where they brewed what he considered a decent cup. He'd been here often enough to form an opinion. Mercy General was Nettie's hospital, where the clan usually brought anyone injured badly enough to need surgery. Rule had met Lily there about fifty minutes earlier, escorting his own small group of casualties.

She took the foam cup in both hands. Her left wrist was wrapped in an elastic bandage, all snug and tidy. It throbbed, but she'd been lucky. She had a sprain, not a break.

Luck was one weird and capricious mother. "Gil is doing okay?"

"Excusez-moi un instant," he said to the person on the phone, and he told her that Gil was doing very well and already on his way home—"somewhat against the surgeon's wishes, but he'll rest better there." He switched back to French as he sat beside her. Casey—who'd gone with him, along with two other guards—handed him his cup. Rule laid his arm along the back of the couch in a way that let him play with her hair.

Lily sipped and smelled coffee, baby lotion, and blood.

The baby lotion had come from Cynna's tote. Cynna had woken up on the way to the hospital and winced and started rooting in her tote, but she hadn't been focusing too well. Must have been a bad headache. Lily had located the ibuprofen for her. While digging for that she'd noticed the baby lotion, so she'd asked if she could use some, thinking it might cover up less pleasant smells. Like blood.

Which she should not be smelling. She didn't have Rule's nose. She'd cleaned up in the restroom, and while she hadn't been able to get rid of the blood splatter on her clothes, there wasn't that much of it, and it was dry. Chances were the smell was all in her head.

A crowded and unpleasant place, her head. She leaned into Rule and closed her eyes and tried to notice only the smell of the coffee.

"C'est bien," Rule said, messing with her hair. *"Oui, je vois que vous comprenez . . .* Mercy General. *Vous le savez? Oui. Merci, monsieur."* He disconnected.

"I guess that means Philippe is back on board."

"Complete with *feuilles des pommes et grenades*, which he assures me will outshine even the *feuilles de brick avec fruits de la passion."*

"Grenades? We're serving grenades at our wedding?"

"Grenades is French for pomegranates."

"Oh, good. I'm feeling real fond of grenades right now, but can't see serving them sautéed in butter or whatever." She tipped her head. "Is Philippe really French? I figured that was just part of his image and his name was really Jim Bob or something, but the way you were chattering at him, maybe not."

"Belgian, I think, though I'm no expert on accents. I promised to tell you that he is desolated that he bothered you at such a difficult time. I was barely able to dissuade him from rushing here immediately to throw himself at your feet and beg your forgiveness."

In spite of everything, her mouth twitched. "I don't know. That might have been fun."

"I could call him back."

"That's okay."

"I could call him back," Rule repeated in a different tone. "Are you sure you're okay with keeping him on?"

She shrugged, uncomfortable. "The wedding's too close to get another caterer."

"I'd rather serve Spam and Vienna sausages than have you unhappy about this."

She turned her head to look at him. The dark fans of his lashes hung lower than usual, and she could see brackets down his cheeks. He was exhausted, worried, hurting. Just like her, but somehow he'd found the patience to deal with the damn caterer. She touched his hand to tell him thank you. "I'm going to say no on the Spam. Mother would have a fit, if she was herself. She's not, so it wouldn't be any fun."

Rule sifted her hair through his fingers. "It's not a victory if your opponent isn't fighting back."

Her opponent? Huh. Was that how she saw her mother? Lily took another sip of coffee. Not exactly, she decided. Her mother didn't oppose her so much as want to fix her, or fix her life, or just hold on to the time when Lily was small and things could be fixed. How odd to think no one was trying to fix her now. Odder still to find that, on some level, she missed it. She felt as if she had to pick up the pieces her mother had dropped—plans, quirks, attitudes. As if she could hold on to those pieces now, then hand them back at some point.

Better be careful of what she held on to. Becoming her own opponent wouldn't be fun, either. "'Sparring partner,'" she decided, "fits better than 'opponent.' As for Philippe . . . I shouldn't have fired him. Hung up on him, maybe, when he wouldn't listen, but firing him didn't solve anything. I was just . . . Santos didn't listen, either. I was angry at him, and took it out on the guy who thought the worst news I'd get today would be about passion fruit."

"Ah. Yes. I need to discuss Santos with you." He glanced around the waiting room. It was crowded that afternoon, especially with so many lupi lurking nearby. They'd pretty much claimed this whole side of the room. "Scott, remain here. The rest of you need to wait out of easy earshot."

Scott had a quick word with the others. They were hip-deep in guards pulled from both Leidolf and Nokolai to minimize the depletion of fighters at either location. Casey had been allowed to stay as part of the Leidolf contingent in spite of some minor wounds—minor to a lupus, anyway—so he could hear about José the moment they did.

Santos had not. He'd been sent to the barracks to await judgment.

Another attack so soon seemed unlikely, but until a few hours ago, they'd have thought dworg were unlikely, too. Unlikely verging on impossible, like opening gates in four places at once. Or flat-out impossible, like creating gates without a node to anchor them.

Someone had done it, though. Someone had used ley lines to open three gates. He, she, it, or they had used a node for the gate at Nokolai Clanhome—sheer destructive greed on their part, Isen thought, that had led to their defeat. If they'd been willing to settle for just killing him, they could have used a ley line and a smaller gate and sent three or four dworg without needing the node. That might have succeeded. Instead, those twenty-two dworg had had to race down from Little Sister, giving him time to prepare.

That was an assumption, of course. They knew their enemy had used a node for the gate at Clanhome; they were only guessing about why. Maybe they'd needed a node there because Clanhome was somehow a harder nut to crack, arcanely speaking. Guessing, too, about their enemy's goal. But that was a strong guess. Four attacks, with three of them on those who held or could hold the Nokolai mantle? The aim seemed clear: destroy the mantle and you destroyed the clan.

Lily figured the attack on her had been gravy. The Great Bitch knew how to hold a grudge.

Since reaching the hospital, she had called or been

called by several people. Karonski first. He was working the scene with the Big A, and he had a good news, bad news deal to report. Miriam had succeeded in removing the contagion from Officer Crown, which was great news. Crown had even woken up. And screamed, and kept screaming . . . they were keeping him under heavy sedation.

Then she'd talked to Ruben again. And Li Qin, who said the children—by whom she meant Julia as well as Toby—were frightened but well. And Isen, who told her he'd spoken with the other Rhos and none of the other clans had been attacked. And finally Benedict, who'd answered some of her questions.

Sam hadn't hung around to chat after dispatching the two dworg at the hospital, but he had told Benedict a couple of things before he left: That it was impossible to open a gate within his territory without his knowledge, which was how he'd known about the dworg. And that the gates hadn't truly opened simultaneously, but within the span of four seconds.

Dragons were hell on wheels at multitasking. In those four seconds Sam had sensed the gates; identified the first dworg to leap through; sent Grandmother a warning; taken telepathic note that Lily, Benedict, and Isen were aware of those gates; and chosen his target. By the fifth second he'd leaped skyward, heading for the hospital at top speed.

Why there, rather than one of the other sites? The pediatrics ward, Benedict had told her. Then he'd explained exactly why that mattered. Lily had nearly thrown up.

She hadn't been able to ask Cullen about node-free gates yet. By the time Rule called and told her about the attack at their home, Cullen had been on his way to the ER. When she and Cynna got there, Cullen had been wobbling on his feet. He'd kissed Cynna, which seemed to energize him—not through pure eros, though. Cynna had slid him some clan power, enough to keep him going a little longer. Then the two of them had hurried off to scrub.

Anesthetics didn't work on lupi. Sleep spells and charms did, but their duration wasn't predictable. Cullen and Cynna were alternating between the operating rooms, making sure no one woke up on the operating table.

Lily didn't have a complete casualty count, but a lot more lupi had been wounded than were transported. Wounded wolves do not deal well with hospitals, so only the truly critical had been brought there. That included José and Andy, but not Joe. Lupi didn't consider a broken leg serious, and he'd stopped bleeding before blood loss became an issue. Eric, who'd fought beside Rule, had a bad head injury, and two Nokolai from Clanhome had needed surgery. One had lost a leg. One had nearly bled out through a throat wound.

That was Gil, the one who was on his way back to Clanhome now. He'd healed enough by the time he arrived at the hospital that they'd patched him up in the ER. He'd needed fluids, blood, and stitching, all of which could be handled there. The one who'd lost a leg was out of surgery and would probably be discharged soon. Fielding, too, was out of surgery, if not out of danger. He'd been moved to recovery when Ackleford called Lily. José, Eric, and Andy were still in surgery.

So far, Isen had lost one of his fighters. Rule hadn't lost any. Lily had lost two.

So far.

Soon, Lily's pulse whispered. *Soon, soon, soon.* Her tidily wrapped wrist throbbed in time with that mantra. Surely the surgeons would be done soon and she'd know if her tally of dead held steady or moved up.

"About Santos," Rule said once most of the lupi had moved out of earshot. "I need you to repeat, as precisely as possible, what you told him about following José's orders."

She did. She remembered clearly, so it wasn't hard.

"He indicated that he accepted this."

"He didn't like it, but he nodded. Steve and Joe did, too."

"And you heard José tell him to fight alongside Steve and Joe."

"Yes. When he didn't—when he followed and grabbed

me—I told him to let go and get back there. He didn't follow that order, either."

Rule looked at Scott, who hovered close. "Scott?"

Scott was as grim as granite. "Clear failure to obey. It's my fault. I knew he had a problem recognizing authority in a woman. Most of Leidolf do until they've been around Lily awhile. They obey anyway, because you've been clear about that, but at first that's all about you, not her. I thought Santos . . . but I was wrong. I shouldn't have assigned him to her. With your permission, I'll take care of it."

"No," Rule said. "That will be my duty, should it be necessary."

"Wait a minute," Lily said. "What duty?"

"One more question, then I'll answer yours. If Santos hadn't obeyed when you held the gun to his throat, would you have shot him?"

Scott made a small noise. She glanced at him and wondered why Rule wanted him to be part of this discussion when he'd sent the others away. "Not where he thought I meant to," she said, "but yes. I was thinking I'd put the bullet in his front shoulder, if he needed more persuasion. That way he'd still have the use of both legs and one arm after he Changed."

"You had no intention of killing him, then?"

"Does it matter?" And why did she put it that way? Of course she wouldn't have . . . but memory barged in. She'd been ready to pull the trigger when she jammed her gun under Santos's jaw, into his vulnerable throat. She'd told Rule she'd been angry with Santos. She had, but that had come later. In that moment, she'd felt cold. Focused. He *would* obey her, whatever it took.

"It may."

"I don't know." With all those lives on the line and the others fighting monsters, no action had seemed too extreme. Anything was justified. "I don't know," she repeated, her voice cracking—a small hairline fracture, barely there at all. "He was no use to me dead. I needed him alive to get Cynna to safety."

"You—" Scott stopped, started again. "Excuse me, Rho, but I didn't know about this. If I may ask Lily for more details?" Rule nodded. "Lily, can you describe exactly what you said and did when you threatened Santos?"

She wanted to talk about almost anything else, but she did as he asked. Her voice held steady this time. When she finished, he looked *pleased*. He glanced at Rule. "I shouldn't be surprised, I suppose."

"Why not? She surprises me regularly."

"Still," Scott said, "it does complicate things."

"It does. It also gives me options. I haven't decided yet if I want them."

Lily looked at the two of them. "You realize I have no idea what you're talking about."

Rule's face was expressionless. "There are only two punishments possible for deliberate disobedience during battle: death or expulsion. I am not cruel enough to expel Santos from the clan."

Her stomach twisted. She'd expected Santos to be punished. He deserved it. But this was too much. "Santos was wrong. He was really wrong, but he was trying to do the right thing. He wasn't cowardly or traitorous. He thought he was saving me. He didn't know about the Uzi in the trunk. I did, but there wasn't time to . . ." Time to explain. Which was precisely why he'd needed to follow orders. Battle seldom offers the leisure for explanations.

"You are not obliged to consult your guards over the orders you give them."

With a jolt, Lily realized that Rule was furious. Coldly, quietly furious.

Rule went on, "Some Rhos have made exceptions to the death penalty—"

"Victor sure didn't," Scott muttered.

"—usually when the clansman had information his superior lacked, and obeying the order would have caused great harm. Santos may have believed that's what he was doing, but he had no special knowledge, only his own conclusions. He decided José was wrong, you were wrong, and he could disregard you both. That he would, in fact, be a hero for doing so."

Since that was exactly what had happened, Lily couldn't argue.

"He went on to ignore your direct order. He knows better. All of the guards know. They are to treat your word as mine. There are only two exceptions. If your order contradicts mine, they follow mine. And regardless of what you tell them, they are not to leave you unguarded."

"He might have thought that because Cynna and I were separated from them, we were unguarded."

"Santos may be a fool, but he isn't stupid. Engaging the enemy is not the same as leaving you unguarded." Rule drew a slow breath. "It's true that I have encouraged our Leidolf guards to think for themselves more than they're used to doing. This may have confused Santos, so I share some responsibility. I didn't make sure he understood the difference between initiative and disobedience."

Her stomach was churning. She'd lost two under her command today. She didn't want to add Santos to her tally. She was sick of death. "Scott said I complicated things by threatening Santos. He looked downright happy about that."

"Not about the complication." Briefly, Rule's eyes warmed, though the smile didn't make it to his mouth. "He's pleased for the same reason I am. You didn't have time to plan the best way to deal with Santos, yet you did so perfectly."

"You're glad I threatened to kill him?"

"That distresses you now."

She didn't say anything. He knew damn well it did.

"That makes no sense to my wolf, but I understand that your experience and culture tell you that such a willingness to kill is wrong. It is, however, exactly right for a lupus in that situation. You took Santos by the throat and let him know that his life was yours. Because you had a use for him—a use vital to the Lady, I should add, protecting one of her Rhejes—you spared his life. You treated him precisely as a dominant treats an erring subordinate, or one who has Challenged."

That was really weird. She'd reacted like a lupus? But she wasn't one. She was human and . . . and really confused. She shook her head and tried to set the problem aside. "How does that complicate things?"

"If your word is to be treated as mine, then your actions also speak with my authority. In effect, by choosing to use Santos rather than kill him, you rendered a partial judgment."

Half a dozen questions bubbled up in Lily's mind. She bit her lip to keep from speaking any of them, afraid that if she did, she'd tilt Rule toward the death penalty.

"But only partial," Rule said. "His life is mine—to protect when possible, to take if necessary. If José dies . . ." His face turned hard. "If that happens, I doubt I'll find much mercy in me. If José lives, I will ask for his wishes. Steve's death and his own injury give him a stake in my decision."

Would Steve be alive now, if Santos had obeyed? Maybe. All Lily could say for sure was that events would have unfolded differently, but Santos was supposed to be one hell of a fighter when he was wolf. One of the best. That was why José had set him to fight alongside Steve. If Santos had obeyed José, Lily wouldn't have been in the line of fire when José got his hands on the Uzi. How much would that have changed things?

She didn't know. Couldn't. She knew one thing, though. "I have a stake, too. And I don't want you to kill him."

Rule looked at her steadily. "So noted."

"The clan needs fighters."

"Not if they can't be trusted. Enough, Lily," he said when she opened her mouth. "Your opinion matters, but the decision is mine. I haven't made it yet, and I don't wish to discuss it further."

She wanted to keep arguing. She was so damn tired, though. Tired and sick. She closed her eyes and leaned her head back against the wall. "We'll talk about it again later."

The voice that responded wasn't the one she expected. "Rough day, huh?"

She jolted upright.

"What is it?" Rule demanded.

"Drummond," she said and sighed. "It's just Drummond."

TWENTY-EIGHT

～

"**JUST** Drummond," the slightly see-through man standing in front of her repeated. "Right. Good to see you, too."

"Like you said, it's been a rough day. Unless you're here to alert us to imminent danger—which, I might add, you didn't do with the dworg—"

"I know. I'm sorry."

He looked it, too. Regret wasn't an expression she was used to seeing on Drummond's saturnine face. "I guess I shouldn't expect you to turn into a precog just because it would be convenient." Not that precognition guaranteed anything. Even Ruben had been hunchless today.

"The gates . . . took us all by surprise."

Us meaning everyone on his side of death? "Not everyone. Hardy had some kind of warning, though by the time it reached me, it was kind of garbled."

He shrugged. "Saints are different."

"But he's getting his information from your side of things, right?"

"Yeah, but I probably can't hear what he does. See, in order to talk to you, I have to be aware of your world more or less the way you are, and when I'm like this I don't . . .

I can't . . . hell, just take my word for it, okay? While I'm working with you, I'm not in the right state to hear the, uh, the sort of beings that talk to Hardy. It's like trying to be ice and water at the same time. Doesn't work."

She struggled to follow. "Unless you're a saint?"

"Saints are different."

"What's he saying?" Rule asked.

"That unlike Hardy, he's not talking with angels."

Rule's eyebrow lifted. "This is news?"

Drummond shot Rule the finger without looking away from Lily. "Look, I need to tell you a couple things, and I don't know how long I can stay manifested. That's getting hard to do. First thing is, you've got to . . ." His mouth moved, but silently. ". . . marigolds and . . . popcorn. No time to lose."

"Wait, wait. Marigolds? Popcorn? What are you talking about?"

"Shit." He rubbed his face, glanced to one side, and said, "*This* is what I can't tell her? Jesus." After a moment he added, "No offense intended."

"You're sure polite these days."

He rolled his eyes. "You can hear me talking to . . . and can't hear me talk about . . . Great. Never mind the first thing, then. The second thing is that you've got two enemies."

"We've got more than that, but I assume you mean Friar and the Big B."

"Assume is for assholes. While you were fighting those dworg, you were also under attack spiritually. I saw it. Now, I'm not real experienced with this sort of thing, but I'm pretty sure it came from a different source."

"The Great Bitch."

"I don't think so. At least, the, uh—call it the spiritual signature—on the attack didn't look like what I saw on the monsters. Something protected you. I don't know if it was your bond with the wolfman or that ring or—"

"Which ring?"

"The one with that weird little charm on it."

The *toltoi*? Her thumb rubbed it absently. "How did it—"

"It's Cullen," someone called from the hall.

Lily was on her feet before she knew she meant to stand up. Rule was faster. He was already halfway across the room when Cullen wove inside, green scrubs covering up the jeans and T-shirt he'd arrived in. For once, he didn't look gorgeous. He looked like he needed to be admitted to this place, stat.

Rule got to him before he'd taken more than a couple of wavering steps and propped him up. Cullen frowned blearily at him. "Rule. 'M sorry. Eric didn't make it."

Rule's face went tight. "Ill news."

"Yeah. I beat the doc here?"

"You did."

Cullen nodded—and kept nodding, like a deranged bobblehead. "Cynna's with José. He's holding on. *Not* used to surgery. Bloody business. Didn't throw up, though."

Lily guessed he meant Cynna, being unused to watching an operation, had been shaken but hadn't thrown up.

"Good for her. You need to sleep."

"Yeah." Cullen ran a hand over his face. "Andy's in recovery. Renewed his spell . . . should sleep another thirty, forty minutes." He stood there, swaying, and frowned. "What was I saying?"

"That you're going to come lie down."

"Right." He swayed some more. "Cynna . . . she's got power, doesn't have healing. Not like Hannah did. Can't do much. Eating at her. You'll talk to her."

"I will. You're going to lie down now."

Cullen studied the floor in front of him. "Lie down here."

Rule picked Cullen up as if he were a child and carried him back to the small couch where he and Lily had been sitting. Cullen was asleep before he laid him down.

Rule straightened, looking down at his sleeping friend. "I'll call Isen." He said that, but he didn't take out his phone. Lily went to him and put her arm around his waist. He sighed heavily and rubbed his cheek along the top of her head. "One of the dworg had me cornered. Eric jumped it."

She knew how he felt. She knew so very well. "It doesn't

help much to know you'd have done the same for him. A little, but not much."

She felt him nod. He didn't speak.

Someone else arrived in the waiting room. She wore scrubs, too, and looked tired, though not as wrung out as Cullen. But she hadn't been fighting dworg, just the damage they'd left behind. "Mr. Turner?"

Rule's call to his father was postponed as the doctor gave Rule the bad news he'd already heard from Cullen. Then another scrubs-clad person arrived, this one male and beaming. Andy's surgeon. Dr. Alexopoulos was full of good news, questions, and amazement. He was new to Mercy General and had never operated on a lupus before. He found their ability to heal fascinating. He hoped to confer with Dr. Two Horses on the subject . . . "Oh? So sorry to hear that. Who's her surgeon? Good man, good man . . . she's recovering well, then? Ah! Didn't realize that these, ah—what did you call them? Didn't know they showed up in more than one spot . . . no complications, then? Excellent. I understand she's quite an expert on your people. Now, I have a few questions about . . ."

Rule eventually pried him off with a promise to let Nettie know he looked forward to conferring with her. Then he took out his phone and tapped the screen. "I need to get down to recovery. Andy can't wake up alone."

"I should let Casey know about Andy," Lily said. "Shall I tell him and the others about Eric?"

"Scott is. Isen," he said into his phone, "I have news."

Lily hadn't noticed Scott leaving the waiting room. Someone else was gone, too, she realized. She checked up near the ceiling. Sometimes Drummond didn't stay fully manifested, but hung around as a drift of white no one else saw.

No sign of him. He was having trouble manifesting, he'd said. But he'd made the effort because he had two things to tell her, only it turned out he couldn't say the first thing. Not intelligibly. Marigolds? She grimaced. But the other thing that mattered from his perspective was that they had a second enemy. One who'd mounted some kind of spiritual attack on Lily.

What did that even mean? Someone was trying to pull her over to the dark side? Or did he mean the kind of mind control that had affected poor Officer Crown? And God, she hadn't thought about him in hours . . . she needed to check on him.

But the attack on him had been magic-based—grimy, yucky magic that she'd touched. What had been done to her mother and the others . . . that involved spirit. Or *arguai*. Same thing, according to Cullen. Had someone been trying to wipe out her memory? Why would their enemy—or enemies—want anyone's memory wiped out? Lily scrubbed her face with both hands. *Think, damn it.* Her brain felt clouded, fogged by grief and guilt and exhaustion. Even her relief about Andy was distant. In the midst of all that dimness, a tiny little question nudged up.

Had someone wanted her to kill Santos? Tried to make that happen?

Rule squeezed her shoulder. "I need to head to recovery, Lily."

"Hmm? Oh, yes. Of course. I'll stay here and wait for news."

"You looked very far away just now, and not in a happy place."

"Trying to think. Not doing a great job of it."

"You probably need to eat." Rule sighed. "We all do. I'll have a word with Scott on my way out. I should have seen to that before. Do you have a preference?"

Rule and those lupi who'd been involved in the battle had grabbed various foodlike substances from the vending machines earlier, but Changing made them *hungry*. So did healing. Chips and peanuts were a small, temporary stopgap.

Lily, on the other hand, had no appetite whatsoever. "Whatever's easy. You go see Andy. I told you what he said, didn't I?"

A small smile touched Rule's lips. "He didn't freeze."

"Yeah. He . . ." Her phone hooted like an owl. Her eyebrows shot up. "That's Isen."

"He said he wanted a word with you." Rule brushed his lips across her cheek and headed off, trailing three of the guards.

Lily took out her phone. "Hi, Isen."

"Lily." Isen's voice was a deep, true bass. The phone didn't do it justice, but did allow the warmth through. "When we spoke earlier I was somewhat distracted, but something you said has nagged at me. You said that Cynna identified the dworg immediately. You realized she must have recognized them from the clan memories."

"Yes." Where was he going with this?

"It occurs to me that you haven't heard our stories about dworg."

"Ah . . . no. No, I haven't." Maybe that was why she'd lost twice as many men as Rule and Isen had. She didn't know how to fight dworg. Hadn't been able to fight them. Which was why she'd tried to stay out of the way of those who did, those who'd fought and bled and died . . .

"In the old days, it took ten or twelve lupi to kill one, and even with those numbers, several were always lost. We always tried to fight them in the open. We needed room to maneuver. Your men lacked room, in that parking lot. In spite of that, your casualties were amazingly low. José was quick and beautifully competent. So were you."

"Competent?" Her voice rose and cracked. "José, yes. Me? I couldn't fight them. I did nothing."

"You sent for backup before you even knew what you faced."

Which got one person killed, another badly hurt. Though it had also alerted Ackleford, who'd gone for the RPG as soon as he looked out his window . . . "It was the candy frog. Toad. Whatever. I saw that and thought about Hardy's warning."

"For which I have thanked him. Once the monsters arrived, you recognized that you couldn't personally engage with them and trusted José to do his job. You got Cynna to safety. You drew the dworg away from José so your compatriot could fire his RPG. How is it nothing, when you did all these things right?"

A huge lump rose in Lily's throat. She had to swallow twice to get rid of it. "That doesn't feel true, but thank you."

"Feelings are not always a guide to truth, and guilt is an indulgence you cannot afford. It clouds the mind. Set it aside and think. What would you do differently?"

Several impossibilities rose to mind immediately, like never leaving the house without an Uzi in her hands. She let those bubbles rise to the surface and pop, then said, "From now on, we park as close as possible. I've got the authority. I've been reluctant to abuse it, or seem to be abusing it. We had AK-47s in the trunk of the car, but it was too far away to do us any good. They don't have the stopping power of Uzis, but they would have been a damn sight better than the handguns we did have." And maybe she'd see about getting a couple of Uzis, too. Could Ruben pull some strings, make that a legal acquisition somehow?

Which reminded her—she needed to check with Karonski, see if he'd been able to keep those Uzis off the record. She had a couple of ideas about that. Her fingers twitched. Where was her notebook?

"Excellent. Remember that José and the others were not fighting your enemy, Lily. We were, all of us, fighting *our* enemy. Today that enemy struck using an ancient horror. We not only won, but won handily. They failed to achieve a single one of their objectives. Thirty-two dworg were sent against us. In the old days, that many dworg would have meant at least a hundred lupi deaths, and many times that in human casualties. They were our enemy's most feared and potent weapon. Today, thirty-two dworg managed to kill only three of us before we killed every one of them."

"Modern weaponry beats teeth and claws. Admittedly, it took major firepower to bring them down. If we hadn't had the Uzis, the story would've had a different ending."

"And somehow the Great Enemy failed to take modern weapons into account?" Isen paused for a moment, letting that sink in. "*She* spent an enormous amount of power today, power on a level she has not used against us in thousands of years. And achieved . . . nothing."

Lily opened her mouth. Closed it again. And said, "Shit. We're missing something."

"I think so, yes."

Could the dworg have been a diversion? Maybe, but you didn't use that kind of power for a distraction unless you had something even bigger planned, and nothing else had happened.

That wasn't the only thing that didn't make sense. "The Azá. Last year, *she* needed them in order to open a gate. Them and a whole lot of death magic. How come she's suddenly able to pop open four gates—bam, bam, bam, bam!—with no helpful ritual on this side? Three of them without nodes, too. We have to ask what's different now. Friar, yeah, she's got him all supercharged, but he wasn't in four places at once, opening gates. I don't think he could open even one. If Sam can't do it himself, I can't believe . . . hold on a minute. Hold on. Cynna's here."

Cynna's scrubs were pink with little bunnies on them. It made for an odd look with her tats. Her face was tired and a bit grim, but she smiled the moment she saw Lily heading for her. "José's out of surgery. He should be okay. No guarantees—I'm not Nettie, I can't check him out myself—but his surgeon has operated on lupi enough to make a guess about his recovery, and he thinks José will make it. Oh, and I saw Rule in with Andy. I told him about José."

This time the relief hit hard and immediately. Lily's eyes filmed with tears. "Thank God. Are you . . . you look tired, but okay. Cullen got up here and crashed."

"He was still so drained after his stint with Sam—he damn near burned himself out just using sleep spells. Where . . . oh, there he is." She moved around Lily and crouched beside her soundly sleeping husband. She watched him a moment, stroked his hair, and whispered something Lily didn't catch. Then she stood and looked at Lily. There was a lot more grim in her expression now, along with a healthy dollop of determined. "Just before the shit hit the fan, I got a decent pattern for your murder victim. I am by damn going to Find whatever I can with that pattern. I'm headed outside now to do that. You with me?"

Oh, shit, was this a good idea? Cynna was a target, and just because—

Drummond popped into being in front of Lily, his face clear, the rest of him fuzzy and indeterminate. "That's it! That's the first thing I wanted to tell you, but couldn't. She needs to do that. You need to go, both of you. And hurry."

TWENTY-NINE

❧

CYNNA could not be talked out of it. Admittedly, Lily didn't try very hard, not with Drummond cheerleading the idea from his side, but Rule did. He was hampered by having to make his case over the phone, since he had to stay with Andy and José until they could be taken home. Cynna told him he'd have to cope, because she was damn well going to finish what she'd started before it rained down dworg on their heads.

"I don't think the dworg were sent on my account," Cynna told Lily as she sat down on a wide strip of grass next to the hospital's parking lot. She untied one shoe. "*She* didn't go to all that trouble just to keep me from Finding your victim's home or whatever. But maybe that was part of the timing. And even if it wasn't"—she took that shoe and sock off and started on the other one—"I'm going to do this."

Lily suspected Cynna was hell-bent on doing her Find because she *could*. This was what she did, what she was good at, and there'd been little she could do for their wounded. Reason enough to follow through, Lily thought, if Cynna hadn't been Rhej. She was, though, which raised the stakes considerably. For that reason and a couple of others, Lily would stick with her. No point in dividing up their guards.

Those guards stood in a circle around them now, facing out. Once Cynna had removed her shoes and socks she stood, her stance wide, knees flexed, arms overhead. Her Gift didn't need anything but her attention to work, but for a tricky Find she sometimes boosted her focus with a sort of barefoot drumming dance. That was what she was doing now.

Slowly she began to stamp the earth with her bare feet. The rhythm picked up as she turned in a slow circle, her hands weaving invisible patterns, her arms gradually descending as her feet punched the ground faster and faster. Her dance paused twice before she stopped, her arms straight out in front of her. She nodded once, satisfied. "Got it."

"LEFT at the light," Cynna said. The words came out a little muffled because her mouth was full of mozzarella, crust, and sauce.

They weren't in the tankmobile, though it hadn't been damaged by the dworg. The shiny paint had gotten a few scratches—maybe when the RPG went off, maybe from the claws of a scrambling wolf—but the car was operational, unlike several others. But none of the vehicles could be handed back to their users yet. CSI was still vacuuming. That wasn't as pointless as it seemed. No one expected to find anything pertinent, but, as Karonski had put it, they didn't want to feed the conspiracy nuts by stinting on the usual procedures.

In the end, Rule had accepted that Cynna was going to do this. So he'd rented them an armored limousine.

That had meant a delay, but a brief one. Just the right amount of time, it turned out, for the pizza Scott had ordered to arrive. That was good, because two of their guards were among those who'd fought dworg that day. They needed the fuel.

Cynna and Lily had the limo's rear seat. They were sharing a large pizza with pepperoni and extra bell pepper. Mike, Miles, and Jonathan sat across from them. Each of them had his own box, as did Casey and Scott up front. Casey was driving.

Lily wasn't hungry, but she'd taken a slice knowing that it might be hours before she had time for supper. Then she bit into it and was suddenly ravenous. That first piece was gone now, as was the second, and she was finishing her third. She glanced out her window. They were on Market Street, passing Mount Hope, the cemetery where the first person she'd killed was buried. "We getting close?" she asked Cynna.

"Still a little over ten miles."

That should be enough time. Lily washed down the last bite with Diet Coke. "I've got a question."

Cynna was eyeing the box, where one last slice remained. "Go ahead. You want the last piece?"

"I'm full. It's a couple of questions, actually. The first one's for you as Rhej."

Cynna's eyebrows went up. She took the last slice. "Okay."

"It seems as if all of the Great Bitch's agents we've run across have been psychopaths. We're known by the company we keep, right? I can't help wondering if the Big B is literally crazy."

"Well, sure!"

Lily blinked. "Then she is a psychopath?"

"Oh, no, I don't think so. I think that's a purely human malfunction, and whatever else *she* is, she's a lot more than human. I wouldn't be surprised to learn that exposure to her causes psychopathy, though. Why do you ask?"

"Because what happened today doesn't make sense. Unless she's really around-the-bend nuts, not operating logically—"

"That's not her kind of crazy."

"What kind of crazy is she, then?"

"Um . . . she's not human, so I guess I'd say she's crazy the way her peer group defines insanity."

Her peer group being other Old Ones? "Can you narrow that down for me?"

Cynna glanced at the three men facing them. "Most of the stories are shared with all the clan, but the thing you want to know is from the *primus memorias*. First Memories. First Memories are from when lupi were created, and they're shared only with lupi, and they're spoken while the Rhej is touching the memory itself, in order to keep the telling as close to the original as possible. Can't do that perfectly because the language they're in is hard to translate, but we do our best. But it's considered safest to touch or enter those memories only at Clanhome."

"So you can't—"

Cynna flapped a hand. "Let me think this through." She did that, frowning. Then nodded. "You're Lady-touched, so it's okay for you to know the *primus memorias*, but I don't want to tell them without touching them. I'd be paraphrasing, and it's okay for others to do that, but not me. But the guys can talk about them." She looked at the three men facing them. "Someone want to tell Lily what the Lady told Aswan about the gods going insane?"

For a long moment, no one did. Miles and Jonathan exchanged an uncomfortable glance. Oddly, it was Mike who finally spoke . . . odd because he was Leidolf, so Cynna wasn't his Rhej, and Mike was not exactly a shining example of liberated thinking.

"I'm not going to say this right," he warned, "but here's what I remember. The Lady was talking about why we aren't ever to worship her. She said that it's normal for the new races to worship those like her, who'd stayed on from the last cycle to help with this one. Like when a baby thinks his mother's breast is the whole world, see? But that time ends. When he becomes a toddler he learns the word 'no' and can't stop using it, and the older he gets, the more he becomes his own person. Only something went wrong this time. I didn't understand, but somehow the godhead got sticky. It stuck to them when it wasn't supposed to, and that was wrong. It would keep the younger races from knowing themselves fully, which is how God comes to know Himself—"

"Herself," Scott put in.

"The universe," Miles said. "The way I heard it, it's how the universe comes to know itself. Through everything it creates, but especially the sentient races."

"You're all mostly right," Cynna said. "The word from the memories doesn't have an English translation, so your Rhejes would have used whatever felt closest. That could be 'God' or 'the universe' or even just 'life.'"

Mike nodded, accepting that. "There was a big argument. Some of the Old Ones thought the sticky godhead must be the way God—or the universe, or whatever you call it—wanted to know Himself this time around. They thought it would be terrible and wrong to abandon their power and leave the new races without help and guidance. But most of them didn't think like that. The new gods didn't have that stickiness, and—"

"New gods?" Lily asked, then wished she hadn't interrupted.

Scott answered that from up front. "Gods who weren't Old Ones."

"Like the Native American gods?" Nettie had said something about that once.

Jonathan nodded. "They weren't as powerful as the old gods. Maybe that's why they remained more like counselors and elders, worshiped but . . . differently. That's not something the Lady said," he added quickly. "That's just me thinking about it."

Mike picked up his thread again. "So the Lady and most of those like her stepped back from their godheads. It's not just that they renounced being worshiped, though that's part of it. They, uh . . . this part I don't remember very well."

"I do," Miles said suddenly. "'And so we sundered ourselves from the being and power of gods. Reft and bereft, we grew smaller and more vast, and slowly returned to ourselves. In our return, we saw that we had started to slip toward madness, and we looked at those who had not renounced godhead. We watched them, and we saw that they were insane.' "

"Right," Mike said. "You've got a good memory. So that's why we don't worship the Lady. It would be the opposite of serving her because it would harm her."

"You need to go left at the intersection," Cynna told Scott, then glanced at Lily. "Does that help?"

"Some. Sort of." There was one hell of a lot of information in those few passages, but most of it didn't apply to the immediate question, as far as Lily could tell. "It doesn't tell me what kind of crazy *she* is."

"The kind that thinks they have all the answers," Miles said. "That's in another one of the First Memories, but it's still the Lady talking to Aswan. Aswan was the first Rhej," he added, in case Lily didn't know that. "The Lady was explaining about submission and how we need to understand it because the crazy gods didn't. It went something like this: 'The unsundered gods, in their insanity, forgot surrender; they submit only to what they already know and confuse will with purpose. And so each is certain that her or his aspect encompasses all wisdom, with all others being lesser, or distortions, or lies.' "

Mike frowned. "Did she say wisdom, or truth? Or maybe I'm thinking about what she said about rainbows."

This time it was Scott who quoted quietly. " 'Which color of the rainbow is the most true? Is red more true than green? Is blue the best path to understanding, and should you therefore outlaw yellow cloth and purple vases and the soft blushing sky awakening to day?' "

"Yeah, that bit. She was talking about how the clans are to respect each other, but it applies to lots of other stuff." He paused, glancing at Miles sitting beside him. "I guess we haven't always done a great job at respecting each other."

Everyone got quiet. Nokolai and Leidolf were prime

examples of clans not respecting each other. Lily decided to return to her question. "So you're saying that the Great Bitch is the kind of crazy that doesn't tolerate disagreement. My way or the highway." This wasn't exactly news.

"Pretty much," Cynna agreed. "The interesting thing is that the other Old Ones considered that insane."

Lily's eyebrows shot up. "It is interesting, isn't it? In a weird and startling way." It also didn't seem to help much. "If the Big B is acting rationally, however screwed up she may be, then she had a purpose for what she did today. Only I don't see it. Sure, she'd like to wipe out Nokolai, but she didn't. She didn't even come close, however tight things seemed at the time. And she used an awful lot of power trying. And how come she can open gates that way all of a sudden? Last year she couldn't."

"Slow down, Scott," Cynna said suddenly. "It's just ahead on the right." She frowned at Lily. "What are you saying?"

"Drummond thinks we have a second enemy. At least," she corrected herself, "he thinks I do. He, uh, saw some kind of spiritual attack directed against me while we were fighting the dworg."

"Shit. That's not good."

"It's sort of what my other question was about." More than one question, really, but with the guards here she wasn't sure how to bring up the second one.

"Ask quick. We're nearly there."

"He thought that either the *toltoi* protected me or the mate bond. So I wondered . . . does the bond have some kind of spiritual component that could do that?"

"Yes."

"That was a quick answer."

"I should qualify that. The mate bond is a magical construct similar to an artifact, but it's, ah . . . how do I put this? It's fashioned around a spiritual component instead of a material one. I don't know what kind of spiritual attack he saw—"

"He didn't tell me, and I haven't been able to get him to show up again. He's having trouble manifesting."

"Hmm. I think—I don't know, mind—but I think the bond might be able to protect you from direct attack, like if something tried to take you over. I'm not sure it could help with the kind of spiritual interference that doesn't rob you of choice, the sort the Church calls temptation."

Lily had wanted to kill Santos. She hadn't done it, but she'd been tempted, and it hadn't been moral reasons that held her back. He'd been trying to rescue her at the time, however mistakenly. Did that mean—

"Stop," Cynna said. But she wasn't talking to Lily now. "We're there."

THE man who'd been staked to the ground and ritually murdered had lived in a brick-veneer ranch-style house in Alta Vista—a nice enough neighborhood, the kind where vacations were more likely to be Motel 6 or camping than anything involving airfare, but most of the time most of the people here could take a vacation. Like much of the city, Alta Vista had been hit hard by the foreclosure crisis, but it was beginning to come around. Not as many For Sale signs dotted the streets, nor were there many walkaways standing empty and forlorn.

This house hadn't been abandoned. Someone had added a pricey metal roof in the last five years, and the landscaping was well tended, if uninspired. A wide driveway leading to the two-car garage left little room for the yard, which was all grass except for the kind of foundation plantings beloved by builders fifty years ago. The grass had been cut recently and looked like it got watered as often as the city allowed. "Anything?" she asked Mike, whom she'd sent to peer in the high window in the garage door.

"No car, if that's what you mean."

She nodded. "Head around back, keep an eye on that door." There was a fence, but that wouldn't slow him down.

No toys on the lawn or the drive, Lily noted as she headed for the small front porch. No potted plants or lawn ornaments, either. The porch's only decoration was a slumped sack of fertilizer topped by a pair of dirty gardening gloves. The welcome mat provided the single note of whimsy. "Hop In!" it said in bold black letters surrounding a cheerful green frog.

She rang the doorbell.

"If anyone was here, wouldn't they have reported your guy missing?" Cynna asked.

"You'd think so." Lily rang again, to be sure. It wouldn't be hard to get a search warrant, but it would take time, and—

"Lily!" Mike came loping from the side of the house. "Something's wrong. There's a window cracked open around back. I couldn't see in because of the blinds, but I could smell it. Piss and shit and sickness. Not death—I didn't smell decay, and I heard breathing. Someone's in there, and it's bad."

Lily hammered on the door with her fist. "Police! Open up! We have reason to think someone inside is injured or ill, and will break in if you don't open the door!" She let two heartbeats pass, then said to Scott, "Get me in."

Scott stepped back two paces, eyed the door—solid core with a dead bolt—and said, "Mike! Get in through that open window and let us in."

Mike spun and raced back around the house. A moment later she heard glass break. Apparently Mike hadn't been able to just push the window up. She drew her weapon. Her heart pounded. She waited, waited . . . heard feet running on carpet, coming near. The click of the dead bolt being turned.

The door swung open. "She's in bad shape," Mike said. "No sign of anyone else inside."

Lily decided to trust his senses and holstered her gun. She ran after him, gathering quick impressions—a small, neat living room flooded with light from the picture window, a darker hallway with four doors, where the sewer stench that had alerted Mike grew thick in her nostrils.

Mike turned into the second doorway on the left. She followed.

It looked like a little girl's room, all pink and white, with stuffed animals on the shelves and a frilly bedspread on the double bed. But the woman lying in that bed, stinking of urine and feces, must have been at least twenty. Her hair was dusty brown and braided in twin plaits. Her eyes were closed. She lay on her back with her mouth open, one arm limply cradling a bedraggled stuffed dog, and she looked more dead than alive. She had the small chin, the broad, flat face, and the flattened nose of Down syndrome.

THIRTY

~

DRUMMOND came to slowly. He was lying down . . . in bed. Yeah. He was in a bed, and he felt like hell—sick and woozy. A lot like he had that time he got concussed. That wasn't the worst of it, though. His arm hurt like a mother. He'd taken a chance . . .

A foolish risk, someone had told him. *Very brave, but foolish.*

Yeah, that's right. She'd told him that while she was patching him up. Had it been her who snatched him, pulled him away before—

He shuddered. He'd known that damn knife worked on both sides. He hadn't understood what that meant. He'd been trying to . . .

He couldn't remember.

This wasn't the kind of forgetting he did about stuff that was too separate from the mortal world to bring with him when he was working here. This was cold and stark and terrifying.

Because the knife was wielded only on this side, it did no harm to who and what you are. You have lost some memories of your actions on this side, but your sense of self remains strong. The damage to your function is more of a problem.

To his function? Drummond shook his head, trying to shake himself awake. That was one of the shitty things about this side. No coffee. He sat up and looked around.

He was in Lily Yu's bedroom, in her bed. Hers and that Turner guy's. He'd been to her place a couple of times, so he recognized it, but that didn't explain why he'd woken up in her bed. He didn't need a bed to sleep. Right after he died, when he'd been so screwed up, he hadn't known how to rest without the trappings he was used to—beds, chairs, whatever. Not anymore, though. Now he just sort of slid sideways into whatever struck him as a restful spot—a tree, a drop of water . . .

A tree? A drop of water? What the fuck?

But that was what he'd been doing. He remembered it, but now it struck him as straight out of Bizarro World. He started to rub his face and hissed in pain.

His right arm *hurt*.

It was in a sling, but he could see the bloody bandage wrapped around his biceps. Not that it was really blood, or a sling, or a bandage. Not really an arm, for that matter. But he knew arms and blood and bandages, so that was how he saw and felt it, was maybe why he'd woken up in bed. When you were hurt, you rested in a bed, so some part of him must have dragged him here.

That was . . . that was good, actually. At least he remembered that much about how things worked. What else?

He spent a few minutes sorting through his memories of the time since he died. He couldn't find anything missing except for what he'd been doing when he got into a fight with someone who held an ancient artifact. Someone on *this* side. He was sure of that. Someone on this side had taken possession of the spirit side of that damn knife, and he'd . . .

That part was gone. Wiped out. No, cut out. Drummond grimaced.

Another memory rose, this one very recent. He'd been

injured on the job. They wanted him to take medical leave. That wasn't how they put it, maybe, but that was what he understood. Medical leave meant going home to Sarah . . . a pang of longing shot through him. He missed her. Missed her a lot. He looked at his left hand, where her ring . . .

The ring was gone. The glowing gold ring that had followed him into death, that tied him to Sarah. His hand was bare.

"Nooo," he moaned. The ring couldn't be gone. It couldn't.

It's part of what was removed, a gentle voice said. *Keep to your path, and all will be restored.*

His path? What the hell did that mean? Drummond scrubbed his face and found it wet. But . . . apparently he wasn't alone. He didn't see anyone that voice might belong to, but it was familiar. He knew it. Trusted it.

Keep to his path. Right. He remembered a little more. He'd turned down the medical leave. They didn't have anyone else with his skill set available. They couldn't have replaced him, so he'd opted to stay on the job, but there was a problem. He'd lost function in some way, yeah. And the ring. The ring was gone, and that hurt all the way down, but he'd also lost memory. Not much, but any loss sort of loosened his connection to other memories. He was going to default more to his in-body ways and find the in-spirit stuff a bit slippery.

Like wanting a bed for rest instead of a leaf or whatever. Grimacing, he got out of the bed he didn't need but thought he did. Better see what was going on. He felt sure he'd been drawn here for a reason.

It was pitch-black in this room, but that didn't bother him. He didn't see the way he used to, and whatever was wrong with his functioning, his spirit eyes worked fine. When he got to the door, though, he automatically tried to open it.

Stupid. At least he'd reached out with his left arm, not the right. He rolled his eyes at himself and passed through it. On the other side, he saw Turner sitting in the living space, stropping a wicked-looking knife. Drummond had never been one for knives, but cleaning his weapon used to soothe him sometimes, and Mr. Wolf Man looked like he could use some soothing. His face was stony, but his spirit was all agitated. No surprise, after everything that had happened lately.

Must be late. No one else seemed to be up. He'd check on them, he decided, and did so, passing through walls and doors with no problem. Yeah, all asleep, and they all seemed fine, though Julia was having some kind of bad dream. He watched her a minute, but he didn't see any kind of outside influence, and regular nightmares weren't his job. He wasn't clear enough to help with those.

Lily Yu wasn't here. That bothered him. He'd figured he'd been drawn here because she was, but she was gone, and everyone but Turner was asleep.

Maybe he'd better have another look at Turner. And that big knife.

This time he took as long as he had with Julia, checking all over. And this time he saw it and cursed himself for having missed it before. It was small, yeah, thin as a thread, but once he'd spotted it, it was damn obvious, starkly black against the man's shiny soul-stuff. It slid around in all that turbulence, somehow anchored in Turner's spirit without being static. It kept dodging out of the way of the other thing hooked into the man, that glowing white cord they called the mate bond.

Drummond watched for a minute. It didn't look like the bond was going to block this slimy bit of interference. Someone was trying a different technique, maybe, or else it was Turner's own turbulence that let the black thing keep moving away from the bond.

Now what? He wanted to grab hold of the nasty thing and yank it out, but he knew better. There were those who could touch filth without it sticking to them, but he sure as hell wasn't that pure. And he couldn't tell Turner he was under spiritual attack. He needed Lily to do that, but she wasn't here.

Hell. Only one thing to try.

Drummond zipped into one of the bedrooms. Two women slept there. One was small and wrinkled and sound asleep—and ablaze to his spirit eyes. The other was just as deeply asleep. Her glow was also beautiful, but in a different way. Clear, clear, all the way down she was clear. Every time he saw her, he wanted to slow down, to just look at that quiet glow awhile . . . no time for that.

Drummond crouched next to her side of the bed and tried to settle his mind. He wouldn't actually enter her dream. That would take too long. But she'd given permission for him to contact her this way, if only he could remember how . . . oh, yeah.

He reached out his left hand and touched her spirit in the spot some called the third eye, right over the center of her forehead. "Li Qin, I'm, uh, I'm sorry to intrude, but I need your help. I need you to wake up and go stop Turner. He's about to make a big mistake, but it's not really him. Not just him. Something's influencing him. Don't let him leave until Lily gets here. Please, if you can hear me . . ." He said it all again, but she wasn't stirring, wasn't opening her eyes. He must be doing something wrong. Or maybe she could hear him, but wasn't able to wake up. Why hadn't he thought of that?

Turner's phone chimed in the other room. He cursed and zipped back there. Turner had set down the big knife to pick up his phone. "Yes?"

"Lily turned in off the highway," a voice on the other end said.

"Thank you." Turner glanced toward the TV—no, at the DVD, where the time showed. Twenty minutes past midnight. "It's later than I thought. I'm leaving now. Assemble the others, and remind Barnaby to give her my message."

"Will do."

Turner put down his phone, stood, and slid the knife into a sheath fastened to his belt. He was wearing jeans. No shirt, no shoes. His spirit was still all stirred up. Was that nasty black thread thicker?

It was. Shit. That meant the influence had gained ground,

probably because he'd made up his mind, and in the wrong direction. He hadn't acted yet, so there was still time—but time to do what, exactly?

One of the bedroom doors opened and Li Qin limped out, using her crutches.

Turner's eyebrows flew up in surprise. "Is everything all right?"

"I am not sure. I had a dream."

"A bad dream?"

"An important one, I think, though I remember little of it."

Turner looked puzzled. "Can I get you something? Some water or juice?"

"I would appreciate a glass of juice. Thank you." She sighed as she reached the closest chair and set her crutches aside, then lowered herself carefully. "Where is Lily?"

"She'll be home any minute. Is orange juice all right?"

"That would be lovely."

Turner knelt in front of the minifridge where they kept cold drinks. He took out a bottle of orange juice, grabbed a paper cup from the stack on top of the fridge, and filled it. "I'm afraid I can't keep you company right now. There is clan business I need to take care of right away." Three steps took him to the plain, middle-aged woman whose soul was starlight and water. He held out the cup.

"Thank you." She took the cup, but didn't drink. He started to turn away. "Rule. I have a request."

He paused, clearly impatient. "This is not a good time."

"Perhaps you could wait for Lily to arrive before you leave for this clan business."

His brows pulled down. "That isn't practical, I'm afraid."

"Rule." She leaned forward. "I have not asked a favor of you before."

The frown was a twitch away from a scowl, but he didn't hightail it the way he clearly wanted to. "You haven't, no."

"I am asking now. Please wait for Lily. I feel it is very important."

"I would honor your request if I could, but this is clan

business." He spoke courteously, but the unspoken ending was clear: *and none of yours*.

"Is this something you need to conceal from Lily?"

"I'm not concealing anything. She will have to know, but it will be easier on her if . . ." He stopped. His head turned. He sighed. "It looks like you're getting your wish, unless I want to bail out the window. Lily just pulled up out front."

Li Qin's smile spread soft and slow. "I am so glad."

Turner clearly was not. Drummond wanted to high-five Li Qin. "Damn good job," he told her, knowing she couldn't hear him.

Turner gave Li Qin a brusque nod and headed for the stairs. Drummond followed him.

The first floor was a wide-open construction zone. Not a single wall in the whole space, though some were framed in. There were tarps, tools, lumber, sawhorses, a pile of drywall, spools of electrical wire, conduits, and what he thought was a wet saw. A single overhead light left plenty of room for shadows.

Lily came in just as Turner reached the bottom of the stairs. Drummond zipped over to her and manifested so he—

Oh, shit, goddammit, that hurt! He was panting from the pain—pain in his arm, which made no damn sense. What did an arm have to do with it? And he hadn't come close to bringing himself far enough into her world for her to hear him. She might be able to see him if she tried. He had to be a tiny bit into her world to see and hear things, but at this low a level, he'd be so diffuse she could easily miss him.

And what good would it do for her to know he was here if he couldn't talk to her? Cursing, Drummond withdrew slightly.

Her attention was all for Turner, anyway. "Barnaby said you'd left to deal with clan business."

"I was delayed. I'm headed for the barracks now."

She stopped a few feet away from Turner and looked him over. Maybe her gaze lingered a moment on the sheathed knife. "What kind of clan business?"

Turner didn't answer right away. He had a stone face as good as old Montgomery's—a supervisor who'd scared the crap out of Drummond when he was a wet-behind-the-ears agent. "Santos."

"You've decided to kill him."

"It's necessary."

"Is it?" She studied him a moment. "Okay. Let's go."

That shook the stone right off his face. "There's no need for you to see this."

"When I first became Nokolai, I read a lot of stories. Histories and stuff. I got the idea that it's traditional for all clan who are nearby to attend an execution like this."

"You're Nokolai. This is a Leidolf matter."

She snorted. "Talk about a mental block. I thought being your mate made me clan, with or without one of those *gens* ceremonies. If you're Leidolf as well as Nokolai, then so am I."

Turner's mouth opened. Closed. Finally he murmured, "Clearly, I hadn't thought things through. You're right, of course, and at some point Leidolf needs to hold a *gens salvere iubeo* to welcome you. But tonight—"

"I'm going with you."

If Turner's spirit had been agitated before, it was in the spin cycle now. His voice was low and pained. "Why are you doing this?"

"If you were heart-sure this was the right thing to do, would it bother you this much for me to see it?"

"Right is a damn blurry standard to spot in the middle of a war," he said bitterly. "Necessity is an easier mark."

"Is killing Santos necessary?"

Drummond expected Turner to trot out whatever arguments he'd been making to himself while he stropped that knife. Instead he was silent for several long moments . . . and suddenly, for no reason Drummond could figure, his spirit calmed. His mouth quirked up and he reached for Lily and held her tight. "How is it that you never run out of questions?"

"Practice."

Hallelujah. Drummond started looking for that damn thread. He couldn't find it. Of course, he couldn't see through Lily, but he was pretty sure the nasty thing was gone. Had Turner banished it himself by getting his thinking straight? Or had the mate bond finally caught up with it? He should've been watching it. He'd forgotten to, caught up in the moment . . . distracted by the embodied world when he should've been keeping his eye on spirit stuff. Now he didn't know any more than he had before about how to defeat that kind of spiritual attack.

"I'd convinced myself it was necessary," Turner said, low voiced, "though I no longer wanted his death. My anger had turned to ash, but it seemed like weakness to allow him to live simply because I felt such distaste for killing him. Now it seems as if I've spent hours pacing the same rutted circle without noticing that it took me nowhere."

"Mmm." She nuzzled him, then pulled away slightly. "What did José say when you asked for his preferences?"

"In the politest way possible, he let me know it was my decision and he didn't care to have it pushed off on him."

"Well, then."

"Yes." He sighed and straightened. "Though it's a risky sort of mercy I'll be showing."

"What will you do?" Lily asked.

"He'll be shunned for a full week."

"That's the maximum, isn't it?"

He nodded. "He may be wishing I'd just killed him before the week's up. Shunning is . . . difficult for us. Do you still mean to accompany me? They're waiting for me."

The two of them headed for the door together. Drummond hurried ahead so he could check Turner again. The black thread was definitely gone.

"Shunning is harsh," Lily said, "but it's got to be better than dying."

Turner opened the door. "It will be hard on everyone, not just Santos. Including you. If you see him collapsed on the ground and sobbing, you'll have to behave as if he isn't there. Will you be able to . . ."

The door closed on the rest of what Turner was saying. Drummond could figure it out, though. Maybe shunning was harsh, but it wasn't going to give that nastiness a hold on Turner. That was what counted. He'd done the job. Enough of it, anyway—the part that he could do.

The glow of satisfaction faded. He ran his thumb over the bare finger where a ring should be. How was he going to be any damn use if he couldn't contact Lily? He frowned at his arm and gingerly flexed the muscle. Winced. It sure as hell felt as if someone had sliced through the muscle with a knife. But knife wounds heal. Maybe this would, too.

Of course it would, he told himself. But would it heal in time?

No way of knowing, and he was suddenly exhausted. That was how it went when you were injured. You ran out of oomph. That empty bed upstairs sure sounded good, but Turner and Lily would be back, and even though they'd never know it if they climbed into it with him, he would.

There was a big, oversize chair up there, too. He could sack out in it for a while. He'd figure out something about how to communicate, he thought as he drifted up. Tomorrow.

THIRTY-ONE

EIGHTEEN hours later, they knew a lot about the man who'd been staked to the ground and killed . . . and more about their amnesia victims, too. He'd been the key, all right. Plug his life into the puzzle and a picture finally began to take shape.

Alan Debrett had been fifty-seven years old when he was killed. He'd grown up in San Diego, attending Hoover High followed by a semester at a now-defunct community college. Apparently the academic life wasn't for him; he'd dropped out to join the Marines. After a stint there he'd gone to work at Achilles, a firm that made custom pipe fittings. He worked at Achilles for twenty-eight years, the last ten in management. He'd lived in the same house for twenty-five of those years.

Alan had been thin on family. An only child, he'd lost his father when he was forty-two. His mother was in a nursing home with advanced Alzheimer's and his wife died five years ago. He was survived only by two cousins—one in Denver, one now living in Belize—and by his aunt and uncle.

And by his daughter, Mary.

Mary Debrett was twenty-seven years old. She had a thyroid condition, a heart condition, an IQ of 30, and many friends, both in her neighborhood and at the training center where she went once a week. She remained in ICU in a deep coma.

None of Alan's coworkers remembered him.

One was among the amnesia victims. Upon closer questioning, several more coworkers reported gaps in their memories. A few of them had been concealing this out of fear—no one wants to think they're losing it. Others had simply not been aware of the gaps. Yes, they knew someone used to work in that office. Couldn't think of his name right now. Was it a he? Might have been a woman. Odd, now that you mention it, but they simply didn't remember.

None of Alan's neighbors remembered him.

The couple on one side had only lived there for four months and said they didn't know any of their neighbors; the family on the other side was out of town. The SDPD was tracking them down. But several of the others remembered Mary and a few recalled Alan's deceased wife, but not Alan. The house across the street belonged to his aunt and uncle, who were in their seventies. They'd been in bad shape when the officers knocked on their door. Both were in the hospital now, suffering from dehydration and severe disorientation. Questioning them was difficult, but it was obvious neither remembered their nephew . . . or large parts of the last fifty-seven years.

None of Lily's family remembered Alan Debrett, either. But she did.

Not his last name, nor had she ever met him or seen a photo of him . . . at least she didn't think so. But her mother had once talked about her high school boyfriend, Alan, when trying to impress upon a teenage Lily the need to date nice Chinese boys.

Alan hadn't been Chinese. Julia's father had been furious when he found out. He and her aunt had forbidden the relationship—with little success, Julia had admitted. She and Alan had gone steady for nearly two years, using any number of subterfuges she had refused to divulge to her curious daughter. His parents hadn't approved, either. "In the end," Julia had said, her lips tight with remembered anger or pain, "Alan came to agree with them." And that was all she'd been willing to say on the subject.

Shortly after seven o'clock on the night after she found Mary, Lily was at her new home, which was currently a bit crowded. In another half hour they needed to leave for Isen's house. Karonski wanted everyone to meet there for a combination briefing and brainstorming. But for now, for once, for just the next thirty minutes, Lily wasn't doing a damn thing.

They'd turned the TV off. Someone in the insurance building on the east side of the parking lot had gotten video of almost the entire battle with the dworg. Lily had watched it all the way through online, which may have been a mistake. She didn't want to see it again, but all the news programs kept showing snippets from it. No TV news for her for a while.

Music was better, anyway. Yo-Yo Ma was making love to his cello at the moment, and Lily was curled up in the chair-and-a-half that had been her total seating in her old apartment. Their current living area was composed of the original second-floor landing plus one of the tiny bedrooms with one wall removed. There wasn't much room for a couch, but her old chair fit nicely.

Most of her sat in the chair, anyway. Her legs were draped across Rule's lap. "I was so curious about my mother's big youthful rebellion," she said softly. "I didn't think she'd rebelled at all, you see."

"Mmm." He combed her hair with his fingers. "She wouldn't tell you more than that?"

"No, so I asked my father about Alan. I was sure he'd know. It didn't occur to me she might not have told him about an old boyfriend . . . these days, cynic that I am, I'd probably assume every married couple had secrets, but it turned out I was right to think she'd told him about Alan. He knew who I meant, but he pretended to think I was trying to shop for a different dad. Teasing me, you know, in that dry, straight-faced way he has. When I pushed—I was pushy back then, too—he said something about letting the past stay in the past."

"Bah," Grandmother said.

Lily paused to see if that was addressed to her. Grandmother, Li Qin, Toby, and Julia were playing mah-jongg in the "office"—the room with the dining table. Grandmother had brought her mah-jongg set with her. Not the good one, which was over two hundred years old, but her everyday tiles. In spite of that "bah," Grandmother was undoubtedly winning. She always did, and she didn't believe in cutting any slack based on trivialities like age or experience.

When no further comments came, Lily went on. "So when I saw his name on the papers in his home office, I felt this little tug, as if I ought to know who he was. The memory didn't float up to the top of my mind until we found his high school yearbook, though. There was a picture of him with my mother, and bam! I remembered that whole conversation. It had left so many questions unanswered—that's why it stuck, I think." She looked at Rule. "Only I shouldn't have remembered, should I?"

"Something protected you from the memory loss others suffered." He was winding one strand of her hair around his finger. "Whether it was the *toltoi* or the mate bond, clearly something kept your memory from being damaged."

"Probably the mate bond." Lily wanted her mysterious protection to be the mate bond. If it could protect her, it ought to protect Rule, too.

"We don't know enough to say for sure. Whichever it was, I'm very glad you have it."

Trying to get Rule to agree with her wouldn't make it so . . . but she wished he had. "I wish Drummond would show up again. And that's something I never expected to say."

"No sign of him?"

She shook her head and shoved her hair back from her face. And winced. She'd taken the elastic bandage off her wrist after supper to let it breathe, but maybe that had been a mistake. It was pretty tender still. "What would you do if I cut my hair?"

His eyebrows went up. "Do you want to?"

"Thinking about it. I don't usually let it get this long. It takes forever to blow it dry these days." And when she was one-handed, doing anything with her hair was a bitch. Rule had washed it for her that morning.

"It's your hair, so it's your choice."

"The way you're always playing with it, I thought you might go into shock or something."

He smiled. "I think I could cope if there were less hair to play with. As long as you don't decide to shave your head."

"Not going quite that far. Maybe I'll wait until after the wedding, though." Her mother had been happy Lily had let her hair grow out, thinking she'd done it for the wedding. Mostly Lily just hadn't had time to mess with it.

That reminded her. "I meant to tell you earlier. My father called this afternoon."

"Did he?"

"At first he wanted to know about the wedding, if we'd postponed it. But then . . . he's sorry he said that about not wanting to hear from me. He . . ." Tears stung, making her feel foolish because this was good news. "He said cutting himself off from me was both wrong and stupid. It was like he'd had his foot amputated and decided to blame his hand for that and cut it off, too."

Rule pressed a kiss to her hair. "Like I said, he's a good man. What did you—"

"Did not!" Toby cried, indignant.

"Did so!" That was Julia, very loud. "You're always bragging—'my dad *this*, my dad *that*, my dad is soooo wonderful'—"

"I just said you didn't need to be all scared because Dad is here, and it's true! He killed the dworg and kept us safe and—"

"What do you know? You're just a stupid little kid!" Julia's voice rose to shrill, but Lily could hear the tears in it. "Too stupid to be scared when there are monsters that want to *eat* us! They wanted to eat us!"

"But Dad didn't let them."

Julia shrieked in rage. A chair scraped, then clattered.

"Julia," Grandmother said crisply. "Pick up your chair."

"No!"

Julia came racing out of the room. She jerked to a stop when she saw Lily and Rule. Her face flooded with a mixture of loathing and longing, then crumpled as she spun and headed for the stairs, thudding down barefoot.

Lily shoved herself out of Rule's lap.

"I'll go," he said, standing.

Grandmother stood in the door to the office. She shook her head. "A bad idea. She will either kiss you or hit you, and either way she will feel worse."

"How come everyone's worried about her feelings," Toby said, "when I'm the one who got called names?"

Grandmother sniffed. "And your feelings are so hurt, are they?"

"Well, no, but . . ."

"Then perhaps this is not about you."

Rule's phone picked that moment to chime. It was his father's ring tone.

"Take your call," Lily said. "I think I know what this is about." Not Toby, and not monsters. Not exactly.

Lily found Julia sitting on the front porch, her arms curled tightly around her legs. She didn't look up when Lily stepped out.

Lily closed the front door, letting darkness wrap itself around them. "One of these days, this porch is going to have furniture." A porch light, too. Also floodlights, but those would go all over the place and were about security, not comfort.

"I'm not going to apologize."

"No?" The stubbornness in that voice was so familiar.

The whine was not. Lily sat on the steps a couple feet away. "Did you think that was why I came out here? To make you apologize?"

"He *is* a stupid little boy," she muttered, turning her head away.

"Do you think so? I . . . ow."

"What?"

"A splinter poked me. These boards are in terrible shape. You're likely to get splinters coming out here barefoot."

"I don't care."

Lily borrowed one of Rule's favorite responses. "Hmm." After a moment, she added, "I heard that your father came to see you today."

Now Julia jerked upright. "For a whole hour. He looked at his watch! Twice! He couldn't wait to get away. He's such a—a—he's an asshole!" Her eyes narrowed. "Why are you smiling like that? You think I'm funny?"

"I was remembering how you sent me to my room once for saying something along those lines. Grandfather Li had called, making his usual excuses for missing my birthday party. I didn't much care, but it upset you, and that made me mad."

"What did you say?"

"I don't recall exactly, but it included calling him a dick."

"That's worse than asshole," Julia announced judiciously. "Not that I'm allowed to say either one." She stole a quick glance at Lily. "Maybe I am allowed now. Who's going to tell me I can't?"

"Grandmother, I expect."

"Oh. Yeah." Her arms had loosened slightly; now she unwound one and began picking at a toenail on one bare foot. "Tell me something."

"If I can."

"Edward Yu . . . is he a good dad?"

Lily's throat closed. She had to swallow before she could answer. "He's a great dad. I don't know if he could fight off dworg, but mostly we don't need fathers for that, do we? He always listened. Still does. He's good at it. He played games with us a lot. Oh, and then there were the Dad Dates. That's when he'd spend all Saturday afternoon with one of us girls, just one, who got his whole attention that afternoon. I loved Dad Dates. We'd do all kinds of things. Movies, miniature golf, the beach . . . anything but the mall. He would not go to the mall, but that was okay. It didn't matter what we did."

"Good," Julia said gruffly. "That's good. I'm glad I . . . the grown-up me . . . picked a good dad for you."

"You did."

"Do you think I loved him?"

Oh, damn, her not-a-mother-anymore was going to make her cry. "I know you did. And he loved . . . loves you."

Silence, while Julia picked at that toenail. Then, "I guess he's pretty sad."

"Yes."

More silence. "I guess it would be okay if he wanted to come see me."

"Shall I tell him that?"

Julia nodded. "But it's still going to just be me, you know? Not that grown-up Julia he remembers, so he'll probably still be sad."

"I guess we can't keep him from being sad."

Julia sighed the kind of long, windy sigh twelve-year-old girls were so good at.

For several minutes neither of them said anything, just sat there together. They weren't really alone, Lily knew. Somewhere in the darkness guards patrolled, some on two feet, some on four. But it felt like just the two of them. She rubbed her arms, which were getting chilly, but she didn't want to go in yet. The sky was clear and splendid with stars, and she was sitting with the girl who had been—had become—her mother. And it was okay. For this moment, it was okay. "It's funny. I always pictured you as a very proper sort of girl. I thought you always did your homework and your chores, that you respected your elders and never talked back."

Julia snickered. "Well . . . I usually do my homework."

Lily smiled.

Julia tilted her head. "What kind of mother was I?"

Oh, damn once more. She didn't want to lie, but the truth was complicated. "You read stories to us when we were little, and you were wonderful when one of us was sick. You'd nag us about how we hadn't taken care of ourselves, but in this really soft voice that was really saying *I love you*, never mind what the words were. Then you'd fix us whatever treat made us feel pampered. Oh, and you threw wonderful birthday parties. For my tenth birthday you rented a bunch of costumes, western stuff, enough for my whole class. We put on a play, making it up as we went along. It was fun." Lily smiled, remembering. That had been her first birthday after the abduction. She hadn't wanted a party, but her mother had insisted, and she'd been right. Not about everything, but about the party. Lily had been the sheriff.

"Was I strict?"

"About some things, yes, because you wanted what was best for us."

Julia nodded. "Were we close? Me and my mother were really close."

Lily licked her lips and tried. "I think you and your mother were unusually close. That's the impression I had."

"Yes, we were. But you and I weren't." Julia nodded again, decisively, and stood and dusted off her rear with both hands. "Good."

"Ah . . . it is?"

"That's a mistake, being too close. My mother was . . ." Julia's voice thickened. "She was wonderful. She really was, and she didn't know she'd die like that, so it's not her fault, but . . . but it's better if there's a little distance. Mothers should take the very best care of their children, but they shouldn't make it so it hurts so much when you lose them."

With that, Julia headed for the door. "I am going to apologize," she announced, "to Grandmother and Li Qin because I was rude, and to Toby because I shouldn't have said that about him being stupid. Even if he does brag too much." She opened the door and went back inside.

Lily didn't move. She just sat there, robbed of speech. Had her mother always thought this way? That the truly loving thing was to keep some distance between her and her daughters so they wouldn't hurt too much when they lost her?

Oh, Mother. She rubbed her chilly arms and stared up at the starry sky with damp eyes. *You were wrong. It still hurts. It hurts a lot.*

THIRTY-TWO

HOME.

That was what Rule felt as they drove down the familiar asphalt road . . . in spite of the subtle push-away that began the moment they passed the gate. In spite of the fact that he had his own home now, however unfinished it might be. He didn't really know every twig and rock here. It just felt like it. Nor had he been away for long, only since their move.

It just felt like it.

"What does it feel like?" Lily asked quietly.

Startled by the echo of his thoughts, he glanced at her. She was watching him, her eyes dark in the shadowed car. He decided she was asking about the dissonance between Leidolf's mantle and the way the Nokolai mantle claimed this land. That dissonance only affected Rhos, and only when they were on another clan's clanhome. If he was wrong, if she was really asking if he ached from the rejection he felt every second . . . no doubt she'd let him know. Whether he wanted her to or not. "Rather like walking into a wind that blows from every direction. It's not a problem."

She cocked her head. "Maybe it will be okay to visit

your dad sometimes, then. Eat some of Carl's lasagna. See some of the people you've missed."

"Perhaps." This place had been the center of his world for most of his life, and now it pushed him away. *Home* didn't want him here.

"Does it help to focus on the portion of Nokolai's mantle you hold? It must be happy to be here."

Lily always personified the mantles, in spite of all his explanations. "I'm fine, Lily. It's a minor discomfort, one I can easily ignore for the short time we'll be here." Though he'd done poorly at that so far, allowing himself to be distracted. That needed to stop. "It looks like Abel is here already."

"We're late."

She sounded so grim he had to smile. Lily hated to be late. "By less than ten minutes. I think they'll forgive us."

His father had left the porch light on in the universal sign of welcome. The van—which held Toby, Julia, Li Qin, Madame Yu, and six guards—pulled up behind Abel's government car. The van had been an airport shuttle in its previous life. They could have all ridden in it, had Rule been willing to bring fewer guards. He wasn't.

No one had attacked them on the way, though, and he wouldn't need Leidolf guards at his father's house. He'd arranged for them to enjoy a nice four-legged run with a few Nokolai. The two clans needed to get used to each other. Some of his guards had stayed with him here at Clanhome before the move, but most had not.

He should have come here sooner, he realized as the car pulled up behind the van and stopped. He should have been bringing his men here all along to train with Nokolai the way he'd been doing in D.C. If he had, Santos might have accepted José's authority better. Which made Santos's failure his, as well—a failure he would have cemented in his soul if he'd killed the young man who was currently deeply miserable, but alive.

Thank God Lily had shown up in time. Stubborn woman. He smiled as he stepped out of the car and inhaled, which told him several things . . . Isen had had spaghetti and meatballs

for supper. Home still smelled right, however it might push
at him. And . . . "Sam doesn't seem to be here."

"He watches over Nettie," Grandmother announced as
she climbed down from the van, "so Benedict may attend."

"Hey, Dad!" Toby shot out of the van at his usual pace.
"Can Danny and Emmy come over? They'd like to meet
Julia, I bet."

Rule's gaze flicked to the five-foot-nine twelve-year-old
exiting the van behind his son. "I'm afraid not. We'll be
discussing confidential matters. Would you like to go to
Danny's?"

The excitement leaked out of Toby's voice. "I guess not.
Carl's probably got cake or cookies or something."

Toby was as interested in sweets as any other boy, but
that wasn't why he didn't want to go to his friend's house.
He didn't feel safe away from Rule. Rule understood that.
He didn't want to let Toby out of his sight. When he thought
of how close Toby had been to those dworg, how differently
it all might have ended . . . best not to think about it. They'd
have to get over their mutual clinging, but for now, Toby
stayed with him. "Let's find out," he said cheerfully enough
and roughed up Toby's hair.

"C'mon, Julia," Toby said and set off for the front door
at his usual clip.

The door opened and Isen stood there, solid and sturdy
as a tree, beaming at his grandson, arms opening for a hug.
"Toby!" he boomed happily, as if he hadn't seen the boy in
months. Toby barreled into him.

Then it was Rule's turn. His father was a world-class
hugger, and for a small pinch of a moment Rule felt as safe
as Toby must have when those strong arms closed around
him. *This, too, I could have lost . . .*

Enough of that, dammit. Rule moved on into the house,
hating the anxiety that had trailed him like his own shadow
since the dworg attack. Normally he would have slid closer
to his wolf to relieve it. To the wolf, it was simple. He'd won
that battle. His mate and his brother and his Rho had won
theirs, as well. What was there to be anxious about in that?

But the man was too aware of how easily it might have gone differently for any one of them. The man kept thinking of that, dammit, no matter how often he pushed those thoughts away.

And here at Clanhome, the wolf couldn't help because that part of him was much more sensitive to the push-away. It made the wolf nervous and jumpy and distracted. Here, the wolf needed the man's help to be calm.

Isen had intercepted Lily on her way in to give her a hug. Lily's family didn't touch easily and often the way Rule's did, but she'd gotten used to Isen's greetings. She might even, Rule thought as he watched her hugging Isen back, have grown to like them.

Isen did not attempt to greet Madame Yu with a hug. He gave her the sort of nod he would have given another Rho and told her she and Li Qin were welcome. "And this is Julia." His voice softened with his smile. "You'll call me Isen. It's not what you're used to, I'm sure, but what choice do you have? Courtesy demands you address me as I wish, and that's my wish." And he took Julia's hand and tucked it into the crook of his arm and patted it. "Come, come, and let me introduce you to Carl. He's going to let you and Toby help him make tarts. Apple, I believe. Do you like apples?"

Julia was happy to talk about apple tarts, happy to go off with Isen. Lily stopped there in the entry hall and shook her head, smiling. "Your father does have a way with . . . well, with just about everyone."

Because he liked just about everyone. Each person mattered to him. Some more than others, yes, but Isen's heart remained open. Even now, even in the midst of war and loss . . . "He risks so much," Rule murmured. "I haven't half his courage."

Lily cocked her head in a silent question.

He slid his arms around her and pulled her to him. "I need a moment." Because this, too, he could have lost. He could have lost Lily. Friar had tried to kill her—again— and would keep trying. His heart beat fast in fear that

threatened to swamp him, drown him . . . how could he be
with both Toby and Lily every moment? He couldn't.
Couldn't protect them both, couldn't keep them safe . . .
Can't, can't, can't pounded in his mind with every too-hard
beat of his heart.

Gradually his heartbeat slowed. She was here now, and for
once not asking questions. "Anxiety attack," he explained.

"You?" Her eyebrows lifted, as did the corners of her
mouth. "Must mean you woke up on the wrong side of perfect yet again."

"I believe I did." He smiled down at her dark eyes, the
beautiful oval of her face . . . her skin was soft, but nothing
like porcelain or ivory or anything so fragile and protected.
His *nadia* was a California girl who'd been impatient with
her mother's lectures about sunscreen when she was young,
and still forgot it more often than not. Often on purpose, he
suspected. Her skin was sunshine and honey, not cream,
and right now she smelled of toothpaste, of almonds from
her lotion and apple from her shampoo, and Lily. The love-
liest smell in the world.

A smell that stirred him . . .

"Wrong time, wrong place," she told him. That wasn't
telepathy. If his face hadn't given away his reaction, his
body certainly had.

"True." He eased away, but took her hand. "End of time-
out. Let's go deal with something other than my delicate
feelings."

She snorted softly, squeezed his hand, and went with him.

LILY liked Isen's house. She liked it even better now that
she wasn't living here anymore. Though that, like most
truths, had layers. Because she had lived here for a few
months the place felt homier to her now, which was funny
because it hadn't felt like home when she was staying here.

Minds are weird, she decided. Hers included.

They'd assembled in the great room at the back of the
house. It was large and flooded with light in the daytime;

now the windows were covered by remote-control-operated blinds that hadn't been there a month ago. Isen was showing off his new toy—the remote—to Karonski. One of the blinds started to lift, paused, and headed down again.

Rule headed straight for the new toy. Lily paused, looking around.

Near the fireplace, Li Qin smiled at Hardy, who seemed to be singing something to Cynna. At the far end of the room, Cullen sat at the big table with Arjenie, both engrossed in their discussion—magical shit, no doubt. They both loved to talk about magical shit. He had little Ryder on his shoulder. She was asleep. Grandmother sat at the other end of the table, and as Lily came in, Benedict handed Grandmother a cup and saucer.

That would be tea, not coffee. Grandmother detested coffee. Lily had never seen anyone in this household prepare or drink tea, and Grandmother was extremely particular about hers. She moved closer to listen.

Grandmother held the cup near her face. She inhaled, then sipped. Her eyebrows lifted in surprise. "It is good tea."

"Carl," Benedict explained.

"You may sit beside me," Grandmother informed him. "I wish to hear about your daughter. She is recovering?"

Benedict didn't talk much. He didn't smile much, either, but when he did, it transformed him. He sat beside Grandmother now, all but glowing. "The doctor let her wake up this morning and try some healing. She did great. She says there's nothing wrong she can't fix, given time and rest. They've taken her off the sedatives so she can keep herself in sleep most of the time. That's better for healing."

From out of nowhere, Lily was hit by this wave of *feeling*—feeling both vast and weightless, universal and utterly particular to this room, this moment, these people. Every one of whom she loved. Every one of whom had woken up this morning on the wrong side of perfect, just like Rule, just like her, each of them capable of annoying, delighting, or disappointing her; capable of heroism, misunderstanding, quarreling, laughing, or sitting stubbornly on some stupidity he or she refused to abandon. All of them so different, and so connected.

The feeling ebbed, then passed. She thought: *Love? Karonski?* And of course that was ridiculous, but even as she shook her head at herself, she knew that it could be both ridiculous and true. This . . . all this, the room, the people here, the odd little pairs and groups they'd formed, the ways each was finding to connect to the others . . . this was what she fought for. For these people, yes. And for moments like this, punctuated by coffee or tea, with a baby on one man's shoulder and a saint humming over by the fireplace . . . everyone gathered together to work toward their common goal. She fought for them, and for people she'd never met and never would, people who deserved a chance to make their own moments, built from their own flawed choices, with the people they found.

If everyone is here, a crystalline voice announced in her head, *we should begin.*

THIRTY-THREE

~

JUDGING by the sudden silence in the room, that had been a Sam-to-everyone communication. Judging by their expressions, they'd been as startled as Lily was. Even Grandmother's eyebrows shot up.

Lily hadn't known Sam could do something like this—talk to all of them when he was about thirty miles away keeping a telepathic eye on Nettie. "I want some coffee first."

Attempt to do two things at once. I have serious matters to impart, but wish to know what you have learned before I do so. Abel Karonski, you may begin.

"Fine," Karonski said. "First I want to bring everyone up-to-date on the victims, because that's where we've been focused, now that we know how they're all connected. We're up to three hundred and twelve. They aren't all in San Diego. Debrett's cousins, for example . . ."

Lily listened with half an ear as she headed for the kitchen. He wasn't saying anything that was new to her, though the others probably hadn't heard it in detail. Debrett's cousins, for example, were in bad shape, though not comatose like their parents. The one in Belize was being flown back here. The other was being treated in Denver. But they'd found more, so many more—Debrett's coach in high school, who'd moved to Albuquerque and had thought he was going crazy; people he'd served with in the Marines; friends from college and from church. Many of them were only slightly affected, like the ones at the pipe company, but some were more seriously messed up.

Two of the victims had died. Barbara Lennox had slid from a coma into death; records showed she'd been Debrett's first grade teacher. And a man in San Francisco who'd gone to grade school with Debrett had been killed in an auto accident right about the time someone slit Debrett's throat. He'd suddenly and inexplicably lost control of the car. Not drunk, not on drugs, no obvious medical condition. Lily figured he'd suddenly forgotten how to drive.

In the kitchen, Toby was turning the crank on a gadget that peeled, cored, and sliced apples. Julia stood at the restaurant-style range stirring something under Carl's supervision. She flashed Lily a quick smile. Lily filled two heavy mugs with coffee, knowing Rule would want one, too. She'd rewrapped her wrist before they left, and it didn't hurt at all to carry a mug in that hand. Maybe her left hand wouldn't be out of commission too much longer.

She got back just as the others were seating themselves at the big table. Isen had a pad and pen ready. One of his more unexpected skills was shorthand.

Rule took the mug with a smile. Lily sat and pulled out her own notebook. Isen's notes would be more complete, but she still wanted her own.

Karonski was finishing his summary about the victims. "Those affected the worst seem to be the ones who either knew Alan Debrett as kids or who had a strong emotional connection, like his aunt and uncle, though there are exceptions, like the former teacher who died early this morning. We don't yet know if there was another, deeper connection between her and Debrett, or if her physical frailty—"

Physical condition means little, Sam informed them. It was amazing how well a voice that was no more than iced thought could cut off normal conversation. *This is one of the two subjects I need to introduce. Your supposition that the chief predictors of major damage are an early connection to Debrett or a deep emotional connection is roughly correct. I will state this with more accuracy, although your terms do not allow real precision. The level of damage depends upon the way the excised memories were woven into subsequent memories and the individual's sense of self. A visual metaphor may be helpful. Imagine an elaborate house of cards with many levels. Some cards may be removed, particularly in upper levels, with little damage to the overall structure. Remove cards in the middle or lower levels, and some or all of the levels above the point of excision collapse, and the lower structure may be in turn damaged by the falling cards, creating instabilities that do not immediately reveal themselves. Remove foundational cards, and the entire structure collapses.*

Lily spoke slowly, keeping her voice down so she wouldn't be heard in the kitchen. "The part about how removing cards from a lower level makes the top levels crash and damages the lower structure . . . that's my mother."

In a lamentably imprecise way, yes. The memories she lost were substantial, emotionally charged, and were formed at a time when she was building her understanding of identity, community, and sovereignty. At the moment of injury, her mind instinctively reverted to its most stable configuration prior to the excision. It was not, however, truly stable; such extensive collapse had damaged the underlying structure. I reinforced certain foundational structures and performed other alterations that do not fit the card house metaphor.

So Julia was a stable twelve-year-old . . . if that wasn't a contradiction in terms.

I describe the damage in this imprecise manner in order to increase your understanding of the process that is under way in the victims of memory excision. I will also offer generalizations about their prognosis so you may prepare for the most likely results. I am generalizing about a process that is highly individualized, and therefore will not apply in every instance. These generalizations refer to matters as they stand now, and are as follows.

Those who are now in a coma will die. Those with substantial damage to early memory formations will continue to deteriorate, which for most will mean coma followed by death. Many, but not all, of those with light to moderate damage who seem to be stable are not. They, too, will deteriorate. Some of them will reach a point of stability; others will not, and will eventually slide into coma and death.

Everyone waited for a moment to see if Sam was done. Apparently he was.

"Well," Karonski said, "that's a grim prognosis. I'll let Ruben decide who needs to know. Those who are caring for the victims, obviously. Others in emergency management. The president, of course, which brings me to something I suspect some of you aren't going to like. Ruben called me as I was on my way here. People were already on edge about the amnesia victims, and the sudden appearance of dworg has made it worse. The president plans to give a prime-time speech to tell everyone about the Great War and *her*."

"What?" Rule exclaimed. "The market's volatile, yes, but—"

"Is she nuts?" Cullen exclaimed.

"I don't know," Arjenie said. "Maybe it's time to level with people. Have you seen the news lately? They're talking about the end times and plagues of locusts—as if dworg were some kind of giant locust!—and alien invasion. The reputable channels are trying to pooh-pooh those ideas, but—"

"And this is going to help how?" Cullen said. "I can see it now. 'Don't worry, folks—we're not dealing with an alien invasion. Just a crazy goddess who's been trying to take over since before the dawn of recorded history.' Yeah, that'll do wonders for the Dow."

"They're also talking about conspiracies and cover-ups," Karonski said dryly. "Which may be part of the reason the president decided to reveal more. She did run on a platform of increased transparency."

Rule muttered something Lily didn't catch.

"True," Isen said, "but I don't believe the president has solicited our opinion. We'd do better to focus on how the clans should handle this. We'll need to get in touch with the other Rhos."

"Who are not going to appreciate the fact that the president knows about the Great War."

"The Lady never forbade our speaking of it. That's tradition, but Nokolai broke no covenant by revealing historical facts the rest of the world was unaware of."

"Until now. Or soon, anyway." Rule looked at Karonski. "When does she intend to speak?"

"Tomorrow night at nine Eastern. She'd like to have you and possibly some of the other Rhos join her electronically afterward, if you could be at a local television studio."

Rule scowled. "I don't know if that's wise."

Isen spoke. "Will the president insist on a script? If not, this would be a chance to spin the revelation the way we wish."

Rule cast his father a glance. "It might, if we knew how we wished to spin it."

Both Benedict and Cullen started to say something at the same time.

Delay this discussion, Sam told them in a voice sharp enough to cut. *I need to relate the other matter that brought me to join your council tonight. I have learned much concerning the artifact in Friar's possession.*

"You heard from that agent you sent to the sidhe?" Lily asked.

In a manner of speaking. I suspected that the artifact disrupts time, which—

"It *what?*"

Everyone else reacted, too. Cynna repeated, "Disrupts time?" Arjenie exclaimed wordlessly. Isen frowned. Rule asked what that meant. Karonski said, "Son of a bitch!"

And Cullen sat bolt upright. "It's named?"

That was an odd reaction even for the magic-obsessed Cullen. Never mind that the artifact disrupted time—he was worried that it had a name. Lily frowned at him. "Why did you—"

Be quiet. I do not have time for endless questions. Your sorcerer's astonishment denotes a decent grasp of reality. A number of spells and rituals cause a minor disruption of time, either intentionally or inadvertently. Gates, for example. However, time is resilient and extremely difficult to damage in a meaningful or sustained manner; most such workings have no lasting repercussions, except at times for the practitioner who attempts them. I was not, initially, alarmed by the flux. It was quite minor. Even among those capable of discerning such phenomena, very few who are not dragon would have noticed it.

However, it was still present after I finished working on Julia Yu's mind. This did alarm me. In addition, I observed a troubling flow in the probabilities. I sent an inquiry outlining my observations via an agent to one of the sidhe— you might call him a historian—whom I know in Iath.

This time it was Arjenie who was startled into speaking. "Iath? The Queens' home realm? But their time is completely different from ours. It will take months to hear back, surely."

Arjenie did not get told to be quiet. *Iath is highly dissynchronous with our realm, making communication difficult, but there are ways of managing this. My agent planned to travel through multiple dissynchronous realms, managing her route in a manner that allowed her to arrive in Iath at a now that corresponds roughly to three days ago in our time.*

Lily looked at Rule. "Did you understand that?"

"If I did, then Sam's agent arrived before she left."

Sam ignored them. *My agent did reach the historian. I have not, however, spoken with her myself. I received her report from the emissary from the Queen of Winter who arrived outside my lair approximately two hours ago. Winter invites me most courteously to visit her and discuss this matter in person.*

Lily's breath hissed in. That was . . . good? Bad? Major, anyway. "Is that the kind of offer you can't turn down?"

Naturally I could turn it down, if I wished. I do not. I have been in conversation with Winter's emissary. Much of what I will tell you comes from that source; I judge it to be incomplete but accurate. The artifact in Robert Friar's possession is almost certainly a knife called Nam Anthessa. I refer to it by a call-name; its true name has been lost for centuries. Its existence violates Queens' Law. It is used to tamper with the dead.

"Oh," Arjenie breathed. "That's bad."

Yes, in ways you do not comprehend. It means, first, that Alan Debrett is not simply dead. The knife cut him out of time, making it as if he never existed. You will note that this loss does not affect the material world; his daughter still exists. Records of his life exist. Memories of him do not.

I will not attempt to explain the relationship between reality and sentience. A few of your physicists have begun to approach this subject, though their grasp remains limited. Accept that this relationship exists, that tampering with the dead—removing a sentient being from the time stream—disrupts time, and that the excised memories mean the disruption will not heal on its own. Put simply, the fabric of this realm is in danger. The existing disruption has not worsened, so the realm is not yet unstable, but even a single additional use of the artifact could destabilize it. The artifact must be destroyed so time can heal. It must be destroyed before it is used again.

"Mage fire," Cullen said promptly. "I've used it on—"

You have not used it on a named sidhe artifact possessed of vast amounts of magic and arguai. Mage fire might damage Nam Anthessa, but only to the extent that it burns through the restraints laid on the blade. The likely outcome of such a loss is the utter destruction of this realm.

"Oh. Right. No mage fire, then. So how do we do it?"

To destroy Nam Anthessa, one must wield its true name, which no one now alive knows. The name might be discovered were the knife in the possession of one with sufficient skill and patience who is firmly guarded against it, but that is a slow process. We do not have time for me to undertake it. We need Winter's assistance.

She also needs us. The Queen of Winter has sought Nam Anthessa for many centuries. She wants badly to destroy it.

"If it can't be destroyed without its name," Rule said, "and it would take more time than we have to discover that name, I don't see how involving her helps."

I will explain, and you will understand why I accepted Winter's invitation. This is not one of the Queens' Realms, and the Queens have good reason not to act here. If Winter believes Nam Anthessa is here she will act, but in a way that minimizes her cost and risk. She will seek to take possession of it so she may spend the necessary time and focus to uncover its name, then destroy it herself. She is capable of doing so more quickly than I, but it is unlikely she would finish before the stability of this realm breaks down. Therefore, I will negotiate so that she will send a Hound.

Lily frowned. "A hellhound, you mean? We want that?" According to Arjenie's half sister Dya, they were bad news.

There are hellhounds and there is the Queen's Hound. The second begins as the first. I will not explain the distinction now. Both are dangerous, and either will do for our purposes.

"And what will you negotiate with?" Rule asked.

Good question. What did they have that the Queen of Winter might want? The knife, yes, or at least its approximate location, but she must have guessed that, or she wouldn't have sent the mysterious emissary.

How I choose to bargain with Winter is not your affair.

Cynna spoke. "If this knife can't be destroyed without its name, what can a Hound do?"

Hounds are exceptions to many things. They are Wild Sidhe, all of whom are dangerous, but hellhounds are feared more than most due to the nature of their powers, which are limited in number but absolute within those limits. They cannot be corrupted or turned aside from a hunt given them by their Queen. They are not true immortals, but they are extremely difficult to kill. And they can kill anything.

"Anything?" Rule repeated.

"Even immortals," Cullen said, "according to stories I've heard. Even a semi-sentient, semi-immortal artifact, I guess . . . because that's what it means for that damn knife to possess a true name, isn't it? It's alive. Aware. Sort of."

Yes. Because Nam Anthessa is aware, it can employ its own power. It is highly dangerous. Magically, it can compel. Spiritually, it can persuade and corrupt. If you should encounter it before I return, do not, under any circumstances, touch it. Immediately remove everyone from its vicinity, including yourselves. The emissary suggested the equivalent of sixty-one feet for a safe distance, but his knowledge relates to sidhe. I do not know if humans would be more or less susceptible than sidhe.

"Would wards help?" Cullen asked.

Certain types of wards would diminish the effect of the knife's compulsion. They would not affect its ability to persuade and corrupt, which is based on arguai, *not magic. A holy person should be proof against that. I do not know if holiness on the part of one would protect others.*

"If it's that dangerous," Cynna said, "how can one of these hellhounds be trusted to destroy it? Unless they're saints—"

Hounds are immune to persuasion. I do not know the mechanism for their protection, but I trust its efficacy.

Isen was frowning. "There must be some reason Winter hasn't set one of these Hounds on the trail of that knife already."

She has. They haven't found it. Hounds cannot be turned away from the hunt, but they require what you might call a scent or a trail to follow. Nam Anthessa is good at hiding its nature. It is worth noting that its call-name translates roughly as Eater of Truth. This is why Winter will not send a Hound of either sort unless she is convinced the knife is here. She is fond of them. If she sends one to us and it fails

*to find Nam Anthessa before the damage to our realm be-
comes irreversible, it might be lost to her.*

When Sam paused this time, Lily jumped in. "But why
is Friar doing this? Why does he want to tamper with the
dead, mess up time, and destabilize the realm? How does
that help *her*? She wants a realm and lots of people to rule
over."

Apparently what I thought obvious is not. There was a
distinctly acerbic flavor to that thought. *If the agent of hers
who wields Nam Anthessa—presumably Robert Friar—
chooses the right victims for the blade, it will create a rent
in the fabric of our realm such that* she *is able to enter.
This is like causing an earthquake in order to knock down
a locked door. The door may come down, but there will be
considerable additional damage. It seems she is willing to
accept such damage in order to gain entry.*

The Great Bitch wanted in. She wanted in badly enough
to destroy some part of their world to get here. This was
really, deeply, seriously bad. "And if this Hound comes
here and finds the knife and destroys it, will that restore—
dammit." Her phone was vibrating.

But Lily didn't have to finish her question out loud for
Sam to hear it. *I do not know. Time itself will heal. I suspect
that the spiritual damage connected with the lost memories
will heal as well. I do not know if this means that the victims will regain their memories.*

Not what she wanted to hear, but better than a flat "no."
She took out her phone and looked at the display and huffed
out a breath. "I have to take this."

She listened first, then asked a couple of questions. As
soon as she disconnected she turned to Karonski. "That
was an SDPD homicide detective I used to work with. He
wants me to check out what looks like a ritual murder in
case the body's contaminated the way the other site was.
Only it doesn't make sense. There's two victims, one dead,
one critical. But they were gunned down, not throat-slit."

"That doesn't work," Cullen said.

"I know. But if something other than gunplay went

on . . . they got the living victim transported quickly, then pulled back because of the risk of contamination, which is exactly what they needed to do, but that means they haven't examined the scene or the body. Maybe this Nam Anthessa was used in some way other than cutting the throat, and they didn't see the wound."

I sense no additional troubling of time. I do not believe Nam Anthessa has been used tonight.

"That's good. I still need to go."

"Go," Karonski said.

Lily shoved back her chair.

So did Rule. "You mean *we* need to go."

THIRTY-FOUR

~~~

THE Torrey Pines Reserve was closed at night, but people interested in committing murder often don't worry much about park rules. Maybe the killer hadn't realized that rangers sometimes work late. Two rangers had been busting some asshole for camping on the beach below the bluff when they heard gunshots. When they checked that out, they found a bloody scene complete with arcane symbols.

"You sure the EMTs knew to keep latex between them and their patient?" she asked T.J. as they headed up the Guy Fleming Trail. The body was at the north overlook; no one waited there but the dead. Once T.J. arrived, he'd kept everyone away except for the EMTs.

"I told 'em. Sent word to the hospital, too." T.J., aka Lieutenant Thomas James of the San Diego Police Department, looked less like Santa Claus than he had a few months back, when he'd grown a beard. He'd made a saggy Santa, but he did have the white hair and twinkle. Behind that twinkle was a canny and suspicious cop's brain. The SDPD had been warned about the steps to take if they found an apparent ritual murder. T.J. had followed that directive.

"I guess you haven't heard anything more about Ms. Ward's condition."

"Not yet. You a fan?"

"I saw *Duck Walk* five times when I was a kid." Not to mention the *Pygmalion* remake a couple years ago, plus a dozen other movies that every person in the country must have seen at least once. Angela Ward was an old-fashioned, capital *S* Star. Four Oscars, more than any other living actor; four husbands, too, though she'd been single for years now. She called herself retired, though this or that director was always coaxing her back for a part. She'd chosen San Diego for one of her homes, though she spent most of her time in Hawaii.

She'd be wishing she'd stayed in Hawaii, if she lived to make wishes. She'd been tied up when they found her. Unconscious. The EMTs said she'd damn near bled out. Bullet wounds in the abdomen and upper arm.

"You see anything?" she asked the man ahead of them.

"Trees."

Trust Cullen to find an excuse for sarcasm. She needed him along, though, and for the same reason he was up front now. He'd see any icky magic before stepping in it. They made quite a cavalcade. Cullen first, then her and T.J. with Rule right behind. Behind Rule, two cops with some of the gear they'd need at the scene if they were able to enter it. Behind them, the six lupus guards Rule considered necessary.

Lily hadn't argued. Not after the dworg.

On the way over, she'd tried talking to Sam. Either he was finished chatting or he hadn't heard her. The latter was possible. Likely, she supposed. Even the black dragon might find it hard to eavesdrop telepathically on so many people in different locations, none of them near him, while keeping watch over Nettie. She hoped he'd be available for questions when she finished with the scene. She had several.

The two rangers who'd found the victims were back at the park road. So was the scene-of-crime squad. Lily had checked the rangers for traces of icky magic. Nothing on them. Maybe no icky magic here at all. Maybe she wasn't needed. "Doesn't make sense," she muttered. "Bullets?"

"That part doesn't," Cullen agreed, "but the location does. There's a baby node on the lookout."

She wondered if Cullen knew the location of every node in a hundred miles. Probably. "They used a ley line the first time. Why change? Maybe this isn't the same bunch."

"Maybe, but not for that reason. A lot of spells and rites can use either one, depending on the skill of the caster. They could've used a ley line the first time because it was their first time. Ley lines aren't safe, but they're safer than nodes. Even a small node has a lot of raw magic."

The trail wound around and up. They moved slowly, giving Cullen time to study both the trail and the area near it. The wind off the ocean was strong and cold, whipping Lily's hair around and making her think again about cutting it. Assuming the fabric of time held together long enough for her to get an appointment . . . she dug in her pocket and pulled out an elastic. A couple of quick twists and one problem was solved.

What happened when time was damaged? When the fabric of the realm was damaged?

What did the Great Bitch *want* to happen?

It was, maybe, a mistake to try to get inside the head of a being older than the cosmos, due to being impossible. Lily still had to try. G.B. thought her goal was noble. She wanted to save humanity from itself. Therefore, she didn't want to destroy humanity . . . but anything short of utter annihilation might work for her. Might work out great. Knock everyone back to the Stone Age, flash some power around, start helping the survivors of the devastation you'd caused, and bingo. Before you knew it, you had everyone worshiping you, just like they ought to.

Maybe understanding that much helped, but trying to figure out what kind of damage might occur was a distraction. She didn't need specifics to know it would be a heaping helping of world-class horrible. She didn't need to prepare for the horrible. She needed to stop it. That meant stopping Friar. How did you stop someone if you couldn't find them? If—

"Now I see something," Cullen said.

Lily stopped, her arm flashing out to bar T.J., who'd already stopped. "What?"

"Leakage from the node. It looks . . ." He tipped his head to one side. "Well, that's not good. Wait here." He left at a run.

Lily tucked her flashlight under her arm, pulled off her shoes so she'd know if she hit a patch of icky magic, and jammed them into her purse. "Do like he said. Wait here." She gripped the flashlight and set off the way Cullen had, only slower. Three footfalls later she added, "Dammit, Rule!"

"You'll let me know if there's contagion." He ran easily just behind her.

"I could lie."

"You won't. Not about that."

Wisps of power brushed her face as she ran—overflow from the node. Her feet didn't touch anything icky, just rocks and sticks that jabbed. There wasn't much brush at the crest of the trail, but the lookout was at a high point and it was dark. Lily didn't see what waited there until she reached it.

A man's body lay facedown on the flat, sandy ground. Near one outflung hand was a small wooden altar, tipped on its side. Near his feet was a small duffel bag. A large shape—a pentagon? No, a hexagon had been drawn or painted on the bare ground of the overlook. Under the beam of her flashlight it glowed a bright, cheery yellow. Six dark candles were distributed evenly around the painted shape, which enclosed the body and the toppled altar. Cullen stood in front of it, glaring at them. "Does anyone listen to me? Does anyone ever freaking listen to me?"

"There's no contagion."

"No, there's a goddamn major working that got interrupted at the worst goddamn time possible, so instead of dissolving like it ought to, it jammed. Then it got fed a lot of blood. And it's still tied to the goddamn node, and now it's about to blow up. So sit down *out of my way* and shut up." He began pacing around the hexagon, eyes narrowed as he studied the ground.

Sometimes you really had to listen to the experts. Lily sat on the trail. Rule dropped down beside her. After a moment, she turned off her flashlight. It might be a distraction.

Cullen made a slow circuit of the hexagon. There was barely room for him to stay outside it in one spot; the overlook was enclosed by a low pole-and-cable fence meant to keep idiots from straying off the trail or falling off the cliff on the ocean side. He crouched twice, tilting his head, and muttered under his breath now and then. At last he stopped, nodded briskly, and raised his arms. He began chanting too low for Lily to hear the words. All at once he snatched something invisible out of the air, flung it up, and shouted, *"Ak-ak-areni!"*

Fire shot up from the candles—fire as red as molten lava. It leaped from candle to candle, then inward to the center of the hexagon, where the six crimson flows collided with each other—and with a seventh, this one from Cullen's other hand. Rainbow fire, that one, green-blue-orange-purple-yellow, every color but red. It merged with the lava fire and exploded into eye-searing white. White that shot straight up in a brilliant column three or four stories tall . . . and gradually dissipated, like the slow, shiny fade-out of fireworks.

THREE miles away, a woman sat cross-legged on the beach, her head tipped back, her mouth round in a silent "oh" as the brilliant white light faded. It was time to go, and yet she lingered. The wind off the ocean was chilly. It felt good on her hot cheeks . . . hot cheeks, shivery stomach. She'd felt so odd ever since she picked up that knife. For just a moment longer she'd sit here and smell the ocean . . . brine and fish, the Mother's moist breath. Only she wasn't thinking of the Mother. She was wondering if anyone had died in that beautiful flash of light. If she'd killed people she didn't even know.

You are sad, F'annwylyd?

"A little." Apologetically she added, "I've never killed anyone before."

They would die anyway. Does it matter greatly when?

It did to them. And to her, too, though he wouldn't understand that. She hoped no one had been near when the node exploded. The others . . . no, she didn't regret them. She'd been shocked by how loud the gun was, that was all. She'd owned the weapon for ages and dutifully took it to the firing range two or three times a year to make sure she stayed familiar with it, but she'd never fired it without the protective gear at the gun range. She'd never really thought she'd shoot it anywhere else.

You grieve. A ghostly warmth stroked her cheek. *Though it is not the dead who grieve you. I wish I could put my arms around you. Comfort you.*

Tears sprang to her eyes. Ah, look at her, indulging in melancholy when there were important things to do! Vital things. "Soon. Soon I'll feel your arms—and all sorts of other parts of you, too." She laughed, suddenly flooded with a wild, exuberant energy, and bounced to her feet. She had places to go, things to do.

People to kill. On purpose.

LILY was still blinking bright spots out of her vision when Cullen plopped to the ground with a satisfied sigh. "Glad that worked."

"So am I," Rule said dryly.

"The node's still not entirely stable. I think . . ." Cullen tipped his head, studying something only he could see. "Yeah, it's settling down. Should be safe enough, but I'll keep an eye on it."

"My turn, then." Lily stood. "I guess you don't see any power radiating from an ancient artifact or you'd be rooting around, looking for it."

"No, but if this Nam Anthessa is as good at hiding as Sam said, maybe I wouldn't. If you see a knife, don't touch it."

"Sam made that clear. It's safe to cross the line?"

"Sure. Not a whiff of power left in it. I may have damaged some evidence. Couldn't be helped, so don't bitch at me about it. But the missing blood isn't my fault."

"What missing blood?"

"There's no blood on the ground inside the hexagon. Some outside it, but none inside. I think the *übrik* rune drank it."

That was seriously creepy. Lily flashed her light over the ground. "I don't see any runes." Though there was a drift of ashy residue of some sort she hadn't noticed before. And the once-yellow line of the hexagon was burned black.

"No runes?" Cullen stirred himself to come look. "Huh. That's weird."

"Meaning?"

"I guess my pyrotechnics burned them up."

Lily decided not to worry about it. The scene was already thoroughly compromised—first by the rangers, then by the EMTs, and now by Cullen's efforts to keep something—either the runes or the node, she wasn't sure which—from exploding. "Rule . . ." She realized he'd moved. He was a little ways down the trail, talking to Scott. And when had Scott come up past T.J. and his two cops?

Rule looked at her. "Scott, Barnaby, and Mike are going to stay with you. I'm going to take the others for some four-legged sniffing."

"Okay. Before you Change, would you let T.J. and the rest know they can come up?" Time to put her shoes back on. Lily took out the baby wipes she kept in her purse for occasions like this. By the time she'd wiped both feet—which were scratched and tender in spots, but she didn't find any blood—and put her shoes back on, Scott and T.J. were coming up the trail together. She didn't see Rule, but she knew where he was—about forty feet away, and not sticking to the trail.

"I've got to say," T.J. said when he reached them, "you do know how to mess up a scene, Seaborne."

"Would've been a bigger mess if the node had exploded."

Lily shivered. That answered that question. "T.J., you said you took some pictures from the scene earlier. We need to document what's changed. Can you have your guy snap some more while I look things over?"

"Will do. We need the SOC squad. They're going to bitch enough as it is."

"You can send for them now."

T.J. called the scene-of-crime people in and gave instructions to his two cops—a woman whose name Lily hadn't caught and a grizzled sergeant named Armstrong whom she knew slightly.

While the woman set up a pair of small floodlights, Lily pulled on a pair of the disposable gloves she kept in her purse. She approached the body carefully, avoiding the ashy smears that had been runes, and crouched.

The burned smell was strong. Some of it was from the dead man's exposed skin.

He lay facedown in the dirt. Might not be much face left of it to see when they turned him over, judging by the way the back of his head looked. High-caliber rounds made a mess. A couple feet from his outflung hand lay a weapon—a Sig Sauer P226, either new or nearly new, she thought, playing her flashlight over it. Good gun, but no weapon's much use if you're shot from behind. She directed her light at his head, hoping to learn his hair color, but he'd worn a ski mask. What was left of his head was covered by knitted stuff.

The rest of his body seemed unmarked, aside from postmortem burns. He'd been maybe one eighty, one ninety, and under six feet. Dark turtleneck, dark slacks, dark athletic shoes, all good quality. His right hand was underneath the body. The outflung left hand lacked a wedding ring. No visible calluses. No sign of defensive wounds.

And the wrong build for Friar, dammit.

The floodlights came on. Lily put away her flashlight. Sergeant Armstrong began snapping pictures.

"I'm going to check out the spot I picked for the shooter," T.J. said.

Lily looked at him, then studied the way the dead man had fallen. The bullets had to have been fired from the east . . . she shifted to check. "That patch of brush about thirty feet southeast of us?"

"Not a bad spot to hide while waiting to pick off your targets." T.J. turned and headed for it.

Shooting uphill could be tricky, but the slope wasn't bad there. "You think the perp was already in place?"

"I don't see how he could've gotten there without being heard," he said without turning around, "if anyone had been around to hear."

Some lupi could move that quietly, but otherwise he was right. So why had he or she waited until the rite was under way? Could the shooter have wanted to create the instability Cullen had shut down with his pyrotechnics?

A large, black-and-silver wolf slid out of the darkness to meet T.J. at the brushy spot. T.J. froze. "Uh, right. Which one are you?"

"That's Rule," Lily called and went back to studying the scene.

No knives of any sort visible. The altar, singed now, was next to the body. Things had spilled when it tipped over—a metal chalice and some other stuff too crispy to identify right away, but no knife. "Why didn't they use a circle?" she asked Cullen.

"They had one. It poofed when the rite was disrupted, leaving the hexagon. Which is not a stable array for a node."

"They didn't drive stakes through Angela Ward's hands and feet like they did Debrett's. Or this guy's, for that matter." Though she suspected he'd been one of the ones throwing the party, which someone else had crashed.

"It's all in the timing. Look in the duffel. Uh . . . carefully. Just in case something else is there."

She moved to the dead guy's feet, where the duffel sat, unzipped. Sure enough, it held four metal stakes and a mallet. She rooted around, checking. No knife. "Why hadn't they used these?"

"Most rites have three stages," Cullen said. "First stage is traditionally called the invocation, though I prefer the term 'definition.' That's when you invoke or define the powers you'll work with and your intent. Second one gathers power. In this case, that meant tying in to the node, which would have happened at the very end of that stage. Third stage shapes and directs that power. They didn't get that far, but it says nasty things about the kind of shaping they had in mind that it called for a form of crucifixion and murder."

She chewed on that a moment. "You think they were planning to use the knife the way they did on Debrett."

"Looks like, yeah."

"But they were interrupted at the end of the second stage, when they'd tied in to the node. That's why it went unstable?"

"Basically. I'll spare you the long explanation of why this rite would do that when others wouldn't. Short version: nodes are not safe."

"I'm wondering if the shooter knew that would happen. Picked that moment on purpose. If the node went boom it would get rid of the bodies, wouldn't it? And any other evidence the shooter might find inconvenient. Would he or she need to be familiar with the rite to know when they reached the end of the second stage? Or would they have to be able to see magic the way you do?"

"Huh." Cullen's eyebrows lifted. He looked over his shoulder at T.J., who was crouched on the near side of the brushy thicket, shining his flashlight over the ground. Rule was sniffing nearby. "From that distance . . . maybe not. It depends on a lot of variables, but it's certainly possible he could feel it when the node was brought in. Likely, even, if the shooter was an experienced spellcaster himself."

"Or herself."

"You have someone in mind?"

"No, just keeping mine open." Lily stood. "Would this hypothetical spellcaster know how long it would take for the node to go boom?"

"Without the Sight? No, and even with the Sight you're just guessing. There are spells that would tell him it was unstable, but not how long it would take to hit the threshold. Well, there's one that might, but it takes a couple hours to cast. He'd have to be remarkably stupid to hang around an unstable node that long."

"Not to mention a body or two." She nodded, satisfied. "Our perp didn't hang around. He or she got the knife and got the hell out. Either he didn't bother to make sure both victims were dead or he didn't care. When the node went, it would take out anyone nearby. He wasn't counting on the rangers hearing the shots. Or on you being able to do whatever you did."

"I am a wonder and a half," he agreed.

"Rule thinks he's found something," T.J. called, "but damned if I know what."

Lily turned to see Rule loping up the slope toward them. The young patrol officer squeaked like a mouse, but she didn't reach for her weapon, and the sergeant was made of sterner stuff. His eyes widened, but that was all. Rule stopped at the edge of the hexagon, his head lifting in surprise. His nostrils flared. He walked up to the body and lowered his head.

"He isn't going to, ah . . ." The sergeant looked worried.

Lily pretended he wasn't wondering if her fiancé was likely to eat the victim. "Wolves' sense of smell is better than just about any other mammal's, except for bears. His nose can be very useful."

After giving the body a thorough sniff, Rule moved outside the hexagon—this time to the side near the drop-off. He sniffed that thoroughly, too, then peered over the edge. The drop-off was steep there. A cliff, really, with a rocky bit of beach below.

He Changed again. The patrol officer squeaked a second

time, probably because Rule was now very naked. "Lily," he said, "the dead man is Armand Jones."

"Friar's lieutenant?" She turned to look at the body. It was the right height and build. She'd hoped it might be Friar, been disappointed that it wasn't, but Jones . . . that fit, too. "You're sure."

"Oh, yes. I made a point of learning his scent."

"A falling-out among thieves, then. Not the way I first thought. Jones must have taken the knife. Sam did say it's persuasive. Maybe it called to him or something, or maybe this was a power grab, pure and simple. Friar wanted the knife back. He would have known exactly when to fire to make the node unstable—"

But Rule was shaking his head. "Friar was here, yes. I found some of his blood outside the hexagon. I suspect he spilled quite a bit more inside it. He was among those shot, not the shooter."

"But—is there a trail? Did he—"

"I think he went over the edge. I don't see a body."

She chewed on that in silence a moment. "Friar's dead or badly hurt. Jones is dead. And whoever shot them must have the knife." It didn't make sense. Had the Great Bitch decided to ditch Friar and sent a new henchman to get the knife?

"T.J. and I found bullet casings by those bushes. That's where the shooter was. That's what I came to tell you. The scent I found there belongs to Miriam Faircastle."

THIRTY-FIVE

~

"**WHAT** do you mean, you aren't going to pick her up for questioning?" Lily wanted to reach through the phone and shake Karonski.

"Pipe down, Lily. You heard what Sam said about this knife. If she's got it—and it sure as hell sounds like she does, or maybe it's got her—we do not want to get close enough for it to start with the compelling and corrupting. We want Miriam Faircastle and that knife contained. Once she is, I can question her over the phone."

Okay. Okay, that made sense. She was maybe a little excitable. "How do you plan to contain her?"

"Ruben has to sign off on this, but if he does, I want guards, armed guards, outside her home. We'll evacuate her neighbors. We can't let her leave and we can't let anyone in there with her until Sam gets back."

"Wait. He's already left?"

"Right after you did. He wasn't sure how long he'd be gone. Well, he said it would be at least two weeks for him, but from our perspective he might return anytime between now and a couple weeks from now. Something to do with the way he'll travel through those dissynchronous realms."

"Can Ruben authorize holding someone under . . . I guess it's an extreme form of house arrest . . . for a week?"

"Looks like we'll find out."

Lily disconnected and frowned at the activity around her. The SOC crew had arrived and were having a meticulously grand time. Two were on their hands and knees, sifting the scrubby grass near the lookout point. One was carefully scooping bits of blood-soaked soil from just outside the hexagon into baggies. Friar's blood, according to Rule's nose, which Lily trusted at least as much as any DNA analysis. Rule and T.J. stood near the edge of the drop-off gripping one end of the rope Barnaby dangled from, sniffing at places a falling body might have hit on the way down.

Barnaby had an unusually good nose, even two-legged, but they didn't expect him to find much. When Friar got supercharged by his goddess a few months before, he'd acquired several useful skills, including a trick like the demonic ability to go out-of-phase. *Dshatu*, demons called it. Friar had used it to get away before. From what Lily could tell, it was an immaterial state, which was probably handy if you found yourself falling off a cliff.

There was no shot-up, smashed-up body at the foot of the drop-off; therefore, Friar had probably gone immaterial when he fell. While he was out-of-phase, he wouldn't leave a scent or blood trail. But he couldn't drive a car while he was *dshatu*, and getting away would have been a priority. Rule had sent two of the others off four-footed to check spots where he might have parked a car.

Thirty feet away, two SOC officers were checking out the bushes where Miriam Faircastle had apparently waited on the best moment for murder.

The corruption must have leaped from Officer Crown to Miriam when Miriam was trying to remove it. In retrospect, that was obvious. He'd woken up screaming, but free of the taint; she'd gone on to plan and execute murder. Had they been wrong about the icky magic only being able to travel through organic substances? Had Miriam been stupid enough to ignore that safety precaution? Had she just been careless?

Whatever had gone wrong, Lily was kicking herself for not checking Miriam herself. It seemed so bloody obvious now. The corruption left the officer, so where did it go? Only that still didn't explain everything. Why had the corruption compelled Miriam to shoot Friar and Jones and Angela Ward and steal the knife? If the corruption was connected to Nam Anthessa, then the knife itself seemed to be acting against Friar.

Lily huffed out a breath and told herself to brood later, when she had time. She turned away from the busy scene and headed for the south side of the trail.

Normally there was a bench on the lookout. Friar and Jones had moved it to make room for their rite, parking it on the smooth sand a little ways down the southern end of the trail. Cullen was sitting on it, eyes closed, either meditating or asleep.

"Got a question for you."

"I'm busy."

"Yeah, I can tell. Squeeze me into your schedule. Those fireworks you set off . . . they'd have been visible from a long ways off. If Miriam was watching, would she have known what you did? Or would she have thought that was the node blowing up?"

His eyes opened. He tilted his head, thinking it over. "Good question. It's not something she would've seen before, probably not something anyone she knows has ever seen. Nodes don't go unstable often, and when they do, they don't often leave witnesses. I've read a description in an old journal, but she probably hasn't. She doesn't share my interest in old documents relating to the Art. So . . . yeah, she could easily have assumed her plan had worked."

"Then she thinks she got away with it. Good." Miriam would head back to her condo—was probably there now—and Karonski would station however many officers were needed to keep her from leaving. Would they be armed with tranq weapons? Should she call him and . . . no, she told herself, though her fingers twitched with the urge. Karonski was in charge, and he was certainly capable of thinking of that himself.

When her phone chimed, she immediately thought it was Karonski. Like most assumptions based on coincidence, that was wrong.

"Glad to learn that you didn't blow up," a familiar voice said.

Lily stiffened. She touched the mute. "Get Rule. Fast," she told Cullen—who shot off the bench as if he'd been fired from a cannon.

"Shocked you speechless, have I?" Robert Friar said. There was an odd, breathy quality to his voice.

She unmuted the call. "I was trying to think of a polite way to say that I wish you had."

"You'd settle for such an impersonal death? We are different, you and I. I'd find it deeply unsatisfying if someone else killed you."

"I'm not picky. You took some bullets. How badly are you hurt?" She heard Rule call out something to Barnaby.

"Not fatally, obviously, but you will be pleased to know that I'm in a great deal of pain. Why don't I tell you why I called?"

"I am curious about that. Among other things. You calling from a disposable?"

"Of course."

Rule arrived at a run. Cullen was right behind him. She made a hushing gesture and pointed at the phone. In this form Rule couldn't prick his ears, but he looked like he wanted to. She didn't put it on speaker; no need on Rule's behalf, and the microphone might pick up sounds she didn't want Friar to hear.

"I wish to make a deal," Friar said.

She snorted. "Yeah, that'll happen." Rule had gone on high alert the moment he heard Friar's voice. He leaned close. Cullen crowded up to Lily's other side, making sure he didn't miss anything, either.

"You need me and I, unfortunately, need you. I'm too

badly injured to save the world on my own tonight. I propose to put myself in your hands, entirely at your mercy, so we can do that together."

"Saving the world being so high on your priority list."

"I was attacked." His voice was lower now. Rougher, with real emotion leaking through. It sounded like fury. "Nearly killed, although I'm quite difficult to kill these days. Armand *was* killed. The knife was taken from me and will be used by one who will place this world forever beyond the dominion of my mistress by destroying it. Yes, saving the world is high on my priority list tonight. Revenge is near the top as well." He paused, and when he spoke again his voice had smoothed out. "I'm assuming you're aware that I had an artifact—a knife—and that someone took it from me. I can find it."

She met Rule's eyes. So far, Friar seemed to be telling the truth. "Can you, now?"

"Because of the previous ritual, I'm linked to it. You want to find that knife, Lily. I will lead you to it. In exchange, you will refrain from harming or imprisoning me. Together we will take it from the person who now holds it, thus saving the world."

"You trust me to keep my word?"

He chuckled. It turned into a coughing fit, which continued painfully for a moment. "Ah, that hurt," he said at last. "My lung hasn't healed yet. No, I don't trust you. You and I are different, but not in that way. You're a practical soul. You'll kill me if you can, but not until you've gotten what you need from me. I will, however, trust the word of Rule Turner. He would also like to kill me, but if he gives his word, he'll keep it. Is he listening, by the way?"

Lily looked at Rule. *Should we admit that?* He raised his brows. *Up to you.*

"Why should we believe you?" she asked, tacitly agreeing that Rule was with her. "Seeing as how your word isn't worth used toilet paper."

"I could, of course, be lying in order to lead you into a trap, but it's unnecessary. If I'm telling the truth, I'll be taking you to someone who's channeling the power of a god. Someone who will certainly try to kill you, and may succeed. It's quite amusing, really. By telling the truth, I may lead you to your deaths—and you want me to do that." He certainly sounded amused, in a breathless way. A bullet to the lung? "I will, however, do my poor best to keep you alive until the knife is retrieved. I can't do it myself, not in time."

"What's this business about channeling the power of a god?"

"What do you know about the knife?"

She wasn't about to hand him everything, but she could prime the pump by telling him what he already knew or could guess. "It's an ancient sidhe artifact you got from Benessarai. Lots of magic and what the sidhe call *arguai*. When you killed Debrett with it, it sucked up every memory of the man."

"Almost every memory," he corrected her. "Choosing him for the first sacrifice was a mistake. A natural one— who would have thought you'd have any memory of a man you never met?"

"What makes you think I do?"

"Come now, Lily. Just because I can't eavesdrop on you doesn't mean I can't listen elsewhere, and cops are a talkative bunch."

And with his magically powered luck, it would have been easy to Listen to the right person at the right time. "Why did you pick Debrett?"

"Why do you think?" There was a strong flavor of smirk in that statement. "But I shouldn't have allowed my desire to make you suffer bias my choice. Not that I had any way of knowing you would be somehow protected, and I confess I do not understand that. Still, it was a mistake. Whatever memory you retained of Debrett created an imperfection, a tiny knot, that allowed someone else to hitch a ride on the power generated by the ritual."

"Someone else?"

"A sidhe god. The one to whom the knife is linked."

Sam hadn't said anything about the knife being tied to a

god. He had indicated the sidhe probably weren't telling him everything, though. He'd called the information they gave him accurate but probably incomplete. "That's bad news for you, since you want it for the Big B."

"Bad news for all of us, since the god's resurrection will destroy our world."

"His resurrection."

"Dyffaya áv Eni is the sidhe god of chaos, compulsion, and madness. Or he was . . . either present or past tense applies, since his current state is ambiguous. The sidhe killed him over three thousand years ago, you see. But life and death are not the same for gods as for mortals, and they vary even among the gods. If one who was born a mortal assumes a godhead, it is possible to kill the god's body. Difficult, but possible. The sidhe achieved that much, but the individual who occupied the godhead retreated into it. Godheads may fade or change over the centuries, but they cannot be destroyed. Dyffaya áv Eni . . . that's a call-name, of course. It means Beautiful Madness. Dyffaya still exists, but not in a manner that would make sense to you and I. He wants more than that limited existence. He wants to walk in the world again."

"I'm sensing a contradiction. He wants to walk in the world, so he'll destroy it."

"It wouldn't be destroyed instantly. It would degrade. Using the knife creates a certain instability. Perhaps your sorcerer is aware of this? I used it in a way that minimized the instability. My mistress wants to save this world and all who live here, not destroy it. Dyffaya won't be so careful. The—" He stopped with a gasp and wheezed painfully for a moment. "I will be glad when that bullet finally works its way out. Dyffaya will enjoy himself here—the chaos of a disintegrating realm will feed him. Before the realm dissolves completely, he'll leave. He has enemies in the sidhe realms he will wish to rebuke. You have, I believe, heard of the Queens."

"Yes." She exchanged another look with Rule. What Friar said fit with what Sam had told them. Did that mean it was true? Some of it, she thought, but how much and which parts?

"Have I persuaded you, Lily?" Her name sounded greasy and overly intimate in his mouth. "You and your inhuman lover? I think you can't afford to dismiss me. Am I right? Shall we make a deal?"

She saw Rule's opinion in his scowl. He shook his head to make sure she understood. For herself . . . Friar was right, damn him. She couldn't afford to dismiss him. "I need to think about this."

"I'll call you back in a few minutes. Don't delay, Lily. We haven't much time. I arranged the second sacrifice for tonight for a reason. Whoever holds the knife now will use it tonight."

"You can't trust him," Rule said the instant she disconnected.

"I don't. That doesn't mean I can't use him." That sounded way too close to what Friar had said. She hated the idea that she and he were alike in any way. "It fits. Everything he said fits. He may be lying about some of it, but we know the knife is bad news. We know we need to stop whoever has it from using it. And we don't have a clue how to do that, how to find the blasted thing."

"Dark moon," Cullen said.

"What are you talking about?" Rule snapped.

He shrugged. "That's the obvious reason for the rite to take place tonight. It's the dark of the moon. If I were summoning a god of madness, that's when I'd do it."

Lily felt she had to point something out. "Friar wasn't summoning a crazy dead god, though. He was trying to make enough of a rip in reality to bring *her* in."

"Magically speaking, dark moon means two things—the period when the moon isn't visible, which lasts from one-and-a-half to three-and-a-half days, and the distinct moment when the moon and sun are in conjunction. We haven't hit that moment yet, so Friar must have opted for the broader period, when reality thins out."

"Which doesn't make anything he said true," Rule said

evenly. "We don't even know for sure that someone stole the knife. He may be luring us to him so he can use it on one of us."

Lily opened her mouth to argue . . . and closed it again. He was right. He was right, and she'd missed that possibility entirely. They'd assumed that because the knife was missing, the shooter—Miriam—had taken it. But Friar was missing, too. He'd been hurt, sure, but he'd gotten away. What if he'd held on to the knife?

Her mind clicked through the possibilities that thought opened up . . . and came up with the same answer. "If he's got the knife and is luring us to him, we still have to go. It doesn't matter who has the knife. We can't let them use it."

"I could go alone."

"If you're serious—which is hard to believe—then remember that Friar called me, not you. Do you think he'd agree to a deal that left me free to arrest him or shoot him or whatever? He'll want me under his eye."

"Because he wants you dead."

"Yeah, and I'm sure he'd honor any deal he made with you and let you just walk away with the knife."

"The knife we aren't supposed to come in range of, you mean?"

She just looked at him. He wasn't really trying to talk her out of this. He knew the stakes . . . the ones she was trying hard not to think about. Phrases like "the fabric of the realm" and "destroy the world" were likely to set loose the gibbering fool at the back of her brain if she let her attention pause there. Finally she said, "You make the deal when he calls. You're good at that sort of thing." She held out her phone.

After a long moment, Rule sighed and accepted both the phone and the necessity. "All right, but you seem to be pretty good at closing a deal yourself."

THIRTY-SIX

～

LILY was glad she'd handed the phone to Rule. It would never have occurred to her to have Friar swear by his mistress's name. One of her names, anyway.

The deal consisted of three terms that applied to both sides and two just for Friar. First term: If any of them broke their word, the deal was off. Second term: The deal lasted until the knife was recovered and placed in the custody of a saint—a stipulation that startled Friar. Either he didn't know about Hardy, or he faked surprise really well. Third term: Everyone agreed not to harm or cause harm to the other side. Harm included physical harm, magical assault, arrest, drugging and other forms of incapacitation, imprisonment, and duress. In addition, Friar would allow them to search him, and he would not engage in any illegal actions except with Lily's express consent. "You don't jaywalk unless I say it's okay," she told him.

That had made him wheeze with what might have been amusement. "I don't walk at all at the moment."

Friar swore to abide by those terms, swore using a name Lily didn't know. Rule did, though. Then Friar gave them an address and Rule disconnected.

Lily said, "He never mentioned the 'compel, persuade, corrupt' deal."

"I noticed that. Nor did he say that the knife is named. Either he doesn't know, he doesn't understand the significance, or he's hoping to use his knowledge in some way." Rule put his fingers in his mouth and let out two loud, piercing whistles. That was the recall. Lupi could hear such a whistle for miles.

They started back to the lookout. "Do you think swearing by one of *her* names will really make Friar hold to the deal?"

"It may. He's tied to *her* strongly now, and she doesn't forswear herself."

That startled Lily. "That's oddly virtuous of her."

Cullen, a few paces ahead, said, "Words shape magic, create a flow. Those with a great deal of power experience repercussions if they break their sworn word. *She* might be really unhappy with him if he broke a vow made in her name." He shrugged. "Doesn't mean he won't, but he'll avoid it if he can."

"If he does," Rule said, his voice dropping into something close to a growl, "I'll no longer be bound by my word. Apparently he can now survive and heal bullet wounds. He wouldn't survive what I would do if my word didn't hold me back."

How desperate did Friar have to be to place himself in their hands? Unless, of course, he had no intention of doing that. They might show up at the address he'd given them and have it blow up. She reminded herself to keep in mind that Friar might still have the knife, but she didn't believe it. Her gut said he was genuinely, deeply pissed about having the knife stolen. "If he can go out-of-phase whenever he wants, he's going to be hard to sink your teeth into."

"I'd have to be quick, wouldn't I?" He said that softly, maybe because there were cops around them now. Maybe because he was warning his wolf not to linger over the kill.

"T.J.," she said as he turned to look at them, "I've got to go. Woo-woo stuff."

His eyebrows lifted. "You and Turner taking all your sniffers with you?"

"I am, yes," Rule answered without stopping.

As they reached the trail, Cullen pulled ahead and Rule dropped behind. No room to go abreast. Together all three of them shifted into an easy lope. Lily couldn't take the trail fast, not at night . . . but she wanted to. She wanted to race as fast as she could. She felt twitchy, as if she'd drunk way too much coffee.

Nerves. Jitters. This wasn't like her. Normally at this point in an operation she'd be tense but focused—on what she was doing, what her next step needed to be. She had the tense part down. It was focus she lacked. She couldn't seem to get her mind to pay attention. "If Friar doesn't have the knife, he means to use us to get it back. Once we get it away from Miriam, he'll try to take it."

"I'm still trying to work out how we'll get it away from Miriam."

"There is that." Maybe that's why she was so jumpy. They didn't have a plan. Showing up was necessary, but it wasn't a plan. Only she couldn't think of where to start.

They hit the first sharp bend. Scott and Mike joined them. Rule told Scott to have the rest of the men meet them at the cars.

From a few feet ahead of them, Cullen said, "Polyester."

"What?"

"The contagion couldn't pass through inorganics, and it came from the knife, so maybe the knife has trouble working through inorganics. We need polyester."

"I've got latex gloves."

"That's a start. We need more."

Lily's phone started on the opening bars of the polka tune she used for Karonski. She pulled it from her pocket just as Barnaby joined them at the rear. "Yes?" Her heart kicked once and started pounding, which made no sense. She could run at this pace a lot longer without her heartbeat going crazy.

"Fairchild's not at her condo. I've got an APB out. Can

you get over here? I'd like you to check the place out with your magical fingers. Maybe Rule could sniff around, too."

"Can't. I'm headed off on . . . urgent Unit business."

He was silent a moment. "I see. Advise me when you can."

"Will do." She disconnected, feeling vaguely dizzy.

Karonski had known what she meant right away when she said "Unit business." She hadn't referred to the legal Unit Twelve, whose investigation he was heading, but to the one that operated in the shadows. The Shadow Unit.

Cullen was right. They couldn't touch the knife. They had to stop Miriam from using it, but they couldn't touch it. It would be best if they didn't get near it. And that was why she'd had trouble focusing. She didn't want to go where the facts led her. But her unconscious had gotten there just fine, without the rest of her noticing. She'd told Karonski this was now something for the Shadow Unit to handle. That, in effect, she planned to act outside the law.

The best way to stop Miriam without getting close was obvious, wasn't it? Shoot her from a distance. Don't risk letting the knife take over any of them. Kill Miriam and leave the knife wherever it fell. Maybe have Cullen put up wards around it. Keep everyone away—could they leave Hardy near to keep an eye on it?—until Sam got back with the Queen's Hound.

Lily had killed to save her own life. She'd killed to stop someone from killing others. But to kill someone who was a victim herself . . . Miriam had been taken over by the knife or by the god it was linked to. Just like Officer Crown. That made her a victim, not a bad guy. Could making Miriam a victim twice over possibly be the right thing to do?

Lily wasn't sure. She was deeply, desperately unsure. Stack up the fate of the world against one woman's life, and it ought to be obvious. It wasn't.

Ruben had put her in charge of the Shadow Unit's role in this because she would try her damnedest not to see killing as the only solution . . . but he expected her to do that if she had to. Or order it done.

Did she have to? Wasn't there always a choice?

Behind her, Rule was giving crisp instructions to Scott for the men. Bound by his word, he said nothing about Friar or a crazy god or the deal they'd just made. He told Scott that he and the rest were to follow him, Lily, and Cullen to an address he could not give out at this time. Earlier, on the way to the scene, Rule had briefed the men on what Sam had told them; now he asked Scott to emphasize to the others that the knife was their most urgent priority. He said there was a good chance that Miriam Faircastle had the knife, but it was not a certainty. Yet.

When he finished, she told him that the call had been from Karonski. "Miriam isn't at her condo."

Rule was silent a moment. "That tends to support the information we just received."

It did, though it wasn't proof. But if Miriam did have the knife . . . Rule had said he was trying to think of how to stop her. Either he hadn't seen the obvious, either, or he meant that he was trying to find another way. One that didn't involve a rifle. Rule saw nothing inherently wrong with assassination, but he didn't hurt women. Killing one would rip him up inside. It would rip up any of the lupi.

What was right?

What do you believe? That's the gist of what Karonski had said when Lily picked him up at the airport. *What do you know in your gut about goodness?* She hadn't known how to answer. Maybe it was time she figured that out.

She believed in the rule of law. Individual laws might be wrongheaded, but the rule of law was a definite good.

And yet that wasn't her bedrock. At one time she thought it was, but she couldn't see it in that black-and-white way anymore. She'd been brought to accept the need for a Shadow Unit to deal with matters the law couldn't. Tonight she'd indicated to Karonski that this was a matter for that Unit, not the legal one. She'd been happy to circumvent the law, too, about the Uzi José had used on the dworg. She didn't want him jailed for using the only weapon he'd had that stopped the monsters.

Stopping the monsters. Yes. She believed in that. Heart, gut, and mind, she knew that was right.

But *stopping* was not another word for *killing*. Sometimes that was what it came down to, the only way she could stop them, but killing monsters was not the goal. Stopping them was.

And Miriam wasn't a monster. At least, not of her own free will.

Sam had told Lily once that the fundamental value for dragons was freedom of will. She believed in that, in free will and choices. That was what lay behind the whole rule-of-law thing, wasn't it? People got together and decided that those who made bad choices, ones that harmed others, were subject to consequences. Cops, laws, courts, prison . . . if you didn't believe that every person was responsible for his or her choices, there was no point in any of it.

They'd reached the road where their car was parked. Gray and Joel were there, but Ronnie hadn't made it yet. He'd been the farthest away, but he'd be there any minute, Rule said. They'd wait.

And with that, another piece of her beliefs fell into place. Lily wasn't a dragon. Free will mattered hugely, but so did teamwork. Cops, like soldiers and lupi, knew about working as a team. Other groups did, too. Families, churches, nonprofits, even businesses . . . at their core, each was about people getting together to do things no one could on their own. About working together. Helping each other the best they knew how. Their best was a long way from perfect. Even the good guys were full of flaws and foibles, and they swam in a society made up of people—every one of whom thought they didn't have enough of something. Beauty, friends, love, sex, money, food, whatever.

Sometimes you truly didn't have enough. Sometimes all the choices open to you were bad. That was what the law called mitigating circumstances, wasn't it? You were responsible for your choices, but sometimes those choices were so limited you couldn't find any good options.

You did the best you could. You *tried*. And you kept trying.

Ronnie showed up running flat-out in wolf form. Rule

told him to stay four-footed for now and get in the van. Cullen was going to drive Rule's car. He'd heard the address.

Lily slid into the backseat beside Rule and shut the door. She fastened her seat belt and said, "Ruben put me in charge of the Shadow Unit for this case."

Rule gave her a long look. "He did."

"Which of the men with us is the best with a rifle?"

"Gray. I don't think he'd ever fired a handgun before he joined us on this side of the country, but he's excellent with a rifle."

She nodded. "If Miriam has the knife, we'll do our damnedest to save her. She isn't one of the monsters by choice, is she? But if we can't . . . if the knife gets its claws in us, or if Friar tricks us somehow . . . I want Gray stationed well back with a rifle. Far enough that he should be safe from the knife's effects. He's to take her out if I signal him, or if it's obvious I've fallen under the spell of the knife."

"I agree with you in theory, but in practice . . . if Miriam can use that knife to compel or corrupt us, we don't have any business getting close to it."

He wasn't going to like this. "It can't compel me. It tried. The contagion tried to get into me, and it couldn't. As for the corrupt or persuade part . . . either the mate bond or the *toltoi* gives me some protection. We don't know how much, but some. Miriam's no fighter. If I can take her down quickly, get the knife away from her—"

"You don't seriously think I'm going to let you go in alone."

"If you're with me, what's to stop her from compelling you to stop me from stopping her?" That came out tangled. "You know what I mean. What's to stop her?"

Rule's face turned dark. His eyes did, too, in the way that said he was fighting for control. He didn't speak.

Into his grim silence, Cullen chirped, "Polyester?"

THIRTY-SEVEN

❧

FRIAR didn't like Lily's plan any better than Rule had, but for different reasons. "You have fucking got to be joking."

The address he'd given them turned out to be a florist's shop. They'd taken elaborate precautions getting inside, all of which turned out to be unnecessary. He'd had help getting there, according to Ronnie's nose, but he was alone now. Alone, unarmed, and a bloody mess. Lily's first sight of Friar had startled her into an instant's pity. He'd taken several bullets. Someone had wrapped his chest and shoulder in gauze, but they must have run out. His right arm had an old T-shirt tied around it. His left leg wasn't bandaged at all, so it was easy to see the damage there. The kneecap was gone. Pulverized.

The first thing they'd done was remove the gauze and the bloody T-shirt along with his clothes. They didn't find a damn thing except for the two bullets that his body had apparently expelled from his chest. But no weapon or wallet, just the phone he'd used to call them. Friar declined to explain the lack of a wallet.

They had a stash of medical supplies in the trunk, so they'd used some of their gauze to rewrap his wounds. No point in letting him bleed all over the leather seats. While Mike bandaged his arm, Friar told Rule to order his men outside so he could tell them something "not for public consumption." Rule ignored him. Friar then told him to "send the sorcerer away, at least. He'd find information about the knife entirely too enticing."

"The sorcerer," Cullen had said, "already knows about the knife. Both what you told me—I listened to your conversation with Lily, you see—and a few tidbits you left out. Which part did you think I'd find unbearably enticing?"

Lily had almost heard Friar's teeth grind. Maybe he was truly desperate. He looked royally pissed, but he'd gone ahead and told them at least some of the truth about the knife, ending by saying that obviously they had to shoot its current holder from a distance. That was when Lily told him she meant to go in alone . . . though that wasn't entirely settled. Cullen was pushing to go with her. He was sure his shields would protect him. She didn't mention that Gray would be staying back with a rifle.

"This is not my joking face," she said now, "and you don't have a veto."

"And I thought you were the practical one. If you—hell, you don't have to wrap it that tight."

Mike had started rewrapping Friar's chest. "Shut up," he said and kept winding.

Friar looked at Rule. "Are you going to let her throw away her life? And with it yours and everyone else's? Your clan will not survive what happens to our realm if the god is brought through."

Rule hadn't spoken much. He was crouched near his enemy, his eyes never leaving Friar's face. He was, Lily thought, about halfway into his wolf, though his voice was civilized enough. "It's surprising that a man of your intelligence—one who has had reason to learn what he could of Lily—could believe it is within my power to *let* her do anything."

Friar had quite a sneer when he made the effort. "Perhaps you'll feel differently when I tell you that the next victim is almost certainly one of your people. One or more."

"You didn't choose one of my people for your rite."

"I'm not constrained the way the god of that knife is, nor do I want to destroy our realm."

Lily wanted to smash his face in. "Shut up. Just shut up about how you don't want to destroy the world. Do you think if you say it often enough we'll believe it? You don't want that dead god coming in and taking over your playground, but you had every intention of messing it up yourself. You were going to sacrifice Angela Ward. Millions of people have memories of her. Millions. That's why you chose her, isn't it? She's loved and she's famous and cutting her out of time would create millions of victims. It would damn sure destabilize the realm, and that's exactly what you wanted."

Friar didn't answer right away. He was thinking, dammit. She'd given away more than she meant to, letting her temper lead instead of her brain. He was wondering how much more they knew and how they knew it. "Reality would have wobbled a bit," he said at last. "Nothing my mistress couldn't fix. Dyffaya áv Eni will destroy it."

"What kind of constraints is this Dyffaya under?" Rule asked.

Friar's gaze flicked to him. "Because of the way the knife was awakened and fed, its god is bound to act . . . if not precisely according to my plans, then in league with them. At least until he pulls himself fully into our realm." He shifted as if uncomfortable, but he was breathing a lot better, wasn't he? Probably because he'd expelled those two bullets. His chest was still pretty messed up, though. "If you're not going to be reasonable, you'd better call that shaman of yours. We're dealing with a sidhe god. The only chance short of bullets we have of stopping him is to invoke a deity native to our realm."

Lily was staring. "You don't know. How could you not know?"

"What are you talking about?"

Cullen's eyebrows looked like they were trying to climb

off his face. "He doesn't. He really doesn't know. And he talked about the god being bound by his rite, not the knife. It isn't just Lily's secondhand memory of Debrett that let this semidead god take over. You used the wrong bloody rite."

"You don't know what you're talking about."

Cullen gave a single, harsh bark of laughter. "Oh, don't I? Then why didn't you know that a police officer was possessed by the corruption left behind by your rite? That the corruption compelled him to shoot Nettie Two Horses?"

Friar's eyes widened. Only for a second, but it gave him away.

"You didn't know," Cullen said, leaning forward, "because you thought the knife was still in your control at that point. You thought you didn't lose control until later, but you were so bloody wrong. You used the wrong bloody rite. That knife is a *named* artifact, you stupid asshole—and you didn't know that, either, did you? A named artifact, and you didn't bind it when you woke it. Which gave this Dyffaya áv Eni a big, fat loophole to squirm through."

Silence.

"Now that," Lily said, "is interesting."

Friar's dark eyes glittered. "Almost as interesting as the fact that you knew the knife was named. Since you're so interested in us sharing information—"

"Uh-uh. You want us to take care of this little problem you've created. You're just along for the ride, so your part is supplying information. I need to know why you didn't use the knife to compel others. You carried Alan Debrett to the ritual site. You could have just told him to follow you."

He gave Lily a disdainful glance. "Had I used the knife's ability to compel, it would have strengthened the god's presence in the knife."

"Oh? And why weren't you compelled or persuaded by the knife while you held it?"

"I am wholly dedicated to my mistress. She protected me. If you're thinking your *Lady*"—he looked at Rule, making the title sound like an obscenity—"can offer you the same protection, you're wrong."

"That," Rule said pleasantly, "was a lie."

Lily smiled. Not pleasantly. "He can smell them, you know. Lies."

"Which part?" Cullen asked. "Because I'm betting it's his shields that protected him, not his devotion. Whoever crafted those shields does very nice work. They're not quite as sweet as mine, but still, quite decent work. Of course, you could say his bitch mistress protected him because its *her* power in those shields. Is that what you meant, Robert?"

"We don't have *time* for this," Friar said through gritted teeth. "Smell the truth when I tell you this: the world is at stake. If we don't stop whoever has that knife from using it, we are all doomed. We need to leave now."

"Actually, we do have a little time," Cullen said. "Assuming tonight was chosen because it's the dark of the moon—is that correct?" Friar didn't answer. Cullen went on as if he had. "I've been thinking about that. Robert here could perform his rite at any point during the dark moon period, but bringing through a dead god—that's different. You need one whopping big hole in reality to pull that off, which means the knife-holder will wait for the moment of conjunction. That's reality's sleep apnea moment. It doesn't just thin out then, it pauses. And the conjunction isn't due for . . . ." He paused, looking at Rule. "You hear her better than I do when she's veiled. How long?"

"A little over three hours."

"So there's time to make plans. Share information."

Lily looked at Cullen. "You're sure about this?"

"I could explain, but that makes you testy. Yeah, I'm sure."

"Okay." She looked back at Friar. "I want to know why you lied about the Lady's protection. And how you kept the knife from taking over Armand Jones."

Friar closed his eyes. "I will pray that, when the time comes, I'll be able to kill you very, very slowly. A quick death may have to suffice, but it will not be satisfying."

"Indulge in daydreams later. Right now I need some answers."

Friar kept his eyes closed. For a long moment he didn't speak, either gathering strength or trying to figure out how to lie without Rule smelling it. "All right." His eyes opened. He looked at Rule. "The extra magic Rhos carry may protect you. The individual who told me about the knife is sidhe, and they know almost nothing about werewolves. Half of them think you don't exist. But there's some *arguai* mixed in with the Rho's magic, and that's what might protect you. Or not. And it won't protect your men. And don't think that cut-rate compulsion you use on your men will override the knife's compulsion. The knife is much, much stronger."

"What a Rho does is not compulsion," Rule said evenly.

Wasn't it? Lily didn't let herself look at Rule. She wasn't going to give Friar the satisfaction of knowing he'd unsettled her. But how, exactly, was it *not* compulsion when Rule used the mantle to make his people obey?

Either she'd done a bad job of keeping her cop face on or she smelled upset, because Rule glanced at her and smiled slightly. "Santos," he said.

What the hell did he mean by . . . oh. Santos had been ordered to obey Lily. He hadn't. If he'd been compelled, he would have had no choice. She nodded to tell him she understood. She still wanted more of an explanation, but this was not the time.

"Whatever you call it," Friar said, "it won't stand up against what the knife can do. As for you"—he looked at Lily, his dark eyes glittering with hate—"your Gift may protect you from compulsion, but that's not certain. The knife is powered by a god, you overconfident fool. Is your Gift stronger than a god?"

"A god who just yesterday opened four gates—three of them using only ley lines, which is supposed to be impossible. That's probably a heavy lift even for a god. I'm betting he's tired right now."

"You're betting more than your own life on that assumption, and compulsion is only half of what you'd face. You are not immune to spiritual power."

"And yet I remember Alan Debrett. I must have some trick you don't know about, huh? Look"—Lily leaned forward—"you might as well accept that we're doing this my way, and we're not budging until we know more. How do we protect ourselves from the knife? Benessarai must have told you how to shield from its power. He wasn't under compulsion from it. Neither was Jones."

"Benessarai was an ass. The knife had slept for centuries in his family's vault, and he had no idea what it was. Admittedly, when asleep it's mostly inert, its nature hidden, but he knew it possessed *arguai*. He simply accepted his family's story about it, too incurious to investigate."

"So when it's asleep, it doesn't compel?"

"That's what I said. Were you listening?"

"And Jones?"

"I shielded Jones."

"Another lie," Rule observed.

"I wonder," Lily said to Rule, "if we have time for coffee. I could sure use a cup. I saw a coffeepot by the sink."

"I'll put some on." Rule rose.

"All gods damn you," Friar muttered. "All right."

STEPPENWOLF'S "Born to Be Wild" blared from the speakers of Miriam's beautiful little 1970 Karmann Ghia. Tonight she'd learned that Dafydd, her perfect, incredible Dafydd, just loved rock 'n' roll.

That wasn't his name, of course. She didn't know that, but he'd given her permission to call him Dafydd. It was the Welsh form of David and meant Beloved. A perfect call-name for her lord and god. Miriam sang along with the music, laughing when she skidded on the turn. "Oops. Guess I'm going a little fast." She felt his amusement like a chuckle in her mind—and his agreement, so she eased off on the accelerator.

He was so *close* now. So wonderfully close. She felt his nearness all the time, and he could talk to her . . . sadness pricked her. He could talk to her now, because of that poor officer.

She had no regrets about tonight. The loudness of the gun had shocked her, but killing was easy, after all. And didn't they deserve it? Robert Friar was responsible for hundreds of deaths at the Humans First rallies last year, and the other man had been part of that, too, she was sure. And they'd wanted to block her Dafydd, keep him out, keep him imprisoned and alone. The woman hadn't deserved what happened to her, but she was their fault, not Miriam's.

But the officer . . . she felt bad about him. Dafydd understood her regret, but he didn't share it. Not really. To him, they were all so ephemeral, so insubstantial . . . he took delight in them, as she might in the beauty of flowers or sweet-smelling herbs. But if you need rosemary for your dinner, you pluck it. So with that officer. He'd been needed to anchor her lord in this realm until she could take over that task. But he hadn't been prepared for it, as she had, and he worshiped elsewhere. By the time she had removed the anchoring energy, he was badly damaged. Poor man. She wondered if her lord might do anything to fix him . . .

You have a saying about eggs and omelettes, my love . . . the man's shell is too badly cracked. Even I can't get the yolk back inside.

She giggled. Wasn't it just like him to think of it that way? Perhaps later she'd go back to the hospital and finish the man off. It would be a kindness. She hadn't dared do it before. She couldn't afford to draw that kind of attention to herself.

But everything would be different soon. Everything. She reached over and stroked the knife that lay in the passenger seat. Delight shimmered through her . . . and power. Ageless, endless power. It was true that at first the feel of the knife had unnerved her. But the knife was like Dafydd. The more she touched it, the more she wanted to touch it.

What couldn't she do with this much power?

THIRTY-EIGHT

⤸

TURNED out Cullen had been right.

Armand Jones's ski mask had been acrylic, but polyester would work, too. Not perfectly, and nothing would help if any of them were fool enough to touch the knife. Friar was the only one who could do that safely. Or so he claimed, and Rule hadn't smelled a lie, so probably Friar believed that. But he claimed that synthetic fibers did offer some protection.

So they headed for Walmart.

There was one not too far out of the way—that is, as much as they knew which way they were going. Friar wouldn't tell them; he wouldn't even say how far away the cursed knife was. No surprise there. The bastard wanted to make sure they took him along, didn't he? It would be hard to double-cross them if he wasn't close by. He told them what road to take, when to turn. Otherwise he sat in grim silence, his injured leg stretched out on the seat.

Rule sat back there with him, watching him. He'd wanted Cullen watching Friar, too, in his own way, and he didn't want Lily crowded in between him and their enemy. So it was Lily behind the wheel when they pulled into the parking lot of a Walmart just off I-805. Scott and the others were behind them in the van. One of the men would run in for their synthetic headgear.

Persuasion, compulsion, and corruption. Those were the powers the knife conveyed. Friar had only talked about two of those. Lily was thinking about that as she parked the car on the outside edge of the lot. The van went on by, heading for the front of the store.

Compulsion she was pretty clear about. That was the instant, violent overthrow of free will. Persuasion and corruption were more slippery, but corruption had to be about morality. Doing wrong when you knew it was wrong. Friar didn't know the difference between right and wrong, so maybe he discounted the knife's corrupting power as meaningless. He'd maxed out on corruption already. Persuasion . . . that would be more like trickery, wouldn't it? Becoming convinced that the sky was yellow instead of blue, that up was down. Making a mistake because you weren't thinking clearly.

When she was under spiritual attack during the fight with the dworg, had that been persuasion or corruption?

Her mind had felt clear. She hadn't been tricked into making a tactical mistake. But for a few moments, it had seemed okay to kill Santos if he didn't obey her. Maybe that would have been right and moral behavior for Rule. It wasn't for her.

It sure sounded like corruption.

Cullen spoke suddenly. "Let's stretch our legs a minute."

"I think I'll pass," Friar said dryly. "Oh—you didn't mean me, did you?"

Cullen rolled his eyes and opened his door. Lily climbed out on her side, and Rule, frowning, did the same. "I don't know how good his hearing is," he said, "but I don't want to move far from the car." He headed for the back of the car, stopping a few feet from the trunk.

Lily followed. As Cullen joined them she said, "Does anyone else wonder if he's laughing at us? I mean . . . I know Jones wore a ski mask, so Friar's probably telling the truth, but the idea that cheap ski masks or knitted caps will stop this god he says is so powerful . . . it seems ludicrous."

"Hmm?" Cullen was clearly preoccupied. "No, that makes sense. It's not the magic they stop. It's the vector."

"Unpack that," Rule said.

Cullen was surprised. "I didn't explain already? I got that figured out finally. The compulsion is magical, but it has a spiritual vector. That's the only thing that fits. The contagion couldn't travel through inorganics because it's vectored—mobile—only through spirit. It's like the plague that way, where fleas were the vector. Maybe one in a million people were actually immune to the plague the way Lily is immune to the compulsion, but the trick to avoiding the plague wasn't having a superpowerful immune system. It was avoiding flea bites. That's what we have to do—block the vector. Keep those spiritual fleas away from our crown and brow chakras. I'm pretty sure the brow chakra is the key," he added, "but best to protect them both, just in case."

"Just those two chakras need to be protected?" Lily said dubiously. "The contagion didn't have to get rubbed over Crown's third eye to take him over."

"That was like someone catching the plague by sticking their fingers in diseased tissue instead of through a flea bite. And that's not a great analogy, but . . ." Cullen ran a hand over his hair. "If I tried to really explain, we'd be here all night. Just take my word for it, okay? This isn't what I wanted to talk about."

"Okay. Talk."

"Friar doesn't heal the way we do."

"What do you mean?" Rule asked.

Cullen waved toward the car and the man in it. "The magic's the wrong color, for one thing. And he's using way more power than a lupus would. Spending power like crazy."

"*Her* power." Rule's lip curled with distaste. "I feel it, sitting so damnably close to him. Are you sure he's using it for healing?"

"He's got shields. One of them makes it hard to see details, but I can see the general flow, and huge amounts of active power are localized at his injuries. So yeah, I'm pretty sure that's what he's doing. Only I'm not sure I'd call it healing." Cullen frowned, tipping his head. "It's almost as if he's remaking his body instead."

This time it was Lily who asked what he meant.

"I think he's using what the elves call body magic. Healing and body magic are . . ." Cullen wobbled a hand. "The magic is similar, but they aren't the same. Like, ah . . . you can do lots of things with your hands, but catching a ball and painting a picture are very different skill sets. Body magic's not the same skill set as healing. And using body magic to heal is like having a hole in the drywall and, instead of patching it, you take down the whole wall and rebuild it."

Lily could relate to that metaphor. She'd been living with it for over a month now. "Maybe the Big B's power can't be used for healing. Given the way she likes to gobble down death magic, that would make sense."

"Yeah, probably, but the point is that I don't know much about body magic. I've never watched someone using it and I don't know how long it will take him to finish. He might be all rebuilt a lot sooner than we're expecting. I can keep an eye on him, see if he stops spending power in the injured areas, but he could be healed enough to be a problem before that happens."

Rule frowned. "I'd hoped we could simply walk off and leave him when we got near the knife. If there's a chance he's healed or mostly healed, we'll have to keep him with us so we can watch him."

"We don't have to guess how much he's healed," Lily said. "We just take the bandages off and check."

Rule shook his head. "Only with his permission. The terms of the deal don't allow me to search him a second time."

She stared. "They don't say we can't, either!"

"If he doesn't cooperate with the search, we'd have to hold him down. That's a clear violation of the terms."

Oh, God. No wonder Friar had wanted Rule's word

instead of hers. She wouldn't have a problem bending that part of the deal. If it saved all of them from a sneak attack by someone who didn't just want to kill them, but make it last? No problem at all. But for Rule, the line was clear and absolute. "If you changed your mind about that," she said slowly, "it would probably be corruption talking."

Rule's eyebrows shot up. "What?"

"Earlier I was thinking about the difference between persuasion and corruption. Our, uh, our source didn't exactly define the terms, did he?" She didn't want to mention Sam in case Friar could hear them. As far as they knew, his hearing was only human . . . but maybe Her Bitchiness had upgraded that, too. "The way I've got it figured, persuasion messes up your thinking. Makes you lose your common sense. Corruption would make us lose our moral sense. For you, bending your word would mean a loss of moral sense."

"My word, once given, has no 'bend.' I keep it or I break it."

"That's what I mean."

Rule thought that over, then nodded. "We can use that as a canary in the coal mine. If, once we're close to the knife, I suddenly decide it's okay to break my word, we'll know that is corruption speaking."

"That would be one . . ." Lily's eyes widened in sudden dismay.

"Lily? What is it?"

She swallowed and reminded herself to keep her voice down. "You know what Drummond said about when I was fighting the dworg. There was a spiritual attack. Was the knife nearby?"

After a moment Cullen said, "Oh." And, "Shit. No one acted like they were under compulsion, did they? The dworg would've bloody won if, say, Scott had been compelled to stop fighting."

"Which means," Rule said slowly, "the knife was not nearby."

"Yeah," Lily said. "But someone was able to mount a spiritual attack anyway." And if the knife or the god could do that, how did she know any of her decisions tonight were truly hers? She wasn't corrupted. Surely she'd notice if she made a decision that ran counter to her understanding of good and evil . . . wouldn't she? But persuasion was a sly and sneaky bastard. Persuasion crept in and put thoughts in your head.

Could she trust her own thoughts? How could she tell?

MIRIAM slowed as she neared the gate, pleased with herself for finding the place. She'd only been here that once. A barbecue, that had been. Rule had invited her and others from her coven, and his people had been very welcoming . . . one of them in a most personal way. Memory made her smile, but it faded. A pity, what would happen to them all.

The guard was quite young and looked serious as only the young can. He also looked very fit. No shirt, so she could see just how deliciously fit he was. He had pretty blond hair, and she did have a weakness for blonds, so the little leap of lust didn't surprise her. Its echo did. "You want him, too? Oh, that would be lovely." She sighed. "The time's wrong, though, isn't it? Priorities, priorities." She pulled up to a stop and shut off the music.

The fit young man came up to her window. She lowered it and smiled at him. "I'm Miriam Faircastle. I need to see Isen about something I learned when I was trying to help that poor officer."

"Ma'am, I'll check, but we're not admitting anyone with weapons except for officers of the law. You'll have to either leave the gun and knife with me or lock them in your trunk."

Oh, rats, she'd forgotten how well they saw in the dark. But how did he know about the gun? It was under the seat. Had he smelled it? She reached for the knife and laid her fingers lightly on the hilt. Power surged up her arm, filling her. "Forget about the knife and the gun."

He blinked. "You need to see Isen?"

"That's right." She could just make him admit her . . . that was a giddy thought. She could make him do anything at all. Priorities, she reminded herself. She mustn't alarm Isen Turner by showing up unannounced. Dafydd said the knife wouldn't work properly on a Rho. He hadn't said why, but it didn't matter. Isen Turner would have to be put to sleep, and that would go so much more smoothly if he wasn't wary of her. "Oh, before you call . . ."

He'd taken out his phone but paused, waiting just like she wanted him to.

She beamed at him. "You're such a nice young man. You want to help me in every way possible." Her fingers tingled where they rested on the knife. "Are Lily and Rule at their house?"

"I don't know. They were here, but they left about an hour ago."

Well, they'd planned for that. Or Dafydd had. "Thank you. Now you can—"

Ask if the sorcerer and the old woman are here.

"One more question. Is Madame Yu here? Or Cullen Seaborne?"

"No, ma'am, they left."

"Thank you. Forget that I asked all that." Not that she understood why Dafydd was worried about Lily Yu's grandmother.

Not worried, love. However, we would need different tactics if they were present.

That made sense, she supposed. The old woman had some kind of Gift. Miriam doubted that she knew much spellcraft, but Gifts could be difficult to counter. As for Seaborne . . . he did know a great deal about magic, but he didn't have the kind of power available to her now. Nor did he have a god to guide him in its use. She stroked the knife again and savored the thrill.

The guard put away his phone. "Isen says you're to come ahead. You know where his house is? Just keep on the road. It dead-ends at his place."

"Thank you. Touch your nose and stick out your tongue, please."

He did.

She giggled.

F'annwylyd, Dafydd said, rebuke mixing with amusement in the Welsh endearment. She didn't know why he favored Welsh, but it was certainly a beautiful language to listen to while making love. *You will have time to play later.*

He was right, of course. She smoothed her expression to an appropriate solemnity. Reminding herself that this guard would probably be dead soon helped. "Forget about that, too," she told the lovely young man and put her window up. A moment later, he'd opened the gate and she drove through.

Her face felt chilly. How odd. She touched her cheek. It was wet. She was crying? But that made no sense, no sense at all. Soon, very soon, her Dafydd would be with her, in the flesh and forever . . . or for the rest of her life, anyway. Which might be short, given how careless her love could be even with those who mattered to him. Like her.

But that didn't matter. His happiness was all that did. She touched the sleep charm in her pocket, assuring herself it was ready. Isen and Rule Turner were protected in some way, but Isen had no defenses against a simple sleep charm—especially one with the power of a god behind it. And his men had no defenses at all.

She giggled again and turned Steppenwolf back on.

JULIA brushed her teeth as slowly as possible. She already had her pj's on, so toothbrushing was the only thing standing between her and bedtime. And she did not want to go to bed. There was too much going on. Though it was not likely, she thought bitterly as she spat toothpaste spit into the sink, that anyone would tell her much. But if she was awake when Mr. Turner and Lily got back, she'd surely learn something.

Eavesdropping on the grown-ups' conversation in the great room hadn't worked all that well. Carl turned on some music, for one thing, so she only heard little bits of what people said, but everyone had seemed to be talking to someone she couldn't hear. It took forever for her to figure out that the dragon must be talking to them in their heads.

To them, and not her, when she was the one who'd had all her memories stolen. It wasn't right. They made all the decisions and didn't tell her anything.

Not much of anything, anyway. She did know why Mr. Turner left with Lily. Someone had been killed and they were supposed to investigate. The gorgeous man who wanted her to call him Cullen, not Mr. Seaborne, had gone with them. Then Grandmother wanted to leave so she could protect the people at Mr. Turner's house, who were in a different clan and couldn't come here, where it was safer. The scary one—Benedict—and his girlfriend, who had a weird name Julia couldn't remember and a ton of curly red hair, had given Grandmother a ride. As soon as they left, so did the woman with all the tattoos and the beautiful little baby, and Julia never got a chance to ask if she could hold the baby.

Julia spat one last time and rinsed her mouth with water and sighed. Everyone had important things to do and no one wanted her to do anything but go to bed. If she were really fifty-seven . . .

The bathroom door opened without anyone knocking. Julia turned and scowled—but it was Li Qin. That made Julia's eyes widen. Li Qin was the politest person ever, and not in a fake way. It was just how she was. She breathed out courtesy the way a rose gives off scent.

Li Qin held her finger to her lips and motioned for Julia to come.

Curious and a little bit scared for no reason she could tell, Julia did. That crazy guy who sang because he couldn't talk right was in the hall, waiting. He patted her on the shoulder. Li Qin made that shushing gesture again, and the come-along gesture, and limped to the door to Toby's room.

She had a big boot on her broken foot now, but she still needed to use one of her crutches. She opened Toby's door.

Were they going to have a secret party? Stay up late after all, only Toby's grandfather wasn't supposed to know? Julia grinned and paused in the doorway.

Toby was just sitting up. He looked bleary, as if he'd been asleep, which maybe he had been because he'd had to go to bed half an hour before Julia. "What—" he started.

Li Qin hushed him.

Hardy pushed on Julia's back, getting her to move all the way into Toby's room. He closed the door.

Li Qin whispered, "A very bad person is coming. Hardy tells me we must leave."

Toby whispered back, "If it's someone bad, we have to warn my grandfather."

Julia entered into the whispering. "How could Hardy tell you anything? He can't talk. And how would he know?"

Li Qin smiled. "The angels speak to Hardy, and he sings their meaning. Toby, your grandfather will need our help. We must not be caught here, or we cannot help him. How do we leave without being caught?"

Angels? Li Qin thought the crazy guy listened to angels?

"Grandpa says Hardy walks with angels." Toby gave the man a careful look as if he might be able to see angels hanging around him. He bit his lip, then nodded. "We could go out the window. The guards will hear us or smell us, but we aren't hiding from them, are we?"

Li Qin looked at Hardy. "Hardy?"

He tilted his head. His eyes looked sleepy, not like he was worried or anything. After a moment he hummed some song Julia didn't know.

"We wait for the bell," Li Qin whispered.

"What bell?" Julia whispered back.

The doorbell rang. Julia jumped.

"Quickly." Li Qin limped to the window. "Toby, you go first, please."

THIRTY-NINE

WHEN Friar had Lily turn onto an all-too-familiar road heading out of town, she knew where they were going. Rage swam up hot and strong. Her fingers tightened on the steering wheel, making her turn jerky.

She wasn't the only one. "You son of a bitch," Cullen breathed. "You knew where it was all along. You knew, and made sure we didn't call and warn anyone."

Lily didn't dare take her eyes off the road, so she didn't see exactly what happened. One second Cullen was staring at Friar. The next there was the smack of flesh on flesh and Cullen bounced back into the seat, having left it so abruptly Lily missed it.

"Cullen," Rule said. "No."

Cullen subsided, breathing heavily. "I didn't swear to anything."

"I did," Rule said. "And you're under my authority. You will not cause me to forswear myself. And neither," he added in a voice dropped straight into arctic cold, "will he."

No question who *he* was. Lily flexed her hands on the wheel, encouraging circulation to return. "You might as well admit it," she told the bastard in the backseat. He was gloating. She was sure of it, though she couldn't see his face. "The knife's at Clanhome, isn't it?"

"I did warn you," the bastard in question said in a silky voice. "I said the next victim would probably be one of your people, and where else does one find your people?"

Yeah, he'd known all along where the knife was—and he'd made sure they didn't call and warn Isen. That had been part of the goddamn deal. Lily breathed deep, trying to keep calm. She was driving. She couldn't fling herself over the seat the way Cullen had tried to do.

"Perhaps we don't need you now," Rule said. "We know where we're going."

"Clanhome's a big place, and time is short. Do you want to waste some of that time hunting the knife?"

"Cullen," Rule said, "will the knife's holder need a node for the rite?"

Cullen was silent for a long moment. "I don't know. I don't bloody know. I'd think they would want one, but that damn dead god managed to open gates without a node."

"You see?" Friar sounded much too smug. "You can't assume you can go straight to that node of yours. What if they're using a ley line instead? Plenty of them to choose from."

Lily wanted to grab his tongue and yank it out. She could imagine doing just that. Get a pair of pliers, grip that slimy, lying tongue with them, and rip it out, then watch him choke on his own blood and . . . and what in God's name was she thinking?

She'd long wanted Friar dead. She could have killed him, given the chance. Right or wrong, she knew she was capable of that, but to imagine torturing him . . . that wasn't her. Surely that wasn't her. She shuddered and wished she knew how to pray, but the only one she remembered from her religion-averse childhood started *Now I lay me down to sleep*, which was no help at all.

What do you believe in?

Try. And keep trying. "Now that we know roughly

where we're going, we can start making plans," she said in a voice that surprised her. She sounded a lot more level than she felt.

MIRIAM stood in the open French doors. Outside on what was left of the deck, five brawny men pried up the last boards. They were shirtless and lovely to watch, but she felt so . . . so impatient. Restless. As if parts of her were trying to fly away even while the rest of her stood here, watching. She couldn't begin laying out what was needed for the ritual until the earth was bare and had been raked to remove any nails that might have fallen.

There's time, a beloved voice said soothingly.

He was right. Of course he was right, though she glanced at her watch anyway, to see how much time. An hour and fifty minutes until the conjunction, and really, the ritual required very little prep. "I don't know why I'm so jittery," she said apologetically. "I can't seem to think clearly."

Their plans had changed after she got here. Originally, Miriam had intended to use a node that was halfway up a rocky hill, but just as she could now hear her beloved and feel his presence, he could now perceive the world through her. Yet he hadn't sensed the node behind the house until she was almost on top of it, which had intrigued him greatly. He'd changed the location for the ritual. There was something about that node, he said, that he needed to understand. Something connected to Isen Turner . . . who she would sacrifice atop that node in an hour and fifty minutes.

If they ever got all those stupid boards removed.

Love, you're shaking.

Was she? How odd. "It's a bit unpleasant," she whispered. "What I must do to him is . . . I know him, you see."

He crooned to her in Welsh—a beautiful, lilting language she didn't know, but that soothed her in one way even as it roused her in another. It was the language he used for lovemaking. She forgot to be shaky and upset and licked her lips. "That both helps and doesn't."

He chuckled. *There was a man you were eyeing earlier.*

"The one in charge of security?" She'd forgotten his name, but she remembered him quite well otherwise. Long and lean, very masculine, with straw-colored hair and the most beautiful way of moving . . . she turned, knowing exactly where he was.

Everything had gone perfectly, and all she'd had to do was follow Dafydd's plan . . . which was just as well, because for some reason she couldn't plan well herself right now. But Dafydd had thought of everything. First put Isen Turner to sleep, then have the guards nearby come in. They'd told her who was in charge of security; they'd summoned the man by saying his Rho wanted him. The security man—what was his name?—had done as he was told, too. He'd brought twenty of the guards here and made sure those currently patrolling wouldn't interfere. The knife could control more than that, but Dafydd was reserving most of its power for the ritual. Miriam had given those twenty guards her instructions—Dafydd's instructions—and told the security man to wait right there, next to the table.

And so, of course, he had.

Go work out your fidgets, little one. And he goosed her right between her legs with a flare of heat.

She laughed out loud and wiggled, delighted with the hunger that spread out from his touch, and walked up to the tall man watching her silently. She ran a hand up his chest. "Mmm. What was your name again?"

"Pete," he said, never taking his eyes off her.

"Well, Pete, I have something else I'd like you to do." She took his hand and led him to the closest bedroom.

LILY stopped the car beside the sign that notified people they were about to run out of public road. Just ahead, the road swerved around a tall, stony outcrop, then ran straight for a half mile, right up to the gate to Clanhome. Rule leaned forward to squeeze her shoulder, then climbed out. Cullen got out, too. The van pulled in behind her, but Joel didn't shut off its engine. Everyone but him piled out; Mike, Barnaby, Gray, and Ronnie headed off with Rule and Cullen into the brush. Scott joined Lily in the Mercedes. He sat in back with Friar and pulled out his knife to have it ready. Just in case.

The gate guards would have heard them coming, but with luck the van's louder engine had hidden the sound of the Mercedes. The last turnoff before Clanhome was about four miles back, and people who'd missed it sometimes noticed the sign and turned around here. Joel would imitate them, turning the van around and heading back up the road for seven minutes. He'd then turn around again and drive back, timing his arrival for fifteen minutes from now.

Fifteen minutes had to be enough. The conjunction was only an hour and twenty minutes away. Lily settled herself to wait, her phone in one hand.

When they started making plans, it was immediately obvious that they didn't know enough. Friar still wouldn't tell them more than "turn left" or "go straight." That had to change, but they also had to find out more about the situation at Clanhome. Any or all of its residents might be under Miriam's control, and they didn't know enough about how that worked. So they'd decided to grab a couple of Nokolai and find out.

The gate guards, to be specific. The gate was far enough from any of the houses that no one would see what happened there. There were always two guards there, one four-footed and one on two legs. The four-footed guard often patrolled along the fence, staying within hearing range of the gate so he could speed back if needed. He would have heard their cars, so if he wasn't at the gate now, he soon would be.

It was really hard to subdue a wolf without hurting him. Lily didn't know how Rule planned to handle that, but he and his men shouldn't have a problem capturing the two-legged guard. When he had both of them, he'd call Lily. All she had to do was wait. And wait. And try not to keep checking her watch because that would make her crazy, but . . .

Her phone vibrated. She checked the screen, huffed out a sigh of relief, and started the car. "On my way," she told him.

The gate was open. Rule stood near it. Gray and Barnaby held a blond young man named Cory whom she'd met a few times. Ronnie and Mike gripped the arms of the other man, whose name she couldn't remember, though she'd seen him around Clanhome. Not as much of him as she was seeing now, though. He was naked.

Lily shut off the car and got out. "He was wolf when you arrived?"

Rule nodded. "I told him to Change. He did. He and Cory tell me that Pete called about an hour ago and told them that Clanhome was closed. No one was to be admitted, no exceptions—yet he didn't give them an alert code. He also told them to call him immediately if you, Cullen, or I arrived."

Her eyebrows lifted. "Did he, now. What did you tell them?"

"Nothing yet, except that you're going to check them for magic, and they are to hold still while you do."

Better get it done, then. Lily went up to the naked guy first. "I'm afraid I've forgotten your name."

"Gene." He looked more puzzled by the odd behavior of his Lu Nuncio than upset.

She put her left hand on his bare shoulder. Fur-and-pine tingles . . . typical lupus magic. She checked his face in case this was one of those rare magics that localized, though the contagion hadn't done that with Officer Crown. "Nothing." She went to Cory and his two attendants.

Her first touch, on his arm, told her this magic didn't localize. Ugh. She checked his face, just to see if that made a difference, then stepped back and gave Rule a nod. "Feels just like what was on Officer Crown, but he's only got a smidgen of it."

"I've got what?" Cory asked, confused and alarmed. "There's something on me? Some kind of magic?"

"I'm afraid so," Rule said. "Cullen?"

Cullen stepped close to Cory and walked around him, looking him up and down. Finally he made a square of his hands, using his magnifying spell to study Cory's forehead. "It's damn subtle," he said at last. "I'd bet it gets brighter if she gives him an order—more power coming in then—or maybe if he's carrying out an order. But right now there's only a slight blurring over his brow chakra. Hard to spot without magnification."

Damn. It would've been handy if Cullen could have checked people for compulsion from a distance.

"What is it?" Cory said, really worried now. "What's wrong with me?"

Rule looked at him. "I'll explain in a moment. Did Miriam Faircastle come to the gate tonight?"

"Yes. Around ten, maybe a little after. I could check the log."

"Tell me what you both said and did."

"She wanted to see Isen—something about an officer. 'That poor officer,' she said. So I called to ask. Isen gave permission and I told her to go straight ahead and the road would end at his house."

Rule looked at the other man. "Gene? Is that what happened?"

"Yes, except that he left out the part about the weapons. And, uh, a bit of flirting. Miriam likes to flirt, and so does Cory."

"I didn't flirt with her," Cory said, indignant. "And what weapons are you talking about?"

"You told her she had to either put her knife and gun in the trunk or leave them with you."

It turned out that Gene hadn't been at the gate when Miriam arrived, but on his way back to it. He hadn't seen Miriam or her car, but he'd heard them talking. What he reported of that conversation didn't match what Cory said. But according to Rule's nose, Cory wasn't lying. He truly didn't remember some of the things Gene said.

Like being told a couple of times to forget things. That was part of what Gene had assumed was a flirtation. "What kind of flirty things did she say? At one point she told him he was a nice young man for wanting to help her out. I think she said he wanted to do anything possible to help her."

"Do you remember that, Cory?" Rule asked.

"Yes." Cory was pale.

"Do you remember Miriam asking where Lily and I were?"

Cory shook his head.

Miriam had asked about Grandmother and Cullen, too. Cory didn't remember that. Then Rule questioned Gene about where he'd been when Miriam and Cory were talking. More than two hundred yards from the gate, Gene thought. He was sorry, but he couldn't be more precise. Not more than three hundred yards, though. He was sure of that, because he hadn't yet reached that abandoned rabbit burrow near the twisted pine.

Three hundred yards was close enough for lupus ears to hear every word spoken. It was not, apparently, close enough for the knife to make Gene obey Miriam's order to "forget." Not close enough to leave the taint of its compulsion on him.

Lily shot Rule a tight grin. The delay here had been very much worthwhile. "Three hundred yards. We can assume that's the knife's limit. It might be less, but we can work with that."

"That's important to know." He paused. "She's got Pete."

That took her grin away. "And Isen, I suppose. And . . . everyone who was at Isen's house when she got there." Toby, Julia, Li Qin, Hardy, Carl, the guards who'd been stationed there . . . Cynna? Had she been there? Cory and Gene both said that Grandmother had left with Benedict and Arjenie before Miriam arrived, but Cynna might have still been at Isen's house. With Ryder.

She glanced at Cullen. He looked as grim as she felt.

Rule spoke crisply. "However many she might have placed under compulsion, we've no reason to think she's harmed anyone yet."

He was doing that I'm-in-control thing with his voice to

make Cullen and his men feel better. Damned if it didn't work on her, too. "That's true. And I'm betting she doesn't have everyone under compulsion. Maybe not even most of them. If she did, wouldn't she have had Cory kill or capture us instead of just giving Pete a heads-up? And logistically, it would be hard for her to get everyone together so she could put them under compulsion. Plus, it would take time, and she's got a ritual to prepare for. If she's using the more distant node, just getting there will take time. If she's using the one behind Isen's house, she'll have to get rid of the deck."

"If she's using a ley line," Cullen pointed out, "she won't have those problems."

"Yes, but . . . she went to Isen's house."

Rule nodded slowly. "She did, didn't she? I find it interesting that Pete ordered Clanhome closed without giving an alert code. That's standard. Omitting the code sounds as if he repeated what he'd been told to say."

"I'm not sure what you're getting at."

"I'm not sure either, except that it sounds like he did what he was told to do, and not one bit more. He didn't tell Miriam there was a code he was supposed to use."

"So he has to obey, but that doesn't really put him on her side?"

"I think so. In which case, a lot depends on the exact wording of the orders she gives."

"Another thing we learned," Cullen said. "The compulsion remains in effect after the knife's gone. Cory's still contaminated, and he doesn't remember anything he was told to forget."

"Ah." Rule frowned. "Yes. We need to take that into account."

"Rule?" That was Cory. "Can you tell me what's going on now?"

"Miriam has gotten hold of an artifact. She used it to place compulsions on you. That's why you don't remember some things. She told you to forget, and you did. I'm sorry, Cory, but we're going to have to tie you up for now. You're subject to Miriam's control. We can't trust you."

"But I wouldn't do anything against you or the clan. I wouldn't!"

"How do you feel about Miriam, Cory?"

"I want to help her in any way I can, of course, but . . ." Horror widened his eyes. "Why do I want that?" he whispered.

The answer was obvious to all of them. Gene got a length of rope from the back of the old truck they kept near the gate for the guards' use. While he tied up his friend, Rule told Gene, "Stay here with Cory. You're not to call Pete or obey any orders he gives you until Isen or I tell you it's okay."

Lily heard the van coming. "Our other ride's nearly here. We need to decide if we're going with plan A or plan B." They'd laid out two general plans depending on where the knife was. She paused. "I'm betting on plan B. Miriam did go to Isen's house."

"Yes, she did." Rule looked at his car. His smile was slow and cold. "I'll have a word with Friar about that. I've an idea how to persuade him to talk."

FORTY

~

RULE crouched low, using his hands now and then to assist his descent. Smells filled him . . . creosote, cypress, and sumac. Wild mustard and cholla. The warm, dry smell of the dirt. The scents of home welcomed him and the mantle tied to this land pushed him away.

Off to his left, a pair of shadows drifted stealthily down the slope. On his right four more did the same . . . unless Gray had found his spot already. Even to lupus eyes it was dark tonight, too dark for Rule to be sure Gray still descended with them. Some kind fate had drawn a skim of clouds over the stars, and the moon was dark.

Behind him, on the other side of the ridge, he'd left the man he wanted to kill almost as much as he wanted his next breath. Almost was not enough, not with other priorities crowding it out. He'd left Friar there, knowing the man might be lying about being unable to walk. The easy sound of Friar's breathing suggested he'd knitted up his damaged chest, so it seemed his body magic did indeed work more quickly than lupi healing.

Friar hadn't wanted to tell them where the knife was. Rule had told him he might as well, because he was no longer necessary. He'd prefer not to endanger Cynna by involving her, but if Friar wouldn't cooperate, they'd have to. From this close, Cynna could undoubtedly Find the knife.

That wasn't true, of course. Cynna was a powerful Finder, but an artifact that could hide from a hellhound might be able to fool her Gift, even this close. But Rule had been convincing, and Friar had bought it.

They'd been right. Miriam was at Isen's house with the knife.

Rule had decided to bring Friar with them most of the way so Friar could tell them if Miriam left the house with the knife. According to Friar she'd stayed put, so when they reached a certain steep-sided gully on the other side of the ridge they were crossing, Rule had deposited Friar in it. This didn't violate their deal; he hadn't been harmed, and the gully was no prison. Even if Friar's knee was still as damaged as he claimed, he could make his way out. Slowly and painfully, perhaps, but Rule hadn't sworn to make the bastard's life easy.

It made Rule twitchy as hell to have his enemy behind him, but what lay ahead worried him more. Below him lay his father's house . . . and at least fifteen Nokolai guards. Rule didn't think that was a complete count, but at least fifteen superbly trained Nokolai awaited them, all of them certainly under compulsion. He had six Leidolf.

They wouldn't be enough. Not enough to take Miriam down. Probably not enough to even get close. For all their care and the boon of the breeze, which carried their scent away from the house, they'd surely be spotted soon. He refused to think about how many might die tonight. But they were, he hoped, enough to distract Miriam. Enough, he prayed, to let Lily and Cullen arrive undetected.

One of the night's ironies was that the plan Friar had fought so hard for—the one Rule had to admit made the most tactical sense—would never have worked. No sniper could take Miriam out if she stayed near the node. He'd known that from the moment they'd realized she meant to use the node behind Isen's home . . . the one linked to the mantle, making this land Nokolai.

Isen's house was tucked up against a rumpled fold of the mountains that sheltered this valley. It was impossible to come at the house unseen from the front or sides; Benedict had run enough tests of his security for Rule to be certain of that. The only possible approach was from the rear, where there was a lower deck, an upper deck, and this rough, rocky hill dotted with trees and low-growing brush.

The node was next to the house, beneath the lower deck—and the lower deck was roofed. That roof blocked any line of sight a sniper might have used, so shooting Miriam from a distance had never been an option.

Shooting others was. Gray and his rifle would still come in handy. He wouldn't charge with the rest of them, but would wait above them and pick off as many guards as possible. *Avoid head shots,* Rule had told him, knowing Gray might have no choice but to put a bullet in the brain of one of Rule's people. His other people.

He checked his watch. He could get a little closer before they stood and charged.

There was no way to reach the deck silently. The slope wasn't bad here, but close to the house it varied between steep and perpendicular. They'd have to jump down the last fifteen feet or so—if they made it that far. No great distance, but it couldn't be done silently, so the plan included stealth only up to a point. Then they'd be obvious as hell.

And then men he'd lived and played with, men he'd fought beside and loved for the kin they were, would try to kill him. Or so he had to assume. He'd told his men—his Leidolf clansmen—to avoid death wounds if possible, but they, too, might have to kill.

And all of that assumed that the cheap acrylic caps they wore worked as they were supposed to. So far they had. If that changed, they would all die tonight.

Not yet, he begged the Lady, for whatever luck her grace might bring. *Don't let me die yet.* If he could live long enough to give Lily and Cullen a chance . . . and with them, his son, his father, his clan. And everyone and everything else.

There was only one way to reach the node behind Isen's house . . . from the outside. But there was another way, of course. Through the house. Which could be reached through the tunnel that opened up in Isen's study.

LILY sat on the cool dirt floor of the tunnel and checked her watch. Seven more minutes. She swallowed and told her heartbeat to settle down. It didn't listen.

It was dim here, but not dark. A mage light bobbed up near the low ceiling. Cullen's doing. He was pacing, moving cat-quiet but too restless to stop.

Cullen had many talents. Waiting wasn't one of them. Lily, on the other hand, was normally pretty good at it. Cops got plenty of practice in the fine art of waiting.

Nothing was normal tonight. *You've done this sort of thing before,* she told her jittery heartbeat and checked her watch again. Her hand shook, a fine tremor that seemed to begin in her belly. Dammit, dammit, dammit . . . She'd gone into bad situations before, yeah. High-stakes situations, when she had no idea if her plan had any chance of working But she'd never imagined going into a fight not knowing if her plans were even *hers*. If her thoughts were her own.

She was immune to compulsion, but like Friar kept pointing out—damn him—not to persuasion or corruption. How could she trust the decisions she made tonight?

Lily sucked in a shaky breath and rubbed the *toltoi* with her thumb. Was it warmer than usual? She wanted that to be true, wanted to think it was protecting her. She wished like hell Drummond would show up and tell her if someone or something was influencing her. She thought his name as hard as she could.

Nothing.

Getting here had been simple enough. Nerve-wracking, but simple. This tunnel was larger and more elaborate than the one they were putting in at their place. It had three arms leading to three access points: one at a stand of trees only thirty yards from Isen's house; one under the water tower; and one at the general store.

Lily and Cullen had driven up to the general store and walked in. Simple.

They hadn't used the Mercedes. The clan kept an old truck near the gate. Supposedly it was there for the guards, but people borrowed it all the time. The old truck was such a familiar sight that Rule thought no one would pay any attention to it, but if someone had—if they'd been stopped—Lily would have pretended to be Cullen's prisoner. Cullen would have pretended to be among the compelled, delivering Lily to Miriam.

It was Rule who'd seen that the problem with trying to figure out who was under compulsion went both ways. No doubt Miriam knew who she controlled, but those she'd compelled into obedience couldn't know who was like them or what she'd told others. At worst, Cullen figured they'd confuse anyone who tried to detain them long enough for him to use a sleep charm.

As it turned out, they hadn't needed to do anything but drive up and go inside. No one stopped them; as far as they could tell, no one saw them. The store was closed at this hour, but it was never locked. People went there after hours all the time and left a note about what they'd bought along with cash or an IOU. The entrance to the tunnel was in the floor of the storeroom in back. The storeroom was locked, but locks didn't slow Cullen down. The trapdoor there was warded, but Cullen had created the ward, so he could take it down pretty quickly. That was one reason he was with her.

The other reason, of course, was his shields. The shields he'd mysteriously acquired almost two years ago had withstood the illusions of an immortal Chimea and the power of another ancient artifact, one created by the Great Bitch herself. They'd probably hold against anything the knife could do, as long as he didn't actually touch it.

Rule's approach was much harder, coming at the house from over the ridge. She and Cullen couldn't know exactly when he'd be in place, but they'd set a time for when he should be ready. They'd have to hope Rule's distraction got under way on schedule.

Lily checked her watch again. This time her breathing hitched. She stood and nodded at Cullen.

He swarmed up the rungs set into the wall that led to the trapdoor. He'd go through first because he was faster, stronger, and able to throw fire, among other things. She'd follow when he gave the all clear. He paused at the top of the ladder, listening, then pushed the square door open a crack. It wasn't locked, but it was thick and a Persian carpet covered it on the other side, so it would be heavy. He paused to listen again. Maybe he was sniffing, too. If so, he clearly didn't smell anything he wasn't expecting. He lifted it a bit more and slithered up and out.

Lily climbed the first two rungs of the ladder and waited. Cullen had left the trapdoor slightly askew, but the rug still lay atop it. She couldn't see or hear a thing.

Suddenly the mage lights behind her winked out. It was utterly black. "Don't shoot!" Cullen said loudly.

Oh, God, oh, shit—

Another voice—male, but too low and muffled by the rug and trapdoor for her to make out the words.

"Sure, okay, on the floor, I hear you. No bullets needed." And Cullen flopped down on top of the trapdoor, telling Lily plainly to stay put, stay hidden. "Not giving you any trouble, Pete. Do you and Jim really need those handcuffs?"

Pete must have come closer, because his voice was a bit louder. She recognized it now and heard some of what he said: ". . . told me to . . . what she says."

"I understand. You do *exactly* what Miriam says, right?"

"That's right." A pause. "Jim, hold your gun to his head. Cullen, I have to gag you so you can't cast."

Muffled but clear, a woman's voice: "Oh, look what you've found."

Miriam. She sounded delighted.

"Yes, ma'am. Just as you said." Pete's voice was as flat and uninflected as a robot's.

Miriam moved closer. She must be only a few feet from the trapdoor. "Cullen, did you really think you could come so close without my lord sensing all that lovely, hot magic of yours? Oh—you can't answer me, can you?" She giggled like a little girl. The sound was jarring. "It must be hard on someone as arrogant as you, being trussed up like this. But don't worry—you may be a bit uncomfortable, but Dafydd doesn't want you killed. He's not at all bloodthirsty and would spare everyone if he could, but he particularly wants us to keep you alive. He's curious about those shields of yours. They remind him of some he saw a very long time ago, but there's no way you . . ." A pause, then, contritely: "You're right, love. I'm sorry. I do run on, don't I? And we are rather short of time. Pete, please have your man take Cullen to one of the bedrooms and make sure he can't get loose."

Pete gave exactly those instructions—"Take Cullen to one of the bedrooms and make sure he can't get loose." Lily heard Cullen lifted off the trapdoor . . . which was still ajar. There'd be a lump in the rug from it, but that wasn't telling them anything they didn't already know. Pete certainly knew about the trapdoor. Miriam must, too. Any second now Pete would push back the rug and move the trapdoor aside. He'd smell her then. Did she draw her weapon now or ease back down the ladder first?

He'd hear her if she moved. Lily forced one sweaty hand to release its grip on the rung by her shoulder and pulled out her weapon. She couldn't shoot Pete in the head. He'd open the trapdoor and look down here, offering her an easy shot to the head and no clear shot otherwise, but she couldn't take that easy shot. If she could have asked Pete, he'd have given her a mildly disgusted look because the answer was obvious. Only that wasn't her answer, which was probably weakness on her part, but she'd try for another spot. One he might survive. She got her Glock up and ready.

"Pete." Miriam's voice was full of reproach. "Why didn't you tell me about the tunnel?"

"I didn't know you wanted me to."

A quick, impatient huff loud enough for Lily to hear. Her left wrist was starting to hurt. She tried to huddle in closer to the ladder so that hand wouldn't have as much weight to support. "That limited sort of thinking is why Benedict is in charge instead of you. Well, put the trapdoor back and lock it up and—"

"There's no lock on this end." The rug rustled as if it had been moved. The trapdoor lifted a fraction—and dropped snugly into place.

Pete had done what Miriam told him to do. *Exactly* what she told him to do, and not one bit more. Lily realized she'd been holding her breath and exhaled, trying to do so quietly.

Miriam's voice was more muffled now. Lily missed some words. "That's hardly . . . leaving this unlocked. What was Benedict thinking?"

Pete was still beside the trapdoor. She heard him clearly. "The other ends of the tunnel are warded. Seaborne's created the wards. He wouldn't have had trouble getting in, but others would."

He'd phrased that so carefully—did he suspect she was down here? Yes. Suspect or hope or pray—he wanted someone to be down here. Someone who could actually *do* something . . .

"Well, at least one . . . unlocked now. You'd . . . put something heavy on top . . . That bookcase should do. It's heavy enough . . . ." The rest was indistinct, but then she said in a different, sharper tone, "What is it?"

"Fighting." Pete's voice was tight. "Out back."

"Our company's arrived!" Miriam laughed, all breezy and glad. "I need to get out there and—no, no, get the . . . then come with me."

Lily heard Pete grunt with effort. Two seconds later there was a loud thud right over her head.

Slowly Lily holstered her gun. Her heart pounded and

pounded as she climbed higher. She pushed at the bottom of the trapdoor with her right hand. Maybe Pete had managed somehow not to block it . . . no. She hadn't a chance of budging it. Miriam had been explicit that time, and Pete had followed orders.

There was fighting out back. Miriam had laughed when Pete said that.

Tears of frustration burned her eyes. Rule had charged the house right on schedule, but Cullen was a prisoner and she was trapped in a tunnel as dark as Jonah's sitting room. Rule would do his damnedest, but he only had six men with him . . . and Miriam had sounded so pleased. What did she have planned?

Lily sucked in breath and told herself to *think,* dammit. She wasn't really trapped. There were three exits. She could head for the closest one, but then what? She'd be spotted as soon as she came out from the trees. Unless every guard under Miriam's control had been sent out back to fight Rule . . . could Miriam be dumb enough to do that?

Probably not, but Lily didn't see what else to do. She climbed back down the ladder in a darkness so profound she might as well have been blind. Not a sliver of light, no shades of gray here at all. She cursed herself for an idiot for not bringing her purse, or at least the flashlight that was in it. There hadn't seemed any point when Cullen could make mage lights so easily, and . . . and she was still being stupid. She had her phone.

Lily pulled it out, hit the power button, and the screen lit. Not much light, but enough to get her moving—walking fast at first, then running, because Rule was fighting for his life right now and she wasn't there, wasn't with him, and when she got to the exit by the trees what the hell was she going to do? Try to shoot her way into Isen's house?

Maybe it was the inadequate light or the uneven surface, or maybe it was the way tears suddenly blurred her vision. Whatever the cause, she tripped and fell, dropping her phone and landing on her sprained wrist.

The sharp pain startled a cry out of her. She choked it

off, but too late, too late . . . had someone heard? There was a lot of dirt between her and the rest of the world, but lupi ears were keen. If one of them was nearby . . .

What would happen if a Nokolai lupus heard her in the tunnel?

She sat in the dirt cradling her throbbing wrist and at last her mind began working. Furiously.

Assumptions, she thought a moment later. Everyone makes them. Miriam did. She kept assuming that because people had to do what she said, they'd do what she wanted. The two weren't the same, were they? Lily grabbed her phone off the dirt floor. Miriam didn't always get her orders right. She'd told one person simply that he wanted to do everything he could to help her. And it worked; he still wanted to help her.

"Help" was such a fluid word.

Lily touched the screen of her phone. She and Rule kept their phones synced, so if he had Cory's number, she should have it, too . . . not that she knew Cory's last name, but she could do a search on the first name and . . . nothing with that spelling. She tried again, this time looking for Gene's number. Bingo.

"Gene. It's Lily. I need to talk to Cory."

FORTY-ONE

~

THERE was no sound of fighting at Isen's house anymore.

It had taken too long to put her plan into action. Lily was horribly aware that it had all taken way too long, and besides, this was insane. What had made her think this would work? No doubt she stank of fear to the lupi around her.

The guard who'd stopped them was named Rick. Rick was over sixty and had one grown son, two lupus grandsons, and a young daughter. A rich man, as lupi counted wealth. "He just came marching up with her, sir," Rick said to Pete. "Says he wanted to help Miriam."

Surely this hadn't been her idea. That damn half-dead god must've put it into her head. He must be laughing his head off right now. But she'd follow through anyway. She'd stand here stinking of fear with her arms pinned behind her back and follow through. Cory wasn't holding her arms tightly enough to hurt, but she had no chance of getting free.

Pete had come from the back of the house when Rick called. The floodlights were on, so she had no trouble seeing him. He was cradling his right arm with his left and his face lacked all expression. Normally Pete had one of those mobile faces that shows everything, but tonight he was as stone-faced as Benedict. "Cory. Why aren't you at the gate? What the hell are you up to?"

"Someone called and when we were chatting she said Lily had gone to the store," Cory said earnestly. "I knew Miriam wanted to see her, and I wanted to help Miriam, so I checked and sure enough, Lily was there."

"You and Gene were told to call me if Lily showed up."

"Yes, sir, if she came to the gate, but she didn't. She was at the store."

Pete's gaze flicked to Lily without meeting her eyes. "And she just came along with you?"

"Well . . . not exactly." Cory did a good job of sounding abashed. "And I had to take her gun. I didn't hurt her, though. I was careful. I mean, it's *Lily*."

Pete sighed. "Better give me her weapon."

Cory shifted his grip on her arms so he could free one hand. He gave Pete her Glock. "I hope I did the right thing."

A longish pause. "I expect you did what you were told to do."

"Yes, sir."

And that was true, as was everything else Cory had said. When Lily coached him, she'd emphasized that he had to tell the truth. If Miriam were to ask him about his story directly, he'd have no choice but to answer, so they'd come up with a story that was, word by word, true . . . just not all of the truth.

Someone *had* called him to say Lily was at the general store. She had, when she arranged to meet him there. Cory had taken Lily's weapon without hurting her—easy enough to do, since she'd given it to him. He did know that Miriam wanted Lily. And he wanted to—had to—help Miriam.

But what would really help a woman who'd been taken over by a god willing to destroy an entire realm in order to be fully alive again? That was what she'd asked Cory to think about. She'd let him work through it himself, come up with his own answer. He had to believe it or this wouldn't work. He couldn't not help Miriam, Lily had said to him, but, she added, "That dead god has taken away her free will, so she wants what her god wants. Should you help her get what she wants? Or would something else help her more?"

Cory had thought it over for a painfully long time, but once he decided, he'd spoken with real certainty: "She needs to be free of him. That may not be what she wants, but it's what she needs. I want to help her get free."

Now Cory held Lily firmly. Everyone had to see that she was restrained, not a danger. But when the time came . . .

"Lily." For the first time, Pete looked directly at her. His face was stony. His eyes were anguished. "We're all doing what we're told."

"I know." She nodded, trying to tell him it was all right. This was all part of her plan—her insane plan that couldn't possibly work, but somehow it hadn't blown up in her face yet. "What happened to your arm?"

"Rule broke it. It would have been better if he'd—" Pete stopped and stood rigidly still, frozen by whatever internal cataclysm he wasn't allowing—or couldn't allow—to erupt in words. Abruptly he turned away. "Better bring her around back. I have to see what Miriam wants me to do with her."

Cory marched Lily behind Pete, who led the way to the side of the house. They passed three more guards on the way. Two of them had been injured . . . or maybe the blood on that second man's arm wasn't his. But whoever had bled tonight—whoever had died—they were hers. Leidolf or Nokolai, compelled or free, they were hers to protect if she could, and to grieve if she couldn't. But not now. She refused to count her dead until this was over, one way or another.

One she knew for certain had survived the fight. She knew where he was, too, as clearly as she knew her right hand from her left. Pete was taking her to him now, taking her behind the house . . . where Rule was, according to the mate-sense. Right by the node.

They rounded the corner of the house. The path they were on was higher than the lower deck; four stone steps led down to it. She could only see this end of the deck; the roof blocked her view of the rest. The upper deck was roughly level with her waist, supported along its length by a stone retaining wall. Floodlights lit it.

Lily glanced quickly at the upper deck, so brilliantly lit—and horror iced the blood in her veins, freezing her in place. It held bodies. Rows of bodies. Maybe twenty. Maybe more. A second later relief punched through the ice, leaving her dizzy. Some of them, at least, were alive. She saw makeshift bandages wrapped around chests, arms, legs. Four lupi moved among the injured—one with water, one with food, and a pair who seemed to be performing some kind of crude surgery on one motionless body.

She knew two of the men tending the wounded fairly well. One was Sean, a cheerful redheaded Nokolai who actually was as young as he looked. One was Mike. One of Rule's Leidolf guards. Mike, who'd remembered a lot about crazy gods when she asked . . . a blood-soaked cloth was tied around his thigh. His head was bare. The garish green-and-orange knitted cap from Walmart was gone.

Pete stopped at the bottom of the stairs, looked at them over his shoulder, and made a come-along gesture, followed by the Nokolai hand sign for *quiet*.

No one was speaking, she realized as she obeyed Cory's nudge at her back and started down the steps. No one made a sound. Even stoic lupi moaned in pain when hurt badly enough, but all of the wounded were silent, as were the men tending them. So were the four guards on the lower deck who moved aside to let Pete pass.

Under the roof were more shadows. For some reason Miriam hadn't turned on the lower floods, just the small porch light. It was enough to see by. The French doors stood open as they so often did in the evening. On the other side of them, the decking was gone. The boards had been pried up, the support beams cut and removed, leaving a large swath of bare ground. Miriam crouched there in the dirt, shaking something from her palm onto the ground.

But Lily didn't pay attention to Miriam. Her eyes went

to the other side of the hole in the deck. That was where Rule lay, his eyes closed. And Isen beside him.

Both men were naked. Carl sat between them with a hand on each man's chest. Rule's head was bloody. His arm was, too. Lily couldn't tell how badly he was hurt. She could barely see Isen, with Carl in the way, but he was as motionless as his son. Not as bloody, though.

Were they unconscious? Spelled?

Her breath was coming fast and jerky. She tried to steady it. Rule was *alive*. That was what counted. She'd guessed he was a prisoner when she knew where he was, so seeing him there—so still!—shouldn't be such a shock. He was alive, and if he'd been hurt, he'd heal. If he'd been spelled . . . that was it. That was why Carl sat there with a hand on each man's chest. He must be holding sleep charms to their bare skin.

If they needed a sleep charm to keep Rule knocked out, then he wasn't wounded too badly. Lily's breathing finally evened out.

Pete made the "halt" sign at her and Cory. Cory stopped, so Lily had to. Pete walked to the edge of the hole in the deck and stood there, saying nothing. Everyone must have been told to be quiet while Miriam did her thing.

Lily tore her gaze away from Rule to study the woman who held him prisoner. Whatever Miriam held in her hand was white and powdery. She was shaking it onto the ground to mark a large circle that seemed almost complete. Her hair was loose, a frizzy brown cloud hiding her downturned face. There were other marks on the ground inside the circle, though Lily couldn't make them out. They'd been drawn in black and didn't show up well. Lily also saw two objects familiar to her from all the times she'd worked with the coven leader: a small portable altar and a quilted tote. The tote held Miriam's spellcasting supplies.

It was large enough to hold metal stakes, too.

"There." Miriam stood, placing one hand at the small of her back and stretching. She wore something white, long, and loose that left her arms bare. Lily had seen the robelike gown before, and the woven belt Miriam wore at her waist, but the scabbard was new. Lily couldn't see it clearly from this angle, but that was definitely a scabbard fastened to the belt. It must hold the knife. Nam Anthessa.

Miriam heaved a sigh. "Almost done. For goodness' sake, Pete, what is it this time? No, unless it's urgent, wait a moment to tell me. I need the dedicates brought into the circle." She looked around, frowning vaguely. Her gaze passed right over Lily. "Oh, you figure out how to do it. Isen and Rule need to be laid in the very center of the circle with their heads north, feet south. Arrange it. Tell your men to be sure the sleep charms stay in contact, skin to skin, the way I explained. They must be very careful not to step on the circle itself. They can't damage the runes, but they must stay off the circle. Oh—they should be barefoot."

"Yes, ma'am." Pete called four names and began giving instructions.

Miriam stepped up onto the deck and dusted her hands together—and seemed to notice Lily for the first time. "You! Oh, this won't do. This won't do at all. You don't want to see this. Pete! What is Lily doing here?"

Pete finished giving his orders. The four men he'd addressed bent and took off their shoes. "Cory found her. He says he knew you wanted to see her, and he wanted to help, so he brought her to you."

"I don't want to see her," she said crossly. "I wanted to know where she was. I wanted her stopped and held, but I did not want to see her."

"Oh," Cory said sadly. "I'm sorry. I thought . . . you asked where she was, and then Pete wanted us to let him know if she came to the gate, and I thought . . . I'm sorry. I thought I was helping."

"You . . . oh. I did say that, didn't I? He meant well, but what do I do with her?" Miriam tipped her head as if listening. "Yes, of course. Cory, why didn't you call Pete like you'd been told?"

"She wasn't at the gate. She was at the store. Someone told me she was there, and when I went to see, I found her and brought her here. I took her gun," he added, hopeful as a puppy trying to wag his way past some misunderstanding about the puddle on the floor. "Pete's got it."

Miriam looked at Pete. "And you couldn't just lock her up or something? You had to ask me?" She huffed an impatient breath. "I would have thought someone in your position would have more initiative. Well, you can just take her to—"

Lily could not let Miriam finish giving that order. "I want to stay with Rule."

"That is not a good idea." But at last Miriam looked at Lily directly. Their eyes met. Miriam's were . . . odd. Too bright, too wide. A junkie's eyes just before the crash. "I'm not at all happy with Rule right now, but you weren't part of it. You don't deserve to watch this."

"Part of what?"

"He attacked his own people! Shot them! It was horrible. I wanted—I was trying so *hard*—and of course I needed him to come here, but not like that! Now all those people are hurt. Some of them died. I didn't want people to die, but he made everything so *difficult*."

"You don't think he had reason to fight?" Lily said mildly. "Considering you intend to sacrifice his father and all. Him, too, it looks like. Hammer stakes through their hands and—"

Miriam flared up. "You should know me better than that! I am not like that man. That Robert Friar. There will be no torture, no . . ." Her mood switched as suddenly as if someone had flipped a switch. She giggled. "True. But I'm glad I don't have to."

"What don't you have to do, Miriam?"

Miriam spoke slowly, as if to a rather dim child. "Use those nasty stakes. Friar needed them to bind my lord to his goals, which is why we're here." She waved widely. "It's all Robert Friar's fault. If he hadn't bound Dafydd that way, I could have killed strangers instead of . . . I'm really very sorry about the clan, but we have no choice. The stakes, however, are obscene. I would never bind my beautiful Dafydd."

She needed to keep the woman talking. "Tell me about Dafydd."

Miriam's face lit. "You'll see," she said eagerly. "Very soon now, you'll see. He's so beautiful, so much *more* than anyone or anything else. And he's been so alone, so terribly lonely. He found me in my dreams. Or I found him. He . . ."

Miriam liked talking about the god she called Dafydd. Lily listened with half an ear as she babbled on about how wonderful he was. Was it time?

Pete was close, which wasn't good, but he was watching his men. A pair of them carried Rule into the circle while another man held the charm to Isen's chest. The fourth man waited beside Isen; Carl still had charm duty there. They were the only ones other than Pete who were close enough to be a problem. Miriam stood right in front of the French doors, about ten feet away—farther than Lily liked, but this might be the only chance she got. If she didn't try to jump Miriam, but instead—

Around the side of the house, a husky baritone voice started singing: "'We shall overcome . . .'" A second later, his voice was joined by others—a child's high voice, and Cynna's? Could that be Cynna singing? And a voice Lily knew intimately. Her mother's soprano came in strongly.

Miriam jolted as if someone had shot her. "What's that?" she cried. "What's that singing?"

"I'll find out." And Pete set off at a lope.

Pete was gone, Miriam distracted. This was her chance. She'd arranged two signals with Cory for when it was time for him to release her—one spoken, one nonverbal. But she didn't just want him to release her. She wanted him to throw her at Miriam. "Cory—"

Drummond popped into sight in front of her, more see-through than usual. And frantic. He was waving his arms, shaking his head, saying with every motion *Stop! Danger! Don't move!* His mouth moved, too, but Lily couldn't hear a thing.

Why? she wanted to scream. Every muscle was tight with the need to move, to act—but Drummond knew things she didn't. He'd helped more than once, and he kept being right. She panted with conflicting needs and made herself stand there, just stand there, even as her mind screamed that this was nuts. She was losing her best chance.

Drummond faded out with his arms still waving.

Lily tried to look behind her, but Cory was in the way. He shifted and she could see the steps up to the path. She heard Pete's voice faintly, and someone responding to him, and the singers continued to come closer. She waited, her body taut, wanting to act, to do—and then it was too late. Pete leaped down the four steps to the deck and ran up to Miriam to report.

"It's Cynna, Toby, Lily's mother, Li Qin, and that homeless guy who was staying with Isen," he said. "They approached the house. When Dave and Mitchell stopped them, they said they wanted to see you. Orders are to bring anyone suspicious to me, and they thought it was suspicious for them to ask to see you. How did they even know you were here? They've been searched. No weapons."

"What homeless man? Who's Li Qin?" Miriam was baffled, tense, distressed. "No, never mind. Why are they singing?"

"I don't know."

"They need to stop. I can't hear him. I can't hear my lord. They're singing too loudly."

They weren't that loud. Not loud enough to drown out a voice you heard with your ears, but maybe . . . maybe the singing was happening someplace else, too. A place that Drummond was aware of and Lily wasn't. A place that a saint might know about.

Without thinking, she started humming along. A moment later Cory started humming, too. And others. All around them, lupi joined in, humming the old civil rights anthem: *We shall overcome . . . we shall overcome someday . . .*

And Miriam did nothing. Her face was as pale as the white powder she'd used to lay her circle and she swayed as if tranced or about to faint. But her lips were moving. She made no sound, but her lips moved: *Deep in my heart, I do believe* . . .

The singers came down the steps to the deck as calmly as if they'd been in a processional at church. Hardy held Toby's hand; behind them Cynna and Julia walked hand in hand, too. Li Qin brought up the rear—and behind her were two guards, their guns trained on their odd assortment of prisoners . . .

. . . who didn't seem to notice the guards, the guns, or the peculiar tableau they approached. Toby looked like he was concentrating the way he did when he played soccer or computer games. Cynna wore a small smile, grim and defiant. Julia seemed caught up in the song, and Li Qin might have been pouring tea, she was so matter-of-fact. And Hardy . . . Hardy looked utterly at peace.

"Stop," Miriam told them. Her voice shook. "Stop now, all of you."

The guards stopped. The singers didn't.

"I forgot," Miriam whispered. "Of course, I forgot to . . ." She fumbled at the scabbard and pulled out one wicked big knife—bigger than Benedict's hunting knife, smaller than his machete. Maybe eighteen inches. And black. Whatever it was made of, it was all one piece from hilt to tip, and a dull, solid black. "Stop!"

They didn't. And Lily knew why. As the singers had drawn closer she'd seen the silver charms they wore—charms the previous Rhej had created based on ancient spellwork from the Great War, workings no one alive today knew except those able to reach into clan memories. Charms that Nokolai clansmen had worn the previous year when they went to war against the Chimea.

Charms against the most potent of mind magic.

Her heart leaped in her chest. Of course! Why had none of them thought of that? Lily herself, Rule, Cullen—they all knew about the charms. It was blindingly obvious now, but she hadn't once thought about them . . . Persuasion? Could that be used not just to plant ideas, but to keep you from thinking clearly, seeing the obvious? If so, nothing she'd done tonight was likely to work.

But it didn't have to. The saint was winning this battle.

Lily and Cory stood near the house. There was plenty of room for the singers to pass them, and at first it seemed they would. But as Hardy and Toby drew even with her, Hardy stopped and made a patting gesture with one hand. Without a break in their song, the others moved to form a semicircle slightly behind Lily and Cory, facing Miriam. They kept singing . . . and Hardy kept walking.

Alone, he walked up to Miriam, who turned so she could keep her eyes fixed on him—eyes wide and wild, but now their brightness looked like tears, not mania. She shook as if she might fall over.

Hardy stopped in front of her. "What have I done?" she whispered. "What have I done?"

He held out his hand. He'd stopped singing. Lily wasn't sure when, but it didn't matter. His face was so full of compassion and love—it radiated from him like heat from a fire. He held out his hand and Miriam looked at the knife she held in hers. And shuddered.

A shredded and sorrowful calm descended on Miriam. Her face relaxed into it. She stopped shaking and stretched out the hand holding the knife, hilt first—then cried out in an anguished voice, "No!" Fast—too fast for Lily to react—she gripped that wicked big knife with both hands. And plunged it into her own chest.

Hardy cried out wordlessly. Miriam collapsed.

Lily gave the nonverbal signal. She stomped on Cory's foot.

He let her go and she dashed forward, but Hardy—who'd fallen to his knees beside Miriam—held up a hand urgently, saying without words to stay back. Lily stopped. "I'm not going to touch it. The knife. I want to help her."

Hardy shook his head sadly. He stroked Miriam's face, crooning softly. Her eyes were open and staring. The knife must have gone straight to her heart. Lily wouldn't have thought Miriam knew how to deliver such a tidy death stroke. But it hadn't been her who did it, had it? That triple-damned god had directed her hands. She'd been about to get free of him, and it had pissed him off.

Hardy brushed her eyelids with his palm, closing her eyes, singing to her softly.

"Stop!" someone behind her called. One of the guards. "Cynna, don't move, for God's sake. I don't want to shoot you. Pete, what do I do? She said to obey you, and you said—"

"Put your weapons up." Pete's voice was low and hoarse. "Lily, I can't move. I still have to . . . she's dead, but the last order she gave was for all of us to stop. Her other orders, too—they didn't go away when she died."

Shit. Miriam was dead, but the knife wasn't. "Can you tell them to take the sleep charms off?"

"No." He sounded agonized. "The others . . . she didn't give them specific orders, except to obey me. She made her orders to me more explicit. I can't give orders that counter hers."

The knife was still enforcing Miriam's orders, but was that all it would do? It was alive, in a sense. Able to act on its own. Any second now it might tell one of them to slit Rule's throat.

Hardy had turned to listen to them. Now he cocked his head, then nodded. He turned back to the body that had been a woman moments before and gripped that black hilt. He grimaced as if in pain.

"Oh, shit. Are you sure you should . . ." But he was the saint. Lily had to hope he was getting instructions from someone who knew a lot more than she did. Maybe taking the knife out would cancel Miriam's orders. Maybe if a holy person held it, it wouldn't be able to compel people.

Hardy placed one hand on Miriam's chest and pulled the knife out. It came free slowly, glistening with Miriam's blood. He looked at it with the expression of someone holding a fistful of stinking, oozing shit.

A gun went off inside the house. Hardy's eyes went wide in astonishment. His hand opened and the knife clattered onto the deck as a red stain spread across his chest. He toppled over.

FORTY-TWO

~

ROBERT Friar darted through the open French doors. Gauze still wrapped his chest and leg, but the son of a bitch wasn't even limping.

Lily launched herself at him.

He got there first and scooped up the knife, but he didn't have time to do more before she piled into him. He went over on his back. She gave him a quick, hard chop with the heel of her hand, delivered under his chin. It snapped his head back, but didn't discourage him nearly enough. He struck at her with the knife and she had to roll off, but she grabbed his arm and tried to wrench it behind him. Any second now he'd go *dshatu*. He'd phase out, and she might still be able to see him—she'd seen Gan in that state, back when Gan was still a demon—but she wouldn't be able to touch him. To get the knife away from him.

To *kill* the bloody bastard who'd shot a saint.

But he stayed solid. All too solid, as he used the arm she held to flip her up and over him with inhuman strength. He sent her sailing right off the edge of the deck to land in the dirt four feet below. She landed hard and badly. It knocked the breath out of her.

As she struggled to get her paralyzed diaphragm to work, Friar jumped down beside her, grinning nastily. He pulled a gun from the waist of his ruined slacks and took aim. And eighty pounds of determined nine-year-old boy hit him from behind.

The gun went flying. Lily's diaphragm suddenly remembered what to do and she sucked in air as Friar flopped onto his knees, but he didn't go all the way down. He twisted and knocked Toby away.

Someone was yelling. More than one someone. She didn't have time to look. She got her feet under her and sent a kick at Friar's head. He ducked and tried to grab her foot, but missed. It kept him busy for a second, though—giving her time to go after the gun he'd dropped. It was right beside Rule. She got her hand on it—and Friar landed on top of her, knocking her flat on her stomach.

He grabbed her hair and jerked her head back, exposing her throat. Toby screeched and must have done something—Lily couldn't see what—because Friar let go. She bucked hard, trying to dislodge him, keep him from hurting Toby. He fell off and she turned over quickly.

A flash of searing pain sliced through her leg. And she was sucked away—away from her body, from the world, sucked off into . . . gray. Endless gray, where she floated for a time without time . . .

Slowly the gray resolved into trees. Black trees. They were tall, impossibly tall, and they were made from shades of darkness. They loomed over her where she lay in the dirt. Glowing dirt. All the light in this place came from the ground, not the sky.

Fear sank talons into her heart and ripped. She whimpered. Was she dead? She remembered fighting, but not . . . who had she fought? What had happened to her? What was this place?

"Welcome to my domain."

The voice was rich and fluid, a mellow and very male voice, one that captivated. That made her want to hear more. She didn't trust it, not at all. She managed to shove herself up, though her arms and legs shook. She felt weak and dizzy, but she got to her feet.

He was a god. She knew that the moment she saw him. He stood about twenty feet away in a small clearing, naked and perfectly shaped. And large, too large for a mortal man—he must have been twelve feet tall. His pale skin gleamed faintly. His ears were pointed, like an elf's, and his face was elfin, too—narrow at the jaw, broad through the cheeks—and he had long, straight, silver hair. Literally silver. It gleamed, too. From the crown of his head to his bare feet, he was supernally beautiful.

She didn't trust that, either. She couldn't remember much—not how she got here, not what had happened to her. Not—oh, God. Not even her name. Fear spiked impossibly high until she panted with it. But however much she'd forgotten, she knew she did not trust this beautiful being.

"You're silent. I don't like silence. I get too much of that here."

"You're . . . the god who murdered Miriam." She remembered that suddenly, the way Miriam's hands had plunged a knife into her chest. The way she'd cried *no* even as she did it.

Sorrow flooded his perfect face. "My lovely Miriam. She wanted so much to be with me, and now . . ." Rage washed away sorrow. "Now she never will, and it's your fault." He took a single step toward her. "You will have a long time, a very long time, to apologize. To try to make it up to me for losing my lovely Miriam. And everything else."

A ghost stepped out from behind one of the too-tall black trees. He was dark haired with a receding hairline. He wore dark slacks and a white button-down shirt and he was familiar . . . but he looked solid, she thought, bewildered. Why did she think he was a ghost?

"Lily," he said, "that bastard is lying to you."

She knew his voice, she knew she did. "My name is Lily?"

"Son of a *bitch*." That came out with such vehemence she took a step back. "No, don't move. It's really important you stay where you are. You can get lost in this place way too easy."

"Lily," that other one said. The god. He was off to her right now, only ten feet away. She hadn't seen him move. "Why are you listening to him? He tried to kill you once. You don't remember? You listen to bad counsel all too often, don't you?" He smiled and whispered, "It's all right to kill Santos. He deserves it."

A flash of memory shivered through her. A face, a man's face. Her hand holding a gun to him, the barrel jammed in his throat. Had she shot him? What had she done?

"You killed him at my suggestion," the god said in his wonderful voice. "You're mine, Lily. You made yourself mine the first time you listened to me. You've been mine all along."

"He's lying to you," the ghost said again, moving so he was in front of her. "He's trying to persuade you, but all he's got is lies." He stretched out a hand beseechingly. "You have to listen to me."

A gold ring glowed on that hand. On the third finger, the one connected to the heart, according to the old tales. A glowing gold ring . . . memory cascaded in on her, so swiftly she gasped. Rule. Isen, her mother, Toby, Cullen, Cynna, her father and her sisters . . . and Rule. Oh, God. "Drummond. You're Drummond."

"Part of him, anyway." His grin was quick and feral. "That shiny bastard behind me sliced a bit of me away from the rest. Thought he was being clever, but we tricked him. The bit he cut out is the part you need. I've been waiting here for you."

"Do you remember him now, Lily?" The god was on her left now. He spoke mockingly. "He tried to kill you. You and so many others. And you trust him?"

"I . . ." But she did remember. Drummond had done terrible things, but he'd redeemed himself. He *was* on her side—and the beautiful god most definitely wasn't. She remembered the fight now. She remembered Friar and Toby and a hot, terrible pain and being sucked out, away . . . "He got me with the knife. Friar did. I've . . . been cut out of time."

The god chuckled. "That's where we are. Out of time. You've worried about running out of time for so long, and now you'll stay out of time. With me."

"No." Drummond came closer. "He cheated. He's sidhe. What do sidhe do best?"

Her eyes widened. "Illusion."

"This"—he gestured widely—"this is real to him and me, because we died. But *you didn't*."

That terrible, slicing pain—it had been in her thigh. Not her chest, not her head—

"He had enough power to suck you here, but he can't keep you. See how he pops here and there, but never gets close? He can't touch you because you're still alive and he isn't, and as long as you don't believe in him—"

"Believe in the god of chaos?" She snorted. She'd spent her life fighting against chaos. "Not happening. But I—can I get back? How do I get back?"

Drummond grinned again. "You've got a heavy hitter of your own. One who operates on your side of things, so she can't come here, but she can help. She's waiting to help. Just focus on that bond of yours."

Lily felt a sudden warmth on her hands and lifted them . . . both rings were glowing, just like Drummond's did. The engagement ring Rule had given her glowed a soft sunshine yellow, and the *toltoi* charm on her other hand shone with the moon's pale white light. She reached out with her mate-sense—and found Rule. He was right beside her. Never mind what her eyes said. She *felt* him.

She knew what to do. She held out her hand. "Come with me!"

Drummond hesitated. "It won't work. You can't—"

"Hurry!" The gray land was starting to fade.

Drummond put his hand in hers. It felt solid and real and warm, and the shock of that rippled through her. She closed her fingers tightly around his and closed her eyes and focused on what the mate bond was telling her . . .

Reality popped like a soap bubble.

She was lying on her back in the dirt—dirt that did not glow—with her leg hurting like fire and Rule beside her and people shouting somewhere, and she knew that here, no time had passed. Because where she'd been there was no time, so she hadn't really been gone at all. Two Drummonds, both misty white and grinning widely, hovered above her . . . and drifted together, until there was just one. Just one, with a glowing gold band on his left hand.

He gave her a quick salute and faded out.

Lily's gaze cut to the sleeping man beside her, and beyond him, the lupus who held that damn sleep charm to his chest. She sat up and knocked the man's hand away. The charm fell off and Rule's eyes flew open.

Toby screamed.

By the time Lily saw that Friar had Toby around the neck, Rule was on his feet and diving for the enemy who threatened his son.

Friar went ever so slightly fuzzy. Rule's hands passed right through him. And the knife, that terrible black knife, fell to the ground. Rule scooped Toby up in his arms, patting him frantically. "You're all right? Are you all right?"

"I'm okay." Toby's voice wobbled. "He scared me more than he hurt me. I thought—he cut Lily and I thought—" He clung to his father.

"Lily?" Rule's head swung toward her.

"I'm okay enough," she said. "Toby saved my life."

Friar tipped back his head and howled in frustration. Lily couldn't hear him, but there was no doubt that was what he did.

Triumph brought a tight grin to Lily's face. Friar couldn't hold on to the knife when he was *dshatu.* That was why he'd stayed solid when they fought. He didn't dare stay material to fight Rule, though, and he couldn't take the knife with him when he wasn't. His clothes, shoes, that gun—all those went out-of-phase with him, but the knife did not. Maybe because it was a named artifact. Maybe it didn't want to go with him.

Lily clambered to her feet. Her leg was bleeding freely and hurt like blazes, but it held her. "Friar's still here." She pointed at him. "He's gone *dshatu*, but I see him."

Cynna yelled, "He's *dshatu*?"

"Yes!" Lily's head swung that way. The guards had put up their weapons, as Pete had told them to—but other orders remained operative. One guard gripped Cynna's arms. Another held Julia and Li Qin. And that, she realized, was what some of the shouting had been about. Cynna did not like being restrained.

"Then I'll exorcise the hell out of him. *Om redne ish n'vatta—tol harvatay nil ombrum. Ils sevre—*"

Friar's eyes widened in sudden fear. He climbed back up on the deck and took off, jumping onto the upper level.

"He's getting away!" Lily wobbled forward a step.

Cynna chanted faster and louder. It wasn't Latin. It wasn't any language Lily knew.

Rule was scowling at her. "Your leg."

"Hurts, but I don't think it's serious." She peered down at it. The slash was long but shallow, for all that it had nearly persuaded her she was dead.

Rule held Toby in one arm with the boy's arms wrapped around his neck, but he had another arm. He wrapped it around her and put his face in her hair and breathed in deeply. "I don't know what the hell has been happening. My father—"

"Is okay. Carl's holding a sleep charm on him because Pete told him to, or maybe Miriam did, so he can't not do that. Uh—most everyone can't move because Miriam told them to stop. Plus, they're all compelled to obey Pete, and he's compelled to follow the orders Miriam gave him before she died. And Friar—" She couldn't see the man anymore. "He seems to be gone." He'd been heading for the slope, but she'd looked away for a moment. Probably he'd vanished into the darkness . . . unless Cynna really had exorcised him. Would that send him to hell? To the realm where demons lived, anyway. Could Cynna do that to someone who wasn't a demon? God, she wanted to think so.

Friar had seemed to think it was possible. He'd run like
a rabbit. She snorted at the memory, but sobered quickly.
Six feet away, a long black knife lay on ground marked by
black runes. All around her were lupi frozen in place because they'd been ordered to stop. And Hardy . . . she'd
forgotten to check, and no one else was able to move.
Maybe he was still alive. "I need to see about Hardy," she
said, pulling free from Rule.

She was too late. She saw that right away. Maybe it had
been too late from the moment Friar blasted a hole in Hardy's chest. Probably. And she couldn't have done anything
differently, but regret squeezed hard at her heart as she
looked down on the empty face that had held such life.
Hardy looked peaceful still . . . but dead. No more songs.

Rule had come up onto the deck with her, still holding
Toby. He was asking Pete exactly what his orders from
Miriam consisted of. Good. If they knew what they had to
work around, maybe they could figure out a way—

"Halt!" someone called from the upper deck.

Oh, good, more company.

"Who or what is it?" Rule demanded.

"The Queen of Winter sends us here, with Isen Turner's
permission," a man called back from somewhere farther up
the slope. "Winter and the one you call Sam."

"Let—" Rule stopped. Scowled. "Pete, tell him to let the
Queen's people pass."

Apparently that didn't contradict Miriam's orders, because Pete repeated it. A few minutes later a man and a
woman jumped down onto the upper deck. They looked
oddly alike—brother and sister, maybe? Both were tall and
rangy. He was darker; she was more striking, with an an-
gular face, a stern blade of a nose, and warm brown hair
pulled back in a braid. She wore a long tunic, a heavily
embroidered vest that reached her knees, and baggy pants
tucked into boots, all in shades of brown and gold. The
tunic was belted in brown leather; a knife-size scabbard
hung from the belt, partly hidden by the vest.

Her shoulders were broad for a woman. His were

broader. He wore similar clothing in shades of blue but without the vest, and he had two scabbards—one at his waist like hers that held a knife, and one fastened to a harness crisscrossing his chest that held one honking big sword on his back. His face lay on the ordinary end of attractive—pleasant but unmemorable—except for his eyes. They were a clear and startling gray.

His eyebrows lifted above those clear gray eyes. "That was easy," he said to the woman. He spoke ordinary American English.

"You're disappointed."

He glanced at her without answering, but his mouth tucked up in a small smile.

Not brother and sister, Lily realized. Not when he looked at her like that.

"It's here, then?" the woman said.

"They have it." He looked down at them. "I had expected a hunt, and I see you have the knife waiting for me. But you are much too close to it. You need to get away. Quickly."

"If you mean Nam Anthessa," Lily said, "you might say it has us. Some of us. The woman who wielded it is dead, but the knife's still enforcing her commands. I'm free and so are Rule and a few others, but the rest . . . before she died she told them not to move, so they can't. Where's Sam?"

The man glanced at the woman beside him. She gave a small nod. He looked back at Lily. "On his way. He travels differently than we do. I was told Isen Turner was in charge of this land and people. I would speak to him, or to the one named Li Lei."

Rule spoke. "I'm Rule Turner. Under these circumstances, I can speak for my Rho, who is currently caught by a sleep charm. The man holding it to him is one of those who can't move. Li Lei Yu isn't here now."

"I'm unsure how to proceed. I was given a way to identify myself to Isen Turner or to Li Lei."

"Hey, I know you!" Cynna cried. "Rule, I know them both. They helped us in Edge. They're cool."

"If you've come to destroy the knife," Rule said dryly, "you're welcome. But I was expecting a hellhound."

"I am the Queen's Hound. Do you accept my authority to deal with Nam Anthessa?"

Rule hesitated, but only for a second. "I do."

"Then—"

"Nathan," the woman said, her voice strained, "Nam Anthessa is reaching for me, and I can't—"

Just like that, chat time was over. The man launched himself as fast as any lupus, drawing a dagger the color of bleached bones as he raced forward and leaped from the upper deck to land on the bare ground below. Right next to the black knife.

He didn't look ordinary now. His face contorted in a snarl. His eyes blazed, shedding color until they were as pale as the blade he raised overhead, gripping it in both hands as he growled—words, there were words in that loud growl, but none Lily knew, nor were they spoken in a man's voice—and plunged his bone white blade *into* the black one.

Nam Anthessa shattered.

The sound of its breaking was small, like the crunch of a cracker. The feel of it . . . Lily reeled as shards of power stung her face, her hands, every bit of exposed skin.

All around them, lupi staggered. Some went to their knees. Some moaned. "It's gone," Pete whispered. "It's gone. Oh, God, oh, God . . ."

The woman came forward then and jumped onto the lower deck. "We didn't finish introducing ourselves," she said apologetically. "He's Nathan. Nathan Hunter. I'm Kai Tallman Michalski. I think you have need of me, too. I'm a mind healer."

FORTY-THREE

❧

THERE weren't that many places to hold a really large wedding in San Diego. Tres Puentes Resort, slightly outside the city, was the poshest and one of the most beautiful. It was named for the three bridges crossing the artful little creek that wandered through the large, open lawn and lush gardens, any or all of which could be reserved, along with the banquet hall, ballroom, smaller dining rooms, and one or more rooms to get ready in before the ceremony. Tres Puentes was usually reserved for over a year in advance, but somehow Rule had booked the place anyway. Part of the deal was that the resort wouldn't provide the food or serving staff, due to having a smaller event that had already booked the kitchen . . . hence Philippe and the *feuilles des pommes et grenades*.

And she was not, Lily told herself firmly, going to think about what it cost. Not today.

"Hold *still*," Beth said—not for the first time.

"I am."

"No, you aren't. You're as fidgety as I've ever seen you. Twice as fidgety." Her sister yanked on the hair she'd brushed back from Lily's face. "I could almost think you're nervous."

"I'm supposed to be nervous—"

"That's right," Susan said. "It's traditional."

"But I'm not." A bit jittery, maybe, but not nervous. They weren't the same thing at all. "What time is it?"

"Five minutes since the last time you asked," Cynna said. "Which proves what a puddle of amazing calm you are. If you were nervous, you'd be asking every minute instead of every five."

"Don't complain. You're the official timekeeper. It's your job to tell me what time it is."

"There." At last Beth released Lily's hair. That was her third attempt. "All done but the orchids, and you need to have your gown on before I put them in."

Lily studied her reflection. Her hair was pulled back from her face and fastened in a deceptively simple way at her crown. It hung down in back, long and perfectly straight—at least that was what Beth told her after wielding the straightening iron. "You don't think it's too severe?" she said in sudden doubt, raising one hand to touch it.

Beth swatted her hand. "It's perfect. Don't touch."

"Lily," Aunt Deborah said, "I brought my diamond drops, in case you needed them."

Lily touched one bare ear. The hairstyle called for earrings, but . . . "No. Thank you, but no."

"She'll be here," Aunt Mequi said. "There's still time. She'll be here."

"Of course she will." Lily said that as if she believed it. She almost did.

At the instant of the knife's destruction, memory had rushed in on the amnesia victims. That sudden restoration did not instantly heal the trauma their minds had been through, however. Kai Michalski had been very busy. Not all of those who'd lost then regained their memories needed her, and not all of those who needed help would let her give it. As long as the person was competent to make a decision—and Kai had some way of determining that to her satisfaction—the mind healer wouldn't act without permission. But she'd helped a lot of them. She'd also helped a few of the lupi who'd been under the knife's control. She'd even been able to help Officer Crown, though he would need additional therapy, she said.

But she couldn't help Julia Yu. Not until Sam returned, anyway, and maybe not then. She had Julia's permission, but ironically, the restructuring that had saved Julia's mind now kept her from being able to access the memories that Kai said were present, but buried. Until Sam loosened things up, Kai had said, she couldn't do anything . . . and she wasn't sure if Sam could undo what he'd done. She'd never seen anything like it.

The black dragon had finally returned that morning. When he did, Rule and Lily had offered Julia a choice. Did she want to attend the wedding as her twelve-year-old self? Or did she want to undergo Sam's ministrations first, even though it might mean missing the wedding?

Julia had chosen door number two. Sam and Kai had been with her all day. No word on how it was going, and the ceremony would start at four thirty—though they needed to be down ten minutes before that. "What time did you say it was?" Lily asked.

Cynna sighed. "Two minutes until four."

"You'll let me put on the necklace now," Aunt Mequi announced as if Lily had argued against this.

"Don't mess up her hair," Beth warned.

Aunt Mequi ignored that for the unnecessary comment that it was. She came up behind Lily and carefully shifted her hair so she could place a single strand of pearls around her neck. It was choker-length and much older than Lily. Lily's other grandmother—the one who'd died long before she was born—had worn it at her own wedding.

The necklace was part of a set. Mequi had inherited the choker; Deborah had gotten the bracelet, though she'd broken it years ago; and Lily's mother had been bequeathed the earrings. Pearl drops. Julia had worn the necklace and earrings when she married Lily's father . . . and Lily would either wear those earrings, too, handed to her by her mother, or none at all.

"The timekeeper says it's time for the dress," Cynna said.

Lily didn't move. She didn't want to put on her dress. Her mother wasn't here.

"Do not cry," Mequi said severely. "Your mascara will run and you will have to clean it off and redo it and—"

A knock on the door interrupted her, followed by her father's voice. "Someone with me would very much like to come in." Having said that, he didn't wait for permission but swung the door open and stepped inside.

Julia Yu came in with him. She wore the sunny yellow suit she'd bought for the ceremony months ago. Hair, makeup, nails—all were perfect. She looked like Lily's mother, not like the twelve-year-old girl Lily had gotten to know and like, but . . . Lily stood slowly, her heart pounding. "Julia?"

"I do not approve of children addressing their parents by their first names, Lily. You know that." And Julia Yu opened her arms to her daughter.

"**. . . AND** so now I have *seven* friends!" The small orange being beamed up at Rule. Gan wore a blue-and-green-striped gown that plunged nearly to her waist in front, revealing a great deal of her truly amazing breasts. She'd accessorized the gown with a purple vest, seven bracelets, five rings, and two necklaces. One was the medallion of her office in Edge. The other was an absurdly large sapphire pendant surrounded by diamonds. She was about an inch taller than the last time Rule had seen her, and she'd started growing hair. Blue hair. He'd complimented her on it the moment he saw her. She'd looked smug. Hair, she'd said, was very tricky, but she thought she had the hang of it.

"You are becoming quite wealthy," he told her now.

"Well, yes"—Gan touched the large sapphire that dangled between her breasts and scowled—"I'm rich these days, but that isn't why they're my friends!"

"Rich in friendships," Rule explained. "My people consider that true wealth."

"Huh!" She thought that over. "Your people are weird. Does Lily think about it like that, too?"

"I believe so."

She thought some more, then announced, "Lily's richer than me, then, but I don't think *all* these people are her friends." She waved broadly to indicate the guests all around them on the resort's wide green lawn. "I bet a lot of them are just half friends."

"Half friends?"

"You know—people you like, but you don't really trust. Like you and me."

"Ah." He smiled. "You know, I suspect we are on our way to becoming actual friends, not just halves."

Gan's eyes widened. "You do? I'm not at all sure about your wolf. Do all these humans trust your wolf, even when it's really close to the top like it is right now?"

That startled Rule. Surely Gan was just guessing. "What do you mean?"

The former demon snorted. "As if I couldn't see! He's right there in your *üther*. In your eyes, too."

Apparently Gan saw more than Rule had realized. "My wolf is good at waiting. He's helping with that." He glanced at his watch.

"You really are eager to get married with Lily, aren't you? Even though it means you don't get to fuck anyone else."

"Even so," Rule agreed solemnly.

"Huh."

"It's almost time for me to take my place for the ceremony. Can I introduce you to someone before I go?" Gan had come with Max, but Rule didn't see his half-gnome friend anywhere. He didn't want to abandon Gan in the midst of a crowd she didn't know who were wary of her.

Gan pointed. "That woman in blue with the big breasts. She has a good laugh. I can hear it all the way over here."

Gan had been a hermaphrodite and a demon for most of her life before waking up fully female one morning when they were in hell. She was now the chancellor in Edge—an extremely important position, as she enjoyed pointing out—but she still had a great appreciation for breasts. Abel Karonski's wife could handle Gan's conversational style, Rule decided, unlike many of his other guests. Everyone had hung back when he started talking to the small orange person who'd stopped being a demon when she started growing a soul. Because of Lily, her first friend. "Come on, then. You'll like Margarita."

Rule deposited Gan with Abel and Margarita and started making his way toward the small grove where his attendants should be waiting. It might take awhile. Everyone wanted to speak to him.

Rule had wanted a traditional wedding. For the most part, it would be. He'd wanted to underscore that this was a true marriage, and for all that the size and cost of their celebration had flustered Lily, deep down she, too, felt the pull of rites that went back centuries. And many of the human traditions were lovely, a pleasure to adopt, but he did not like the custom of the groom hiding away from his guests until the ceremony began. Rule couldn't ignore guests that way.

Besides, greeting people had kept him busy. Waiting was difficult.

"Ha! Rule!" A hearty clap on the back didn't quite send Rule staggering. "You're looking very James Bond in your tux. Smooth and sophisticated. Hiding those nerves well, at least from all these humans."

Rule turned to grin at the slim man with the sledgehammer punch. "What, Andor, can't you smell the difference between nerves and eagerness for the hunt?"

Andor laughed. "You're comparing a wedding to a hunt? Maybe you're not so far off, but are you sure you're hunter, not prey?"

Rule smiled. "I think Lily and I hunted each other, without knowing it. And now we hunt together."

"Hunt partners?" Andor pursed his lips. "Well, Lucas has seen your Chosen on the hunt. She impressed him, and my son is not easily impressed, so I won't argue with you. Tell me about this fight with Friar that you think sent him underground."

Lily had worried that not many lupi would attend, given how controversial their union was among his people. In the end, forty-one Nokolai had accepted their invitations. That had surprised and pleased Rule and angered Lily, who thought the others were being—as she put it—dicks. Many of his Leidolf were here, too, but as guards. They were needed for security, but he'd made that decision for other reasons. Leidolf was a very conservative clan. His Leidolf were more comfortable in their usual role than as guests to a wedding that appalled, angered, or confused most of them.

Very few from outside the two clans had come. Two of the Rhejes were here—Etorri's and Leidolf's—as well as an old friend from Kyffin, and of course Ruben, who was now Rho of Wythe as well as being Lily's boss. But no one would take Ruben's presence as a political statement. As a former human, Ruben was married himself and saw nothing controversial about Rule becoming a husband. Another Rho, Tony Romano of Laban, had offered to come, if Rule thought it would help . . . "But I don't know if it would. People will think you ordered it, and Laban isn't used to me being Rho yet. If I go, it will cause problems. I haven't had to kill anyone yet, but there are a few who . . . but I'll come if it will help."

All of which was true. Not only was Laban subordinate to Nokolai, but when Tony became Rho, he'd submitted *plene et simpliciter*. Without reservations. Rule had excused him from attending.

So there were four present from other clans—four plus the man currently questioning him about recent events. Andor Demeny was Rho of Szós. His presence was a mark of distinct honor as well as a strong political statement. Rule had rather hoped Andor's Lu Nuncio, Lucas, might attend; Lucas was a friend. For Andor to accept the invitation himself had been a huge surprise. "But she's your Chosen," Andor had said when Rule called to thank him. "That's different. Doesn't affect the rest of us. I don't see why we haven't let mates marry all along, if they wanted to. Seems obvious. Married or not, you won't be spreading your seed anymore."

". . . so while we're staying alert," Rule finished, "it's unlikely that Friar can muster any kind of effective strike force this quickly. He may not even be in this realm."

"Your Rhej couldn't be sure she banished him?"

"No, she said—"

"There you are." The voice was warm and slightly exasperated.

Rule turned, smiling. "Jasper. Aren't you supposed to be—"

"Yes, and so are you. Your father sent me to fetch you."

"Clearly I must obey." Rule turned to Andor. "Andor, this is my brother Jasper Machek. Jasper, this is Andor Demeny, Szós Rho."

Andor's eyebrows lifted slightly. Jasper was human, the son of Rule's mother with a human man. Rule should have named him *alius* kin, or perhaps *ospi*—clan friend. Not "brother," which was reserved for a lupus sibling. Andor politely forbore commenting on Rule's unconventional choice. "Good to meet you, Jasper."

"I'm pleased to meet you as well, and chagrined that I have no time to further our acquaintance. Rule?"

"Please excuse me, Andor. As you heard, I'm ordered to my place."

Rule headed toward the small grove at the west side of the lawn with Jasper. He glanced at his watch. "I'm not late."

"Not yet, but you're pushing it. And I, uh . . . I wanted a chance to give you my news." There was suppressed excitement in his voice.

Rule cocked his head. "Good news?"

"You'll be getting an invitation to my wedding soon. We haven't set a date yet, but—"

Rule stopped. "But this is marvelous! Congratulations, Jasper. I take it the Supreme Court decision—"

"Yes." Jasper was flushed and happy. "I wish everyone

could have this chance, but now Adam and I do, and we're by damn taking it."

"I'm glad."

Adam was waiting with the others in the small grove of white alders. Rule made a point of shaking his hand and congratulating him, though he had just about run out of patience with all this *waiting*.

Isen had been talking to Benedict. He turned, his eyebrows lifting. "You're on time, but just barely."

"Andor wanted to speak with me."

"Ah. Can't offend there." Isen looked as smug as if he'd arranged for Andor's presence.

Maybe he had, in his own sneaky way. Rule looked past his father, out across the lawn . . . and felt her. Lily was coming out of the building, heading along the path that led to the small copse of trees opposite this one. Her trees, though, were gold medallions instead of alders . . . and they were blooming. Which they generally didn't do in March. Rule wondered if one of their friends or relatives had tinkered with the trees. "She's almost there." His heartbeat kicked into high gear. His mouth went dry.

"Then we'd best get in position," Isen said.

Rule walked to the path at the front of the grove. His family arranged themselves behind him.

He and Lily had wanted a mostly traditional wedding . . . but not entirely. Neither of them liked the symbolism of the bride being handed over to the groom like a parcel, but they didn't want to leave family out, either. They'd decided that instead of the usual processional of the bride, they would both walk forward to meet in the middle, accompanied by their attendants. Their families. She had her father, her mother, her sisters, her brother-in-law, and Cynna. He had his father, his brother Benedict, and Nettie, plus his newly found brother Jasper and Jasper's new fiancé, Adam.

It had been harder to come up with the answer to another question. Who did they want to officiate? Neither of them were traditionally religious. In the end, though, there had been only one person who was exactly right. Fortunately, California made it easy for nonclergy to officiate at a wedding.

Cullen waited for them now, standing on the small, arched bridge in the middle of the lawn, wearing the flowing white tunic and trousers he'd worn for his own wedding.

The string quartet, positioned slightly east of and behind the bridge, started playing. The crowd—all five hundred of them—began to quiet.

"You forgot your mike," Benedict said.

"Oh. Right." Rule couldn't look away from the spot where . . . and then there she was. Lily. Standing opposite him in a long shimmer of satin silk.

Benedict chuckled and fastened the small microphone to Rule's collar. "Don't forget to turn it on."

"Right," Rule said again.

"Or I can," Benedict murmured and moved back behind him again.

The violins soared into the crescendo of "Gypsy Airs" . . . and Rule stepped out into the sunshine.

He walked slowly. That was what they'd planned, but now he cursed himself for an idiot. Slow was hard when he wanted to be there *now*. But he was a Lu Nuncio and a Rho and he understood control. He forced himself to hold to the pace they'd practiced.

He stopped on his side of the bridge. Lily stopped on her side. He could barely see her, what with the arch of the bridge and Cullen standing right in the middle of it.

"Friends," Cullen called. His voice was picked up by the mike he wore and carried through speakers along both sides of the lawn. "We are here to witness the union of two people, who today will blend two families—and two sets of customs. This ceremony is a human custom, but in keeping with the lupi belief that important public observations are most complete when they are kept simple, the rite itself will be short. Rule Turner, Lily Yu, come forward and marry."

Rule stepped up onto the bridge. Across from him, Lily did the same. And now at last he saw her face clearly, and gods, but she shone so brightly . . . his heart hurt with love and joy.

As planned, they met in the middle. They'd flipped a coin to see who would go first. Rule had won. He started to reach for her hands—and remembered the mike. Hastily he fumbled with it. Lily laughed at him with her eyes. Finally he got it turned on. This time, when he reached for her hands they were held out, ready for him. "I, Rule Turner, take you, Lily, for my mate, my partner, my lover, and my wife, in sickness and in health, for richer and for poorer, cleaving only unto you."

"And I, Lily Yu, take you, Rule, for my mate, my partner, my lover, and my husband, in sickness and in health, for richer and for poorer, cleaving only unto you." Lily pulled her right hand free. Cullen placed a ring in it. Lily's hand shook ever so slightly as she slid the ring onto the third finger of Rule's left hand. "With this ring I thee wed."

Rule held out his right hand. Cullen supplied the other ring. He concentrated hard and managed not to drop it before he could slide it on Lily's finger. "With this ring I thee wed." And then he just looked into her eyes, a smile starting from his toes and spreading all over him. *Mine.*

"And I," Cullen said, seizing their joined hands and holding them high, "declare the two of you well and truly married!"

Fire burst out on their joined hands—fire as green and joyous as spring, a warm, laughing fire that didn't burn— the *ardor iunctio*, the joining fire, used in the ceremony when a newly adult lupus was brought fully into the clan. Cullen danced that happy fire down their arms, then washed them in it, head to toe. Together they turned, hands still upraised and both of them bathed in green fire, and greeted their guests as husband and wife.

USA TODAY BESTSELLING AUTHOR

EILEEN WILKS

MORTAL TIES

A NOVEL OF THE LUPI

~

FBI agent Lily Yu is living at Nokolai Clanhome with her fiancé, lupi Rule Turner, when an intruder penetrates their territory, stealing the prototype of a magical device that the clan hopes will be worth a fortune—if a few bugs can be worked out…

But the prototype can be dangerously erratic, discharging a bizarre form of mind magic—and it looks like the thief wants it for that very side effect. Worse, whoever stole the device didn't learn about it by accident. There's a Nokolai traitor in their midst.

Lily and Rule have to find the traitor, the thief, and the prototype. One job proves easy when the thief calls *them*—and his identity rocks Rule's world.

As they race to recover their missing property, they find Robert Friar's sticky footprints all over the place. Robert Friar: killer, madman, and acolyte of the Old One the lupi are at war with—an Old One whose power is almost as vast as her ambition to rock the *entire* world…

PRAISE FOR THE LUPI NOVELS OF EILEEN WILKS

eileenwilks.com
facebook.com/ProjectParanormalBooks
penguin.com

M1284T0313